Readers love the *Fish O*
by AMY LANE

Fish Out of Water

"*Fish Out of Water* delivers an intense plot as well as a sizzling relationship between Ellery and Jackson."

—Gay Book Reviews

Red Fish, Dead Fish

"Deliciously tense… a satisfying mix of sweet angst and steamy suspense."

—Karen Rose, *NYT* Bestselling Author

A Few Good Fish

"*A Few Good Fish* is a riveting page-turner with high-stakes action scenes, an intriguing plot and two compelling, incredibly likeable central characters."

—All About Romance

Hiding the Moon

"This whole series is amazing, and this book is the cherry on top!"
—Paranormal Romance Guild

Fish on a Bicycle

"The problem for me with an author like Amy Lane is that she continues to exceed my expectations… Thank you, Amy, you're the best."

—Rainbow Book Reviews

By Amy Lane

All the Rules of Heaven
An Amy Lane Christmas
Behind the Curtain
Bewitched by Bella's Brother
Bolt-hole
Christmas Kitsch
Christmas with Danny Fit
Clear Water
Do-over
Food for Thought
Freckles
Gambling Men
Going Up
Hammer & Air
Homebird
If I Must
Immortal
It's Not Shakespeare
Late for Christmas
Left on St. Truth-be-Well
The Locker Room
Mourning Heaven
Phonebook
Puppy, Car, and Snow
Racing for the Sun • Hiding the Moon
Raising the Stakes
Regret Me Not
Shiny!
Shirt
Sidecar
Slow Pitch
String Boys
A Solid Core of Alpha
Three Fates

Truth in the Dark
Turkey in the Snow
Under the Rushes
Wishing on a Blue Star

BENEATH THE STAIN
Beneath the Stain
Paint It Black

BONFIRES
Bonfires • Crocus

CANDY MAN
Candy Man • Bitter Taffy
Lollipop • Tart and Sweet

DREAMSPUN BEYOND
HEDGE WITCHES LONELY
HEARTS CLUB
Shortbread and Shadows
Portals and Puppy Dogs
Pentacles and Pelting Plants
Heartbeats in a Haunted House

DREAMSPUN DESIRES
THE MANNIES
The Virgin Manny
Manny Get Your Guy
Stand by Your Manny
A Fool and His Manny
SEARCH AND RESCUE
Warm Heart
Silent Heart
Safe Heart
Hidden Heart

Published by DREAMSPINNER PRESS
www.dreamspinnerpress.com

By AMY LANE (cont'd)

Published by DREAMSPINNER PRESS
www.dreamspinnerpress.com

FISH
IN A
BARREL
Amy Lane

Published by
DREAMSPINNER PRESS

5032 Capital Circle SW, Suite 2, PMB# 279, Tallahassee, FL 32305-7886 USA
www.dreamspinnerpress.com

Fish in a Barrel
© 2022 Amy Lane

Cover Art
© 2022 L.C. Chase
http://www.lcchase.com

Trade Paperback ISBN: 978-1-64108-411-6
Digital ISBN: 978-1-64108-410-9
Trade Paperback published July 2022
v. 1.0

Printed in the United States of America
∞
This paper meets the requirements of
ANSI/NISO Z39.48-1992 (Permanence of Paper).

I love you, Mate—thanks for listening when I wrapped this one up. Mary, thank you, as always, for being my repository of lore. Kids, well, you made things rough on this one, but I love you all the same. Dogs, you don't care. I mean I love you, but you will never give a rat's ass if you're in the dedication. Jason? Dude. Thanks for all the chats. Rayna? You keep me sane. Oh! And Bob! Thanks. You'll never read this, but you have been such a lovely friend this year.

Acknowledgments

Jason and Kim—I need to consult with you more, but you do know your criminal justice stuff.

Author's Note

I go walking in the park with Bob (from the dedication) six days a week. We knew the indigent population that camped out under the picnic pavilion in the pouring rain. We knew the neighborhood association that fed them. We knew why they all hated and feared the police. Neither of us would talk to our dogs the way the police talked to those people—and we've got some gawdawful dogs. Around Christmas—after I'd written the bulk of the book—the homeless population disappeared. I don't know where. There was no listing in the paper about relocation of the homeless camp. I know our governor has been working hard at the problem, but those guys just disappeared. Not even the church that fed them knew where they'd gone. I hope it was someplace good. I hope they got to call their families and get clean and dry and warm. I hope their lives have turned the corner. But if anybody wants to know where stories like this come from, I've got a Christmas gift in the back of my minivan—a hand-knitted hat for a guy named Robert—who disappeared from my daily acquaintance the week before Christmas. I'll probably never see him again, and he was afraid of that because the park was what he knew. We need to do better, that's all.

Apple Picking Weather

JACKSON HAD to hand it to the woman; she claimed she was shy and nonconfrontational, but she didn't seem to be afraid to express an opinion.

The courthouse in Sacramento was a newish marble-and-glass structure, the rooms inside were carpeted, and the seats were cushioned. It wasn't exactly designed for comfort, but there wasn't a thunderous echo either, which was helpful when the witness who saw the crime in question hadn't wanted to testify in the first place.

But she had finally agreed because, she said, it wasn't right.

"So, Mrs. Kleinman," Ellery said, looking decisive and articulate in his best gray wool pinstripe. "You say you are absolutely positive that the person you saw holding a knife to the victim's chest was not, indeed, the defendant, Mr. Ezekiel Halliday, seated." Ellery gestured to Halliday in the defendant's chair, still thin from the hospital, dressed reluctantly in a suit that was tight at the shoulder joints and knee joints but loose everywhere else. He had dark curly hair and a close-cropped beard, mostly because it was easier to trim the beard than to shave by himself, and his brown eyes didn't always track the proceedings, although Jackson knew without a doubt he was listening. His narrow face was capable of great joy—Jackson had seen that—but not today.

"Absolutely," Mrs. Kleinman said. Her face softened as she took Ezekiel in. "Zeke wouldn't have known what to do with a knife if he had one."

Ellery nodded. "We'll get back to that. It's important. But how can you be so sure? The police identified Ezekiel after one canvass of the neighborhood. What makes you say it couldn't have been him?"

She gave a *harrumph*. "Well, for one thing, I'd passed Ezekiel about a block before I came to the mouth of Harmony Park, where the incident happened. He was sitting on the sidewalk, holding his foot up to his mouth to suck on a wound."

Ellery had been prepared for this answer—he and Jackson had spent some private time in their office giving voice to the "oogies" as their paralegal,

Jackson's sister, called the intense visceral reaction to something gross. But Jackson still saw his wince of dismay when Mrs. Kleinman said it.

"That doesn't sound... hygienic," Ellery said delicately. "Why would he be doing that?"

The woman was plump and doughy, in her fifties, with graying hair and everything from bad ankles to bad knees to a bad back. None of that stopped her from walking three obnoxious Pomeranians two to three miles a day in her little suburb, and apparently Effie Kleinman didn't miss a trick.

"He'd run away from his care home the day before," she said, shaking her head. "His shoe had come off, and he'd stubbed his toe. Zeke's joints aren't properly formed—it makes him very flexible, but not very stable on his feet."

"Did you offer Mr. Halliday help?" Ellery asked.

Effie sucked air in through her teeth. "Well, that's tricky. I've got the number for his care home by my desk in my house, but I didn't have it on my cell. I talked to him for a bit, and he was feeling fractious, so I told him I'd call Arturo—that's the man who usually comes to get him when he's gotten out—and left him to go on my way."

"So that's the last time you saw Mr. Halliday," Ellery responded.

"That day, yes," she said with a grimace, "because then I was walking through the park entrance, and that asshole with the knife was screaming, and I was trying not to shit my pants."

Jackson watched Ellery as he slow-blinked, trying to digest what she *actually* said as opposed to what they'd been *coaching* her to say for a week.

After a stunned silence in the courtroom, Ellery asked, his voice dry as toast, "Were you successful?"

Effie gave an embarrassed snort. "Not entirely. I did feel a powerful need to go home and change my britches, which is one of the reasons I didn't stick around and talk to the police. Besides," she added, sobering again, "I really wanted to call Arturo. If there was a lunatic loose in the park with a knife, I didn't want Zeke out in that."

"So you didn't stick around to answer any questions?" Ellery reinforced.

"No, sir. Not my scene." She gave a shrug. "Witnesses like me are invisible to police anyway. Just another fat brown woman with too many dogs. They didn't want my opinion."

"So what made you decide to come here and testify?" Ellery prodded, and Jackson let out a breath. They had to make this clear now or the prosecution would turn it into a "gotcha" question on the cross.

"Well, your man there," she nodded toward Jackson, who waved, "got my name from one of the other witnesses. When he told me they'd fingered poor Zeke, I had to come forward. I'd called Arturo, and he was going to come get Zeke, but Arturo's got no obligation to me. He hadn't told me Zeke was in jail, which was the stupidest thing I'd ever heard of."

Jackson Rivers had known Ellery Cramer for nearing on nine years now, and they'd been sharing a bed for over a year of that. Ellery had slick brown hair and sharp features—nose, cheekbones, chin—along with hard, flat brown eyes.

Jackson knew Ellery's every expression, including when those narrow lips went slack and bruised with passion and his brown eyes went from hard to limpid with need, and he knew that if he hadn't known Ellery down to the last nuance, he might have missed the fury he was suppressing as they covered this next line of questioning.

"Could you explain why it's a 'stupid' idea to think Zeke should be in jail for holding a knife to the victim's throat." Ellery asked, keeping that fury in check.

"Objection!" Arizona Brooks, the ADA in charge of prosecution, stood up hurriedly. "This witness is not a medical professional, and she is hardly qualified to tell us what conditions the defendant may have had that would hinder his ability to perpetrate a crime."

Ellery and Jackson stared at her. Arizona was a fit woman, known for her zero tolerance for bullshit, who sported a spiky gray buzz cut, big silver earrings, and liked to wear white men's-cut suits when she was in court.

She was sharp, surprisingly compassionate for an ADA, and willing to deal for the good of the victim and the perpetrator if she saw injustice being committed in the name of the law.

And she never, ever made a mistake.

Until right now.

"Your Honor," Ellery said, yanking his gaze to the judge in the front of the courtroom with an obvious effort, "besides having been a teacher of the moderate and severely disabled for over twenty years, Mrs. Kleinman has taken a compassionate interest in our defendant for several years and has an established relationship with his caretaker. While we will call Arturo Bautista, who runs the Sunshine Care Home, as our next witness, Mrs. Kleinman can speak directly to why it would have been impossible for the defendant to be where the police claimed he was at the time of the crime."

"Overruled," the judge said reluctantly, and Jackson caught the glare the man sent Arizona.

And he didn't like it.

Judge Clive Brentwood *looked* like everything a judge should be—tall, broad-shouldered, distinguished, with the tanned skin of a tennis or golf aficionado and a lion's mane of gray hair tamed by the stylist's comb. Brentwood *looked* like he should be wise and educated and fair. His courtroom presence was formal and impeccable, much like the man himself.

But Ellery had groaned and cursed his luck when he'd seen that he'd drawn Brentwood to try the case in front of, because whereas much of Sacramento was progressive and most of the judges were fair and had the best interest of their constituents in mind, Brentwood was conservative down to his Ronald Reagan leather-soled oxford shoes.

Although he'd never been said to let politics get in the way of a fair ruling, it was still a blow to their case to have someone belonging to a party that seemed fundamentally against mental health and disability care. And they hadn't seen much of his greatly vaunted "fairness" here.

The look he'd aimed at Arizona Brooks had not been friendly, although technically Brooks had done nothing wrong. Her mistake had been in giving Ellery a chance to voice Mrs. Kleinman's qualifications as a judge of Mr. Halliday's condition, and Ellery had taken full advantage.

Jackson eyeballed Arizona, who managed to put an apologetic face on things, but who didn't—to Jackson's eyes anyway—look sorry at all.

In fact as she sat down, Jackson saw her give Effie Kleinman a look that bordered on hope. Like she *hoped* Mrs. Kleinman was the answer to Ezekiel Halliday's prayers.

But Ellery was already questioning their witness, and Jackson's attention was pulled—as it always was—to the magnetic personal force that was Ellery Cramer.

"So," Ellery said, rephrasing for Arizona's sake, because she was a colleague, "could you tell us why it would have been impossible for Mr. Halliday to have been the perpetrator who took Annette Frazier hostage?"

"Well, like I said, Zeke was sitting down, tending to his foot when I passed him. He was bleeding, and it looked like a fierce cut there, and Zeke doesn't move well anyway."

"Could you explain 'doesn't move well'?" Ellery prodded.

"He's got something wrong with his muscles and joints—I think Arturo said it was caused by brain damage at birth, so cerebral palsy of some sort. He's very flexible but not very strong and not very coordinated. If he was the dickhead with the knife who terrorized Annette Frazier, he would have needed to pass me up on the park pathways, and he did not. And he would have needed to have gotten a weapon from somewhere, and then done all of the things the witness for the prosecution said he did: wrap his arm around Annette's chest, hold a knife to her throat, and threaten bystanders. His speech isn't clear enough to threaten bystanders, and if he wrapped his arm around somebody's throat it would be to help himself stay standing. I was there. I saw the guy they were looking for. He was young with brown eyes and brown hair, but that was the only resemblance. Zeke Halliday was not him."

The silence in the courtroom was electric, and Jackson saw the witnesses for the prosecution looking at each other speakingly. The four policemen—Jackson had dubbed them "choirboys"—would not be able to actually speak because courtroom rules precluded it, but their eyeballs were talking daggers. Jackson managed to let out a breath he hadn't known he'd been holding for a month, ever since Arturo Bautista had contacted them on Zeke's behalf to try to get his charge out of jail.

"Why do *you* think Zeke Halliday was arrested?" Ellery asked Effie, and Jackson's eyes darted toward Arizona Brooks to see if she'd object to the question. She should have—it called for speculation on facts Ms. Kleinman could not know—but she didn't, which told Jackson all he ever needed to know about how excited Arizona had been to prosecute this case.

"I think the cops got lazy," Effie said, obviously hurt. "I think the bad guy got away, running through the park's underbrush and down the irrigation stream, and whoever followed them encountered Zeke on the pathway and thought, 'Hey, this guy's obviously homeless. Nobody will give a crap if we arrest him, and that way we can say we tried.'"

Effie's words rang throughout the courtroom, bitter and very true, and once again Jackson looked toward the prosecution to see if there would be an objection.

This time, when Arizona remained stubbornly silent, Ellery met Jackson's eyes in question for a brief second before he turned his attention back to the stand.

"One more thing," Ellery said, before turning the witness over to the prosecution. "You said Mr. Halliday had a wound on his foot. Was he wounded anywhere else?"

"No, sir," Effie said, her eyes seeking out the officers sitting behind the prosecution's desk waiting to be called in rebuttal.

"Were there any bruises on his face, neck, or on his arms?"

"No, sir."

"Was there any blood besides his foot?"

"No, sir," she replied, eyes narrowing.

"Objection," Arizona said belatedly. "Where's this leading?"

"We'll have to talk to the next witness to find out," Ellery said smoothly.

"Withdrawn," Arizona snapped out smartly, and again, that glare.

Brentwood had been going to sustain, but Arizona hadn't let him.

Interesting, Jackson thought. Very, very interesting.

The cross-examination went smoothly, and Arizona pretty much stuck to the script, testing Effie Kleinman's testimony in the places it could—potentially—be weak. Could Mr. Halliday have run through the underbrush in order to take a shortcut to where the incident had taken place?

No, Effie had insisted, he could not have. Between the injury to his foot and his lack of physical coordination, Zeke Halliday couldn't have beat her to the park's entrance where the incident had taken place.

Then Arizona had done more of Jackson and Ellery's work for them. Why, she asked Effie, if Zeke Halliday was disabled, would he be allowed to stand trial?

"He's not *stupid*," Effie had protested. "His IQ is very functional, and I understand he really loves audiobooks—he apparently loves to discuss them. But his body makes it difficult to parse his sentences and difficult for him to be self-sufficient. He's cognizant and able to stand trial, but he's not physically capable of committing this crime."

Then Arizona Brooks had put the nail in the coffin of her own case by asking what sounded like a "gotcha" question—but it got the wrong side.

"You say you were going to go home to call a resource for Mr. Halliday," Arizona said, her voice measured, as though she were weighing every word.

"Yes, and I did. I called Arturo as soon as I got home."

"But there were resources all over the park. The police were already there. Why didn't you call them?"

Effie Kleinman visibly recoiled. "Have you ever *heard* the police roust the homeless? Have you *heard* the way they talk to the transient population in my neighborhood? It's dehumanizing as hell, and it's certainly not help of any sort. No, if I'd realized they were going to come get Zeke, I would have sat down next to him and told them to fuck off when they tried to arrest him. I certainly wouldn't have thrown him to the wolves."

And before the judge could call order, Arizona proclaimed herself done with the witness, and Ellery was up to call the next one to the stand.

Arturo Bautista was a trim man in his midfifties with a square, lined brown face and a sweet smile. His family ran several adult-care homes off Stockton Boulevard, and while the places weren't posh, they were clean, the residents felt safe, and the staff knew everybody by name and talked to them like human beings. Arturo, who'd been sitting next to Jackson during Effie's testimony, gave Jackson a nervous smile as he stood.

"You'll do fine," Jackson mouthed, and Arturo gave a here-goes-nothing sort of shrug.

After being sworn in, he sat, both feet on the floor, and regarded Ellery with bright, alert eyes and a sort of calming presence. Jackson had seen him in action at the care home. Arturo had a big job, taking care of nearly forty residents, each with an assortment of mental and physical disabilities, but he dealt with the challenges using compassion, humor, and a solid dose of common sense.

"Mr. Bautista," Ellery began, "you are the proprietor of the Sunshine Prayers Care Home off Stockton Boulevard?"

"The Sunshine Prayers Care Home for the Moderately Disabled," Arturo clarified. "Sunshine Prayers is the company name. There are different homes for different needs."

"Thank you for the clarification," Ellery said, and Jackson had to keep from smiling to himself. Ellery had originally scripted different wording during witness prep, but once, when he'd been tired, he'd simply left off the remainder of the name. Arturo had made the clarification then, too, and Ellery had liked the way it sounded—as though Arturo was a professional who knew his business and made sure there was no confusion.

"So," Ellery continued, "you're responsible for Ezekiel Halliday?"

"Well, his family is responsible for him," Arturo said wryly, "but we provide the day-to-day care. It's often difficult for a family—particularly one with low income—to provide a suitable peer-interactive environment for an adult with special needs."

Ellery nodded and began to question Arturo about the day-to-day operations of the care home. Jackson's stomach knotted, expecting Arizona's objection at any moment, but none came. In a way, it was a relief; sometimes the prosecution spent the entire trial trying to disrupt the defense's rhythm or vice versa. But as Ellery's questioning—designed for one exclusive purpose—continued, Jackson started getting jittery. When was the other shoe going to drop?

"So your facility sounds very organized," Ellery said. "But that begs the question. How was it Ezekiel Halliday was in the park that day unsupervised?"

Arturo looked sorrowful, as he had during witness preparation. "Zeke's smart," he said with a sigh. "And he gets bored. Some of the residents are cleared to leave unsupervised. They need very little help and are close to being independent. Ezekiel has been begging for the same privileges, but—" Arturo took a deep breath. "—he's easily injured," he said, meeting Ezekiel's eyes in apology. "And his speech is unclear, so it's difficult for him to ask for help."

"How long had Ezekiel been missing from your facility on the day of the incident?" Ellery asked without commenting on Arturo's explanation.

"Two days."

"Is this common, Mr. Bautista? For a resident to be missing overnight?"

"No," Arturo said grimly. "In fact with any other resident, we would have been on the phone to every authority in the book to find him. It's not safe for him to be out there."

"Then why not this time?" Ellery lowered his voice, made it soft, almost invisible, because he wanted everybody to hear the answer. Jackson hated the answer, but it wasn't any less true because Jackson hated it.

"This was his third such incident in two years," Arturo said. "When it happens too often, social services moves residents to a different facility."

"Wouldn't a different facility be a better fit?" Ellery asked. He'd asked that question during preparation to find out why Ezekiel had been in the park that day.

"The state-owned facility is horrible," Arturo told him, voice shaking. "Too many people, too many problems. He could get assaulted, have his possessions stolen, be force-fed medication. He's vulnerable on his own, but that is not the place for him. Neither is jail. There's not a violent bone in his body. He just… just was in the wrong place at the wrong time."

"So you didn't call the police because you were afraid of what they'd do?" Ellery asked.

"Yes."

Ellery pulled a folder from his desk that featured eight-by-ten photos that Jackson had taken when they'd managed to bail Ezekiel out of jail.

"Is this what you were afraid of?" he asked.

Arturo's voice broke. "Yes."

Between the time Effie Kleinman had seen Ezekiel sitting on the sidewalk and Arturo had gone to the jail with Jackson and Ellery to post his bail, Ezekiel had been badly beaten. His face was puffy—one eye swollen almost completely shut—and his jaw had been broken as well. He'd lost two teeth, and there were bruises on his neck and shoulders that showed clearly the outline of hard-soled boots.

Not the soft-soled crocs given to prisoners.

"Objection?" Brentwood asked, looking at Arizona Brooks.

"Of course I object to seeing a man badly beaten," Arizona said smoothly. "And so should you."

"But the pictures are irrelevant," Judge Brentwood protested.

"To why the defendant had a legitimate fear of the police?" Arizona responded. "No, sir, I think they speak very clearly as to why the defendant and his caregiver didn't ask the police for help. It is not your place to object. It's mine. And I don't. I think the defense should continue on."

Brentwood gaped for a moment before looking at Ellery in confusion.

"Mr. Cramer," he said, gesturing vaguely.

"Thank you, sir," Ellery said smoothly, but Jackson could see that Ellery was as boggled as he was. Arizona Brooks was a topflight attorney. Much of the testimony, including the damning pictures that spoke to a painful beating at the hands of the authorities, should have been a tooth-and-nail fight to get admitted.

Arizona was doing everything but leaning back and taking a nap. In fact she was going one better. She was actually putting on her hip waders and helping Ellery cut through the bullshit.

Jackson wondered why. He wanted to excuse himself to go make a phone call or two, but he'd promised both Effie and Arturo he'd be there for the two of them. Effie was sitting next to him now, clenching his knee with stress.

Jackson patted her hand until she let go with a sheepish look, and together they watched as Ellery finished with Arturo's testimony and turned Arturo over to Arizona.

She looked at Arturo reluctantly and continued to give him a very mild cross-examination. Toward the end, she paused and took a deep breath, as though fortifying herself.

"Now, Mr. Cramer showed us pictures of the defendant, and he looked in bad shape. Did you ever, at any time, see one of the officers seated behind me lay a finger on Ezekiel?"

"No, ma'am. I didn't see it happen."

"Then why would we assume that the police are responsible for the bruises?"

"Because when I asked Ezekiel what happened, he said it was 'the bad policemen,'" Arturo said, not backing down.

"But I thought Mr. Halliday couldn't talk!" Arizona was feigning surprise—and not bothering to hide it.

"It's difficult to understand him," Arturo told her. "But not impossible. He knows who to be afraid of."

Arizona nodded slowly. "Good," she said. "It's good somebody does. No more questions for this witness."

The judge looked at the clock. "It's getting close to quitting time. Let's resume testimony tomorrow, 9:00 a.m. sharp."

"All rise!" intoned the bailiff, and Brentwood exited the courtroom, followed by the jury.

Arizona didn't look at them as she packed her briefs into her briefcase and turned to speak to the officers who had been ready to be called as witnesses. The conversation didn't appear to be going well.

The officer in charge, wearing his full blues, hat tucked under his arm, was doing his best to use his six-foot-plus height to loom over Arizona's five eight or so.

True to the woman Jackson and Ellery knew, she sent him a killing look.

"If you didn't want it brought up," she said icily, "maybe you shouldn't have authorized it."

"He fought back!" said a younger officer bitterly. So fair his neck was turning purple with agitation, his voice rang with injured adolescent dignity.

"You were *beating* him," Arizona retorted. "I don't know which part of that you don't understand. I told you this would happen, and I warned you they would introduce the evidence in the criminal trial so they could use it in the civil trial. Well, they have. And when this kid gets let off, expect Cramer's partner to come after you in the most celebrated civil suit in the city. This isn't going away."

"Well, not from anything *you're* trying to do," snarled the taller dark-haired officer. "I swear, it's like you want him to get off!"

"Because even *I* know he didn't do anything," she snapped back. "Now if I were you, I'd go try to find the real perpetrator, or Rivers and Cramer are going to do it for you and make you look even worse. Now go."

They all stared at her and then looked over at Jackson and Ellery speculatively.

Jackson bared his teeth at them in what was definitely *not* a smile. They were working on it. Of *course* they were working on it. But the state was hell-bent on cramming this case through the system, trying their defendant while the bruises from his police beating were still visible and his jaw was still wired, rendering him all but mute.

The witnesses for the prosecution visibly recoiled from Jackson's expression, and the silence in the courtroom thudded like a lead gavel on flesh.

"*Go!*" Arizona shouted, and the clot of cops left, grumbling, leaving a nearly clear courtroom.

"Arizona…?" Ellery began, but she shook her head and held up her hand.

"Win this one," she said. "I can't have any more off days or Brentwood'll declare a mistrial. You know that. See you both tomorrow."

And with that she was gone, leaving Jackson with the distinct impression she was crying.

Ellery met his eyes then, and they had a complete silent conversation that started with "Okay, that was weird" and ended with "We'll talk about it when we get rid of the civilians."

Arturo had already gone around the table to grasp Ezekiel's wheelchair and begin pushing him down the aisle between the banks of seats, and Effie followed him slowly. Arturo, Effie, and Zeke had all come in Arturo's van—he'd been given custody after Zeke made bail, and suddenly Zeke was having to deal with locks on the door to his dormitory and hourly checks to make sure he hadn't tried to fly the coop again.

Jackson got the feeling that after meeting the "good" guys, Zeke wasn't going to want to fly the coop again for a very long time.

October Dreams

THEY'D LEFT their car at their office, which was less than a mile away. After they saw Arturo, Ezekiel, and Effie off, all in Arturo's well-equipped shuttle, they decided to give Ellery's healing leg a workout *not* in the pool and walked back. They didn't hurry, practically the only people on the sidewalk in the surprisingly crisp and cloudy October afternoon.

Jackson had shoved his hands into the pockets of his slacks, and Ellery made a note to himself to steam the creases before Jackson wore that suit again. With some maneuvering on Ellery's part, Jackson had more than two good suits now, but not much more. On the one hand, his protests made sense; most of his days were spent running down leads. People were much more likely to respond to him—open up, in fact—if he was casually dressed, although Jackson tended to take it to extremes.

On the other hand, Jackson, nicely dressed in a fitted suit with a tie the same green as his eyes, quite simply took Ellery's breath away, and Ellery was not above his little indulgences.

Living with Jackson Leroy Rivers wasn't easy. Ellery figured he was due.

They got about a block, the tension seeping from them with each step, before Jackson voiced the question that sat heavy between them.

"What the actual fuck, Ellery? I mean... the actual holy Mary mother of *fuck* was that?"

Ellery blew out a breath, about to say "I don't know," for comfort, when he realized that would be the easy answer and a lie.

They took a few more steps, and Jackson glanced at him sideways. "Spill."

Ah, the benefits of a partner and lover who could read your mind. Fantastic when they were in bed, not so wonderful when Ellery wanted to think carefully about something before answering.

"So," he said after a moment, "remember when you were half-dead from your heart condition and I was half-dead with worry?"

"So, say, most of June, all of July, on into August, until you broke your leg in a car wreck and we had other things to do."

"Yes, that," Ellery said dryly. October was closing fast, with what looked like a hopefully wet November on the other side of the weekend. His leg was mostly healed from a hairline fracture of the tibia, and the bruises from the car wreck that had, they both hoped, saved lives in the long run, had disappeared weeks ago.

And some of the consequences of the two of them being occupied with each other instead of the political climate of their city were coming home to roost.

"I remember," Jackson replied, voice equally dry. "So we were busy. What happened while we weren't paying attention?"

"Trey Cartman," Ellery said, not dropping his voice for respect or fear or anything else, because Jesus Christ, why would he?

"Fuck *me!*" Jackson kicked savagely at a rock, obviously recognizing the name of Sacramento's newest district attorney, recently put into office by the special election that took place in July when Elaine Longley had to resign for health reasons.

"Would love to," Ellery said, keeping his voice light, "but do you really think this is the place?"

Jackson gave him a dirty look. "Now who's being cute." Before Ellery could snipe back, Jackson cut to the chase. "Do you really think Mr. No Broken Windows is the one pushing to put Ezekiel in jail? I mean, it makes sense, but it feels so targeted. Why Ezekiel? He's not going to win Cartman any popularity points."

Ellery shook his head, not sure Jackson was right about that. "No Broken Windows" referred to Cartman's advertising campaign and the well-known law enforcement policy of giving no quarter to the homeless population. The theory was that a house with a broken window attracted people to break more windows and trash the place, and it had been used to terrify homeowners into allowing the homeless to be bullied, beaten, and imprisoned instead of *helped*, which is really what they needed. When Effie had spoken of the way the police department addressed the homeless population in Harmony Park, she was specifically referencing this policy, although not many media outlets made the connection for the voting population that "no broken windows" also meant "no rest or humanity for the poor, hungry, and mentally ill."

"You disagree?" Jackson pushed, and Ellery sighed.

"Everybody says they want to do something about the homeless," he murmured, "but by 'do something' they really mean sweep them under the rug. You know the statistics as well as I do, Jackson—the population is growing and the resources to keep them housed are shrinking. Mental health resources, poverty resources, childcare to help workers earn a living wage are literally laughed at in Cartman's circles. I mean, I can't solve the crisis myself, and I don't know all the answers, but if Cartman wants to make a mark for himself as being tough on crime—Mr. No Broken Windows, as you said—throwing Ezekiel Halliday in prison is the way to do it."

Jackson responded with a grunt and another assault on the rock on the sidewalk. "Fucker," he said, and Ellery had no doubt that if Mr. Cartman had been right there, Jackson would have hauled him by the scruff of the neck to Ezekiel's care home and dared him to watch the man pour his soul into walking down the hallway to the dining room without leaning on the walls and dare Cartman to insist that Zeke had been the one to wave a knife around and threaten police officers while in what appeared to be a drug-fueled rage.

"So," Jackson continued after a few more steps, "Cartman wants to be No Broken Windows—he's young, he's pushing his agenda, and he's Arizona's boss. Isn't she a deputy district attorney? Doesn't she have some say?"

"It would be nice to think so," Ellery said with a shrug. "But she's not elected. She's appointed, and her job rests on Cartman's sufferance. I think she's been trying to tell them the truth the whole time, but nobody's listening. Or they're threatening her job. Judging by the way she was speaking to those police officers, she's been telling them all along that they have no case."

Jackson frowned. "They really don't, so how did they get here?" He found his friend the rock and kicked it some more, down through the beginnings of fruitless mulberry tree leaves that would soon be massive piles along the usually shady sidewalks of the city.

"Same way police get away with everything," Ellery said, because Jackson, with his complicated, often hostile relationship with the police, knew the answer to this.

"No…." Jackson's temper had flared and receded, leaving one of the brightest minds Ellery had ever encountered to work. "No… those cops were entitled. I mean, remember this summer when I was working with some of them? They were unorganized. Their CO was green and didn't know her ass from a hole in the ground, and some of those guys—whoooeee, incompetent as fuck. But this was different."

Ellery narrowed his eyes and tried to see what Jackson was seeing. "They were talking to Arizona like they expected a specific outcome," he said after a moment. "This wasn't disorganization, or even entitlement. This was somebody telling them what should and should not happen to them during the trial."

"Who's in charge of our police union?" Jackson said grimly. "You're right. We got super focused on ourselves, and it's not like we didn't need it, but we're behind on our political landmines, and we're this close to stepping on one."

"Boehner," Ellery said. "Officer Charlie Boehner. I think I met him at that dinner two weeks ago—you remember…?"

"The one I didn't go to," Jackson said, rolling his eyes.

Ellery studied Jackson as they walked, quiet for a moment, appreciating. He'd just turned thirty-one, and his hair was still the color of dark honey. His eyes—bottle green—should have been flat, unfriendly, and bitter, but they weren't. Jackson's life hadn't been a picnic. Born poor, raised by a drug-addicted teenager until he was in middle school, he'd been shown kindness by Jade and Kaden Cameron, who had started out as kids in Jackson's apartment building and who had become, along with their mother, Toni, family. Toni had passed away far too young, but Jackson, Jade, and Kaden had stayed tighter than many blood families Ellery knew. Ellery always wondered at the miracle that Toni Cameron's kindness and decency, as well as the same solid moral compass she'd gifted Jade and Kaden with, had fallen on such fertile ground.

Jackson should have been a product of the streets—and parts of him *were* angry, violent, and impatient for the wheels of justice to turn the right way. But so much of him was grateful that somebody in his life had turned kindness his way and almost desperate to make that count.

He was possibly the best man Ellery Cramer had ever known—but also the most frightening to love. Jackson didn't set a high enough premium on his life, on his person, and both those things were becoming more and more dear to Ellery with every passing day.

"You really don't like those functions," Ellery said faintly, when he became aware too much time had passed.

Jackson shrugged. "That was the night I tracked down Effie, remember? I mean, she let me in the door, but she wasn't going to talk to me if I bolted out again to go put on a suit."

What he meant was that Effie was lonely and prickly, and her tiny barky dogs were the only constants in her life after she'd been forced to take early retirement as a high school science teacher because she actually said, "Creationism is bullshit, and I'm not teaching it," during a staff meeting.

But yes, he'd also probably kept Ezekiel out of jail, and now that Effie was volunteering her time at the Sunshine Prayer Home for the Moderately Disabled, affectionate animals at her heels, he could also claim credit for helping her as well. Not that Jackson would ever claim credit for that sort of thing.

"Jackson?" Ellery said uncertainly, because he'd heard the self-recrimination in Jackson's voice and didn't like where it was heading.

"Yeah?" Jackson glanced at him sideways as they continued their stroll under darkening skies.

"You don't ever have to apologize for not being a political animal. You know that, right?"

Jackson grunted and shook his head. "Talk to me about politics *after* we get Zeke exonerated. He is too damned close to being back in jail for me to even think about going to that benefit dinner tomorrow night."

Ellery sucked air in through his teeth. "Gods. Yeah. I'll beg off—"

Jackson grunted again. "No. Aren't the new DA and the policeman's union there in full force?"

"Yeah." Ellery tried to suppress a shudder. He went every year. Halloween themed, subtly ironic costuming was required. There was a cloaked undercurrent of homophobic bigotry that permeated this particular event every year. Ellery couldn't put his finger on it except to say any costume that was considered in any way "gay" was given a lot of unwanted attention. He and Jackson had been new the year before, and Jackson hadn't been doing well on a lot of fronts. Ellery had skipped it then, but Jackson was right. He couldn't afford to this year.

"Bring Jade," Jackson said. "She can dress as Sister Night, you can go as Doctor Manhattan—you'll cause quite a stir."

Ellery blinked once to try to remember who those characters were, and then again in horror at the implications. "It's a funny joke, Jackson, but the minute somebody figured out what it meant, Jade and I would be in very real danger." Because, of course, those two characters, who did mostly good, had been nearly killed by a psychotic police department on the ultimate power trip.

"You're only saying that because you'd have to go naked... and painted blue," Jackson chided, and Ellery fought the urge to sock his arm like a little kid.

"I *will* take Jade," Ellery said, pondering it. "But I think we can skip the costuming that will irritate the entire police force. We'll have to think of something. What will you be doing?"

"Well, *tonight*," Jackson said thoughtfully, "I'm going to be tracking down the actual suspect. Arizona was right about that. Henry and I have some leads, but I want to be able to subpoena his ass into the courtroom tomorrow. If I have to pound down his door in the middle of the night and truss him up like a turkey, I'm going to have that guy in custody when we need him."

"You're *sure* Henry can help you with that?" Ellery clarified. "Doesn't he have classes?"

Henry had come to them for help proving himself innocent of murder in early June. Fresh out of the military—and out of the closet and an abusive relationship to boot—Henry had been a surly handful when they'd first met. But Jackson knew how to find the wounded human in the most vicious of animals, and when he and Henry had been done with each other, they had somehow become friends and work partners. Henry was as physically fearless as Jackson, but he also had caution, pounded into him by years of active duty. Ellery would feel a *lot* better if Henry was going with Jackson.

"Yeah," Jackson nodded. "Henry's free. Lance is working a double again, and Henry hates being bored. And the little shit is super smart too, for all his 'I'm just a dumb young country boy' schtick. He's getting As, and according to Galen, he's not even studying. Asshole."

Ellery rolled his eyes. "You take classes for fun," he reminded Jackson. "You could probably be a lawyer by now, but you keep insisting you don't want to. I think you like to lord all that knowledge over other lawyers who try to talk down to you, but what do I know?"

"Heh heh heh heh." Jackson's evil laugh told Ellery everything he'd guessed was spot-on true. Well, the man did have his quirks. "And speaking of Galen," Jackson murmured, "is *he* going to this policeman's ball or benefit or circle jerk or whatever?"

When Henry had walked in their door asking for help, Galen had been the irritated friend of Henry's older brother who had herded him in with a stick. Galen—a property attorney from Florida—was in recovery from addiction after a horrific motorcycle crash. He'd come to California to be with his boyfriend, the owner/director of Johnnies, a pornography studio that operated out of Sacramento, and he'd fit into Ellery and Jackson's little start-up law firm seamlessly.

Before Ellery had met Jackson, he might have judged all of them: Henry for staying in the closet, Henry's brother for working in porn, Galen's boyfriend for filming it, and even Galen, the consummate Southern Gentleman, for his addiction to oxy. But one of the side benefits of watching Jackson accept people without judgment was that Ellery had not denied himself a friend and business partner as sharp and as kind as Galen Henderson, and not beating Henry to death minutes after meeting him had turned out to be a plus as well.

But Galen—as brilliant as he was in the courtroom—did not suffer fools gladly, and it showed in his lack of political clout in the city.

"Galen wasn't sent an invitation," Ellery said, grimacing. "And I thought of asking him to come with me if you couldn't, because he deserves the chance to make contacts, but he said, rather pointedly, that I of all people should know why those aren't the contacts he should be making."

Jackson chuckled. "He's got a point. I mean, yes, it's good to have contacts in the police department and the DA's office, but if we don't attract criminals, we don't get paid."

"I'm fully aware of that," Ellery replied. "I merely thought he'd be a fun friend to go with. What are you doing again? Tracking down the actual perpetrator for Ezekiel's crime is on the agenda for tonight. Are you sure you can't come if you get that done?"

Jackson *hmm*ed in his throat as they approached the last crosswalk to their office, a converted Victorian on F Street, painted dark gold with forest-green trim and surrounded by hundred-year-old trees dropping leaves in the crisp wind.

"C'mon," Jackson ordered, pulling his hands out of his pockets so he could latch on to Ellery's fingers, lacing them firmly together with his own. "Let's go." Together they hustled across the street and down the sidewalk toward their office building right when the skies, building gray during their walk, opened up and began pattering rain on their heads.

"Shit!" Ellery complained. "I'm going to have to steam both our suits tonight!"

Jackson laughed outright, still running, careful not to let his leather-soled shoes slide on the fallen leaves as they grew wet from the rain. He held Ellery's hand the entire time as they crossed lawns of other businesses—large converted houses like theirs, set back from the road with family-style lawns and walkways—until they saw their own walkway and turned, the clatter of the rain on the leaves growing louder and louder, like the footsteps of a pursuing god.

They paused for breath underneath the thruway that connected the original part of the offices to a more modern part and also provided an overhang for covered parking.

The thruway wasn't safe at night, and Ellery needed to have Henry power wash it twice a month to purge it of the smell of used wine. But today it was relatively clean, and nobody was seeking shelter in the semiprivate darkness, and as they drew to a stop, breathless and laughing, Ellery had a sudden wish for the two of them to simply go home. They could leave Jackson's vehicle and drive Ellery's Lexus through the rain-drenched streets, and then they could change into their soft pajamas and sit in front of the television with some wine, pet the cats, and allow themselves to be lulled and cocooned by the sound of the rain. They might even make love, but mostly he'd have this beautiful, laughing man safe under his own roof, and tomorrow would be a certainty and not a leap of faith.

Ellery gazed at Jackson, his mouth parted, halfway to begging for a night of quiet, a night of peace, when Jackson lowered his head and captured Ellery's mouth with his own and all thoughts of speech fled.

Intoxicating. Every time. His kiss rushed through Ellery's bloodstream, more potent than any drug, even adrenaline, and his taste sent need blossoming in Ellery's chest.

Ellery returned the kiss, hands on Jackson's hips, pulling them tighter, groin to groin, and Jackson's fingers, biting into his shoulders, were the only thing keeping him from losing all common sense and dragging Jackson to the car.

Ellery was so lost, so caught up in the moment, that when Jackson tore their mouths apart and rested their foreheads together, he felt an almost physical pang of loss.

"Jesus, Counselor," Jackson panted. "You go to my head like nothing else."

Come home with me and let's fuck like bunnies and forget the world is a frightening place that has almost taken you from me more times than I can count.

"Same," Ellery said weakly, his heart pounding out a completely different tattoo. "I don't want to let you go."

Jackson *hmm*ed and took his mouth again, a hard, brief kiss that promised more.

"I won't be too long," he half promised. Even Ellery knew that "not too long" could mean home in time to leave for court the next morning.

"Just let me know where you are," Ellery begged. Jackson hadn't always. One terrible, terrible night almost a year ago, he had disappeared off the grid, and Ellery had almost lost him in a thousand different ways.

"'Course," Jackson said with a wink. Then, obvious reluctance in every muscle, he took a step back. "I gotta go upstairs and change and grab Henry."

Ellery nodded and primly wiped the edges of Jackson's sinfully swollen lips. "Maybe kissing me wasn't your best bet for professionalism," he said, but his heart wasn't in the advice.

"But, Counselor, you looked so delicious," Jackson murmured, voice low and sexy, and Ellery gave it up and groaned, resting his forehead against Jackson's shoulder this time.

"You delight in doing this to me. Fabulous. Thank you so much."

"Heh heh heh heh heh heh."

And that laugh! Gah! Ellery was lucky he remembered his own damned name after that.

"So?"

Jade Cameron was a beautiful woman, curvy, a little on the short side, dark-skinned, with hair that had been styled into long, flowing curls, each one ending in a bold magenta wave. She'd also grown up on the same streets that had helped shape Jackson, so when she asked a question, Ellery tried to answer her straightforwardly.

Which was also why—in the way of siblings—Jackson was the one to yank her chain.

"So what?" he baited.

"Ellery, I'll hurt him."

Ellery scowled at Jackson, who grinned back. Apparently bickering was a hobby that the two of them enjoyed very much. That and inventing new swearwords, which Ellery was starting to enjoy as well.

"No, you won't," said Henry, popping his head out of Galen's office and peering down the corridor to the entrance where Jade's reception alcove stood as the dividing line between the now empty lobby and the three offices and the conference room that made up the practice. One of those offices had yet to be filled, but Galen and Ellery had discussed it and had come to the conclusion that they were both picky and wanted to make sure it was the right person as opposed to just a body. The fact that nobody was in the waiting room—and Henry had been in Galen's office—told Ellery that the last client had probably left a few minutes ago.

"Why won't I hurt him?" Jade challenged. Like Jackson, she enjoyed treating Henry as a much-tormented younger brother.

"Because he's going to tell us, like, right now!" Henry insisted, striding down the hallway to stand in front of the reception desk and glare at Jackson. The reception was a counter-height extension of a wall that sheltered a small alcove. The alcove hosted a shared computer at a tiny student-sized desk that sat against the back wall. A copy machine took up the adjacent wall, and a shelf rack filled with office supplies sucked up all the remaining space. Ellery wasn't sure what the space had been when the whole building was one house, but for their office, it was a combination office/changing room/supply closet.

"No, I'm not," Jackson said mildly, going around the cluster of people standing in front of Jade and into the supply closet space. He started rooting around on a shelf where he kept a set of street clothes to change into for days like today when he didn't want to wreck his suit.

"Dammit, Jackson!" Henry began, but Ellery snorted.

"You two are so easy," he said, not wanting to hear the threats to his lover's person today. "He's waiting for Galen so we don't have to say it twice, because I think this one's going to need big brains."

"If you want to summon the devil," Galen Henderson said in his acid Southern drawl, "you need to call his name two more times." He was taking measured steps down the hallway, no cane in hand. Ellery noticed he did that sometimes when the distance was small, even though it seemed to cost him a great deal. Galen Henderson may have barely survived the accident—and the addiction to oxy that had followed it—but his stiff-necked pride hadn't received so much as a dent.

"Galen," Ellery said with a nod.

"'Sup, Galen," Jackson said from the back of the reception cubby. "If you all want to go to the conference room, I'll be there in a minute." He had his back toward them and was clearly unbuttoning his suit coat as he kicked off his shiny dress shoes.

Galen met Ellery's eyes and raised an amused eyebrow. Henry let out a quiet whuffle, and even Jade raised *her* eyebrows at them all before turning around to enjoy the show. Together, they watched in silent appreciation—and judgment—as Jackson stripped down to his boxers, taking care to hang his suit up right. For a moment, right before he hopped into the legs of a pair of baggy jeans and yanked them up in one smooth motion before donning a T-shirt and a hooded sweatshirt that had a picture of the *Star Trek* starship *Enterprise* painted a la Vincent Van Gogh's *Starry Night*, they all got a look at his pale, scarred, and naked back.

Ellery, who got to see him naked nearly every day, breathed a sigh of relief. Jackson had put on weight this summer after his heart surgery, thank God, and it looked like the weight was staying on. He had muscles in his back now, instead of bare scapula and vertebrae, and his ass had some meat on it to hold up his briefs, whereas in June it had appeared to be mostly pelvic bones. Yes, there were scars—more now than when they'd met—but there were no wounds, no stitches, and no recent bruises. Around him, Ellery could feel the quiet relief of everybody else as they all assessed the health and progress of Jackson Rivers, who was so very good at taking care of other people and so very bad at taking care of himself.

He seemed to be doing all right, and Ellery thought maybe he'd worry a smidge less if Jackson was a little late home that night.

Oblivious to the scrutiny, Jackson started packing up. He placed his suit in the suit bag and added the shoes on the bottom, hung it up again on the shelf with the paper on it, and then turned around, obviously intent on heading toward the conference room, where he thought everybody had gone.

He was greeted by hoots and hollers and a smattering of applause, and Ellery would forever treasure the way his eyes grew wide in actual surprise.

"Oh dear God," Jackson said, holding his hands up in front of his chest in retroactive embarrassment. "I feel a little violated."

"Yeah, well, you're looking a little beefcake," Henry said, voicing what seemed to be the universal opinion. "And thank God. It gets boring telling people to eat, believe me. You don't have to mother a bunch of bulimic porn models like I do. I'm over it. If you can down a cheeseburger without being nagged, my job is *so* much easier."

"I would like to add that we appreciated the view," Galen said, inclining his head regally.

Jackson grunted. "My back looks like a war zone," he muttered. "Not much of a view."

Ellery frowned, surprised, but Jackson was heading toward the hallway, accepting the ribbing of their friends, so he didn't say anything, but he was thinking it.

Jackson's back was scarred, like the rest of him. Ten years ago he'd survived a sniper shot that had vaporized a lot of muscle and bone but thankfully missed his heart. The trauma had still almost killed him, though, and the event was written on his skin. His shoulder and chest were a battleground of scar tissue from countless surgeries, and his back had a fist-sized smooth spot, a crater where the bullet had emerged, ripping what seemed like half of Jackson with it. And for any other man, that would be enough, but Jackson hadn't sat idle. He had stitched knife wounds, bullet grazes, road rash—his back and his front were mapped with an active, violent life, and Ellery had never flinched from seeing those souvenirs of the times Jackson had lived. He'd always been so excited, so thrilled, to have Jackson Rivers in his bed, and he knew the physical scars weren't nearly as painful as the emotional scars his love carried.

He hadn't realized Jackson was embarrassed to wear those marks on his skin.

Given that Jackson was rallying from his temporary embarrassment and giving Henry, Jade, and Galen a ration of crap for looking, it wasn't the time to talk about it, but still…. Ellery filed it for later.

He really wanted to talk about it later.

"Look, Jade lives with an old guy who I don't even want to imagine without a shirt—"

"He's one of your best friends, and he's hotter than hell," Jade retorted, standing up for her unlikely boyfriend, Mike, with the staunchness Ellery had come to expect from her.

"Yeah, I'll take your word for it," Jackson muttered. "But Henry, *your* boyfriend is one of the hottest guys I've ever seen in my life, and you roomed with porn models for *months*. Galen, your boyfriend films them for a living. Seriously, don't you people have anything better to do than watch my scrawny ass in the copy room?"

"Nope," Henry said cheerfully.

"Me neither," Jade agreed.

"It made a pleasant break in my day," Galen added with a smirk.

Jackson let out an outraged sound when Jade took his arm and pulled him back so they could let Galen, Henry at his elbow, go into the conference room first.

"Besides, honey," she said softly, "we've worked hard to see you this healthy—let us revel a little in our achievement, okay?"

Jackson gave her a sweet lopsided smile. "Thank you for getting me this far," he said, completely sincere, before dropping a kiss on her forehead. Looking over his shoulder, he winked at Ellery before swinging into the conference room.

"Now, do you guys want to hear some weird shit? Because Ellery and I have got some weird shit, and maybe some bad news as well."

"How bad could it be?" Henry asked, and Jackson smirked.

"Bad enough for Jade to have to go to the policeman's benefit costume dinner with Ellery as backup tomorrow while you and I run down some leads," he said.

Jade's eyes grew wide, her horror palpable. "I take it all back," she declared. "Jackson, you get me out of this bullshit or I'll kill you myself!"

"No can do," Jackson replied, grimacing at Ellery. "Unless Galen wants to be his plus-one. But you guys need to hear the whole story before you decide. Because Arizona Brooks tried to *hand* us a victory today, and she risked her job to do it. You guys, something *very* frightening is going on in the DA's office, and I think we're going to need to go to the wall on this one. We are *very* close to having Brentwood declare a mistrial and throwing Zeke in jail while he postpones the retrial indefinitely. You may or may not have noticed, but the nice people of Sacramento seem to have put a monster in the DA's office, and if we don't put our collective foot down, there's not going to be anything to do but pick up body parts that he leaves in his wake."

Everybody recoiled, including Ellery.

"Dammit," Ellery muttered, "I knew letting you read *Beowulf* was a mistake!"

"I can't believe I missed that shit in high school," Jackson said wolfishly. "That was some *prime* entertainment!"

"Ha-ha," Galen intoned dryly. "Now tell us what happened."

Ellery took over the conversation from there, and when he was done, the silence around the table was ruminative—and worried.

"So you and me need to get us some ballin' costumes for tomorrow night's do," Jade said soberly. "Because I get it now. Galen can't do this. He's right. People put him on retainer because they trust him not to be too chummy with the police, and he needs to keep that reputation. But yeah, if it's going to be balls to the walls cops and unions and kamikaze prosecutors, we need to have eyes and ears open there to see what's going on." She paused and asked Jackson the question Ellery had forgotten during that breathless kiss under the thruway. "What are you going to be doing, baby boy? I assume you've got a plan?"

Jackson nodded. "So," he said, "given that guys like Cartman and Boehner tend to work on the 'you lick my balls and I might scratch your back' principle, I think we need to find the people who haven't been licking their balls."

"Where would they be?" Henry asked.

Jackson snorted. "Well for one thing, they *wouldn't* be at the policeman's union shindig. Think about it. Where are the cops who don't like the No Broken Windows policy going to be?"

"Working," Galen said, sounding pleased. "That's some very fine deduction, young man. The people willing to dish about the new order are going to be the people not necessarily invited to the party."

Jackson nodded, and while he very well could have looked pleased with himself, he was instead looking grim. "And given that Henry and I made some nice contacts with the cops who don't suck over the summer, I'll bet those are the people we'll run into if we do a sweep of the station and the cop haunts tomorrow night. A little bit of casual conversation on a slow night might net us enough info to keep Ezekiel out of prison, at the very least."

"So what are we doing tonight?" Henry wanted to know.

Jackson grimaced. "We're doing the jobs of the cops who've already sucked Cartman's balls," he said. "Do you know who's not on the witness list?"

Ellery nodded. They'd discussed this over the past week during trial prep.

"I got no idea," Henry said. He shrugged apologetically. "So sue me, I've been taking classes."

"Keep taking them, Junior," Jackson said, "because I'll give you this one for free. Annette Frazier. Zeke is being tried for criminal mischief and assault with a deadly weapon. Someone held a knife to Annette Frazier's throat and ripped it across her clavicle, leaving a gash it took twenty-seven stitches to close. We've got her picture, we've got her statement admitted into evidence, but you know what we don't have? We don't have her in court. And we don't have the right guy. So we're going to start with her and work the facts of the case, and we're going to track down the *right* guy tonight so they don't imprison the wrong guy tomorrow. I swear to Christ, if we hadn't had to work so hard tracking down witnesses and doing trial prep, I would have been on this already, but they fast-tracked this case, and I'm pretty sure it was to keep us off-balance."

"Easier to railroad us if we don't have time to prepare," Ellery said. "And they used the threat of revoking Ezekiel's bail and putting him back in jail to do it. People have spent years in jail awaiting trial. We couldn't take that risk."

Galen let out a pained grunt. "Agreed. As soon as they realized Zeke had decent representation, the DA's office began playing hardball. I hope your friend Arizona isn't putting herself too much at risk. There are plenty of people ready to fill her shoes if Cartman doesn't think she's balling hard enough. And those people won't have Brooks's sense of fair play."

"So we've got to find the guy who really did it, and we've got to put him on the stand," Jackson said, looking at Henry. "You ready for a rough night?"

Henry gave a diabolical grin. "*So* much better than school."

A Few Meager Chances

ELLERY WAS *not* excited about letting him off his leash.

Jackson could admit it. As he headed for the front door of the office and out into the blustery evening, he would have much rather gone back to their posh, spacious house on American River Drive and curled up with a cup of hot chocolate and a streaming service. He and Ellery could put on their pajamas and have foot fights in the middle of the couch, and then, when the movie was over, they could go to bed and spend some time finishing that kiss they'd started under the thruway.

But the risk to Ezekiel Halliday was far too grave for him and Ellery to put their night of snuggle bunnies before his case.

Sometimes they got to prioritize each other, but the thing that had brought them together and welded them tight was fixing the fucked-up they could fix.

It was time to pony up.

But that didn't mean Ellery didn't have one more moment of "be careful" left in him.

"Jackson, wait up," he said as Jackson turned the door latch. Ellery stepped neatly in front of Henry and drew intimately close. He put his hand on the sleeve of the denim jacket Jackson wore over his hoodie and grimaced. "It's raining outside, and this is what you're wearing?"

"Easier to move in," Jackson said briefly. "Now stop nagging me and give me a kiss for luck and tell me you're going to go home and feed the cats."

Ellery grunted. "Stay close to Henry. Don't take any unnecessary chances. And of course I'm going to feed the heathens, because if I don't they'll eat my eyeballs as I sleep."

Jackson choked back a laugh. "They will not! They *like* you." Well, Billy Bob, his battle-torn three-legged Siamese, liked Ellery, mostly because moving in with Ellery had resulted in the swank wet food, and Billy Bob knew that was Ellery's doing. Lucifer, their four-month-old black kitten—also with three legs—was used to being spoiled. He *might* go after Ellery's eyeballs, but not out of malice. Mostly out of curiosity, which really *was* going to kill the cat if he didn't learn to stop being curious about Billy Bob's ass, which he kept trying to lick. Cats—endlessly fascinating, but once you learned the answers to why they were trying to destroy the house at 3:00 a.m., you wondered why you bothered.

"Well, I like you," Ellery said dryly, keeping them on topic. "And I like you not bleeding and not sick. Be careful." And with that, he kissed Jackson quick and hard before backing up and gesturing for him and Henry to proceed.

Jackson stepped into the blustery evening with a sigh, wishing somebody could have contradicted the logic of what he and Henry were about to do.

"Are we taking the crap-mobile?" Henry asked as they headed for the stairs. The building had an elevator that Galen would probably use when Jade took him home, but Henry was like Jackson—his body got twitchy if he didn't use it enough.

"Probably to Galen's immense relief," Jackson said to answer Henry's question. Henry's official job title was Driver and Personal Assistant. He didn't have his PI's license yet, although he'd proven adept at the job, and he and Jackson worked together better than Jackson had ever imagined he could with a partner. But while Henry earned his license, he collected his check from the law firm for, ostensibly, driving Galen to and from the office, as well as running errands, since Galen's mobility was compromised. Henry didn't have a car of his own and went back and forth between driving the town car John had bought for Galen's comfort and whatever car Jackson was driving that hadn't been blown up, crashed, or otherwise destroyed.

This month's version was a "rental." Jackson's newish CR-V had been destroyed in a parking space, and Jackson had given the car to a friend to fix up, under the table since he figured Ellery's insurance would give them the boot if they reported one more claim. His buddy had gotten them a "good deal" on the bodywork and a rental, but after they'd gotten the CR-V back the first time, there had been some electrical glitches, which had devolved into engine work, which had devolved into work on the frame and then the interior and then the cooling system and then....

And long story short, Jackson and Henry had been driving around in a ten-year-old crap-brown Chrysler Town & Country for the past two months, and Galen hyperventilated whenever Henry drove it to his house to pick him up.

It didn't help that the damned thing was haunted, either.

"Has it been acting up?" Jackson asked as they clattered down the stairs, and Henry's snort of laughter told him there was a story coming.

"Okay, so Galen likes to ride in the back," Henry said as they neared the vehicle. "You know, so he can spread out and work. And he's got his briefcase balanced on the island in the middle, between the two back seats, right? You can have either three seats or the island or console or whatever, and he's set up like that. And we are at a complete stop—like, stuck for the next five minutes at the interminable light—and suddenly, and I swear, I didn't touch anything, not even the stereo, the console folds itself up and slides right into place flush with the floor, leaving all his stuff on top. He was gasping for air, trying to explain what the hell happened, and suddenly traffic is moving and there is nowhere—*nowhere*—to pull off and fix it. It's like the fuckin' car *knew* when to mess with him, and it chose the absolutely worst time to do it."

Jackson chuckled, feeling bad for Galen but relieved to have someone else who would believe the damned thing was haunted.

"What did he say when you guys finally got here?" he asked.

Henry guffawed. "He straightened his suit jacket, cleaned up his briefcase and papers, and then he actually *spoke* to the damned car. He was like 'Look, Drusilla, if that is indeed your name, I concede these are not the best of circumstances in which to coexist, but I promise upon my honor that if you do not act like a lady, *I* shall buy Mr. Rivers's next vehicle, and you shall be replaced. So think about that and decide if this sort of attitude is the kind you wish to carry with you into the scrap yard.' And then we were here. I went to help him out, and she started to close the door on him when he was only halfway out, so I think she's pissed and holding a grudge."

Jackson groaned. "Oh my God. That was *today*? She's going to make our life *hell*!"

Ellery thought they exaggerated the minivan's cantankerosity (Jackson's word), but Jackson had never met a car more thoroughly haunted by a pissed-off spirit before.

"I think it was the name thing," Henry said thoughtfully as they drew near the vehicle. "I think if we name her something besides Drusilla, she might not hate us so bad."

A part of Jackson wanted to kick the thing's tires, put sugar in her gas tank and walk away as he had her towed. But that would only cost Ellery *more* money, and somewhere in there, he was pretty sure he'd have to confess to an insurance agent about how he came to be driving the car in the first place.

Nope, making peace was the only way.

Jackson held out a hand as they neared the automobile, and Henry smacked the keys in his palm.

"Okay, girl," he said, walking up to the driver's side. "Remember us? We *love* you. You helped us catch that one perpetrator, remember? Good times. You're a good car. We can give you a better name if you like. Drusilla doesn't suit you, I swear. Maybe something rich-girl, like Stacy? Polly? Courtney/Whitney/Jessica?"

In response, the car's headlights flashed on, and Jackson eyed Henry over the hood.

"Jennifer?" Henry hazarded. "'Cause that's pretty. You've got good taste if you like Jennifer!"

The lights flashed once, and Jackson let out a breath. "Okay, Jennifer. That's good. We're going to go out on a little adventure tonight, so maybe, you know, work with us instead of against us. We sure would appreciate it."

In response, the car's horn beeped briefly and the doors unlocked.

"You're not even touching the key fob," Henry said bitterly.

"Nope," Jackson told him, trying not to shudder. "That's all Jennifer."

"Well, good for her." Henry was obviously trying not to put too much false brightness in his voice. "She's a *good* friend."

Very carefully—she'd been known to slam doors on hands or slide seats suddenly forward—the two of them got into the car. While she was warming up, Henry asked the obvious question.

"So where in the fuck are we going? You're like, 'Let's go get the perpetrator!' and I'm like, 'Yeah!' but, uhm, seriously—how do we know who he is?"

"I've done some of the groundwork already," Jackson said, thanking God, Goddess, and Jennifer for that. He'd been needed in the courtroom today because Effie and Arturo had asked him to be; they'd responded to him during pretrial, and they'd both needed the moral support. But even though the trial date had been pushed up and crammed through, all the better to fit the agenda, he'd taken the list of police interviews provided by the prosecution and tracked down the ones who hadn't been called in. He'd been prepared—and so had Ellery, although Ellery was always reluctant to let their jobs intrude on their off hours—to run down the real perpetrator after the dog and pony show was over.

He pulled out his phone. "Here, Junior, I've got the list of names, numbers, and addresses right here. See Effie's number in my phone? Call the number after hers. It's Annette Frazier, the victim, who purportedly wasn't asked to come in today because of her wounds."

"That *is* a lot of stitches," Henry agreed.

"Yeah, but our supposed perpetrator was there in a wheelchair with his jaw wired shut," Jackson said in disgust. "There's got to be something else. Do you remember your script?"

Jackson and Jade had been working with him on interviewing techniques, starting off with identifying himself and his reason for wanting to speak.

"All up here," Henry said, tapping his temple.

"Excellent. Be sure to mention your colleague—"

"You."

"Exactly, and if they seem to think we're serial killers, remind them that all investigations are done within legal boundaries. Sometimes it makes people think we won't hurt them, which is hysterical if you're the one pushing Zeke Halliday's wheelchair to the restroom, but they don't have to know that." If any one of the four choirboy cops sitting on the prosecution's side had been in sight when Jackson had been helping Zeke that afternoon, he would have hurt someone all right. He would have put them in the hospital and slept like a baby.

Henry's grunt had a thoughtful quality to it. "Is Zeke going to be all right?"

Jackson thought about his quiet presence during the trial and Arturo's gentle, unobtrusive pain management. "Physically, probably. But...." Jackson sighed. "He was sort of a rebel—kept trying to push his boundaries to be independent. I-I wouldn't be surprised if he never pushed another boundary after this, and you know me. I think that's a shame."

Jackson tried the wipers on the car, and after a few swipes, he figured the mostly not-blurry and not-foggy image of the road was about as good as his view as going to get.

"Time to head out," he said. "I looked up directions to Annette Frazier's house. You need to get on the horn."

HARMONY PARK, where the attack had happened, was near the river, close to the bike trail and the levee, and it was no surprise when Annette

Frazier's house turned out to be within walking distance of it. The majority of the park was used for soccer fields, but there were trees and underbrush on the river side of the fields, near the levee, where Jackson had scouted for the place Effie had first seen Zeke. She'd been walking her dogs, hugging the shade, and Zeke had been sitting back underneath a tree.

As Jackson piloted the minivan through ever-slickening streets, he found himself grateful that Zeke was at least cared for right now. He and Ellery had been inside the care home, seen the staff interact with the residents, and knew the level of dedication it took to be patient and professional and kind twenty-four seven.

Zeke might someday get some more independence, but right now he was safe, and safe counted.

"She was okay with us stopping by?" Jackson asked.

"Yeah," Henry said. "In fact, she was surprised nobody had interviewed her before now."

Jackson grunted. "Arizona is too good not to—she must have been acting on orders. God… this whole thing stinks to high heaven."

"You know, the world is a pretty fucked-up place when the DA would rather prosecute a man with a disability than find the actual perpetrator."

"What's fucked-up is that he thinks this makes him look tough," Jackson muttered. "But we've seen it in the news, on TV. Thirty-three percent of the country thinks it's okay to mock the disabled, or scapegoat their troubles on people who need social services. And they're loud and obnoxious about it. If you're the kind of politician who panders to that crowd, this isn't about you being a fucking lowlife bully, it's about you proving you've got the biggest straight white penis."

"My bent white penis objects to these people." Somehow Henry managed to make him laugh, although the fury churning in his stomach was enough to nauseate him.

"God, all penises should object to these people. A penis without compassion and a brain is just a dick. There's our house."

The houses clustered in the blocks around the park were older—they'd been built in the 1960s—and small, but they tended to have adorable gardens. Annette Frazier must have loved her roses, because her yard was full of them, growing rampant without anybody to tend them and reaching out spiked tendrils in the blowing rain.

Jackson parked the minivan in front of the house, and he and Henry fought their way up the walk, much like the prince in the "Sleeping Beauty" fairy tale was said to have done, only wielding their denim-jacket-covered arms instead of shields.

When they knocked on the intricately carved white door with paint barely starting to peel, they were greeted by a white man in his midfifties with a classic dad bod—pouchy little stomach, thin legs in baggy, no-assed jeans, and narrow shoulders underneath a hooded sweatshirt much like theirs, but his read Engineers Do It Repeatedly for Quality Checks. His graying hair was receding a bit, but his smile pushed at the lines by his eyes, and Jackson thought that made him a little bit sexy.

"Come in," he said. "I'm Larry Frazier, Annette's husband. Annie's still taking it easy—no leaping up from the chair for her, is there, Annie?"

Annette Frazier was a soft, round, biscuit-dough counterpart to her husband, with grays peeking out from the dark brown dye job and lines around her eyes that made the hair color a lie anyway. She was holding a black cat on her lap, sleek and imperious, and Jackson had a moment of missing Lucifer, the new kitten.

"Hello, handsome boy," he said softly, extending his fingers. "May I pet?"

"If he'll let you," Annette said, smiling a bit. Jackson held out just two fingers, close enough to whisker level for the cat to feel his presence. Very intentionally he rubbed his whiskers against Jackson, and Jackson smoothed them back again. The cat retreated, and Jackson smiled.

"I think that's enough. His royal highness is satisfied," he said, grinning at the woman. She gave him a tired smile back, and he took in the bandages then, underneath her flowered sweatshirt. They were taped at the neck and along the shoulder and bulged at the front of her chest, before the breast tissue started. Oh, he needed to tread carefully here. This woman, this nice woman, had been hurt. He needed to respect that.

"So nobody has come by to interview you?" he asked after he and Henry had made themselves comfortable on the corduroy couch. The living room was small and structured around a mid-sized flat-screen television, but it was cozy. The furniture was worn but still comfortable, although the coffee table was a heavy lacquered maple relic to a bygone age.

"Not after the initial incident," Annette said, looking worried. "They said they caught the guy, but the sketches I've seen on television haven't looked like him at all."

"Nobody asked you to identify him?" Jackson asked, looking at Henry in dismay.

"No. Is that normal?" Annette was chewing her lip, and Jackson took a breath.

"No. That's not normal at all," he said, pulling out his phone. "Look, I need you to give me *your* version of events that day, and then I'm going to show you a picture and ask you to identify the man in the picture. So far, all I've heard is the police report, and I don't really trust those." He gave his most charming smile. "I work for the defense—I'm not supposed to."

"As you should not," Annette said staunchly. "I teach middle school. We try to tell them to use their critical thinking skills when interpreting literature."

"That's my kind of teacher," Jackson said, winking. "Now I'm going to record this," he said, setting his phone on the table, set to record. He stated the date and the time and who it was in the room. "Now, Annette, all you have to do is tell me about the day at the park."

Annette nodded. "Well, it was early Saturday, late September. I wanted to get my walk in before it got too hot. I usually meet my friend at the park around nine—she's got a big golden retriever—but it's not a rule or anything. We just try to be there at the same time, same place. So I was waiting by the bathrooms, where we usually see each other, right where the underbrush opens out."

"By the toys?" Jackson asked, because he'd looked at maps of the park with Effie during prep.

"Yes. I was standing there when I saw a couple of guys talking."

"What did they look like?" Jackson asked, knowing this was critical.

"Well, they looked like *cops* is what they looked like," Annette said, sounding unhappy about it. "But they weren't dressed like it. One was tall and rangy. He had the haircut and the posture, right? Dark hair, dark eyes, white skin. In his late thirties, I'd guess. I… I've seen the cops who come to the park during the week to roust the homeless. I'm almost positive this man was one of those policemen, but I'm not sure of it. I'd need to see pictures."

Jackson slow-blinked. Well, wasn't often clues like that fell into your lap, was it? He leaned over to Henry and murmured, "Have Ellery send ID shots of the arresting officers to my phone."

Henry nodded, and Jackson returned his full attention to Annette Frazier. "That's fascinating," he said, sincere as hell. "Keep going."

"Well, the other man had longer hair, and it was weird. He started out upright, and as Roger Ramjet as the other guy. But as I was watching, his shoulders seemed to stoop. He started to bounce on his toes. It was like watching an actor, you know? Backstage? Like that film *Get Shorty*, where Danny DeVito becomes a mobster right in front of your eyes?"

Jackson knew *his* eyes were getting big. "Like getting into character," he said, making sure.

"Yes!" She smiled, her round, lined face becoming younger, animated. Jackson bet she was an amazing teacher—he'd learned that the best ones had smile lines and looked like your favorite sweater. "I remember thinking I had to tell Larry, you know, because it was so fascinating. I thought he might be trying out for a play or something."

Jackson nodded, laughing a little. "What play was he trying out for?" he asked.

"*Basketball Diaries*," she said promptly, her laughter fading. "Or a new biography on Lenny Bruce. Or Kurt Cobain."

He heard Henry make a suspicious noise next to him and didn't dare look his partner in the eye. "So, uhm, drug addict."

She nodded emphatically. "I know what it looks like when someone's jonesing, sadly enough," she added. "And this guy did too. He started doing the junkie tap on his thigh with his thumb, started to bounce on his toes, started to look around furtively. I mean, he wasn't doing that when I first saw them talking. It was just two guys, shooting the breeze."

"Hunh," Jackson said, completely lost in thought. "That's… that's something that didn't come up in court today. Keep going."

"Well, the one guy gave a nod—"

"Which guy?" Jackson asked. "The actor guy? And what did he look like?"

"Oh! Yes! The actor guy gave a nod. And he had long hair, like stringy, to his shoulder blades, under a ball cap. He was wearing a T-shirt under a plaid shirt. You know, with the plaid shirt unbuttoned and untucked. But his face was surprisingly young—narrow, high cheekbones. Like if he'd only gotten a haircut and a good shave he would have been a Boy Scout. Like the long hair and the beard were sort of schwacked on."

Jackson felt his lips quirk. "Schwacked on?" he asked.

"Yeah." She stroked the cat on her lap a little faster, as though seeking comfort. "Like when your worst kid comes in with a completely insincere smile on his face and you wonder where the little bugger stowed the bullied kid this time. Is it a trash can? The bathroom? You start calling the janitor and asking for a search before you even know who's missing. Because that smile isn't real. It's schwacked on. That was this guy's hair and beard. I mean, I know they were real, but they weren't really him."

"Understood," Jackson said, thinking *undercover police officer* but not wanting to say it out loud. "So he went to the bathroom. What did the other guy do?"

"He took off."

"What was he driving?"

She grunted in disgust. "One of those big-dick trucks? You know, not the serviceable ones, the F-150 or whatever, but the truck one bigger than that so everybody has to look at it and it doesn't fit in the lanes or the parking spaces."

"F-250," Jackson said, liking this woman more and more.

"Yeah. What'd you call 'em, Larry?"

"Aw, Annie—"

"No, it was funny!"

Larry grimaced apologetically at both of them. "A cock sleeve with an extra cab," he said.

Jackson had to cover his mouth with his hand, and he didn't dare meet Henry's eyes.

"I'm pretty sure we know which model you're talking about," Henry said, his voice strangled. "Color?"

"Red," she said promptly. "Like the end of a fat, red—"

"*Annie!*" Larry wailed, and Jackson wondered if this was going to be him and Ellery when they reached paunchy middle-age.

He sort of hoped so.

"So, moving on," Jackson said, holding on to himself. "What happened *next*."

"Well, the long-haired guy went to the bathroom, and I got a text from my friend that said she'd be there in about five minutes. I started to walk up to the park entrance to wait for her. We usually do the full block around the park—if you add in parts of the neighborhood, it's about two miles."

"Nice," Jackson said, because he knew exercising wasn't always everybody's favorite.

"And as I was walking up, I noticed that the picnic pavilion… you know, the covered tables beyond the toys?"

"Yeah, they were using a power hose on it when I went to scope out the scene," Jackson said, and to his surprise, Annette put a hand to her mouth, a look of anger and sadness crossing her face.

"Of course they were," she said vehemently. "Because now they've got an excuse to kick the homeless out, right? One guy they *think* was homeless goes on some sort of rampage and they relocate everybody to Redding, don't they!"

Jackson blinked at her. "Redding?"

"There's an agreement with the prison system to drop their released prisoners in Redding. Apparently the murder rate there is very scary."

Jackson blinked. "Is that true?" he asked. "Or a liberal urban myth?"

Larry held his hand perpendicular to the floor and wiggled it back and forth in the classic "maybe" gesture. "We have a friend who lives there who swears that the mayor has a thing going with Folsom Prison, but it's true their homeless problem is horrific."

Oh Lord, there went his stomach again. "One city at a time," he said grimly. "Tell us about the homeless population in the park."

"They tended to hang out in the pavilion," Annette Frazier told him. "There's an overhang to shelter them from the elements, and there's picnic tables for socializing. You can…." She grimaced. "You can smell pot there a lot, but, you know, it's not shooting up, so better that. Anyway, a lot of the time they'll hang out there or stash their gear. But it's not comfortable to sleep, so they sleep near the tree line, in the underbrush. The place is almost always in shadow."

Jackson nodded. "And you felt safe walking there?" he asked.

She shrugged. "Well, there's bad people everywhere," she replied, "so I know it's not always safe. But I know some of the folks by name. I chat. In the summer, I bring big flats of water, and in the winter, I'll go early on holidays and bring containers with real turkey dinners in them."

Her smile at her husband was winsome. "Larry helps me put them together, and we buy socks and toothbrushes and things and give them as gifts."

"She makes fleece scarves for everybody," Larry said fondly. "I mean, yes, it's not great, which is why she tends to find friends to walk with, but being recognized there makes her feel safe."

Jackson nodded. He understood too. Homeless encampments weren't safe—there was no escaping that. But like Effie, Annette had refused to drive out people in need.

"So this long-haired guy—the actor—he wasn't a part of the usual crowd?" Jackson asked, to make sure.

"Oh, I hadn't seen him there before," she said. "And the people at the park wouldn't look at him, just like they wouldn't look at the cop in the street clothes."

Jackson was still thinking *undercover*—it practically screamed from his pores—but he had to keep that supposition to himself.

"So he went into the bathroom, and the other guy left, and you went near the pavilion to wait. What happened next?"

"So I was looking toward the street, and I guess the long-haired guy came out of the bathroom. He was there about four minutes." She let out a sigh. "Long enough to get high—I mean, really high. He started charging people, just getting in their face and yelling, like he was trying to incite them to violence. He terrified the people in the pavilion. One guy had a dog, and he was crouched in the corner, hugging his pit bull and sobbing. So I turned and told him shame on him, shame on him for scaring all those nice people like that. And… and it was weird. I swear he was really high. He wasn't faking it. His pupils were the size of UFOs. But he squeezed his eyes shut and rocked back and forth on his feet, and when he spoke, it was from far away. He said, 'Lady, you don't want any piece of this. Please. I beg of you. Go away.'"

Jackson's breath caught. He could see it so clearly. "And then?"

"And I thought I had him." Her voice shook. "I thought… you know, like the emotionally fragile students, I thought I'd talked him down. I said, 'You don't want to do this, honey. Why don't you find a quiet place and let it all simmer down in your head?' And for a minute, I thought he was going to do that. But then…." Her voice hardened. "Then the cops show up, sirens blazing, and they all screech to a halt like they think they're starring in some sort of television show, and suddenly there's six-dozen guns pointed inside that little pavilion. And he said,

'Fuck!' and that's when the knife came out and he had me around the waist and the knife at my throat."

She'd started to cry softly, and Larry, who had moved closer, tangled his fingers with hers in the cat's fur. "And everybody was yelling, and he was yelling back and dragging me away from the pavilion and toward the underbrush. And then, just when I thought it was going to be okay, he was going to let me go, the dog started barking, and one of the young officers—blond and red-faced, you know, like that one actor? Jesse somebody? He turns toward the guy with the dog and shouts, 'I'm gonna shoot you through your fuckin' dog!' and all the officers swivel their heads toward him. The guy goes, in my ear, mind you, 'Sorry, lady. I'm so sorry.' And then he cut me with the knife. Not even as hard as he could. I could feel him holding back, and I started to cry. Just as everybody turned back toward us, he shoved me forward and disappeared, and...." She buried her face into her husband's waist as he stood next to her chair. "I'm sorry," she sniffled. "Maybe this was why they didn't call me to testify. They knew I'd be a big weenie and hurt their case."

"I don't think that was it," Jackson said, and he and Henry exchanged furious looks. "Annette, we're almost done. You've been so brave. Everything you've told us is so helpful. I'm sorry to have to drag you through this."

She shook her head, taking the Kleenex her husband proffered her with a grateful little smile. "I'm sorry," she muttered, her voice a little more solid.

"Don't be," Jackson told her sincerely. "You have helped so much. The police report said nothing about any of this—not the dog, not how you were injured. That's all important stuff. Now I'm going to show you a picture of the guy they're trying for this crime. I know you've seen drawn pictures, but this was taken last month, before all this happened. I need you to tell me your first reaction."

He held out the picture of Zeke that Arturo had taken—apparently he took the residents' photos whenever they had a good day and gave them copies so they had an easier time of it when they had bad ones. Zeke's wide mouth was relaxed in a smile, and he was sitting up, facing the camera. The focus was precise enough so Annette couldn't see any of the physical anomalies—the larger joints, the elongated fingers—that would have marked him as having some sort of disability that would have made moving the way she'd described her assailant moving a chore.

"Zee?" she said, looking at Jackson's phone in wonder. "They're trying *Zee* for this?" She looked at Larry in distress. "The papers said Ezekiel Halliday. I had no idea…. Oh God. *Zee*?"

"You know this man?" Jackson asked, his heart hammering in his chest.

"Yes! His care home brings groups of residents there every week. I wave to them, they wave back. Zee comes out and talks. I say hello. He's very sweet, but…." Her brow furrowed. "The police are trying to say *Zee* held a knife to my throat? How in the hell would he do that?"

"The question we've been asking since we got this case," Jackson responded grimly. "But it helps that you know the victim—I mean, the accused." He grimaced. He couldn't make that mistake. He couldn't.

"Wait," she said, frowning. "The newsfeed said the perpetrator had to be taken to the hospital for injuries sustained in jail…." Her voice cracked, and the cat vacated her lap. "They *beat him*?" she shrieked.

"Which we will address in another trial," Jackson said. "As soon as we make sure he never has to go back to jail."

"*I want blood*!" she shouted, standing up abruptly and swaying a little on her feet. "God*dammit*, Larry, somebody's got to pay. This is *bullshit*. This is a *travesty*. This is—oh my God, this is—*what in the fuck is going on*? Why haven't I been called in to testify?" She glared at Jackson, who gave her a serene smile back.

"Would you like to testify?" he asked, practically batting his lashes. "Would you be prepared to testify tomorrow, for instance?"

She bared her teeth, a pudgy little woman who liked cats, liked to make fleece scarves and Christmas dinner for people who had none, and knew the name of the disabled folks who came to visit the park and the homeless people she saw every day.

"Try to fuckin' stop me!" she snarled.

"Wouldn't dream of it, ma'am," Jackson said. "But we need you to do us a favor and stay hidden until all the witnesses for the prosecution are inside the courtroom. I'll meet you at the side of the courthouse and escort you in, but you can't come in through the main door. Do you understand?"

She smiled a little. "They didn't ask me for a reason, that's what you're telling me. They'll object to me if they know I'm there."

Jackson nodded. "Oh yes, they will. And we want to catch them by surprise." He tried to calm himself down and remembered the other important thing she'd need to know. "And… and this is going to be the hard part. The guy with the knife? The *real* perpetrator? He might be there too. Can you face him? If Henry and I are there to keep you safe?"

She gave a sweet little smile—one of the saddest and bravest things Jackson had ever seen. "I swear to God, he didn't scare me as badly as the police. I think I'll be just fine."

In his pocket Jackson felt his phone buzz, probably with Ellery's text of the officer whom Annette had possibly seen in the park with the perpetrator. Oh yes, things were about to turn Zeke's way.

TWENTY MINUTES later, after Jackson had put Annette Frazier in touch with Ellery and left them conversing about particulars, he and Henry ventured out into the blustery dark.

"Fuck *me*," Henry muttered. "Jackson, that was *nuts*. I mean, I expected it to not be our guy, but… but was I hearing that right? Was that an *undercover cop* who sliced her up?"

"You know what's even more bonkers?" Jackson asked, approaching Jennifer with his hands up. "Sweetheart, you've got to let us in. We've got a few more places to go." And with that he clicked the key fob and the lights blinked and—contrary to every feature the car was supposed to have—the two front doors popped open.

Jackson and Henry stopped, and Jackson swallowed. "Thanks, honey. You're a good girl, and we're grateful. I'll try to get your oil changed sometime this week—how's that? Sound good?" The lights blinked on and off, and he and Henry got in the car.

"Uh, Jackson?" Henry whispered.

"We're not talking about it," Jackson muttered. "We've got shit to do tonight, and if, uhm, Jennifer is up to help us, that's even better."

"Good car," Henry said, patting the dashboard. "Happy to work with you." Then he got back to the matter at hand. "You were telling me what was even more bonkers?"

"Yeah," Jackson said. "The most bonkers thing about that entire scenario is that I think he cut her to keep that young blond cop from shooting the guy with the dog."

Henry let out a low whistle. "I didn't catch that. But it would make sense. Everybody turns around to see the dumb kid cop aiming at the dog and his owner, and our guy…. It sounds like he went in the bathroom to get high on purpose, right?"

"That was my take. He's an undercover cop. He's told by his handler that he's supposed to create a stink in the homeless encampment. He's not happy about it. He goes into the bathroom, gets high as a fucking kite because he's been under too long, and he comes out ready to raise hell."

"And then Annette steps in, trying to talk him down," Henry continued. "And she's good at it. And he's thinking, 'I can just walk away from this and tell my handler it wasn't a good day to fuck around here,' when the cops show up, so he takes her hostage because that was the sort of thing he was *told* to do."

Jackson nodded, accelerating gently through the sopping wet streets of the residential neighborhood. It was exactly the sort of lower-middle-class area where there *should* have been homeless encampments all over the place. They should have covered the park, been sleeping in alcoves near the drugstore he was about to pass, be hunkered down under the carport of the shopping mall, not because anybody should be living like that, but because this was the sort of neighborhood where the cops only came so often.

But they weren't—just like the pavilion at the park had been power hosed, this entire part of the city had been scrubbed clean of the people who would have gone home if only they could.

"It was," Jackson said. "He was obeying orders, but he didn't want to. That's why he got high as a fucking kite. So he's got the knife out, and he's hating the sitch, and he sees the dumbfuck young cop about to blow away the guy and his dog, and he says, 'I'm sorry,' and cuts her. Not her face—did you notice that?"

"Not her throat, either," Henry said. "It was along her clavicle, across her shoulder, and into the meat of her arm."

"Not comfortable—and scary as fuck for poor Annette, who was just there to walk with a friend—"

"But not lethal either," Henry finished. "Yeah. I think you're right. He was there to raise a stink, and he didn't count on getting this super sweet woman as a hostage, and he didn't want to see the guy and his dog get blown away, so he gives her a flesh wound and disappears."

"And Zeke gets the blame because the cops figure him for homeless too. They have no idea he's got people who will go to the mat for him. They're halfway through their case—I swear to God the DA filed charges while he was still getting stitched up from the beating the cops gave him—and they didn't need to interview a soul."

"Oh my God!" Henry exploded. "That's *right*! Those names you showed me. There were mostly cops and Annette's friend, but none of the people on that list were, you know, homeless. And that's where *this happened*."

"Yeah," Jackson said bitterly. "It's like they didn't fucking matter."

He and Henry breathed out slowly and evenly because they were both furious. Then Henry said, "But how do we find this undercover guy?" he asked. "How do we track him down?"

"We got sources," Jackson said, his gut clenching. "Remember?"

"K-Ski's still not working," Henry said, referring to their friend Sean Kryzynski, who had been hospitalized for a punctured lung only days before Jackson and Ellery had been involved in the car wreck. "As far as we know, he's getting fucked into the mattress by that hot nurse you got to take care of him."

Jackson smirked. He was not actually positive Sean was having an affair with the porn model who had volunteered to be Sean's stay-at-home help for room and board, but if he *was*, it might be the most emotionally healthy thing the repressed young detective had done in quite some time.

"And his partner is about through with us," Henry warned.

Well, shit. "That's true," Jackson agreed. Andre Christie, K-Ski's partner, had worked with them over the last two months, and they'd managed to make a number of legitimate busts out of the hash Christie's department had been trying to make of their reputation. But Christie was in hot water for depending on Jackson and Henry so much, and this latest case had given them an excuse to leave him alone so he could do his job without getting hassled by his department, and for him to distance himself from them so when they really *did* need him, and later K-Ski, their reputations would be in good enough shape to give them some clout.

"So not them," Henry prompted, breaking into Jackson's thoughts.

"No," Jackson said. "I was thinking more along the lines of Fetzer and Hardison."

"Beat cops," Henry said, proving that he remembered them from the thing that had gone down in August. "Is Hardison back up and running?"

He'd been shot in the leg—a through and through—but that didn't rule him out as a source of information.

"One way to see," he said. "Find Fetzer's number. She's the leader. Then give me the phone."

"I'll put it on speaker," Henry said primly. "Since you're old-school and all and don't have Bluetooth or earbuds."

Jackson risked a glower at Henry as he pulled to a halt in front of a red light. "Don't talk that way in front of Jennifer," he said meaningfully, because the car had obviously been made before Bluetooth was a standard feature.

"You're right," Henry said through clenched teeth. "My bad. Let me put it on speaker so we can all talk."

"Don't say a word," Jackson muttered, sotto voce. The phone stopped ringing and a woman's crisp voice came on.

"Fetzer speaking. I'm off duty, and I don't know you, and if you're a spam call I'm climbing through the phone lines and—"

"You know me," Jackson said, pouring charm through his vocal cords like whiskey through a bottleneck. "Adele! How's it going?"

"Like molasses until Jimmy gets put back on street duty," she snapped. "Hot Dog, you had better be calling to wish me Happy Halloween!"

Jackson belted out some artificially hearty laughter, aiming his car toward Stockton Boulevard. "Happy Halloween, Adele. What's *your* costume going to be?"

"A very pissed-off cop unless you tell me what you want," she said, but Jackson's eyebrows were still attached, so he thought maybe some of her fire was for show.

"Okay," Jackson said. "Maybe not *your* costume. Maybe another police officer's costume. A detective's costume. Someone who's been off the grid for a month. Probably a decent guy, but he's been under too long. Everybody's worried about him. What's *his* costume right now? Where's he trick-or-treating, Fetzer?"

"Oh shit," she muttered. "Gabriel. Cody Gabriel. You're looking for him?"

"I don't know," Jackson replied, losing all of his bravado in the face of her quiet concern. "Has he been missing since Harmony Park?"

She sucked in breath. "Is *that* why he went under? Was he there?"

"Do you know where he is?" He needed the information—tonight. If Ellery was going to have any chance of keeping Ezekiel Halliday out of jail, they had to have Cody Gabriel's side of the story.

Her voice wobbled. "Look, Cody Gabriel's… it's complicated with him. I-I can't turn him in, but…."

Jackson sucked in a breath, remembering everything Annette Frazier had just told him. "He's on a tear, isn't he?" he asked. "A run. He's been under and using for far too long."

It happened—God, he knew how it did. He'd been asked to wear a wire for months when he'd been trying to bring down his dirty partner all those years ago. And every day he'd gone out on the streets, under cover of being a "good team player," which meant another dirty cop, and he'd had to remember who he was. He'd had to remember not that he was on a wire, but that he *wasn't* the guy taking payoffs in drugs, money, and hookers. He had to remember that he *wasn't* who his partner said he was: a street kid who was doomed to be dirty before he was even born. He had to remember that he was *trying* to be the good guy here, and the whole time he was being played by the people listening in. Those people had hired somebody to take Jackson and his old partner out and had moved in on his partner's turf while Jackson had been fighting for his next breath in the hospital.

When he'd awakened, he'd had scars on his body that looked like his flesh was trying to turn itself inside out and scars on his soul that proved it wasn't only his flesh.

Cody Gabriel had been undercover, probably for a good reason, and somebody on his team had taken advantage of that, leaving Cody to make a shitty decision because it was the best decision he had. If he'd been on the edge, using product to bust the sellers, odds were good, really good, that he'd run away from Annette Frazier and jumped right down the hole.

It was safe in that hole, and the demons wouldn't get you there.

The only reason Jackson hadn't fallen down a hole much like it was that he'd been getting all the good and legal drugs in the hospital, just to keep him breathing.

"Adele, look. I don't want to screw him. I don't want to press charges. I don't think this was his fault. Somebody—somebody on the force—told him to cause a ruckus in the homeless camp. He didn't want to do it. Had to get high to do it. And then shit went horribly wrong and he took off. If he needs treatment, he needs treatment. We'll get him there. But he's not going to be okay until he makes this right. I'm not talking with the cops or the law—I'm talking with himself, do you understand? If things went down the way I think they did, he's a decent guy—"

"He's a *kid*," she said bitterly. "He's twenty-four, fresh out of Afghanistan, joined the force because he wanted to do good. He's a baby, and they sent him undercover, and...." Her voice cracked. "Man, if you can talk some sense into him, he's all yours. But be careful."

"Do you know where he is?" Jackson asked, heartsore.

"We *all* know where he is," Fetzer snapped. "He's in the homeless camp surrounding the fucking station."

Oh Jesus. And everybody knew he was there, and nobody wanted to bring him in because admitting he was on a run and addicted would end his fucking career.

"You suck," Jackson said, the words exploding out of him before he knew they were coming. "Your stupid uniforms suck, your dumb blue line sucks, your fucking hypocrisy sucks. He was better than the whole lot of you before he walked in the door."

"I can't argue," she said dispiritedly. "But I know his mother. If you can bring him home, I won't just owe you one. I'll owe you all of them. Jimmy too. You're right, this bullshit's gone on long enough."

Jackson hung up without signing off, and Henry pulled the phone away from him hastily, probably assuming, rightly, that Jackson was a heartbeat away from throwing it through the window of the minivan.

"The camp around the police station," Henry said into the silence.

"That's what she said." Jackson was shaking.

"I... am boggled."

Jackson snorted. Leave it to Henry to put things so succinctly.

"I am too," he answered, voice thick.

"So," Henry said. "You ready to save a life?" He held up his fist sideways, and Jackson hit it with his own.

"Tots and pears, brother. Tots and pears."

Grimly, they negotiated their way through the dark and stormy night.

Illicit Communication

ELLERY HAD made it home, his laptop in tow, and was living out the pajamas-and-dinner fantasy, but doing it all by his lonesome.

Well, except for Billy Bob and Lucifer, who were currently tussling over who got to get stoned first off a new catnip mouse. So far it was looking like Lucifer would win, but only because he was easy. One or two whiffs of that green herbal goodness and the three-legged black kitten was running around in circles, purring. Billy Bob, the three-legged Siamese cross, would probably eventually end up in a corner, taking long drags off the thing, with Lucifer chasing sparkles in the air next to him— at least, that's how it had gone through the last two catnip mice, and Ellery was starting to see a pattern.

And if he didn't have the cats to keep him company, he had Jade, who was talking his ear off through his earbuds.

"So," she said, "what are we going to be tomorrow?"

"Isn't it too late to get coordinating costumes?"

"You're going to be Dracula, right? Can I be Renfield?"

Ellery laughed. "Don't you want to be Van Helsing?"

"Ooh… yeah. Let me run it by Mike!" He could hear her talking offstage with her boyfriend. One of Jackson's best friends, Mike was a rednecked Virginia boy with prematurely white hair, beautiful blue eyes, and an uncomfortable, non-politically-correct way of looking at the world. How he'd ended up living with one of the most powerful women of color Ellery had ever met was a universal mystery, but Jackson loved seeing his sister-of-the-heart and his friend happy, so they'd stopped talking about how weird it was that they were together and started crossing their fingers that it would last.

Jade came back on the line. "He says that would be great, but he wants to make me a real working crossbow—"

"No!" Ellery protested. Then, before she got offended, he said, "Too many live targets, and I might be tempted too."

Jade laughed at that, and his stomach warmed. He and Jade had worked long and hard to build a bridge of friendship that would span

Jackson, whom they both loved. It had been worth it. She was as much a part of his family now as his sister or his mother or father, and if she and Jackson hadn't quit their old job to work for him, he would have needed to be awfully lucky to have found anyone close to her as an employee.

As a friend, he still couldn't believe his luck.

"Well, maybe Dracula and Van Helsing aren't as witty as we think they are," Jade conceded. "Who else do you got?"

"I'd like to make an ironic statement," Ellery said, "but I've got nothing."

"Charlie Brown and Lucy?" she asked out of the blue, and Ellery guffawed.

And blinked. Because he *was* the overly earnest kid who got caught taking himself seriously too often, and she was just the sort of girl who would yank that football away.

And who sat and dealt with his and Jackson's problems and never even got paid that five cents.

"Done. Do it. Yes. That's us. I like it."

She cackled. "Most excellent. I know where they sell them. I'll stop and get them tomorrow. It'll be awesome. Hey, Mike, get a load of what me and Ellery are gonna dress like!"

As she chattered to Mike—and Ellery stirred the chicken soup he had on simmer—he heard the signal over his Bluetooth for another call.

"Jade, this might be Jackson. I'm gonna switch over."

"Tell him about our costumes!" she said quickly. "Take care, bye!"

"Bye!" he said, before hitting the button of his earpiece. "Ellery Cramer, Attorney at Law."

He expected Jackson to be the one on the other line and to give him shit about being so prissy when he answered the phone, but that's not who he got.

"Hello, Mr. Cramer?" It was a vaguely familiar, distinctly female voice that Ellery couldn't place immediately. There was a great deal of static on the line as well, as though this person was calling from a landline or from out in the rain.

"Yes?" he answered, confused.

"This is Siren Herrera. You know me from work?"

"Yes, Ms. Herrera, but this isn't my work number," he said, which wasn't entirely true. He'd given his cell number out to Siren before, but she was sounding very odd.

"I'm aware." There was an iciness in her voice then, a snort of persnickety "No duh, asshole!" that caught Ellery's attention. What in the hell? "This is… this is tricky. I'm calling on a personal matter. Would you like to meet for coffee?"

"Tomorrow morning?" he hazarded.

"Tonight," came the crisp reply. "It's gotta be tonight."

He looked longingly at the soup, just simmering, and reluctantly turned off the burner. "Where—"

"Lawyers, Guns, and Money," she said. "It's on Howe Avenue."

He blinked. "There's a coffee shop called—"

"Yup. Corner of Howe and Hurley. I'll see you there in twenty minutes."

"I'll be wearing my pajamas," he snapped, because it would take that long to drive there through the rain.

She paused for a minute, as though remembering he was doing *her* a favor. "Half an hour?" she hazarded.

"Sure. Don't get pissed if I'm a little late."

"Bring Rivers with you."

For a moment, Ellery was going to tell her that Jackson was out doing law enforcement's job for them, but then he realized that this was supposed to be covert. "Jackson's a big boy," he said. "He's got his own errands to run."

Herrera's response was immediate and frustrated. "*Dammit!*"

"I'm sorry?"

"Not five fucking minutes, can you? Not five fucking minutes without one of you getting into the thick of it. God*dammit*. Okay. Fuck. See you in half an hour. Don't wreck the goddamned car. Fuck. Me."

And then she hung up, leaving Ellery puzzled—and not a little afraid for Jackson.

And also relatively sure he shouldn't be going to the meeting alone.

JADE AND Mike lived close to the location, but from another part of town, so Ellery met Jade in front of the "coffee shop," which was more like an upscale bar.

"Lawyers, Guns, and Money," she muttered. "Cute." Unlike her usual professional attire, she was dressed in thick leggings and a long tatty brown sweater, topped off by a magenta rain slicker. Ellery wouldn't have dreamed of correcting her fashion sense even under ordinary circumstances, but tonight he was wearing a pair of his own jeans and one of Jackson's new hooded sweatshirts and definitely had no room to talk. He hadn't been able to explain it as he'd gone to pick out casual clothes after removing his dinner from the burner. He just wanted to feel closer to Jackson, whose last communication had been a text to call Annette Frazier and arrange for a conference early in the morning, nowhere near the courthouse. Ellery had done that before his call to Jade, liking the sound of Ms. Frazier very much, but Jackson hadn't been forthcoming about his next stop, only texting that he was likely to be—in his words—"bringing home a can of worms."

Fantastic. That was a wonderful thing to have in the guest room, right? Everybody wanted a can of worms; they were the latest in sheets and comforters.

"Yeah," he muttered, shaking off his unease about Jackson. "It's hysterical. I hope it's okay that I ripped you away from Mike—"

"What ripping away?" she asked and gestured with her chin toward the familiar pickup truck cruising the parking lot. "He's going to park and do some reading."

Ellery tried and couldn't get past the lump in his throat. "He volunteered to come?"

She shrugged. "What can I say? That man loves me." She gave an impish, almost adorable smile then, and Ellery was charmed.

They pushed their way into the "coffee house," which smelled more of beer than caffeinated brew, and Ellery glanced around, looking for Siren Herrera in the dark corners of the establishment—and there were a lot of corners. Decorated in "classic bar," the place had dark paneling, redbrick tiles, and brass fixtures. It came with coasters proclaiming the name of the joint with a howling wolf over the word "lawyers" and some top-notch alcohol on the shelves, none of the bottles dusty, so it wasn't a dive. The clientele was mostly dressed well, and Ellery had seen a lot of Mercedes, BMWs and Jaguars in the parking lot. Mike's truck had looked like a battered pit bull among poodles.

Ellery and Jade, in their hanging-around-the-house clothes, looked poor and, in spite of the CSUS logo on Jackson's hoodie, uneducated.

As they searched the shadows, Ellery was bumped from behind by a man in a silk suit, holding three drinks.

"I'm sorry, are you just going to stand there?" he snapped.

Ellery's eyes narrowed and his lip curled, and he eyed the man up and down with disdain. "Second year out of law school," he deduced. "You've lost that perpetual studying squint, you've had a couple of good paychecks and can afford the suit, and you're young enough to be out drinking on a Thursday night. But you're not old enough to know who's who in your town, and you think it makes you look tough to go bullying people in bars." He sniffed. "Walk around."

The man's jaw dropped right when Jade tugged on his elbow. "Ellery. In the corner."

Ellery turned his head and spied a familiar face, but not the one he was expecting. He turned to walk toward a woman who was most definitely *not* Siren Herrera and missed part of what happened next.

All he knew was that a large body fell past him to the ground, the crash of the glassware on the brick flooring loud enough to stop the entire bar.

"Aw, did you drop your drinks?" Jade asked, standing a little bit behind the guy. "That's too bad. Maybe next time you shouldn't threaten to throw one on a guy with his back turned. He was right about you, wasn't he? Were you stung? Thought you'd teach him a lesson? Yeah." She kicked the guy almost gently in the thigh as he was struggling to get up. "Fuck off."

Then she stepped over his back, taking Ellery's offered hand, and the two of them made their way to the corner where Arizona Brooks sat, hiding her face behind her palm.

They slid into the relatively clean booth, and she eyed them both with disgust.

"You couldn't have brought Rivers with you, could you?"

"Oh, like Jackson would have been any more discreet," Jade said, rolling her eyes. "The only difference between me and Jackson is that boy's going to be able to stand up and finish his evening now that I'm done with him. Jackson would have taken him out. There would have been ambulances. Nobody threatens Ellery. You know that."

"Yeah. I know that. What the hell. It's only my career. Twenty-five years of practicing law. I'll be disbarred, but who cares."

Jade regarded her dispassionately. "Boo-hoo. You're doing something good for once and it's going to cost you. Would you like me to measure my brother's blood in pints, quarts, or half gallons? Because I assure you, he's lost more than that in the last eleven years. Hell, *Ellery's* lost more than that in the last *one*."

Ellery gently bumped her ankle under the table, and she glared at him.

"She's here, Jade," he said. "Give her the benefit of the doubt."

"Whatever."

"No, it's important. If she loses her job, the person who will get it next won't be as principled. Play nice."

Jade grimaced. "Fine. I'm sorry for being shitty. It's a dark and stormy night, Arizona. What are we doing here?"

Arizona had straightened her posture a little as Jade chewed her out. Maybe it was the mention of Jackson's blood, Ellery thought, because she knew—she *knew*—what corruption had cost him in the past.

"Your point's taken," she said with dignity. "And you're right. Look, I'm not supposed to be talking to you, you know that. But something is going down tonight, and it's not good."

Ellery frowned. "Something what? That's vague—"

"It's because I taunted them," Arizona said, sounding upset with herself. "Damned ego—we've all got one. Mine reared its ugly head in the courtroom today when we were walking out. I told them to find the guy who really perpetrated the crime. I knew you and Rivers were looking. I mean, how could you not be? As far as I was concerned, the only reason you hadn't walked into court with him the first day was that you had such blessed little time to prepare. Fucking Cartman—" She sucked in a breath, and Ellery could see her struggling with herself and part of him was warmed.

He'd known Cartman had been playing dirty pool from the start. He'd had Arizona all but threaten to put Ezekiel in jail with no trial date—and no endgame—if he hadn't agreed to the ridiculously rushed trial. He and Jackson had been scrambling to get Zeke out of jail, get him to the doctors, and put together a coherent story almost from the get-go. Their file had nothing but a bunch of police testimony, and as Jackson had announced that first day as they sat in the hospital waiting room speaking to Arturo, it stank like a barrel of rotten fish.

Which was why Jackson had gone out that night. He'd spent the weekend running down Effie and preparing her and Arturo for trial, but nothing—*nothing*—would beat the testimony of the guy who'd actually committed the crime.

As well as a reason—any reason—for the crime itself, or for the DA's terrifying intention to imprison an innocent and vulnerable citizen.

The only reason Ellery didn't join Jade in chewing Arizona out was that he and Jackson had figured out where Arturo had gotten their number. They weren't mainstream yet, and it certainly wasn't well known that they did pro bono work on the regular. The only place—*only* place—for Arturo and Ezekiel to have gotten the information that landed them in Jackson and Ellery's lap was from the prosecutorial goddess herself.

"We're all guilty of ego," Ellery said gently. "Witness the guy with the drinks." Who was currently standing up and looking very wounded in front of a pretty young woman wearing her own second-year suit. Well, she was making a big fuss over him and clucking over the scrapes on his hands and the holes at his knees. Mission accomplished. They'd gotten the guy laid.

"Yeah, but my ego put the perpetrator in danger," Arizona muttered. "Which may or may not be a tragedy, but if he gets dead, Ezekiel is screwed, and that *is* a problem."

Ellery had been with Jackson over a year, and he'd learned since that there was no such thing as a person who didn't count. "Both are unacceptable," he said sharply. "What did you hear?"

"Okay, so the police who I called on as witnesses—you may recall their testimony was very…."

"Identical," Ellery said dryly. "They all said exactly the same thing with exactly the same inflection."

Arizona nodded. "That was *not* my doing. Ellery, they walked into my office with that story all lined up. About how Ezekiel had come bounding out of the bathroom to grab Annette Frazier, and he'd been babbling incoherently and then cut her and run. I mean, you made a hash of that story. You were great. When you asked how all four of them could have seen Ezekiel come 'bounding' out of the bathroom when they hadn't arrived until after she'd been taken hostage, I had to keep myself from laughing. God, nothing about that story made sense, and you ripped it apart. And them. But they only look identical from the stand. In truth, the leader is the tall guy with the slicked-back hair and the widow's peak—Engall Goslar. He's a piece of work. Fifteen-year veteran on the force, has failed the sergeant's exam three times. His best buddy from high school is Charlie Boehner, the—"

"Union rep," Ellery said, seeing the way she flinched when he said it.

"They're like this," she said, holding her twined fingers up. "And Boehner is up to his iron-tight sphincter in this case. But through Goslar, you understand? So we went back to meet in my office today, and Goslar gets a text. He looks at the text and turns to me and says, 'Bitch, when do we put that little puke in jail?'"

"Charming," Ellery muttered. "And people say *I* get all the fun people to work for!"

"You've never had to defend a cop," she said sourly. "So I tell him that it's not going to happen, particularly if you guys find the real perp."

Ellery groaned. "Arizona!"

"Ego," she agreed, mouth pinched almost to nothing. "You're right, and I'm sorry."

"Can't change it now," he muttered, but God, nothing like waving the red flag at the bulls while they're shitting. "So how did they respond?"

She shook her head, looking like she was going to vomit. "Look, you dyke cunt, we've got it taken care of. As far as you know, the retard's the only game in town."

Jade and Ellery visibly recoiled, and Arizona shuddered and knocked back the remainder of the scotch she'd been nursing.

"Wow," Ellery said when he'd caught his breath from the sheer awfulness. He had no doubt the words had burned themselves into Arizona's brain.

"I am saying," she muttered. "That guy's a *prince*. But I don't have specifics. I only know something's going down, probably tonight. I wanted to warn you and Rivers. And at first I was going to let Siren do it, but then I thought I should take my own risks and...." She blew out a breath and met his eyes. Her own were a rather stunning turquoise, and in court, they were lined with kohl to make them stand out even more. But now, they were naked—as was her face—of any makeup. She was dressed much like Jade, only her sweater was a little newer and gray. She even had a hat, a simple black stocking cap, to hide the distinctive white brush cut. Very few people would know her for the high-powered ADA who showed up so often in the papers. She looked like a tired middle-aged woman, a little scared and a lot sad.

"And what?" Ellery prompted.

She shrugged. "And I was hoping Rivers hadn't gone out yet—that I could keep him home. You probably think it's bullshit, but I've gotten rather fond of the two of you. I... this summer when he was sick, that scared me. And it aged the fuck out of you, Cramer. I was hoping to spare you something. Like the woman said—" She nodded to Jade. "—it's not like you two haven't spilled enough of your own blood."

Ellery sighed and pinched the bridge of his nose between his thumb and forefinger, knowing exactly what Jackson would say. "They beat him, 'Zona. They didn't just arrest the wrong guy and throw him into gen pop. They beat him. They beat a disabled man so he couldn't tell anybody he shouldn't be in jail. Jackson's not going to come in because you warned him. He"—*wouldn't be the man I love*—"wouldn't be Jackson if he did."

She rubbed her eyes with her palms, and he could see how much this case had cost her. "I don't know what else to do. Ordinarily, if I thought my witnesses were dirty, I'd report it to the police."

Jade snorted and then sobered. "You'd better be careful," she said. "If they find out you've been talking to us, you're going to be in a world of hurt."

Arizona nodded. "I've taken… precautions." She reached into the bag at her side and pulled out a card and a pen. "I'm not staying at my house, and I picked up a burner phone. Here's my burner number. I don't want to know about any trial surprises. Feel free to knock me on my ass there. But, you know, if you get wind of… uhm…."

"Danger," Ellery said softly.

"Yeah." She looked away. "Once upon a time, a terrified teenager had a daughter. She was… not normal. Too many problems, certainly for a teenaged single mother to deal with. So the teenager gave the child up so she could go to college, thinking that hospitals and care homes would be a better bet. And she visited, brought toys, pretty clothes, and thought, 'This was a good idea. My baby needs more than me.' And one day, the little girl didn't wake up because her heart had a defect in it that nobody knew about, and…." Arizona caught her breath. "And it wasn't anybody's fault, but I keep thinking, it's our job, yours and mine, to protect the vulnerable. And what's going on in our courtroom isn't… isn't right." She swallowed, and before Ellery could say anything, or even touch her hand or offer comfort, she grabbed her bag. "I've got to go. Tell Rivers to watch his back. It would be great to know you two are going to outlive me."

And with that, she was gone, weaving her way in and around the young professionals like a street kid in Rome. She probably could have picked some pockets if she'd had a mind to; the dark blue trench coat she wore over her sweater and leggings rendered her almost invisible, down to her black tennis shoes.

"Goddamn that woman," Jade said thickly, and Ellery turned toward her and realized she was crying. With a sigh, he grabbed some napkins from the dispenser and handed them to her. She took them with a sniffle and looked at him unhappily. "What are we going to tell Jackson?" she asked.

"We tell him to watch his back," Ellery said. He took a deep breath and pulled out his phone. "And we tell Henry the same thing."

"Shit, here comes a waiter," she muttered.

"I want coffee," Ellery told her, starting to text. His stomach rumbled, and he thought woefully of the soup on the stove back home. "Never mind. We'll leave a tip and get the hell out of their booth. I need to eat, and I don't want bar food."

"I've got a casserole cooling on the oven," she muttered wistfully.

"I know. I have a big pot of chicken noodle soup. Made it with cilantro, have some sourdough bread to sop it up…."

"You're killing me. Finish your texts, and let's get our asses home." From outside, they could hear the howl of a particularly determined gust of wind.

Home, where all good boys should be.

Jackson, answer your damned phone.

He didn't, but Henry did.

Hey, Ellery, what's up? popped up on the text box.

Just got a warning from a credible source—cops are looking for the actual perp. They have something planned.

I think Jackson's found him. I'll keep an eye out.

Jackson's found him?

Yeah—homeless camp by police station. Guy's a cop. Undercover too long. Has been high since the park.

Ellery paused to let that sink in. Oh God. What would the witnesses in the courtroom do—what *wouldn't* they do—to keep Jackson and Ellery from getting the actual perpetrator in to testify.

Jesus, Henry. Be careful.

Will do. Watching his back. Wait—they're moving. Later.

Ellery let out a grunt of frustration and moved to stand. He pulled out his wallet and handed the approaching waiter a twenty, apologizing for using the table, and offered his hand to help Jade up.

"What?" she asked as they stepped out into the wind-screaming night again. "We blew that place like we were running from the cops. What did Jackson say?"

"He didn't," Ellery told her tersely. "Henry did. Jade, the perpetrator? Was an undercover cop."

"The actual holy fucking hell?" She came to a stop in front of him and whirled to face him, while he almost ran into her. "Do you think Arizona knew that?"

Ellery shook his head. "I'd bet my diploma she didn't." He swallowed, and Jade voiced the thought that had just hit him.

"Good, because you might be betting Jackson's life."

"Yeah." He shuddered, a gust of wind smacking them both as they turned toward the parking lot. "Henry said they were on the move. I don't know what that means. All I *do* know is that we're meeting Annette Frazier early tomorrow, and he promised to be there." He paused. "Promised."

She patted his hand. "It's not like last time." It sounded like she was making sure, but he answered her like it was a foregone conclusion.

"Not in the least. He... he's in a much better place." Nearly a year before, Jackson had gone off into a dark and stormy night to "investigate a case." Except he'd seen his mother's body on a coroner's slab that day, cut apart by the Dirty/Pretty Killer, and he had not been okay—not even close. And Ellery had lived the longest thirty hours of his life waiting for Jackson to come home. When he *had* come home, after a night of horrors, he'd been half out of his mind with fever and even worse with despair. He'd confessed brokenly to Ellery that he'd only planned on coming home to get Billy Bob and leave, because he didn't want to fuck Ellery's life up anymore—his words. Ellery would never, not in a million years, forget the way his heart had beat in his throat at how close Jackson had been to crawling off into a little hole and dying, alone and believing he was unloved.

The year since had been both unbelievably difficult and full of glorious revelations. The difficult part had been the healing they'd both had to do, both body and spirit, to get to a place where Ellery trusted Jackson to take care of himself and Jackson trusted that Ellery was not going to stop loving him if he screwed up. It had almost cost Jackson his life in June, when consequences from that long-ago fever and all that followed had come back to haunt them both in the form of a heart condition that they could manage, but that would never completely heal.

None of Jackson's wounds would ever *completely* heal, but Jackson had worked hard, so very hard, at being whole enough to sustain a relationship. And Ellery had worked hard at not expecting perfection from a man who had spent much of his life worrying about survival.

They'd both learned so much—and had come to trust each other so very much—in the past year. And as Ellery piloted his beloved Lexus sedan, which he *refused* to trade in for a newer model, dammit, back to the house on American River Drive that had seemed empty and bereft of any life before Jackson had moved in, he realized that this was the test of all that learning.

Jackson had kissed him, told him he'd keep in touch, and had left, promising he wouldn't take any unnecessary risks. Ellery had to trust he'd be back.

And dammit, Jackson had to keep that promise.

Far Away Oceans

"WE READY?" Henry asked as Jackson finished with his transformation. It wasn't much. Jackson kept old clothes and a shaving kit in the car out of habit, and Henry did too, because he'd seen how often Jackson had needed that secret stash. As they'd approached the homeless camp, Jackson had Henry pull over about a block away, in the dark recesses of a vacant parking lot, so he could change. He took off the denim jacket and swapped out his new T-shirt for one so old that the picture of Marvin the Martian was mostly flaked off, and the new sweatshirt, which was still damp from walking up Annette Frazier's driveway and back, for an old gray one with frayed sleeves and a Sac State logo that had been discontinued before Jackson was old enough to be in college.

And he'd swapped out his new jeans that fit his ass, with no holes and a stiff button fly, for a pair of old ones with almost *no* ass and big rips in the knees.

He finished relacing his shoes, which were newish, but it was dark outside and he could do nothing about them, and replaced the denim jacket, because it was worn enough to pass

"Ready *now*," he replied, taking a deep breath. Putting on the old clothes didn't bother him in an aesthetic sense, but God, he was remembering how cold it was to go wandering around in the wind and the rain with his ass hanging out.

"So you got your cell?" Henry asked.

"Got my cell." He should be insulted that Henry was nursemaiding him like this, but he was also reassured. He'd been out in the cold alone before. He didn't have to do that ever again. "And my earbud on. It'll be hidden by the hat and hood, but you'll be able to hear me."

"Thank God for technology. Speaking of, got your heartbeat watch?" Henry asked, and Jackson grimaced. The watch had been Ellery's idea, and it made sense because Jackson *had a heart condition*, but it was also an irritating reminder that he would need to be kept on a healthy leash for a good long time. Per Ellery's nagging, erm, suggestion, they'd keyed the watch into both Jackson's phone and Henry's, and then Lance had promptly bought Henry one so Jackson could have his stats and location too. It was frustrating, and it probably felt like what twins felt when they were harnessed together so they couldn't escape a controlling mother, but, well, the little bastards *did* keep escaping, so he figured he and Henry probably had the damned watches coming.

"It's all charged and everything," he said. It had a two-day charge, and Ellery made sure he charged it every night.

"Good," Henry told him. "So's mine. Keep it hidden, right?"

"Right," Jackson said, tucking it under his sleeve. Many homeless people had cell phones—it was the only way to apply for a job these days, and nearly a quarter of the unhomed population were employed. But the watch was an indulgence—and an obvious one—and it would make somebody look twice at him when he didn't want them to look at him at all.

Which reminded him. "Shitty free stocking cap," he muttered, pulling it over his blond hair. It was cold enough for the hood to go over the hat, which had a slight brim, and put his face in shadow. He was blond enough that his stubble didn't show for a couple of days, so he figured as long as he stayed out of the light, he should pass. "How do I look?"

Henry grunted. "Normally my answer is 'homeless,' but that's not funny tonight."

"It never was, Henry," Jackson told him gently. Then he patted the minivan's front seat. "I'm gonna get out, and you're gonna get in the driver's seat and track me. If things get dicey, I hit Call and leave the phone in my pocket. Hopefully you'll pick up enough to help. Ready?"

"As I'll ever be," Henry said, sounding a little psyched. Well, Jackson was too, so that was fine. With a heave of the door and a shiver as he hopped into the wet, cold night, Jackson was ready to go.

He was soaked before he got that first block to the encampment, and he realized that searching for somebody in the dark and the mud and the rain was not going to be easy. But then, he thought, Cody had been at this for a month; he wouldn't *be* in the dark and the mud and the rain. He'd have figured out a way to keep dry and warm, and he may be shooting up or high as a kite, but he'd been high when he'd cut Annette Frazier. He knew what was what when he was high. Or he had a month ago.

Jackson slouched his shoulders and kept his eyes down, scanning from side to side as he picked his way through shopping carts and mini tents, many of which looked uniform, as though they'd been given out recently so the people would at least have something to keep them dry. There were single men curled up neatly on pads, covered in sleeping bags from head to toe, keeping out of the elements in the simplest ways possible, and what looked to be entire families stuffed inside the tents that were only made for one. The tents were on the sidewalk, pushing into the shoulder, bending and warping the chain-link fence that surrounded the precinct parking lot so they could have a place on the gravel. The fence teetered, and in places had almost gone completely flat, in the area of the encampment that stretched at least two blocks before the building itself. At a recess in the fence, somebody had started a fire in a metal trash can, and mostly men were gathered around it, their faces twitchy and illuminated by the flames.

It was impossible to tell anybody's age, and Jackson knew that the "bathrooms" had to be nearby, because every now and then a gust of wind picked up the smell of human waste and threw the stench back over the huddled humans who had nowhere else to go.

Jackson hadn't been planning to hang around the firepit—he wasn't going to get anywhere asking any questions, particularly since he didn't know Cody Gabriel's name undercover. But maybe if he started asking about the guy who got the chick in the park, he might get answers. He was suddenly unsure of his ability to find the guy on this *particular* night without help.

And then he tripped over him.

He went sprawling into the mud, which was crusted with cigarette butts and old food wrappers, and tried not to retch like a baby as he pulled himself up. Then he turned to see what had caught his foot, and he realized it was a man, not hiding under a tent, not curled onto a mat— only a man crouching on a tiny section of concrete, arms wrapped around his knees.

"I'm sorry, brother," Jackson murmured, squatting down in front of the guy to make sure he wasn't hurt. In the light from the firepit, Jackson could see that he was dirty—as were they all, including Jackson, now— but relatively young. His beard was scraggly, his hair was probably light brown when it was clean, and it was down past his shoulders and hung in tangles. His cheeks were hollow, and so were his eyes, and he looked at Jackson with mute appeal.

"I don't know my name," he whispered. "Can you tell me my name?"

Jackson hissed. High. High as a kite. But so sad. So lost. Jackson only had Annette Frazier's description to go on, but nobody was listening that he could see.

"Cody?" he asked softly. "Cody Gabriel?"

And Cody Gabriel lowered his face into the cave of his arms and started to cry softly.

Jackson drew in close to him, looping an arm over his shoulders. "How you doin', brother?"

"I'm lost," he sobbed. "So lost. I can't find my way home."

"You're close enough to walk," Jackson told him. "Look up. Look past the fence. Do you see it?"

"I can't go back," Cody hiccupped. "I can't. I've... I've done things. They told me to do things. And I couldn't. And I had to. And I'm so lost."

Oh Lord. "Brother, if you stand up, we can go get you cleaned up. I'll get you someplace warm. Get you something to eat. We can find your way home."

"They'll kill me," he said, taking a shaky breath.

"I'll protect you. I swear."

Cody looked up and blinked hard, seeming to see Jackson for the first time. "Who *are* you?" he asked, his voice growing clearer.

"That's complicated." Jackson winked. "But don't worry. We'll get there. First let's get you out of the rain."

Cody wiped his nose across the back of his hand, which looked like it had seen a lot of that action. "Okay," he said, compliant as a child. "I'm so cold."

"Yeah. Yeah, I bet you are. C'mon."

Together they stood, and Jackson looked around again, afraid maybe their conversation and activity had been noted by the other campers.

But *they* weren't the ones causing a ripple. Jackson heard the low mutter of conversation and the buzz of excitement almost the same time he smelled the exhaust of a poorly maintained diesel-run bus. And then he saw the figures, made more ominous in the rain, silhouetted by the pink of the soda lamps: beat cops in rain ponchos, strolling through the encampment, swinging their collapsible batons casually, as though just making sure they were handy.

"C'mon," they urged. "Get out of the rain. Gather your things. We've got a hot meal for you if you get on the bus. Get up, there," and the tap—not brutal, but very, very clear—with the club. "Get yourself up. Food and shelter on the bus. Everybody up."

They were being nice. Too nice. Jackson had heard cops talk to the homeless too, and they were brutal. Inhuman. No empathy, no carrot before the stick.

Jackson remembered the power-washed pavilion in Harmony Park and how there hadn't been a hint of an encampment in the last week.

"Oh God," Cody whispered. "Don't let them see me. Don't let them see me. They know me."

Jackson nodded and wrapped one arm around Cody's shoulders while he pulled his hood and hat over his face with the other hand, checking that his earbud was in place as he did so. He knew them too, from court this last week. Engall Goslar was the tall one—the one who had probably told Cody to cause a ruckus at the homeless camp. Freddy McMurphy was he blond one, the one who'd probably been going to shoot the dog. The one who had whined about Ezekiel "resisting arrest" when Arizona called him on it. With them were the other two policemen who'd been on the list of witnesses for the prosecution—Neil Freethy and Keith Brown, in their thirties, medium builds, brown hair, brown eyes, just average everyday white boys with badges and batons, trying to herd the entire homeless encampment onto two buses that were sitting by the curb.

Jackson kept his arm around Cody and kept their faces hidden, looking for a way around the buses through the crowd of tired, wet, miserable people moving toward a heated place to sleep. Every time he tried to steer them through a gap in the crowd, another cop would show up. At one point, Engall Goslar himself sneered at Jackson, apparently taking the arm around Cody's shoulder for romance.

"C'mon, you two. You can screw when we get where we're going. Get on the bus. Food and shelter on the bus. Get your asses over."

Jackson thought for a moment he was busted, but then he realized Goslar wasn't really looking at his face. At the dirt and mud crusted on his old clothes, yes, but not at his face.

Fair enough, but he didn't see any way out. There was a table in front of the open bus set up with little cardboard boxes. Meals— hamburgers and hotdogs, most likely, with fries, but hot—as well as little paper cups with coffee. People were taking from the pile before hauling whatever sleeping bag or tent they'd been able to grab in the confusion and getting aboard the bus. Jackson heard the first protest from someone who realized he was leaving all his worldly possessions on the ground, and the wail of despair as he begged to go back to the shopping cart and get his little dog.

"He can't stay without me. He needs me… and it's cold and…."

Jackson winced as the baton made contact with flesh and the guy was thrown unceremoniously onto the bus and dragged to the back.

A gasp of shock coursed through the crowd, but not of surprise. It had been clear from the very beginning that this was not a choice.

"Keep moving," Jackson murmured into Cody's ear. "He doesn't see us, and I've got backup. Here, have some food." He grabbed a box and a coffee, handed them both to Cody, and nudged Cody carefully up the steps, fumbling in his pocket for his cell phone as he went. He resisted the urge to tap his earbud, knowing it was there and would pick up his voice, even mumbled. With a furtive look into his hand, he unlocked the phone and hit Henry's preset before hiding the thing back in the front pocket of his hoodie.

"Jackson?" Henry's voice, crisp and concerned in his ear, almost weakened his knees. "The fuck is going on?"

"Involuntary relocation," he muttered, following Cody to the back of the bus. The old man was there, crouching in a corner, arms wrapped around his knees. Jackson could hear him crying for "Poppy, my poor Poppy," and had to fight the sudden urge to beat the holy shit out of every cop involved in whatever the fuck this was.

"Do you need me to get you out?"

"Target acquired. All four witnesses present. Wait and follow us."

"Copy that. Did you say all your witnesses? The cops who beat your defendant? They're *all* there?"

"What are the fucking odds," Jackson muttered, watching as Cody slid into the seat in the very back, some of his cop's instincts apparently kicking in. Jackson followed, angling his body toward the window a little, the better to shield his and Cody's faces from the cop he was pretty sure would be coming to check on the back of the bus. "Need you to do me a favor before you follow us, though."

"Jackson, *you* are my priority—"

"Look, they made an old man abandon his dog. His fucking dog is out in the rain." Jackson's voice rose, and the request was ridiculous and sentimental, which told him that he was not as all right as he was pretending. So be it. "Could you just get the fucking dog?"

"Yeah," Henry said soothingly. "Name?"

"Poppy."

"Groovy. As soon as the buses take off, I'll go check. I've got some beef jerky here—me and Poppy will be fine as we tail your ass into the night. Where do you think you're going?"

The police station in downtown Sac was right by Highway 16, which in turn led to Highways 80 and 5.

Highway 5 could either take them to Disneyland or Redding, and given their conversation earlier that evening, Jackson was betting it wasn't Disneyland.

"Redding," he said and heard Henry suck in a breath.

"Conspiracy theories for the win."

"Bacon," Jackson said, seeing Engall Goslar standing in the doorway of the bus, which was now packed full.

"Roger that. I'll monitor, but don't worry about me."

The bus had grown silent as Goslar scoped out the passengers, as implacable as the Terminator. The only thing missing was the human half of his face.

"Poppy," the old man whined. "Poppy!"

"Would you shut up!" Goslar shouted. "You worthless puke. Why would you even *have* a dog!"

The old man burst into a fresh spate of tears, and Goslar took two strides down the aisle. Jackson swallowed, getting ready to stand up and take this asshole and go down swinging when Freddy McMurphy called Goslar's name sharply.

"We don't got time for that. Both buses are loaded and we gots to go."

"Fuckin' hick," Goslar said to McMurphy, but it was almost affectionate. "You can watch this one, then. I don't see Gabriel, but under all this dirt who could? If he's one of these assholes, remember the plan."

"Yeah, sure. What do I do if someone starts jonesing?"

Goslar gave a rather nasty laugh. "Make them eat their burger box, man. Drink their coffee. You shouldn't have any worries at all."

Jackson sucked in a breath and looked around at the others on the bus, most of whom had already started eating.

Many of whom were already nodding off. Jackson turned toward Cody, who was looking at the food and the coffee with absolute craving in his eyes.

Oh no.

At that moment, Goslar hauled down the steps, and McMurphy took the only seat left in the front of the bus, elbowing the woman next to him. "Get over, bitch. I don't want to smell you." She retreated to the corner, whimpering, and Jackson prayed for two minutes alone with this guy. No baton. No gun. Just Jackson and his unadulterated rage.

But the bus gave a jerk and a puff, the squeal of the brakes telling Jackson this must be a city vehicle, because it wasn't in great condition. He used the noise and the movement to whisper to Cody, who was still staring at his drug-laced dinner.

Jackson could see his hands shaking on the box.

"You hurting, brother?" he asked softly.

"I've got a fix in my pocket," Cody murmured. "But it's a lot of movement and hassle." He gave a shudder, something bone-deep that told Jackson he wasn't going to be able to wait.

"Can you do one bite at a time?" Jackson asked softly. "'Cause I've got to tell you, I don't like where this is going."

"Yeah," Cody whispered. "Me neither."

"How about you take a bite of burger and then listen to some of my story. Can you do that?"

With a slight nod, Cody started to unwrap his burger.

"I'm going to borrow your fries." Jackson took the little box of them in the bottom of the food box and leaned over toward the old man. "Have some," he offered quietly, and the old man gave a whimper. "Yeah, I know. You're worried about Poppy. Don't worry. I've got a friend who will get your dog and make sure he's safe. I can't promise I can get him back to you, but I can promise he'll be safe, okay?"

"Really?" the old man begged, and Jackson could see he was begging for hope more than anything else.

"Really," Henry said in his ear. "Poor thing—tiny black terrier Chihuahua thing, right?"

"A tiny black dog?" Jackson asked him. "A hairy Chihuahua?"

The old man's eyes glistened, and he took the fries from Jackson's hand. "You've got him?"

"My friend does. I promise. I don't know how this will shake out, or if I can find you—"

"Just take care of my dog." The man wept, taking a bite of fry. "That's all I ask." He unleashed a wet cough into the hollow of his elbow and then took another bite of fry, and Jackson could actually hear his breathing start to slow.

God, whatever was in the food, it was potent. Jackson pushed away the memory of being locked in the Dirty/Pretty killer's lair, an abandoned drug house that the serial killer had opened up to every junkie in the area. There had been dead bodies, lying in their own excrement, urine, and vomit, all over the house. Jackson, stoned from a forced injection, could still remember the face of the dead woman he'd stared at while he'd tried to come down enough from the high to escape.

It was like that, but worse in a way. He'd had a year with Ellery. A year of learning what happiness was. A year learning to value his own life, of learning the good he did didn't have to hurt him, body and soul.

And now he was back in that airless room, full of people falling into a drugged stupor, knowing that one wrong move, one wrong word, and the cop with the baton and the gun might just take him out.

He took a deep breath and looked again at Cody, who was sighing and leaning his head back, chewing. Panicked, Jackson checked his cardboard dinner box and breathed a sigh of relief. Three quarters of the burger was still there, although Cody washed down the bite with some of the coffee.

"Good?" Jackson asked, mostly to remind him not to go on the full trip.

"Strong," he said, taking a breath. "God, I hope they didn't give this to any of the kids."

Jackson shook his head. "They were targeting the men and the singles. I didn't see any of the family tents even disturbed."

"Fuck," Cody muttered. "Man, that can't be good. The kids are tracked to some extent. There's teachers and nurses down in the tents for them sometimes. This… us in these buses, I don't even know where we're going."

Jackson peered outside, watching as the bus took the left lane at the interchange. I-5 North. He'd called it. "Redding," he muttered, "at a guess. I swear, I thought it was a conspiracy theory."

"Thanks for that," Henry muttered in his ear. "I'm a little behind you. I would have freaked out."

"Definitely going to Redding," Jackson mumbled, reconfirming. "Poppy?"

"Eating beef jerky and doing fine. Jackson, I don't know if I've got enough gas to get to Redding. What say I pass the buses and stop off for some, then get back on the road? Tell me if you pull off, or when you pass my exit. Sound good?"

"Few more miles," Jackson said softly. "Just to make sure that's where we're headed. Then go for it."

"If you pass the airport, there's nowhere else the buses can go for a while. They're not a good bet for the roads to the coast, particularly not in this rain."

"Roger that. Talk to me when you need to."

"Understood."

"Backup?" Cody asked, sounding more lucid than he had since Jackson found him.

"Yeah," Jackson said, eyes flickering to the front of the bus. Freddy McMurphy was playing on his phone. Jackson and Cody weren't the only ones still awake enough to talk, but nobody was shouting, and nobody was jonesing, and everybody was compliant. Well, the buses *were* warm, and they *were* dry, and the people had been fed, even if it was with drugs. Very fucking convenient, Jackson thought, tempted to go beat the shit out of Freddy McMurphy right there and then.

"Jackson, I'm gonna tell Ellery where we're going," Henry said. "It means I'm going to disconnect for five minutes, but I'll be back on ASAP. Don't panic."

"I'm fine. Tell him hi for me."

"Hi?" Henry taunted. "That's weak shit, Rivers. You know it."

"He knows the important stuff," Jackson said, smiling a little. "You can tell him that."

Henry laughed softly and then clicked off, and Jackson let out a sigh of relief.

"It's good to have a partner," Cody said softly. "I miss that in undercover."

"They keep you from going off the rails," Jackson agreed.

"You promised me a story." Cody took another deep breath. "I'm going to need it. I've been under a long time. The burger might stretch out between here and Redding, but I'm going to need to fix again when it's gone. I'm... I'm going to need real rehab, with the sedation and everything, or withdrawal will kill me." Another shudder. "Looking forward to it. Fun fucking times."

"Better than the alternative," Jackson said firmly. "And before you ask, yes, I've seen the alternative on the coroner's slab. I know what I'm talking about."

Cody grunted. "Always comes down to that. Story, pretty boy. I need something to keep my mind off the chemical mixer in my body."

"Okay," Jackson said, deciding it was time to put his guesses to the test. "This is the story about a good boy who was told to play pretend. He was a hero who was fighting the people on the street who provided poison to the good little girls and boys, but he was left on the streets too long, and he started to taste the poison, just a little, to help him recover from all the dragons breathing down his neck." Jackson paused and checked on Cody's breathing. "How'm I doing?"

"It's a shitty story," Cody muttered. "But you tell it so well. Keep going."

Fair enough.

"So some of the people this good boy trusted told him that they knew he'd tasted the poison. They were going to tell on him to the king of the good boys, and he would lose his job and not be a good boy anymore. He was desperate. He *loved* being a good boy. He loved protecting people. And the excitement of doing that—it was in his blood. He didn't want to lose that. He was afraid."

"Oh yeah." Cody's voice broke a little. "I do know this story. It's like it was my own."

Jackson's earbud clicked, and he pushed the button on the side without hesitation.

"Listening," Henry said softly, and Jackson continued.

"So these trusted people told our good boy that if he wanted to stay with the good boys, he had to do a bad thing. He had to cause a ruckus in a… a beggar's castle!" Jackson was proud of that one, because his knowledge of fairy tales was slim. "He had to lay waste to it—scream and shout and threaten people. And if he did this, they would let him still be a good boy."

"Goddammit." Cody tilted his head back, and through the grime tracking on his face, Jackson could see two tears coursing. Apparently this *was* a true story, but that didn't make Jackson feel any better.

"But he started to do it," Jackson said, "and he saw that he was hurting people. Innocent people. And by the time he realized that the men who told him to lay waste to the castle were bad, all the innocent people were in danger from the men who were supposed to protect them. And our good boy didn't want that. So he cut a very sweet woman who was just at the park for a walk and left her to bleed, knowing that the bad boys would have no choice but to check on her, and he took off."

"Yeah." Cody took a deep breath, and with a shaking hand ripped off a tiny bit of hamburger and popped it in his mouth. Well, they didn't have whiskey, and Jackson figured he was due.

"But that's not the end of the story," Jackson told him. Cody was startled enough to turn to look at him.

"What happened next?" he asked, and through the drugs and the hunger, the high and the despair, Jackson could hear the bright mind of what had probably been a very good officer at one time. Goddamn these people. Goddamn the Goslars and the McMurphys and the Freethys and the Browns who could come along and take a pure heart like this one and curb stomp it until there was nothing left.

"What happened next," Jackson said softly, "was that the bad guys found a disabled man on the sidewalk and assumed he was homeless. They accused him of the crime, beat him, and threw him in jail. And the lawyer I work for caught the case, and to keep him out of jail, we need—"

"Oh dear God." Cody closed his eyes and swallowed. "Disabled?"

"Yes. He'd made a break from his care home to prove he could go to the park himself—"

"Zee? He's always trying to tell Arturo he can do more than Arturo lets him do."

Oh Jesus. Good guy. Jackson had called him a good guy, and good guys knew their community. "Yeah. Ezekiel Halliday. They broke his pelvis and his jaw. He can't walk anymore, and the DA wants to put him back in jail."

Cody wiped his eyes with palms that were grime encrusted and hard-caked with the streets. "Fucking Jesus," he muttered. "Fucking assholes. I'll fucking kill them—"

"No you won't." Jackson's voice came out harder than he intended it to, and he made himself hush it down a little. "You'll come with me, and my partner will bail us out, and we'll clean you up, and you'll testify tomorrow, and then we'll get you to rehab with a twenty-four-seven protective detail if I'm the one standing by your door. You're a good man, Cody, and you got screwed. But you're going to want redemption, because you *are* a good man, and the only way out is through."

Cody took a long, dark, shuddery breath, and Jackson took a risk and squeezed his shoulder.

"Do you hear me?" he asked, to make sure.

"Yeah," Cody whispered. "I hear you. Fucking Jesus. They beat up Zee. I'll never forgive those fuckers. Or the force. Or the world."

"Let's work on getting Zee free and clear," Jackson murmured. "And then we'll work on the world."

"Yeah," Henry said in his ear. "Because we're still missing a big piece of the puzzle. You know that, right?"

"Roger that," Jackson murmured, not wanting to talk anymore. In a wave, some of the adrenaline rush of getting herded on the bus and realizing where he was and what was happening receded, leaving him shaking and miserable. The smell hit him then—all of it, from people stuck in the filthy mud to unwashed bodies, cigarette smoke, and urine. Old alcohol, spilled and allowed to fester.

Cody Gabriel sobbed quietly next to him, and Jackson's heart hurt and his head hurt, and he was trying not to have a giant panic attack as the bus driver earned his overtime piloting this human shipwreck through the storm.

But he was going to have to face it, he knew. They were *all* going to have to think about it. Because those cops had told Gabriel to do what he'd done for a reason, and Jackson honestly didn't think they were smart enough to drive that truck. What was the purpose here behind relocating the homeless camps, behind vilifying the vulnerable populations in the press? Somebody with money and resources and a plan. But who? And what was the plan?

All Jackson knew was that getting Ezekiel Halliday off on trumped-up charges had just gotten way more complicated than they'd first assumed.

The Home Fires

ELLERY'S CELL phone rang as he was letting himself back into the house. He shook the rain out of his hair and pulled the phone out of his back pocket on the way to the bedroom, determined to change back into his pajamas as soon as possible. He was cold, he was wet, he was frustrated, and he missed his damned boyfriend. He was going to need those flannel pj's ASAP.

And then he saw it was Henry and his heart almost stopped.

"Is he okay?"

They were the first words out of his mouth, and he wished he could pull them back. It wasn't fair to freak out all over Henry just because he remembered a dark, foggy night in mid-November when Jackson *hadn't* been okay.

"Yeah," Henry said, with enough of a pause in his voice to make Ellery's hackles rise. "He's fine. I'm in contact with him. He's fine."

"Wait. What do you *mean* you're in contact with him? Isn't the whole point of having backup not being alone?"

"Well, yes, Ellery, but sometimes backup means I'm in the back, trying to catch up! Now I told him I'd be in his ear in short order, so you need to listen to everything I say. Pen and paper?"

"Check," Ellery said, grabbing some from the odds and ends drawer in the kitchen and leaning over the counter thruway to write. In the background, he could hear the thump-whump of windshield wipers and the hum of a car in traffic. Oh God. Henry was calling him from the road, and Jackson wasn't there. *Focus, goddammit!*

"What do I need to know?"

"The actual perpetrator is named Cody Gabriel. He's an undercover policeman. Jackson and I think he was *ordered* to cause mayhem in the park—blackmailed, maybe, because he was tasting the candy he was supposed to get off the streets. You follow?"

Ellery had to blink because even now, corruption still stunned him. "Werewolf fucking Jesus," he breathed.

"Yes, you're following," Henry said on a sigh of relief. "Okay, so the cops who were supposed to arrest him were your guys—the witnesses in the Ezekiel Halliday case—and when shit was going down, one of them was going to waste a civilian and his dog. Gabriel cut Annette Frazier as a diversion. Everybody looked at her, the dog and the civilian didn't get shot, and Gabriel made his escape. Smart thing to do if he didn't want anybody to die, but a hard choice. It fucked him up. He's been on the streets for a month. We've found him."

"You just said *we*," Ellery muttered, "but you're telling me—"

At that moment he heard a distinct sound over the rainy traffic noise that had permeated the conversation—loud enough to make both Billy Bob and Lucifer spring to attention on the couch and hiss.

"Henry? Was that a dog?"

"Mm… well, yes. But Poppy is incidental."

"Poppy? You brought a *dog* with you to a stakeout?"

"We'll talk about Poppy later," Henry said. "Ellery, he needs me in his ear. Listen."

Ellery's hands were shaking. "Listening."

"We found Gabriel. He'd been living in the homeless encampment by the police station. He's been high for a month. But while Jackson was pulling him in, those *same four cops* showed up and rounded up the singles—mostly men, but not all—and put them on two buses. And drugged the food. I'm following the buses now, and Jackson thinks they're going to Redding."

"The actual fucking hell—"

"Yeah, *you* look it up. You're the one at home with a computer and a phone. This is not the first time they've done this. They had drugged food at the ready, Ellery. The whole bus was stoned, and they made the entire encampment by Harmony Park disappear as well. Annette Frazier was really fucking upset about that, but I can't investigate that now because I'm following him to Redding because, like you said, I got his back."

"Fuck fuck fuck fuck fuck…." Ellery sank into one of the kitchen chairs and stared at the words he'd written: *Cody Gabriel, paid to cause trouble, same four cops, GOING TO REDDING.* Where to fucking start?

"Well, yeah," Henry conceded. "It's not ideal. Look, could you call Galen and have him call the flophouse guys? They think I'm gonna be there later for movie night. I don't want them to worry. I gotta go. Jackson was calming Gabriel down and—"

"He needs you," Ellery said, sounding sharp and together when he was anything but. "I'll call Galen. Drive safe."

And with that he hung up and tried to catch his breath.

What to do, what to do, what to do....

He must have hit the button without paying attention. Galen Henderson came on, silky smooth, with all of Savannah sweltering in his voice.

"Why, Ellery, what can I do for you this evening?"

Ellery managed to calm his rampaging panic. "Well," he said, his voice tight, "Henry asked me to have you call the boys he mentors, and possibly Lance, and tell them he had to go out of town this evening and might not make it back in time for movies."

Galen was no fool. "Out of town? Where, pray tell, have Mr. Worrall and Mr. Rivers gotten themselves off to? Did they decide, perchance, to try their luck in Vegas? Visit Disneyland? Take a tour through Central California and inhale the lovely cowshit bouquet? We gave you a semifunctioning, almost literate PI in training, Mr. Cramer. What did you do with him?"

Some people, Ellery thought irritably, could have just said they were *worried* about Henry, but no, not Galen Henderson.

"My boyfriend is on a bus full of drugged homeless people who have been rounded up and shipped off to Redding," Ellery said, still not able to comprehend it himself. "Henry's riding backup. He, uhm, has a dog?"

Silence.

"Galen?"

"I heard you. I just... I'm at a loss."

"*You think?*"

"Hey, hey, don't get testy," Galen said, like suddenly *he* got to be the voice of reason. "What, exactly, is Jackson *doing* on said bus?"

Ellery let out a breath. "Chasing down our suspect," he said. And with that, he told Galen everything Henry had told him, along with Arizona's warning, and when he was done, the silence on the other end of the line was no less worried.

"This... this is not good," Galen said, pondering. "Ellery, somebody had to be giving those trained seals their balls and horns, you know that, right? They were told that somebody was going looking for Cody Gabriel, so they found him first. But more than that—they had a plan. Shoving half a homeless encampment onto a bus isn't a spur of the moment thing. Right down to drugging the food. They've done this before. And this little circus needs a ringmaster. Someone with a higher paygrade and maybe even a guy who owns the whole shebang."

"That's what Henry said," Ellery told him, calming down just having somebody to discuss it with. "He said that the encampment near Harmony Park disappeared as well. We knew there were a number of indigents on the witness list, but they're hard to track down—"

"Those cops were counting on that," Galen muttered. "Counting on how hard it would be to track them down, particularly after they'd been moved."

"They were," Ellery said bitterly. "And they were also counting on us not having time to do anything about it. We had three weeks to prepare, on top of our regular caseload, and that included picking a jury. Arizona didn't challenge a single one of my picks, and that's fishy. It was like she'd been told that rushing the case was more important than the jury selection. That's not right at all."

"They threatened to throw Zeke back in jail indefinitely to await trial," Galen reminded him. "It wasn't fair. You knew that from the start. This is one more way to stack the deck."

"What do we do?" Ellery asked, not wanting to dwell on the basic unfairness of it.

"Ellery Cramer, you know better than to ask a question like that! What were you going to do before this little development?"

Ellery felt his spine stiffening and tried not to gape. "Hold on a minute, Galen. I think my mother just walked in."

Galen's chuckle was positively evil. "Having met that formidable woman, I shall take that as the compliment it was surely meant to be. You know what I'm asking."

"I was going to prep for Annette Frazier," Ellery said, because he *did* know what Galen was asking. "And now I need to prep for Cody Gabriel. Both of those are going to be rough, because I don't know the answer to every question."

Rule number one for a trial lawyer: Never ask a question that you didn't know the answer to, revised, in triplicate, and recorded. He wasn't going to be able to do that here—there were going to be nasty discoveries on the stand, and he had to work to keep things focused. The one thing—

and one thing only—he had to prove tomorrow was that Ezekiel Halliday had *not* committed the crime he'd been accused of.

"You've got your work cut out for you, Mr. Cramer," Galen said, voice crisp. "How about you call me in an hour with your preliminary line of questioning and I'll be there to punch holes in it for you."

Ellery hid a laugh. How very Galen. Nobody else he knew could offer such a valuable service under the guise of being a dick—with the added bonus of making sure Ellery would not be worrying the night away alone.

"Thank you," he said, and he was going for gratitude, but he must have let some of his worry show.

"Your Mr. Rivers is a very capable man," Galen said gently. "I do think you've got this."

Ellery took a breath. He and Galen had worked well together since June, when the man had pretty much pushed his way into Ellery's practice and said, "I do believe I'm needed here."

Galen had indeed been needed, and he'd been a good friend since. But it was difficult for Ellery to confide in people. His mother had been his confidant since childhood, mostly based on her terrifying competence. But Galen had jumped into Ellery and Jackson's quest for justice—real justice—without even asking about lawyer's fees. He'd treated Jade with the respect due a queen, and he'd shown a surprising toughness when things had gotten dicey.

And he'd told Ellery some very personal things when Ellery had needed to hear them to know he wasn't alone, so maybe it was time for Ellery to confide back.

"We caught the Dirty/Pretty killer a year ago," he said gruffly. "Jackson's mother was one of his victims. The things he went through, the night before, the day of…." He shuddered. "I almost lost him half a dozen times in two days, and then… then he fell into a swimming pool in November with a fever of 104. His heart stopped, Galen. And my heart stopped with it. And I know this isn't the same. Henry's riding behind him. He's in touch. He isn't off alone, sick and sad and…." *Suicidal.* He couldn't say it. Couldn't. Not now, when Jackson had worked so hard at wellness. It felt like a betrayal.

"You've had cause to worry in the past," Galen said softly.

"Yes. And he's been working so hard, but… he doesn't make any promises. He never guarantees he won't get hurt, or even that he'll make it back. Only that he'll try."

"It's a hard thing to live with," Galen murmured. "That lack of surety. John and I, we don't make promises of sobriety either. I… overdosed three years ago. He got me to the hospital, kicked my ass in rehab. I stayed an extra month to make sure. But… but we're both addicts. We know what an addict's promise is worth. We only promise to love each other. We promise to try. We work every day to make sobriety better than addiction. And that's all we've got sometimes."

"I know," Ellery replied. "You and John are brave. Jackson is brave. I… I never had to be brave until I managed to talk that asshole into my bed."

Galen gave a filthy chuckle. "Oh, it may have been your mouth, sir, but I highly doubt you were using it to talk."

Ellery sucked in a shocked breath and let it out on a laugh. Of course. Things had been getting entirely too personal between two men who relied on practicality and patience to get them through.

"I object to this line of questioning, Your Honor," Ellery retorted. "Now I'm going to change, because I'm still wet from going to see Arizona, and then I'm going to do some trial prep. I'll call you in an hour."

"I look forward to not sleeping with you tonight."

Ellery burst out laughing, and then, to his eternal delight, heard Galen admit something he'd never thought to hear.

"As God is my witness, I did not mean it that way," Galen protested, sounding awkward for the first time in their acquaintance.

"Well, you should have," Ellery said on a chuckle. "Because that was amazing. Talk to you in an hour."

He hung up and spent two minutes leaning on his elbows, his fingers laced behind his neck. *Oh, Jackson, you'd better not get hurt this time. Come on, baby, give us both a break, okay?*

And then he felt a tentative claw at the still-damp leg of his jeans. He dropped his hand automatically to rub Billy Bob between the ears and was rewarded with another claw at the leg.

"Okay, okay," he muttered, standing up. "Pajamas, laptop, couch. I hear you. You know, you two are getting spoiled."

Billy Bob gave a full-throated "*Mrowl!*" and Lucifer followed up with a tiny half-formed "*Mew.*"

Ellery bent down and scooped the three-legged black kitten up in his arms. "You need to keep him on his toes, you know," he murmured, and Lucifer rewarded him with that fully vibrational kitten purr.

Together they made their way to the bedroom to prepare for a long, long night.

I Can't Find My Way Home

"JACKSON, YOU with me?" Cody had fallen into a light drug-induced doze, as had the rest of the bus's occupants, and Henry's voice in his ear was reassuring. Surreptitiously Jackson checked his phone battery, relieved to see he had more than half a charge. They'd been on the bus for two hours. Henry had filled the tank of the minivan and caught up with them again. Easy to do, probably, given that the buses were chug-chug-chugging along at a maddening sixty-five mph, but it was a relief to know Henry had them in his rearview. Jackson had told him to go in front for a while so he didn't get queasy from the fumes.

"Still here," Jackson murmured. "How's the dog?"

"Sleeping." Henry gave a sigh. "Poor thing. He was cold and wet too, but you can tell he misses his human. I used to wonder why people without homes kept animals, and then it hit me—everybody needs someone to love, right? If you've got something inside you that can help a stray dog when your entire world can fit in a grocery cart, I'm saying go for it."

Jackson had to smile in the darkness. Henry had been raised "old-school." His father, Jackson gathered, had been a classic bigot. Blacks, browns, Jews, faggots need not apply. Henry had tried hard to hold on to his father's beliefs—even when they included Henry himself—but since he'd arrived on his brother's doorstep, he'd worked even harder to let go of those same beliefs and to believe in his fellow humans instead. Hearing him discover things that Jackson had always known was sort of wonderful. It meant that the faith in his fellow humans wasn't misplaced.

"Sometimes a pet is the difference between wanting to live and choosing the alternative," Jackson murmured, closing his eyes against the sodium lights, against the vast agricultural dark and wet beyond the bus, and feeling what he said in his bones. He was never sure what had brought Billy Bob to his door, half-drowned, half-grown, fully determined to fuck all the things in the neighborhood as long as he could make his way back to Jackson's home. He would never admit it, especially to Ellery, but getting the cat fixed had probably done both

Jackson and Billy Bob a favor. Billy Bob would live a longer life, now that he'd declared Ellery's house his domain to rule, and Jackson wanted his buddy with him as long as felinely possible.

"Bah," Henry said playfully. "Who wants a dog when they've got five half-grown porn stars to take care of?"

Jackson gave a weak chuckle. "How *is* Cotton, anyway?" Henry and his boyfriend—who used to be a porn model himself—mentored the models in "the flophouse." The flophouse was an apartment that a revolving bunch of young men used until they could afford rent on someplace less crowded—and less likely to smell like old jizz. According to Henry, sex was *on* at the flophouse: morning, night, and afternoon delight. But just because the kids knew how to use their penises, that *didn't* mean they were adults, and Henry and Lance had picked up on that all by themselves. By mutual decision, when they'd moved out of the place, they hadn't moved far, because they could feel the need for big brothers radiating from that pit of angst and hormones, and they didn't have the heart to let those kids down.

Cotton was a former model who had recently had his heart broken—maybe. He'd been rather forcefully recruited to nurse a soldier back to health when the man had needed to be hidden for a while, and the inevitable parting had hit Cotton hard.

"He's going into nursing school, if you can believe that," Henry said, sounding cheerful. "Some place from down in San Diego sent him a full ride offer. Uhm, the woman who signed the offer was, uhm, Jessica Constant."

Jackson had to work to keep his giggle from escaping. The soldier Cotton had nursed back to health had been Jason Constant, and apparently he had a sister. And both Jackson and Henry knew Jason's classified military base was down in the desert, northeast of San Diego. Well, maybe Cotton wouldn't be brokenhearted for long.

"That's the best thing I've heard all day," he said, meaning it. He, Henry, and Ellery had been called in to give Jason and Cotton an assist right before they'd caught the Zeke Halliday case. Jackson felt like it was the last time he'd taken a deep breath.

"Yeah." Henry sounded self-satisfied. "I know Cotton did that growing all by himself, but I have to admit, I feel sort of gratified being there to see it."

"Don't be modest," Jackson murmured. "That kid might not have made it if you—and Lance and John—hadn't stepped up to be there for him. And he's going to nursing school? He wouldn't have had that confidence back in June. Part of that's you. You need to take the win. It doesn't happen often."

"Says the man who literally had me rescue a puppy from the rain," Henry laughed.

Next to him, Cody Gabriel gave a little whimper and a twitch in his sleep, and Jackson couldn't make himself laugh back. Cody had eaten another quarter of the hamburger, keeping half of it carefully wrapped and rationed, but Jackson knew they were going to be cutting it close. Cody had to fix to make it through the night, and he'd have to fix to make it through court. And after all that, keeping him alive while Ellery begged for protective custody was going to be a challenge.

"Jackson?" Henry asked, his voice unbearably gentle.

"I'm fine," Jackson lied. "Have you been able to figure out exactly where we're going?"

"I've been trying to imagine where the best place to ship people would be, particularly in the winter when nobody's there. There's a lot of empty around Redding, but it turns out the campgrounds at Whiskeytown have been closed since September. If I had to hazard a guess, I'd say out there. I mean, I know the lake is probably nonexistent at this point, but it's still water. And you have to go out of your way to get there. I think the bus could make it down the road, and there's camping facilities. I mean, if *I* was a Machiavellian genius, that's where *I'd* go."

Jackson let out a burst of air, a silent laugh. "Well then, we'll guess that's where we're going. Which means we've got another hour." He gave a tiny, uncomfortable grunt.

"What? What's wrong?"

"I really have to pee."

Henry's laughter in his ear kept him sane for the next half hour, while next to him, Cody Gabriel's restless sleep got less and less peaceful. When he twitched hard enough to drive an elbow into Jackson's ribs, Jackson grunted softly and shook him awake.

"More hamburger," he muttered, and Cody groaned.

"Tastes like crap," he muttered, but he was unwrapping the cold food as he said it.

"Sorry about that. If we were at my house, I'd do hot grilled-cheese sandwiches and tomato soup. My boyfriend cooks the best soup. Fresh ingredients, puts it on simmer. It would warm you to June."

Cody munched moodily on the burger, wrapping up the last precious bit and setting it neatly in the empty box. "You've got someone?" he asked, and Jackson let out that small bit of tension that he imagined everybody LGBTQ had when they let loose with a pronoun or a bit of reveal about their private life.

"Yeah. Your lawyer, actually. Hope that's not a problem."

Cody shook his head. "Swing both ways myself," he admitted, surprising Jackson. "Not that I'd tell those fuckers on the force."

Jackson grunted. "I'm bi too. I was only there for a couple of months, on the force, but I was so damned naïve. Joined the chapter of the union that repped the community, paid dues. Eleven years later it's starting to dawn on me that some fuckers still have a problem with us."

Cody gave him a tired, drugged glance. "You were on the force?" he asked.

"Not for long. You don't want to hear that story."

Cody gave a weak laugh. "Sure I do."

At that moment, the bus took an exit for Hwy 299, bypassing Redding. Shit!

"Henry, we're on 299 now, did you see?"

"*Fuck!*"

"Is there a place to turn around so you can take this exit with us?"

"It's two miles up," Henry muttered, and Jackson was glad he couldn't see up ahead, because if he caught the minivan's lights bobbing and weaving like a drunk butterfly, he might yell at Henry and add to the chaos.

"You get back to us, and I'll keep you posted."

"Goddammit, goddammit, goddammit—"

"You couldn't have known," Jackson muttered. "They didn't even signal, and I doubt the bus behind us did either."

"Shit. I'm gonna concentrate on my driving. You tell me what you see."

"Same thing I've seen for the last two hours and forty-five minutes," Jackson grumbled. "A lot of nothing in the rain at night."

Cody laughed hoarsely, and Henry went "Gah!" in his ear.

"You're funny," Cody said, leaning his head against the window. "Too bad you've got a boyfriend and he's not, you know, a junkie waste of skin. Hard to compete."

"Not a waste of skin," Jackson said softly. "And if you knew what Ellery was—what he's done for me—you'd know it wasn't you. I'm not a bargain. He got me straight from the broken boy collection and has been watching me try to fix myself for over a year. That's a lot of patience."

"Mm. Think there's another one out there for me?"

"I'm sure there is," Jackson said softly. "Half my friends are in recovery, Cody. Sometimes you just need people in your life who get what you've gone through. Shit."

Freddy McMurphy—who had been visible mostly through the game he'd been playing on his phone for nearly three goddamned hours—had suddenly pocketed the phone and stood up. Jackson angled his body and leaned his head back, and Cody dropped his face against Jackson's throat.

Jackson closed his eyes, and Cody evened his breathing, both of them giving their best impression of the drugged sleepers who had so eerily populated the rest of the bus.

Together they waited for Freddy to get back to their area.

He's probably headed for the bathroom, Jackson thought, grateful that the engine noise had partially masked their quiet voices as he and Cody talked.

The old man sitting in the aisle had pulled himself against the back. Fortunately the door from the portajohn angled forward a bit, so when McMurphy clunked back to the bathroom, the old man was hidden. He'd eaten the fries, drunk the coffee, and had fallen into a restless sleep.

Jackson heard the clump of McMurphy's footsteps as he entered and could see the sliver of light under his lids as he closed and locked the door. He shifted enough to let Cody know there'd been a change in circumstance, and Cody grunted, letting him know he was good.

Forever. That's how long it took McMurphy to relieve his bladder. For-fucking-ever.

By the time he was coming out, zipping up without even a little hand sanitizer, if Jackson knew his sounds, the bus had finished a series of hairpin turns and the hydraulic brakes were screaming in protest.

Jackson wanted desperately to talk to Henry, but he had to wait until McMurphy had gotten back down to the front.

Fucking. Finally.

"Henry?"

"Yeah, I'm coming back toward the 299 exit. Where are you?"

"We didn't make any turns, but the road has some twists," Jackson said. "I can't tell if we're coming to the end or not, but we're going pretty slow. Bad news is—"

"One lane road," Henry muttered.

"It's like you're here," Jackson said. "When it starts to narrow, I'd park and wait for them to pass. They're Sacramento Department of Corrections buses. I'd put money on them needing to be back in the garage tomorrow."

"Fair. But whatever goes down, you and Gabriel need to not be alone with any of the cops. Run away, coldcock the bastards—we are a long way from home here, Jackson, and I do not like this one bit. If there was ever a plan to dispose of a body or commit a perfect murder, this place has all the earmarks."

"I hear you," Jackson muttered. He squinted and caught a glimpse of something flat and shiny outside the windows. The rain had eased up in the last forty-five minutes, or more likely, they'd driven past the storm and under a peeping moon. He realized he was seeing water. "We're by the lake. Probably by the campground area."

"Brilliant," Henry breathed. "Look, I need to check my maps, but there's usually a way in and a way out—"

And then Jackson saw something in front of them that made him frown. "And somebody is here in an SUV," he said, squinting through the side windows, which were heavy with steam. "You might not have been the only guy playing catch-up on the freeway."

"Shit." Henry breathed out heavily. He was probably thinking that once the buses left, that didn't mean Jackson and Cody Gabriel were in the clear. "Are you armed?"

"I've got a penknife," Jackson muttered, hoping for a laugh.

"*So* not funny. Hide, dammit. If you two have to find a fucking tree to climb, do it!"

Jackson got another look around under that thin moon. "Not a lot of trees here. Mostly scrub, with some manzanita and some oak. But I hear you. We'll hide and wait for your signal."

And at that moment, the brakes on both buses screamed in protest and they lurched to a halt. McMurphy hopped up and ran down the stairs as the driver opened the doors. He stuck his head outside for a moment, having a brief conversation with whoever was out there—probably Goslar if it wasn't Freethy or Brown, but Jackson couldn't see. Then he came back and had the bus driver turn the lights on.

"Come on, everybody. Up, up and at 'em. Wakey-wakey, eggs and bakey. We need you up and out. Good news is it's stopped raining. More good news, there's some water to wash with. If you're truly lucky, the bears have all buggered out. Now come on, you smelly fuckers, get up and get off the bus. This is where the ride ends."

There were tired moans and confused mumbling, but McMurphy had taken his club out again and was smacking it in his bare hand with an intimidating thud. The people at the front of the bus stood, and he went down the steps to usher them out. Jackson and Cody looked at each other. Cody was starting to shiver—probably adrenaline—and Jackson muttered, "Finish your burger," as they waited their turn.

Cody shoved it in his mouth, practically swallowing it whole, and washed it down with a final gulp of coffee.

"Not gonna last," he said softly, giving a shudder. "I'm gonna need to fix in an hour, maybe two."

"Let's live through the next fifteen minutes," Jackson told him, voice grim. "Remember, you and me are cozy. They could recognize either one of us, so we get close when we need to."

"It's been a while since I brushed my teeth," Cody confessed. "No tongue, I promise."

"It would be a kindness," Jackson admitted. He'd gotten hints of fetid breath as they'd spoken, but everything else in the bus had been so rank, close, and humid, that had been the last thing he'd been worried about. "Okay, that's the end. Up we go."

They stood, and Jackson felt Cody's hand fumbling for his own. Figuring Ellery would forgive him, he clasped it and towed Cody behind him, hoping if there was violence, it would reach him first.

Jackson hesitated at the top of the bus steps, seeing McMurphy and Goslar at the bottom, talking to each other and watching the retreating backs of the majority of the bus's former occupants. When the people in front of them went, Jackson hurried down the stairs, Cody right behind him, keeping his face practically in the ass pocket of the guy in front of him. He'd actually taken two steps, Cody behind him, and had the faintest hope that he'd made it, when he felt a hand on his arm.

"Wait a minute," Goslar said, booming voice practically in his ear. "I know you. You're—*fuck*!"

Jackson didn't give him time to finish, instead yanking his hand from Cody's and socking the guy twice in the nose. At his side, Cody was making quick work of McMurphy, kicking out and popping his knee out of its socket with brutal intent, and as McMurphy went sprawling, Jackson grabbed Cody's hand and went hauling ass into the night.

He'd scoped the place out a little as they'd been emptying out of the bus, and they were apparently stopped not far from the water, near restrooms and tables in what was probably, in the summer, a picnic area. Beyond that was the scrub brush and trees Jackson had mentioned, and while their two assailants were down—and the two cops by the other bus hadn't caught on that they were in trouble—Jackson went tearing for the scrub and the trees, hoping that the darkness and the mud might work to hide them.

Just as they hit the brush, two things happened.

The first was that a shot rang out, going wide but landing solidly in the trunk of the oak tree they were passing at the time, and the storm caught up with them again. The moon disappeared, and the heavens opened, dousing the newly arrived campers in the same torrential rain they'd just escaped.

Jackson and Cody didn't pause and didn't look back. They kept hauling through the brush until they came to a wide dirt road, and Jackson pulled Cody back to the brush for a moment so he could take stock.

"Henry?" He gasped, gulping air, and Henry was, thank God, still in his ear.

"Jesus."

"I don't know where we are. There's a dirt track running down the hill past the picnic area. We've found it, and it seems to be heading deeper into the brush and the woodland. We're running toward cover—"

Jackson and Cody both heard a shout and tramping feet, and Jackson didn't finish that sentence. Hugging the side of the road, risking the rocks and the uneven terrain, they both started jogging toward the darkness of better cover, hardly able to see where they were going in the sheeting rain.

Another shout and a shot—this one going wide again—and Engall Goslar's voice proclaiming loudly, "McMurphy, goddammit, stop shooting at them! Your ordinance can be tracked!"

"Fuck!"

And Jackson used that moment to dodge into the brush, off the path, pulling Cody with him.

It was harder to run this way; the bitter clawlike branches of the manzanita bushes scratched their faces, and the rocks were trying to maim them with every step. Just as Jackson thought their luck couldn't hold out, his foot hit a piece of decomposed granite and his ankle rolled. He went tumbling down a slight hill, coming to a stop with a smack against a leveled stretch of dirt packed too hard for the rain to soften.

He glanced around, figuring he'd landed in a campground of some sort, and looked up in time to see a figure in a yellow rain slicker crash into Cody Gabriel.

Jackson pulled himself to his feet and rushed to Cody's aid, getting behind the figure—he thought it was Goslar but couldn't be sure—and kicking him in the vulnerable place behind the knee. Their attacker went down, and Cody looked up in time to shout a warning.

Jackson felt the blade, hampered by his sodden sweatshirt, as it sliced down his shoulder, ground into bone, and slid down his side as he turned, elbow up, to fend it off. It hit flesh and then ribs before he lunged, elbow making contact with Freddy McMurphy's nose, the crunch satisfying and brutal, right as the full extent of the damage flash-fired through Jackson's brain.

"*Fuck!*" he snarled, and something crashed into his legs from behind, sending him sprawling backward, Freddy McMurphy on him with a three-inch fixed-blade, illegal as fuck and highly lethal.

Jackson had his arm up to block, and McMurphy was fighting like a man possessed, driven by pain, adrenaline, and the promise to kill.

Jackson grabbed his wrist in both hands, scrabbling to stop him, and McMurphy used his other hand to squeeze Jackson's throat. Breathing was getting hard, and Jackson's vision wavered, dark and rippled, but Jackson kept his hands on the hand with the knife in it and raised his knee, *hard*, between McMurphy's legs. McMurphy's grip on his throat lessened, and the dagger—oh thank God—*dropped* from between his fingers onto the mud by Jackson's head.

Jackson raised his knee again, hard enough to rupture this fucker's balls, and McMurphy let out a whimper and collapsed to his side, leaving Jackson to scramble to his feet, looking wildly around to see where the next threat was coming from.

He saw Cody Gabriel on his knees, Engall Goslar behind him with his own fixed-blade inches from Cody's throat, and he had just enough time to think, *I can't get there in time. Oh God, I can't get there in time!* Suddenly Goslar went stiff, as though struck by lightning, dropping his own dagger onto the muddy earth and falling on his face, missing Cody by inches and leaving him, wet and trembling, on his knees.

In Goslar's back, Jackson could see two electrodes and the wires that connected them to Henry's taser.

Henry was standing, feet apart in a classic shooting stance, face contorted in a snarl as the rain washed down on them all.

Jackson's knife wound suddenly lit up like a Christmas tree, and he had to work not to keel over and throw up from shock.

"Nice job," he managed to rasp, moving creakily toward Cody and trying to control his own shaking.

"Ta-da," Henry replied, bringing his arms down and disconnecting the spent taser wires. "Backup."

"There's a reason to have it," Jackson said seriously. "How far away are you parked?"

"Other side of the rise." Henry nodded with his chin. "I watched you guys disappear toward the campgrounds and these assholes follow you. What should we do now?"

"Remove the taser prongs, retract the wires, find the tags—every taser charge has them. They can identify the buyer," Jackson said, voice robotic as he knelt by Cody. "Do you have some plastic bags?"

"Yeah, why?"

"Because we're treating the knives like evidence in a crime," Jackson told him grimly. "Ellery is admitting them into evidence tomorrow, in case they try to use this little incident against us." He placed two fingers under Cody's chin and pulled his eyes up to meet Jackson's own. "Brother, you're okay. You're okay. You're alive, and we need your help."

Cody nodded, but Jackson could see the shakes already start to overtake his body. The adrenaline had probably burnt off the last of the drugs in his system.

Behind him, he heard McMurphy moan, and he stood and reached out imperiously for the plastic evidence bags Henry would have in his cargo pants, because Jackson had taught him well.

He scooped up McMurphy's knife in the bag first, checking on McMurphy long enough to see that he'd live.

"Did I rupture your testicle?" he asked clinically, and McMurphy whimpered some more. Jackson hoped so.

Then, bagged knife in hand, he grabbed Cody's elbow and, while Henry was still cleaning up the taser, started escorting Cody to the car. He'd found it—and Henry had just joined them—when he heard Freethy and Brown shout, probably finding their accomplices disarmed and injured in the mud.

"What now, boss?" Henry asked, panting. "Hospital for you?"

Jackson shook his head no. "Hotel room," he said. "Shitty kind, use cash. Cody and I both need to wash up, I need some doctoring, and Cody…." He bit his lip. He hated this part. "Cody needs to fix," he said, looking Henry miserably in the eyes. "We can't put him on the stand puking with withdrawal."

"We can't put him up there stoned, either!" Henry retorted, dismayed.

"Yeah, but he's been using for a while. We're going to have to help him walk the line." Jackson let a whimper escape. "And yeah, I really fucking want some disinfectant and some fucking anesthetic and some fucking stitches. But if you take me in with a knife wound, I'll be *stuck* up here. Let's get me wrapped up and bandaged, and you can take us both to Med Center. If we can keep him from going into withdrawal right now, I bet they could give us a clinical dose of methadone so he's all legal. But once he starts the process, it's going to take it out of him, and he won't be able to take the stand for Zeke. We have to spring this on the prosecution, Henry, or me and Cody will be too busy fighting off an assault charge to do Ezekiel any good. Just until tomorrow."

"Then we're going where, Cody?" Henry asked sternly.

"Rehab," Cody said gruffly. "That's a promise."

Henry nodded. "Fair enough. Jackson, grab a towel from the back so you don't get blood all over Jennifer's seats. She might get pissy, and you know, the old girl's been a real friend tonight."

"Good girl," Jackson murmured, doing what he needed to get settled as Henry killed the lights and started creeping out of the campground in total darkness. On the other side of the rise, they could see the slashing beams of Maglights, and Jackson imagined that Freethy and Brown were busy making sure McMurphy and Goslar were still alive. There had possibly been more than the four of them—the parked SUV had been *somebody's* ride back, but Jackson figured if Henry could get out without drawing any attention and they could make it back to I-5, they were home free.

"Jennifer," Jackson said quietly, trying to find a way to get comfortable on the seat, "this is Cody. He's had a super shitty month. I know you don't owe him a damned thing, but he sure could use some sweetness about now."

"Wh-who are you talking to?" Cody asked from the back seat. Jackson noticed that the tiny black dog—and Henry was right, it was a Chihuahua mixed with something equally small and delicate to produce a five-pound wonder-mutt—had curled up in Cody's lap while Cody stroked him with a shaking hand.

Jackson remembered what Annette Frazer had said about Cody's reluctance to see a dog get shot—or the person holding him—and while he felt bad for the old man who'd lost his dog, he felt like maybe Cody had needed the dog just a little bit more on this awful night.

"The car," Jackson told him, trying to keep his mind on what was necessary. With a grunt, he leaned forward and tried to grab the power cord they kept plugged into the dash, and it took him a moment to realize that the task was so hard because his hand was dripping with blood from the wound on his back.

"Fuck," he muttered, getting control of the cord and plugging his phone into it. Then, purposefully, he wiped his bloody hand on another of the towels Henry had brought to the front of the van. His back, his ribs, the soft flesh of his flank—all of it was lit like a wildfire from pain, and in the humid heat coming from Jennifer's vents, he could feel every last place a punch had landed or his body had hit the ground.

His ankle, he realized, felt like it had swollen twice its size, which was what he got for rolling it while running in the middle of the wild kingdom.

And still Henry crept over the dirt track, the car bouncing and squeaking unmercifully. Jackson saw figures in the rain, ragged, lost, looking for shelter in the brush, in the campground layout, and he knew from his and Cody's jog through the rain that most of the campgrounds had been flat, on packed hardpan, with no shelter of any kind directly above from the rain.

"Jesus," he said, trying to shove his brains back in his head. "They just… just relocated them out here and left them. Do you see the buses?"

Far off in the distance, going up the hill after the dirt turned to pavement, they could see the brake lights of the now-empty buses.

"Are they going to spot us when we turn on the headlights?" Henry asked.

Jackson shook his head. "They'll think we're the SUV—I think there was a cop on each bus, and the SUV came to take everybody home after they'd dropped off their passengers. Get to the road and go before they get back to the SUV and we're safe."

"Not too safe," Cody said from the back, his voice chattering. "They made you."

"Yeah." Jackson shuddered, knowing it would pull at the wound on his back but unable to stop. "But you're still testifying, right? We'll get you from the courthouse to rehab with a guard. I promise."

"I believe you," Cody mumbled. "If you can keep me alive and lucid, I'll do whatever you need. The only way out of this is to fight through."

"Copy that."

Jackson shifted in the seat and let out what he thought was going to be a grunt, but it came out more of a whimper. At that moment, Jennifer's front tires hit the pavement with a thump, front and then back, and Jackson let out an actual moan of pain.

Henry turned the lights on and accelerated. Not fast enough to peel out, just fast enough to let Jackson know his need for speed was appreciated.

"Ibuprofen," he asked.

"Island," Henry said tersely. "There's a bottle of water in there for you too."

"Oh thank God. I swear, I almost regret not drinking the coffee."

"I thought the coffee was drugged?" Henry asked, surprised.

"It was," Cody mumbled. "But not enough."

"My mouth's been dry since I got on board the bus," Jackson explained, rummaging through the console compartment and coming back with the jumbo bottle of ibuprofen and a bottle of water. He chased one down with the other and tried to take stock.

"Do we have enough gas?" he asked. "To get us back?"

"Roger that," Henry responded. "Even with a stop at a shitty hotel. I've got one in mind—it's a chain, but they're isolated. They look like they'll take cash, and I can park in the back, get you two into the room, and nobody will ask any questions."

"Awesome," Jackson mumbled. He'd shut the console to rest his phone on it, and to his chagrin, the phone lit up with Ellery's photo, a picture of him sitting on the couch, Lucifer in his lap, Billy Bob by his side. Jackson's chest ached to be home, but he didn't answer the phone.

Instead he pushed the Decline button and texted, *We're okay. Looking for a place to clean up.*

The phone rang again, because Ellery was stubborn that way, and Jackson hit Decline one more time.

I can't talk right now—

Can't or won't?

I'm bleeding, Ellery. It's not fatal, but it hurts, and I don't want to—

His phone rang again, and he answered it because damn Ellery anyway.

"I can't be a badass with you in my ear," he said on the pickup. "I was trying to tell you that. I need to hold it together until we get to Sacramento, and there's still some hard shit to get done."

Ellery's voice was thick with hurt and annoyance, but not anger. "You couldn't talk to me?"

"*I hurt*," he said, willing Ellery to get it. "When I hear your voice, I just want to be home."

"I'm sorry," Ellery said humbly. "I'm not trying to get in your way—"

"You're not in the way," Jackson told him. "I just... all the things you want to give me right now—including a giant mug of hot chocolate, 'cause I'm fucking *freezing*, by the way—I want. I want them so bad. But I can't think about how bad I want them. Henry and I got shit to finish."

"Fair enough," Ellery said, his voice relaxing. "Tell me what you've got and what you need. I'll do what I can to make it happen."

"I love you, Counselor," Jackson murmured. "And Cody needs rehab, guarded, private, pretty much the minute he leaves the courthouse tomorrow, and he needs an escort that's not police. They tried to kill both of us tonight, and we can't trust them. If you could get Federal Marshals, that would be fantastic. Otherwise it's Henry and me, but either way, he doesn't go in unprotected."

"I'll do what I can," Ellery said crisply. "What else?"

"We need the hospital to be ready for us. Cody's going to need methadone to get him through tomorrow. He's got enough 'medicine' to get him through the rest of the night, but it's not going to make it until he testifies. He needs to be under a doctor's care to testify under the influence anyway, so we're doing that."

"Fair," Ellery said. "What about you?"

"A shit-ton of stitches, some screen doors, and, as ever, some new paint."

"Oh my God—Jackson! What happened?"

Jackson tried to think about it to explain it, but all he could remember was the two shots fired by McMurphy that went wide.

"They couldn't use guns because they had their department issue and the ordinance could be tracked back to them," he said. "I know because they fired two shots, and then Goslar shouted not to, because the ordinance can be tracked."

"Subpoena McMurphy's police issue," Ellery murmured, as though writing something down. "See? *This* is why you need to talk to me! What else?"

"They were using fixed-blade instead—three inches, so illegal— and we confiscated them as we left the scene."

"Prints? Blood?"

"McMurphy's prints and my blood on one of them, Goslar's prints on the other, but Henry tased him before he could slit Cody's throat."

"Bwah!" Ellery shuddered, loudly, into the phone. "God, Jackson—I… fucking Jesus. Thank God for Henry."

"I'm saying," Jackson said, smiling a little and letting his back take some more of his weight. "Henry, Ellery thanks God for you."

"Good," Henry said cheerfully. "I'm sure God's used to hearing all the bad shit. Give me some good press!"

"Henry says thank you," Jackson told Ellery, trying hard to keep his breathing even.

"So where are you?"

"Right outside of Redding. Our four buddies on the force rounded up half the homeless encampment by the station. Cody pointed out that they didn't take the families, only the singles, mostly the men. Apparently children and families are tracked a little better than individuals. We were in city Department of Corrections buses, and they ran like shit. I'm gonna be coughing diesel for a week, and we were herded out of the buses to Whiskeytown Lake. The buses left without the cops, but I think one or two of the cops may have taken an SUV up to drive everybody back."

Ellery sucked in a breath. "You said it sounds practiced. Was Whiskeytown vacant?"

"No. There were other people there. I didn't get to hear any of the responses, but there was a whole encampment there. Mostly by the lake, but we were running toward the darkest part of the campgrounds."

"Why?" And Ellery simply sounded curious. "You were running for your lives—why there?"

"Cover." Jackson shuddered. "It was like the moon was pointing right toward us."

Another deep breath, and when Ellery spoke this time, his "lawyer" voice had flaked away like old paint, and his tender voice, the one he used for Jackson only, was very much in evidence. "Baby, you make sure you go get checked," he said. "You get washed and irrigated and stitched—don't worry about court. I'll call the Federal Marshals Service if I have to."

"Ellery, I promised Annette and Cody I'd be there. Don't worry about the hospital—they'll be happy to kick me out early. Once tomorrow's done, I'll crawl back into my hole and lick my wounds, promise."

He heard the quaver in Ellery's breath. "I'll hold you to that. Make Henry keep you safe."

"Will do."

"Love you."

"Love you too."

And Ellery ended the call.

Cody spoke into the ensuing silence, his voice shaking with the beginnings of withdrawal. "You... you a bad patient or something?"

Jackson grunted, in too much pain to laugh. "Or something. Why?"

"Why's the hospital gonna kick you out?"

Jackson searched his memory to see when he'd said that. Oh yeah. To comfort Ellery. "I'm loud," he lied. "Flirt with all the nurses. Drinkin', sexin', carrying on—it's terrible. Should be a law."

Cody gave a disbelieving snort, and Henry said flatly, "He's got a heart condition, and the longer he stays in the hospital the more his blood pressure goes up."

"Henry!" Jackson whined. "Do we need to take out an ad?"

"No, boss," Henry said. "We need to let your rookie partner go in sometimes. If you think I'm *happy* about being the guy in the car with the dog, you're fooling yourself."

"Guy in the car with the dog saved my life tonight," Jackson retorted. "Nothing wrong with being that guy." The car hit a rough spot in the pavement, and Jackson winced as his back got bounced against the chair seat.

"You and me are gonna have a talk when this is over," Henry said mildly. "But first things first." He signaled and pulled on the wheel, checking his rearview and his front view to make sure nobody was following. In short order, he'd pulled off the freeway and had parked in the shadows of a small mom-and-pop hotel.

"Well chosen," Jackson said, leaning his head back. "Go get us a room. And some sodas if you can find them—"

"Please," Cody begged. Sugar and caffeine weren't substitutes for heroin, but they were definitely a craving when someone was coming down from a high.

"Groovy. Let's get respectable."

The Other Front

"BABY, WAKE up."

Ellery yawned and stretched, uncomfortable on the couch, and squinted through the light from the television. He hadn't wanted to go to bed without Jackson there but hadn't been able to worry for another minute, either, so this had split the difference. He'd slept shitty, but he hadn't stayed awake.

"Jackson?" God, he'd been waiting. He knew they'd had a long night ahead of them after Jackson had hung up, and even after the text saying they were approaching Hwy 50 and nearing Med Center, sometime around 2:00 a.m., he was almost afraid Jackson was a fever dream.

"Yeah, I'm here. C'mon, it's almost four. If we move to the bed, you can get some sleep."

He was trying to jolly Ellery along, but Ellery could see, even in the faint light, that his face was white with sleeplessness and strain, and blue circles of exhaustion practically reached his cheekbones.

"What did the doctors say?"

"Well, Lance says I should be put in a cage until I'm housetrained, but he wanted me to tell you that if *I'm* ever tasered, that's probably it. My ticker will go tits up, and I'll be cashing it in. The PA who laced up my back asked if she could put her initials in there. I told her to knock herself out, but she said she'd better wait until she found a man who could commit."

Ellery ignored his bullshit and moved in to put his head on Jackson's shoulder and wrap his arms around his too-narrow waist.

"Another close call," he murmured.

"It's been closer." Jackson nuzzled his temple. "Last year—"

"I don't want to talk about last year," Ellery said, surprising himself. Wasn't he the one who was always pointing out the life lessons? The potential for growth?

"Then let's talk about having backup," Jackson said, holding Ellery closer. "Let's talk about having someone in my ear who could talk to you. Who could get the bad guy when I couldn't. *This* year I'm alive and here and… well, maybe not whole and healthy but, you know, not at death's door. It's not last year."

Ellery squeezed his eyes shut and nodded. "No," he whispered. "God, Jackson, I'm so glad it's not last year."

"C'mon. Bed for you," Jackson murmured.

"Gah! Is it really four a.m.?"

"Yeah. Long fucking night."

Ellery gave a mirthless chuckle and allowed himself to be pulled to bed while Jackson turned off all the lights. It wasn't until Ellery had climbed into bed that he realized that Jackson had a calculated reason for doing this.

He started undressing in the dark, and Ellery reached over and turned on the lamp.

"What are you wearing?" he asked suspiciously. "Is that a… is that a girl's pink sweatshirt?" Oversized by at least four sizes, it flopped around Jackson's body like his old shirts used to before Ellery had started throwing them out.

Jackson grimaced and pulled it over his head gingerly by the neck. "I… well, I was out of clothes, and so they gave me some scrubs—"

"Which are soaked through with blood," Ellery sighed, getting out of bed. "Here, let me go get you an old shirt and some dressing."

Jackson snorted. "The old shirt thing is looking like a pretty good idea about now, isn't it!"

Ellery paused to touch Jackson's hip as he passed. "Yes, you're very wise. So they gave you scrubs and… hand-me-downs?"

"Lost-and-founds," Jackson corrected. "This one was apparently from the maternity ward." He held the shirt front-first, and Ellery could see the adorable little picture of a baby bunny and the caption Baby on Board.

"Did you let Henry choose that?" he asked suspiciously.

Jackson grimaced. "Lance chose it, but I suspect they were both on the same page."

"Stop bleeding so fucking much?" Ellery asked, the acerbic edge to his voice a surprise.

"Yeah." Jackson let out a tired sigh. "Can you yell at me for this tomorrow?" he asked, head lowered humbly. "I, uhm, may have mentioned it but—"

Ellery came closer, bandages in hand, and noticed that Jackson was shivering. "You're tired, you're hurt, and you never did get warm, did you." He let out the irritation. "Yes. And no yelling. You did everything okay—I'm being an ass. Come on, turn around. Lift up the scrubs so I don't have to."

Ellery had to suck in his breath when he saw the bandages. From Jackson's scapula down past his ribs to his waist. The cut was mostly superficial because it had skated along bones, and because in spite of maintaining his diet-and-exercise regime, he still didn't have much meat on them.

"Wow," he said, voice shaking. "Did they give you blood?"

"Fluids," Jackson said. "Mostly topical anesthetic with some ibuprofen. Henry dropped me off on the way to his apartment. Thanks for the Federal Marshals to watch Cody, by the way. One of them went to his apartment to see if he could get a suit. He'll text us by seven if Cody's shit has been put in storage." He sucked air in through his teeth as Ellery began the now-familiar task of dressing his hurts.

"Well, it was a long, hard sell," Ellery told him honestly. "I basically had to lay out the entire case to the DOJ. It wasn't pretty."

Jackson grunted. "But they'll take him to rehab? And set a guard until we know he's okay?"

Ellery nodded. "There's… it's like when you were under, Jackson. There's no guarantee he'll be safe after the trial is over. You know that, right?"

Jackson turned, and Ellery put a hurried finger on his shoulder to keep him still.

"We have to keep digging," Jackson said after he was situated again. "Getting Zeke out of jail is our focus now, but once he's safe, we need to—" He let out a breath. "I mean, we *know* what's going on, right?"

"Yeah." One more piece of gauze. One more piece of tape. Ellery helped Jackson into a worn-thin T-shirt with a logo so old he couldn't read it anymore. He thought it might be for a Green Day tour. "Someone—and at this point, it's got to be coming from the DA's office or higher—but somebody, probably the new DA, but that's not provable at this point, is giving orders to move the homeless populations to another county. It's a protocol that was banned a couple of years ago. They used to be escorted to the county borders, and then everybody had the collective bright idea that all they were doing was shuttling people from one place to another and trading populations. But someone's doing it now, moving them out of the capital city to a place with less press and less prestige. Probably so a politician somewhere can claim they got rid of the problem."

He patted Jackson's shoulders, and Jackson turned around this time and pulled him close, swaying on his feet with exhaustion.

"I need to finish saying it," Jackson mumbled, "or I'm not getting to bed. So our douchebag tells the DA, or the DA decides to do it himself, buddies up with the police union, and says, 'Hey, let's make it sort of an underground mission. It will make us look good when reelection time rolls around, right?'"

"Indeed," Ellery said, leaning his temple against Jackson's again, just to smell him, to realize they might not have had a chance to do this ever again, and to be grateful. "And the union leader turns to his cop buddies and says, 'Ship them out of town.' But... that's where I'm at a loss."

"I've got this one." Jackson kissed his forehead. "But you get in bed and let me get out of my scrubs. I need skin to skin, Counselor, and I need to be big spoon."

God, Ellery wanted that more than he could say. He did as Jackson asked, and Jackson stripped down and slid under the covers while he was talking.

"So Harmony Park isn't like the street with the police station on it—it's not all concrete and vacant lots and sidewalks. It's a nice little pavilion and places to camp. The people who visit there are engaged. They bring the homeless Thanksgiving dinner and clean socks and... you know. They watch out for their neighbors. So they don't *like* the police rousting the homeless. It feels like their friends are being assaulted. The cops figure these people need convincing. Let's get a homeless man to go apeshit in broad daylight, they think. Let's let him scare people. And they even know who. How about that young queer cop who's tasting the candy. Sure he's been undercover for far too fucking long, but let's leave him there and use him. So they have him go apeshit at Harmony Park, but he realizes they're too strung out on their own power. They are going to waste somebody—and his dog. He cuts Annette Frazier as a distraction— she swears he apologized before he did it—and then he runs away."

Ellery grunted and wriggled back against Jackson, tangling their legs together, while Jackson wrapped a stringy, powerful arm around his chest and held him tight. It was all a man ever wanted in a lover, that feeling of safety, of intimacy, and Ellery felt it, deep in his bones, that this—this was worth the worry. A man who would talk to him, hold him, try to make him laugh even when things sucked. This *wasn't* last year. Jackson *was* that man. Not "could be." Not "had potential." Jackson was exactly the man Ellery had dreamed of for his entire life.

"So Cody is feeling guilty and awful," Ellery murmured. "And he's already using. He... just sort of drops off the grid."

"Yeah." Jackson's shoulders rippled around Ellery's as he sighed. "He spends the last month in the homeless encampment right next to safety. It was... God, so sad. He stayed there and probably watched the people he'd thought were his family, his home, come and go, and they... they didn't know what to do. Was he undercover? Could they go get him? What was going on? Adele Fetzer had seen him. That's where I got his name, but that's between you and me, Counselor. No giving up sources."

"I hear you," Ellery said. "But how awful. So close to the people who should have helped him. So far away."

"Yeah. So I went to talk to him tonight, and he's just... copping a squat. Getting ready to go fix in a couple of minutes. And I talk to him, call him by name, and he just starts crying. And I was getting ready to bring him to the van where Henry's waiting and... fuck me. Suddenly we're eyeballs deep in supposed witnesses-slash-fucking-asshole-cops who are herding us onto buses and giving out drugged food. I wasn't going to eat, but everybody else was starving. They were halfway asleep before I think it hit anybody that they'd been dosed. Cody figured it out and used it to keep from going into withdrawal, eking a little out at a time on the bus ride."

Ellery felt him shudder, and he also heard the gentle slurring of Jackson's speech. They had to be at the courthouse around eight thirty to meet Annette Frazier, which meant they should be up at seven. Three hours? Two and a half? After a night and a day like they'd both had?

"How's he doing?" Ellery asked, knowing Jackson would want to tell him before he fell asleep.

"Grateful to be clean," Jackson mumbled. "Cleaned up in the hotel room after he fixed. We shaved his head with a beard trimmer, got rid of his beard. I think he shaved his pubes too—apparently there were critters everywhere. Henry's fumigating the back seat of the minivan."

Ellery shuddered involuntarily. "Ew!"

"Yeah, well, I was just glad he didn't need our help to do it. He's not a bad-looking guy, but, you know. Ukus are the suckus." Jackson played with the pronunciation of the Hawaiian word for "lice" to make that rhyme, and Ellery let out a tired laugh.

"What about otherwise?"

Jackson *hmm*ed. "He's going to need people in rehab," he said. "He knows I'm taken. Is it okay if I visit?"

"Yeah," Ellery mumbled. "We can both visit. I'm sure other people will want to. Maybe not cops, but we can tell AJ and Crystal and...." His voice wandered as he thought about the people Jackson had known who'd had substance abuse problems, and of course there was John and Galen. "You know people. You'll make it happen."

"Maybe the Rabbi," Jackson murmured, referring to the man he'd sort of adopted as his counselor. Jackson wasn't religious in the least, but because he was Jackson, and he respected a good heart, the two of them had clicked. "He's good at making you feel better. Or me feel better. Whatever. Sweet guy. Good to talk to."

"Say good night, Jackson," Ellery ordered gently.

"Good night, Jackson," he said, letting out a soft chuff of air at the eternal joke. "Love you, Ellery."

"I love you too."

THE ALARM rang far too early. Ellery climbed out of bed first and felt Jackson's forehead, knowing that a night like the one he'd had often had results such as infection and fever. Warm, yes, but not frighteningly so. An ibuprofen for the day might keep the worst of it at bay, Ellery figured clinically. Jackson had spoken of stopping at a hotel to clean up, and his hair smelled of something cheap and chemical, but it was still clean, so Ellery was going to give him a pass on the shower and let him have another half an hour's sleep.

Long enough for Ellery to shower himself, cook breakfast, and—while Jackson was waking up and brushing his teeth—scroll through the news.

He stumbled out dressed in his second-best suit and sat down to a plate of scrambled eggs with cheese and sausage and toast. Ellery watched him apprehensively for a moment, to see if they were going to have the familiar battle over whether or not Jackson should eat. Most of the time, these days, Jackson ate dutifully, and sometimes even enthusiastically, but when he was upset or hurt, the first thing that went was his appetite.

"Stop watching me," Jackson said quietly, shoveling in a bite of scrambled eggs and cheese. He swallowed and continued, "Food is fuel, and you have important things to do that have nothing to do with me. Don't worry about me, Ellery. Worry about Zeke."

Ellery had glanced up from his tablet to see Jackson eating, and now he nodded. "Thank you," he said dryly. "That's very generous of you. But you know, the law degree comes with a multitasking caveat. Turns out I can do more than one thing at a time, so yeah, gonna go kick ass in court *and* worry about you. It's part of the marriage... I mean boyfriend, rules. They both happen simultaneously."

Jackson pulled up a corner of his mouth in a dry smile. "You think I missed that, but I didn't. Way to stir the pot there, Counselor. Because we don't have enough to worry about today."

Ellery shrugged nonchalantly, pretending his heart wasn't beating a million miles a minute at his M-word gaffe. "Freudian slip," he said blandly. "Finish your toast."

"Freudian slip my toasted white ass," Jackson retorted. "You may notice I'm still sitting here eating eggs, so stop sweating." His voice dropped a little, became silky and intimate. "I'm not sure if you heard this last night, but when I was hurt and cold, all I wanted was you. When I could have stayed in the hospital with Cody last night to prove that I could, I came home for three hours of sleep and a scolding, because Cody was going to make it through the night and I know I can deal with a hospital if I need to, but three hours of sleep in your bed is worth all the pride in the world. You can say 'marriage rules' and I won't head for the hills. Doesn't mean I've got a ring in my pocket, but it doesn't mean I'm not thinking about one either."

Ellery's eyes burned, and he had to force himself to swallow. He'd heard wedding bells the first time they'd slept together, but he'd scrupulously avoided mentioning them to Jackson unless Jackson mentioned them first. Jackson's life—gah! He'd had precious little power in it to wield. It just felt like, as micromanaging as Ellery could be, this one thing had to be on Jackson's timetable.

Ellery would marry him in a heartbeat, but Jackson's heartbeat was irregular, and not only in the medical sense.

"Platinum," he managed to say, treating the matter with an insouciance that fooled neither of them. "With a black onyx band in the middle. I've always thought those looked really classy."

Jackson's smile went fond. "Nothing but the best for you, Counselor. I'll keep that in mind." He used a bit of toast to scoop up the last of the eggs on his plate and finished them off. "There," he said, his tone changing to that challenging, snotty voice he used when he was going to be an asshole on purpose. "I'm done with my food. Do I get coffee now?"

"No," Ellery said primly. "You'll get tea with vitamin C and like it."

"The hell I will!" Jackson sounded properly outraged. "You're having coffee—"

"I'm having the last of the coffee, and you have a heart condition!" Ellery argued. "Now normally you get one cup, but how many have you had in the last twelve hours, Jackson? Come on, fess up."

Jackson swallowed, his forehead puckering irritably. "I do *nobody* any good if I fall asleep in court! I'm gonna text Henry and have him bring me coffee."

Ellery scowled at him. "Henry will bring you decaf! Jackson—"

Jackson shook his head, looking mulish. "I ate like a good boy. I did all the things. I'm tired, grumpy, in pain, and I want my coffee."

"And I want you to live long enough to buy me that ring!" Ellery retorted.

Jackson rolled his eyes. "Ellery, believe me, when something gets me, it's not gonna be coffee. Please." He yawned and looked pissed at the timing. "I'm begging you—let me have some caffeine this morning. The day's gonna suck hard enough as it is."

Ellery took a deep breath. "Fine. But I get to doctor it."

Jackson narrowed his eyes. "Is this like when you told me all tea should taste like codeine-laced grape cough syrup?"

"Yes and no. This is when I tell you I'm lacing your coffee with immune system boosters and actual dairy creamer with sugar. None of that chemical bullshit."

Jackson perked up. "This? This is bad? This is a *deal*! Can it taste like vanilla or something too? Cause vanilla creamer sounds like heaven right now, not gonna lie."

Ellery snorted. "You've very cute, but no complaining about eating the extra vitamins. You get sick after nights like the last one. I can't stop it, but I can head off the worst of it."

Jackson's cheeks went suddenly pink. "You do take very good care of me," he said warmly.

"When you let me," Ellery agreed. "Now let me get your coffee. It's time to move."

Home Team Pitches

ANNETTE FRAZIER seemed so happy to see both Jackson and Henry that Jackson didn't have the heart to ditch out on her testimony. One of them had agreed to stay with Cody when the Marshals arrived, which meant Henry would be the one staying in the hallway with Cody Gabriel until alerted by text. Cody and Annette were surprise witnesses—and Ellery had been gloating a little because they were both on the witness list beforehand. The prosecution had enough witnesses in Goslar, McMurphy, Freethy, and Brown. They didn't need Cody Gabriel, Undercover Police Officer at the scene on their side, did they? And if they chose not to call the victim out of compassion, well, the defense *had* to try this case, otherwise their victim, erm, defendant would be stuck in jail without bail, right?

Well, Ellery was about to shoot holes in all of that bullshit—and use the prosecution's untapped witnesses to do that.

And if he wanted Cody Gabriel to make a surprise entrance to do it, well, Jackson could forgive him for a little bit of drama.

"Ma'am," Jackson said softly, after he'd greeted Annette and Larry at the side of the courthouse and pulled them through to the courtroom where their case was being tried, "are you ready for what's going to come next?"

"Mr. Cramer already told me what he had planned," she said softly. "Is Mr. Gabriel all right?"

Jackson grimaced. "I was planning to go see, but since you're here—"

"Oh no!" She patted his arm, blessedly not the arm he was carrying gingerly away from his stitched-up side. "You go and see to his well-being. If you could just tell me where I'm supposed to go...."

"Mrs. Frazier?" Jackson turned and saw, much to his relief, that Ellery had called in the reserves and Jade was there to help move people.

"Mrs. Frazier, this is our paralegal, Jade Cameron. She's going to get you seated, and I'm going to check on our other witness," Jackson said. Ellery was probably introducing the new witnesses even as they were speaking.

"Mr. Rivers?" Annette said, pausing with a touch to his injured arm. He tried not to grimace, and her sweet face darkened with concern. "Are you okay?"

"Sustained an injury," he replied with a deep breath and then saw that her own injured arm was still in a sling. "You might recognize the pain."

Her eyes widened. "That happened last night? Oh my goodness. That happened after you tracked down Mr. Gabriel? Did he—"

Jackson shook his head. "No, ma'am. Let's just say that the people who ordered him to do what he did were not... pleased that he would be here to testify."

She held her good hand to her mouth. "Oh no. Oh no! Is Mr. Gabriel okay?"

Jackson looked at her sadly. "Was he okay the day he hurt you?"

She shook her head. "No. Oh no. Will he be okay to testify?"

"He wants to. Before that day, he was a part of the community of the park too—he was working undercover. He knows Ezekiel, and he doesn't want him in prison any more than you do. He wants to make things right."

She nodded unhappily, probably because she heard what Jackson hadn't said. That Cody Gabriel was going to have to walk through fire in order to do that and that the police officers who were supposed to be on their side were the ones leaving a trail of blood in their wake.

"Jackson," Jade said, gesturing to the courtroom entrance, and Jackson nodded once more at Annette Frazier and hustled to the front entrance of the courtroom, anxious to get out of there before the judge arrived.

Outside in the main hallway, he took a right, then walked past two smaller rooms, antechambers to the courtroom he'd just vacated. Then he took one more right to the smaller elevators used by the judges and one more right to an alcove where a pay phone, of all things, was mounted to a wall. A tall, well-muscled blond man stood guarding the entrance of the alcove, along with his partner, a woman in a navy-blue suit with cunning little tennis shoes masked as women's blue oxfords. Tucked away in the alcove, a small bench sat next to the pay phone, and Henry and Cody Gabriel were hunkered down there.

Gabriel had his head tilted back and his eyes closed, and Jackson at first wondered if he was asleep and then realized he was working hard to keep his breathing even.

"Where's the dog?" he asked. Henry had smuggled the poor thing into the hospital the night before, and Cody had spent a lot of his time clutching it as the tiny creature licked Cody's hands disconsolately and Henry kept feeding him jerky.

"He's good," Henry said. "Had one of the guys at the flophouse take him to the vet to get him some flea treatment and his shots." He patted Cody's shoulder. "I called the rehab facility John recommended, and you know what? They let you bring comfort animals with you. They've got their own wing. So after we get him all his shots and stuff, you can bring him to rehab if you want. I forgot to tell you that when you walked in."

Gabriel's face lit up. "You-you'd do that for me?" he asked, voice rusty.

"Well, yeah." Henry shrugged. "I figure you need everybody in your corner you can get, right?"

Cody squeezed his eyes shut and nodded, and Jackson gave Henry a proud nod. "Good idea," he mouthed. Then, louder, he said, "You're looking pretty perky today, Junior. What'd your boyfriend put in your Cheerios?"

Henry made a face. "Not *in*—with. Vitamin packs. It was like rinsing down a holistic pharmacy with my orange juice." He looked both ways like he was telling a national secret. "I swear to God, there were, like, a zillion B-complex vitamins in there. I got a *boner* with my coffee!"

Before Jackson could respond, from behind them the male Federal Marshal, North Albright, said, "We can't thank you enough for the coffee, by the way. Your paralegal said you asked her to bring it." He hid a yawn against his shoulder. "Long night."

"And good call on the pumpkin spice," said his partner, Leah Foy. "And the whipped cream." She gave an ecstatic little shiver. "And the donuts. You guys are the best. Saying."

"Hey," Jackson joked, "when we wake you out of bed to guard a witness, we do it classy." He turned to Cody, whose eyes were on him now, wide, limpid brown, red-rimmed with the recent emotion and jittery with strain. Jackson dropped his hand to cover Cody's. "Hey," he said softly. "Look at me. You need to know, Annette Frazier was worried about you. I told her you were not okay. When you walk into that courtroom, you don't need to be afraid of her, afraid of her judgment, afraid of the terrible thing you've done. I told her you were trying to make it right, and I think she knows how much it cost you. Does that help?"

Cody squeezed his hand. "Yeah," he whispered. "It does. Thank you." He swallowed and sat up a little straighter. He'd probably been handsome not too long ago, but now his makeshift buzzcut was patchy and his cheekbones stuck out from hollow cheeks. The skin of his jaw and chin were bright pasty white compared to the weathering of his forehead and the apples of his cheeks, and the hand he used to scrub across his mouth shook. This was a man who had lived on drugs and guilt and horror for too long on the streets.

And then his lean, cracked lips gave a twist. "Thanks for making my coffee that ginormous venti frozen thing. Gotta tell you, between the sugar and the caffeine, I'm gonna be vibrating right into rehab."

Jackson managed a smile back. "Remember that, brother. Plenty of legal substances that'll make your heart thunder in your ears." He gave a conspiratorial grimace. "I just don't get to drink any of them."

"What did Ellery make you drink?" Henry asked, his customary evil grin in place.

"It was so damned cruel. Real coffee—the good stuff. Vanilla cream—like, the best. Sugar up the yang. And this… this *mud* that he called a supplement but tasted like grass without the 'gr.' Seriously, the world's biggest killjoy."

"Why'd you drink it?" Cody asked, eyes wide.

Jackson shrugged. "'Cause when you crawl into bed at four a.m. to bleed all over your boyfriend's sheets, you'd better drink his fuckin' coffee in the morning, you hear me?"

Cody nodded. "I hear you. At least there was sugar and cream."

Jackson's pocket buzzed; it was a text from Jade. *Annette sworn in. Time to make your entrance.*

"Amen, brother. Let's roll."

Jackson had already discussed their entrance when he'd been getting stitched up in the hospital. He had to hand it to Ellery: North and Leah had been waiting for his and Henry's arrival with Cody and hadn't appeared dismayed in the least when they'd gotten Cody checked in first, assessed for health conditions, and given all sorts of vaccinations and vitamins to help get him back to health after his time on the streets.

Jackson had insisted on being in an adjoining cubicle while a PA he hadn't met before had stitched him up, and two nurses who weren't Dave and Alex but *knew* Jackson's favorite nursing couple talked about how he was just exactly what they'd expected.

"I'm going to get them for this," Jackson had responded, talking through his teeth as the PA had worked hard to stitch one section of scarred skin to another.

The nurses—"gaybies" as Alex apparently called them—were Louis and Shane, and they had an obsession with boy bands that Jackson had never seen before or since. Their chatter had been diverting, although Jackson would never agree that the breakup of One Direction had been the "singular most defining moment of music, period, the end," but he'd finally had Henry ask them to give him some time to talk to the Marshals about what he and Ellery would need the next morning.

What they really needed was for Cody to magically appear, in a puff of smoke, right when Annette Frazier was supposed to identify him. What they'd settled on was coming in single file—almost—into the outside of the seats in the gallery behind Ellery. Jade would be there to save a row for them, and if Cody walked next to Henry, they could close ranks and keep Cody's face from the other side of the courtroom. That helped satisfy North and Leah's need to flank their witness, along with the hope that they could keep the prosecution from knowing exactly who they were calling in.

So that's what they did now, North and Leah flanking Cody until they got to the courtroom doors, and then Jackson and Henry sliding in like lettuce and tomato on the suspect sandwich. They walked quietly, making as little fuss as possible, and Jackson was relieved to see that the attention of Arizona—as well as her four rather battered witnesses—was focused in horror on Annette Frazier's testimony, as opposed to the comings and goings in the courtroom.

Jackson rather enjoyed the idea that they thought their worst nightmare was in the witness stand at present, and it was a sweet, doughy-faced woman dressed in her best black suit, her fingers laced tightly together instead of stroking her beloved cat.

Silently they slid into their seats—oddly enough, theater seats with coarse woven red cushions, instead of pews—and sat, while Ellery kept the prosecution's attention riveted on himself and Annette.

"So, Ms. Frazier—you're doing wonderfully, by the way. I cannot thank you enough for walking us through this—you've told us that, as you were waiting for your friend, you saw two gentlemen talking together. What happened next?"

"Well, one man—he's sitting over there, behind the counsel for the prosecution—he was putting pressure on another man, who looked as though he really didn't want to do what the first man said."

"Let the record show that Ms. Frazier has just pointed directly at Officer Engall Goslar, witness for the prosecution, who has given testimony to directly contradict what Ms. Frazier is saying now."

"Objection," Arizona said hotly. "Whether their testimonies contradict each other is for the jury to decide!"

"Withdrawn," Ellery said smoothly, and then he gave a thin smile to let Arizona know she'd walked right into that one.

She rolled her eyes and sat down and then glared at her witnesses as they grumbled. Jackson took a covert look at their four choirboys and noticed that Brown and Freethy were both red-nosed and glassy-eyed, wielding Kleenex like party streamers, and McMurphy's face was a mess. His eyes were black, his nose was taped, and Jackson would hazard he limped when he walked. Goslar's face looked a little worse for wear, but he was also sporting a knee brace, and it looked like he might be catching Brown and Freethy's cold.

"Let's hear it for vitamin packs," Henry murmured, barely loud enough for Jackson to hear, and Jackson shot him an amused look. He had to admit, he and Henry seemed to be doing better than their counterparts, and he was the one with the stab wound from the back of his shoulder blade to his waist.

Then Ellery started to speak again, and they quieted down.

"So, Ms. Frazier, you saw Officer Goslar speaking to another man—could you identify this man if you saw him again?"

"Yes, sir. I could."

"What did this man do?"

"Well, first he went into the bathrooms while Officer Goslar drove away. He was in there for quite some time. I thought he was ill, perhaps. Then I walked down the sidewalk toward the park's entrance to see if my friend was on her way…."

Annette went on to tell the same story she'd told Jackson, right down to the part where Officer McMurphy was going to shoot the dog—and the man behind it.

"Are you sure Officer McMurphy wasn't being threatened from that quarter?" Ellery prodded.

"Most definitely," she replied. "The man was squatting in a corner, his arm wrapped around his pit bull, his hand on the dog's mouth to muzzle him. He was terrified." She looked embarrassed. "You could see a little puddle of urine underneath him. He truly expected that police officer to shoot the dog, and that probably would have killed him too."

"So what happened next?"

"Well, then the man with the knife, the one who'd been pressured by Officer Goslar, he said—and I'm very serious, I remember this very well—he said, 'I'm so sorry' in my ear, and then he cut me, on purpose across the arm and chest, before shoving me at the police officers and running away."

There was a murmur through the courtroom, because this directly contradicted what the four officers had testified to, which was that they had tackled the perpetrator and he had resisted arrest.

"Do you know why he might have done that?" Ellery asked. "Apologized to you before he wounded you?"

"Objection, Your Honor," Arizona said promptly. "Calls for conjecture!"

"Speaks to intent, Your Honor," Ellery responded. "Ms. Frazier is in a unique position to be able to surmise what her captor was thinking. We don't know if he intended to kill her or simply make a mess. This is important."

"Overruled," said Brentwood, sounding legitimately curious, and Jackson frowned. Brentwood had been irritatingly correct almost all the way through the trial. This... this was new.

"I don't think he wanted to be in that position at all," she said, her face softening. "I'm pretty sure—in fact, I'm certain—that the only reason he cut me was to keep Officer McMurphy from shooting the dog and old Paul, the dog's owner. He was between a rock and a hard place. If he used me as a distraction, he could get out of there, and the police officers would put away their guns."

"That's an interesting take," Ellery said, smiling at her to let her know *he* believed her, but he couldn't tell the masses she was speaking

Gospel—yet. "Now, you identified the person talking to your assailant before the incident began. Can you identify your assailant?"

"Oh yes!" she said, and she scanned the audience behind the table set aside for the defendant. Her eyes fell on Jackson and then on Cody Gabriel. She blinked several times, eyes filling with tears. "He's sitting in the row behind Ezekiel Halliday," she said. "He's shaved his head and his beard, but I'd know him anywhere. Such big brown eyes."

And then she smiled sympathetically at Cody Gabriel. "You look so tired, son. I hope you get to come in from the cold."

The entire courthouse took a collective breath, and Ellery said, "Let the record show the witness has singled out Cody Gabriel, an undercover police officer who was on the list of witnesses for the prosecution, but whom I will call as a witness for the defense as soon as Ms. Frazier is allowed to be seated."

Across the aisle, Arizona Brooks began to laugh.

"Ms. Brooks," Judge Brentwood thundered. "Aren't you going to object?"

"On what grounds?" she asked.

Brentwood gaped, and he was obviously racking his brains, trying to think of something.

Ellery stepped smoothly into the silence, keeping everybody's eye on the ball. "So, Ms. Frazier, you are saying that the man who held a knife to your throat and then assaulted you with a deadly weapon is most definitely *not* the defendant, Ezekiel Halliday?"

"No, sir," she said, sounding as certain as Jackson had ever heard *anybody* sound. "You'd have to be a stone-cold moron to think Zeke was the man who assaulted me with a knife."

"Understood," Ellery responded, making a manful effort not to even let his lips twitch. "Thank you, Your Honor. I'm done questioning this witness."

Arizona Brooks gave her four witnesses a look full of fire, brimstone, and contempt for a moment.

"ADA Brooks, do you have any questions?" Judge Brentwood asked.

The four policemen, dressed in full uniform, glared stonily back, not one of them willing to concede that they'd been pushing her to prosecute the wrong suspect for three damned weeks.

"Yes, Your Honor," Arizona said after a long, angry pause. She stood, holding one of the thick-barreled, expensive pens she favored and rolling it between her fingers. "Ms. Frazier, may I ask—how many stitches did you receive after the attack?"

"Twenty-seven," she replied. "Fifteen across my chest and twelve across the meat of my arm."

"So, twenty-seven stitches, and you think your attacker was just 'using you as a distraction'?"

Annette Frazier thought carefully and then nodded. "The doctor who stitched me up said repeatedly how much worse it could have been. She said the cuts were clean and precise and well placed. The edges were very clean, and the cuts were superficial. I remember her musing that it was almost as though the person cutting me had done that on purpose, and I thought about how he'd apologized before he'd done it. I was convinced that day that his whole reason for hurting me had been to get the policeman's attention away from the dog and his owner."

Arizona nodded, her fingers toying with her pen. "Your Honor, we should remind the jury that this is all supposition and not proof."

"Sustained," Brentwood said, before turning to the jury and instructing them to keep that in mind.

Arizona shook her head, as though talking to herself, and tried again. "When you identified Ezekiel Halliday for the police—"

"I never did that," Annette Frazier said.

Arizona dropped her pen. "I beg your pardon?"

Annette nodded emphatically. "That officer there—Officer Goslar, I believe—told me the police would be in touch, but they weren't. The next thing I heard, the suspect had been apprehended, and I was told I didn't need to worry. There were enough witnesses at the park to identify him." She swallowed and looked at Ezekiel Halliday. "I'm sorry, Zee. I didn't realize it was you. I didn't know your last name or make the connection with the first one. I never would have let them arrest you if I'd known."

Ezekiel made a sound—probably "It's okay" from his wired jaw—and she held her hand to her mouth.

"They should be ashamed, those officers. Just ashamed. How could they!"

Brentwood banged his gavel. "Please keep your remarks limited to answers to the prosecution," he snapped.

Annette narrowed her eyes. "Fine, Your Honor."

Brentwood retreated a little, looking almost like a startled turkey. "You will mind your tone."

Annette Frazier's mouth was open, and for a moment Jackson was afraid for her. The judge would *jail* her for contempt if she said what she was obviously thinking of saying, and then Arizona stepped up, retrieving her pen as she spoke.

"Ms. Frazier, are you saying you never identified the suspect?"

"No, ma'am. The first person to interview me after the initial attack was the PI for the defense. He showed me Zee's picture, and I said, 'That's Zee—he wouldn't hurt a fly and couldn't if he wanted to,' and then he showed me Cody Gabriel's picture and I said, 'That's him! Why didn't they get *him*?' That was last night." She frowned and opened her mouth to say something else, but Arizona held up her hand, almost desperately.

"You're absolutely certain it couldn't have been anybody else?"

"Absolutely. Just like I know that Officer Goslar was the one speaking to him before he went into the bathroom for so long, and Officer McMurphy was the one who was taking aim at Paul and his dog."

"No more questions, Your Honor," Arizona said, stepping back.

"You may step down," the judge instructed gruffly. Annette Frazier gave him a long look before she did as she was told, but she eventually left the stand.

"Your Honor," Ellery said, "I move that, given this new evidence, the charges against my client be dropped—"

"Prosecution has no problem with that," Arizona said hurriedly.

"Denied," the judge ordered. "Call your next witness, Mr. Cramer."

On the other side of the aisle, Jackson heard Goslar and McMurphy's harsh, angry tones, and then Arizona's absolutely furious reply, every word distinct. "Because the more people he calls up there, the more you guys look like the assclowns you are!"

Ellery kept his face impassive, and Jackson was incredibly impressed. And also suddenly suspicious of the judge. On an ordinary day, Arizona's witnesses and Arizona herself could have been thrown in jail for contempt for making that much noise. "The defense calls Cody Gabriel."

Gabriel rose and made his way toward the end of the row, and Jackson and North stood to let him out. Jackson squeezed his shoulder as he passed, and to his surprise, so did North. Cody gave them both a "here goes nothing" smile, and walked up to the stand to testify.

Ellery watched impassively for a moment as Gabriel stood to be sworn in, his hand shaking visibly on the Bible as he did so. As soon as Cody sat, Ellery opened his mouth, closed it, took a deep breath, and started again.

"Would you like a glass of water, Mr. Gabriel?"

"That's not necessary, sir," Cody said soberly, his voice firming up a little.

"Let us know if you do. I understand you had a rough night."

"I had a rough month," Cody said, his mouth twisting sardonically, "but I appreciate your kindness."

"Very well—let's begin. You are listed as a witness for the prosecution. Were you aware of this?"

Cody snorted. "No, sir, I was not."

"But you *were* at the park that day."

"Yes, sir."

"In what capacity?"

"I work narcotics and vice, sir, for Sac PD. I was there to see if a new batch of fentanyl was being sold. A lot of folks have been overdosing on it, and it scares people."

Ellery nodded. "Scary job."

Cody nodded back. "Yessir, it is."

"Did you know you were going to be at the park that day?"

Cody's eyes sharpened, and some of the wariness disappeared. It was like suddenly he knew where Ellery was going with this and could help him along.

"No, sir, I did not. I'd had plans to be in another part of the city that day, out in Citrus Heights, but that morning Officer Goslar called my supervisor and said he'd gotten a tip. Asked if I could show up at Harmony Park instead."

"Was this unusual?"

Cody grimaced. "It was. Citrus Heights has its own police department, and I was part of a sting operation. They'd asked for my help specifically and had a whole bunch of people lined up. When I told my supervisor, he said he'd call them and tell them it wasn't my fault, but I still didn't like disappointing them like that. It's frickin' rude, is what it is."

Ellery chuckled, and so did the courtroom. Jackson was starting to see that Cody Gabriel could be charming and personable—and what a crime it had been to drive him onto the streets as he had been.

"So what happened when you showed up at Harmony Park?"

Another grimace, this one tinged with bitterness. "Then Goslar called out to me in the middle of the park, threatening to blow my cover because he's an asshole and doesn't care who he hurts."

"Objection," Arizona called, and she sounded relieved to have something real to object to.

"Sustained," said Judge Brentwood. "Mr. Gabriel, please confine your remarks to the matter at hand and keep the editorial to yourself."

"Sure, Your Honor. Have had a lot of practice doing that."

"Mr. Gabriel—"

"I said I would."

Gabriel glared at the judge with unfriendly eyes, and Ellery started again.

"So he called out to you, and what did he tell you then?"

"He said he had it on good authority I'd been... well, his exact words were 'tasting the candy.' It means sampling the product I was supposed to be taking off the streets." Cody Gabriel looked grim.

"Had you been?" Ellery asked. Jackson had warned Cody these questions were coming—better from Ellery than from Arizona Brooks.

"Indeed, sir, I had," Cody said, his face hard. "I'd been under for a long time. You're told to fake it undercover. Inject saline instead of heroin. Don't snort anything 'cause it's all bad. There's even a special oil to put on your fake pot to make it smell like real pot. But in real life, you can't do that. If the people you're buying from suspect you're a cop, it's bad news all around—and not just for you. The people who introduced you to the buyer—the low-level dealer trying to feed his family, or feed his habit even—he's at risk. The next guy up who trusted the first guy's word. He's at risk. Everybody who ever gave you a tip or sold you a dime bag is at risk for a cold metal enema, and I know people in this courthouse probably think good riddance, but they're people, all of them, and I don't want that much blood on my hands."

"So you were using?" Ellery prompted before Arizona could object.

"Yessir. I was."

"Were you an addict?"

Cody sucked in a breath and chewed on his lower lip, truly thoughtful. "Nossir. I was... well, I was likely heading that way, but I can honestly say that on that day, at that time, I was planning to cash in my undercover chip and stop. I'd already sent in the email to my supervisor, had already talked to my union rep. There's a moment, I think, in that life, when you can walk away. I was right there when Goslar had me meet him at the park."

"What did Goslar want from you?" Ellery asked.

"Well, sir, in his own words, he wanted me to 'be an asshole and piss people off.'"

Ellery paused and looked at Arizona, who waved him on.

"Did he tell you what he meant by this?"

"He said he'd leave it up to my imagination." Gabriel sent a fulminating glare in Goslar's direction.

"Did he tell you why you were doing it?" Ellery asked.

"Yeah." Gabriel's voice grew angry. "He told me that they'd been asked to clean up the park, get rid of the homeless people there, but the neighborhood was too active. People complained if the cops were too forceful, so they wanted to stir up sentiment against the population. They needed somebody homeless to go off the rails and scare people."

The courtroom had grown so silent Jackson could hear Henry breathing on one side and Jade breathing on the other.

"Did you share that goal? Did you want to clear the park too?"

"No!" Gabriel bit out. "I... I had become part of this group of people. I was there for the higher-level drug dealers—not for the addicts, not for the people on the street. I... I knew them. I knew who got food from friends and who had a place to stay when everybody got rousted. I knew who stayed at which shelter and who needed their psychotropic medication. I... this was a community I was well integrated with, and they were not horrible people. Having them picked up and just... moved to someplace they were unfamiliar with—it's cruel and unnecessary. I hated this idea. I didn't want any part of it."

"Then why did you do it?" Ellery asked when the echoes of Gabriel's voice died down.

"Because if I turn myself in to my supervisor and ask for time off to go get cleaned up, that's one thing. But if I get turned in for drug use, my career is over. No health, no dental, no paid rehab. You're done."

"You'd be left out in the cold," Ellery said softly.

"Yeah." Cody took a long, careful breath.

"What did you do?"

"Well, Goslar said he'd be back in fifteen minutes, so I ducked into the bathroom and set my watch for twelve minutes. Three minutes is a lot of time when you're pretending to be crazy—I wanted to have as little time as possible for anything to go wrong."

Ellery swallowed. "Did you do anything else?"

"Yeah," Cody said, closing his eyes.

"What?"

"I shot up. I didn't think I could do what Goslar asked me to do when I was sober. It... it fucking hurt too much."

Gabriel leaned forward and rubbed the stubble on his scalp.

"We've all heard what happened next. I'm going to ask you two more questions now, so I'm almost done. Then we'll get you a drink of water and it's Ms. Brooks's time, okay?"

"Sure."

"Okay, now first question—it's a two-parter. If you were planning to 'be crazy' to stir up sentiment, why did you grab Ms. Frazier? And why wound her?"

Cody looked directly at Annette as he spoke. "The cops showed up, and I thought they'd talk me down, just like she did, but they all had their weapons drawn. I... I realized how vulnerable I was. If they shot me they could simply say I'd shot up and lost my mind. There was nobody to speak for me. I... I'm not proud of what I did when I grabbed Ms. Frazier, but I thought that they wouldn't shoot her. If I could maybe back into the underbrush, it would all be okay." He took a moment. "I'm so sorry. Most cowardly thing I've ever done in my life."

"Thank you," Ellery said quietly, nodding. Jackson saw Gabriel's reaction to Ellery's voice, his expression, his posture, and he gave a silent prayer of thanks that Ellery Cramer was such a good man. "Why did you cut her, after that?"

"Because fucking McMurphy was gonna shoot the fuckin' dog!" Cody burst out. "Goddammit! I was carrying a knife! There was no reason for his hands to be shaking on his gun like that. There was no reason for him to be aiming at old Paul and Zingo—that's the pit bull. They didn't do anything. They were just in the park enjoying one of the last good days, you know? And he was pointing that gun and I couldn't... couldn't just watch him do that. I cut Ms. Frazier and took off, expecting them to run me down, but they didn't."

"What did you do then?" Ellery asked.

"God, I was so high… I don't even remember. I woke up in the corner of a parking lot a little while later. Made it to the homeless camp by the station. Thought… I don't know. Somebody would see me. Come get me." His voice broke. "Help me."

"Who did come get you?" Ellery asked, voice low.

"Your guys, Rivers and Henry. They… they were really kind. Offered to help me get cleaned up. Offered me Federal Marshals for protection. From what I can see, they ponied up."

"They intend to keep ponying up," Ellery promised. "We appreciate your bravery here. Now here's my last hard question—"

"You promised me that two questions ago," Gabriel said, voice thick, but he still got a laugh.

"My bad. I apologize. But here's the last one. I do promise. Are you high right now?"

"Yes and no," Gabriel said.

"Explain that?"

"They took me to the hospital to get checked out, and the doctors supervised a dose of methadone. I'm high, yes, but functional. It's just enough to get me through until the end of today, when I'm going to rehab. I… I've been on the streets for a month. I'm an addict now, hardcore. I'm going to need a whole lot of help to kick."

"I'm sorry to hear that," Ellery said, *sounding* sorry. "But I'm so glad you got brought in from the cold."

"Yeah," Cody said, choked. "Me too."

Ellery took a deep breath. "I'm done with this witness, Your Honor. Ms. Brooks, he's all yours."

Arizona stood, her face composed into a hard mask. Then she shifted her feet and said, "Bailiff, counsel promised this man a drink of water. Can we get him some? This is rough going."

"Yes, ma'am."

The bailiff disappeared, and she turned to Cody Gabriel. "I appreciate what it took to get you here," she said. "But I need to ask— why? Why did you come in? You were on the streets for a month. I assume you were high?"

"As kites and satellites, ma'am," Cody said frankly.

Arizona smiled slightly. "Why come down?"

"Because I didn't want to be there for one thing," Cody told her. "I was cold, I was hungry, I was tired of being alone. I… the whole reason, I think, that I stayed there, by the police station, was that I was hoping my unit—my *brothers*—would come get me. I was hoping they'd see me and help me out." He snorted bitterly. "Apparently once I was used up, they didn't really give a damn, did they?"

"How do you know they saw you?" Arizona asked curiously.

"Because I saw them look away. Yeah, you, Goslar and McMurphy. You couldn't look me in the fuckin' eye—"

Brentwood banged his gavel. "The witness will refrain from talking to the witnesses for the prosecution."

"Sorry, sir," Cody said, his voice laced with contempt. Brentwood didn't call him on it, though—perhaps he didn't hear. Or perhaps he agreed.

"So you saw them looking at you, and they didn't help." Arizona looked at Brentwood and shook her head.

"Was there a question there, Counselor?" the judge asked acidly.

"Oh, there will be," she said—but her anger wasn't directed at Cody Gabriel. "So Mr. Rivers talked you into coming in. Did that happen right away?"

"No, ma'am."

"What *did* happen right away?"

Cody grimaced. "Well, your four buddies over there rounded up all the single men and some of the women on the block, made them abandon their possessions, including their tents, fed them drugged food, shoved them on a bus, and shipped us off to Redding."

Arizona's eyes could not have gotten any bigger. "Redding?"

"Yes, ma'am."

She turned toward her witnesses. "*Redding?*"

They glared stonily back.

"What in the hell were you doing in Redding?" she asked Cody, and although Arizona was one of the most cold-blooded prosecutors in the city, this sounded almost more like an excited utterance than a question.

"Well, they took us to Lake Whiskeytown, and given that there was a fairly entrenched encampment there, it looked like the whole purpose was to get rid of us."

"But… but that's *illegal*!" she exclaimed.

"I'm not arguing with you, ma'am," Cody replied. "And so's drugging people so they won't tell you that they don't want to go."

"How do you know they drugged them?"

"Because eating that hamburger was the only thing that kept me from going into withdrawal during the damned trip," Cody retorted, and Arizona blinked and stepped back, breathing hard.

"You say these men were the ones rounding you up?"

"Yes, ma'am."

"Did you ever think they were looking for you?"

"Well, ma'am, have you ever seen an officer with his telescoping rod out?"

She thought about it. "Sometimes."

"You know how when they smack that thing against their hands, it sounds like a threat?"

She nodded. "Yes."

"They all had their rods out, and they were using them to poke people awake and then smacking them in their hands. The one guy who protested—he didn't want to leave his dog alone in the rain—they beat him around a little and told him to shut the fuck up—their words, so don't get mad. If they were looking for me specifically, ma'am, I did not want to be found. Not by them."

"Did you and Mr. Rivers at any time assault these officers?" she asked. "Either in Sacramento or Redding?"

"No, ma'am. We defended ourselves because they were trying to kill us."

"Likely story!" hooted Goslar, and Cody eyed him coldly.

"We can prove it," he said.

Arizona looked surprised. "Really?" she asked. Cody nodded, but she was already looking at Ellery. "Really?"

"Yes," Ellery said. "But we need to add my PI to the witness list."

"Counselor for the prosecution," Brentwood intoned, "do you have any objection to—"

"No," Arizona said, and she looked over her shoulder, sending Jackson an apologetic look. "No objections at all."

"Then our witness should step down," Judge Brentwood said, sounding as though he was desperately trying to remember procedure. "We'll break for fifteen minutes and then return to question Mr. Rivers before lunch."

"May Mr. Gabriel leave to receive medical care?" Ellery asked quickly.

Brentwood looked put out, but apparently Arizona's refusal to treat the witness badly had put him in a position in which he couldn't enact draconian measures.

"He can't leave town," he declared irritably.

"Sir, he's under the protection of Federal Marshals. I don't think disappearing is going to be a problem." Ellery sounded both smooth and faintly condescending. This—*this*—was the snotty little prick who had gotten under Jackson's skin for *years* before they'd hooked up.

Brentwood opened his mouth in outrage, looking to where Albright and Foy were standing, waiting for Cody to exit the courtroom. "Why does he need protection?"

"Well, sir, I imagine after this the DA will want to bring charges against the witnesses for the prosecution. Just an idea, sir." He turned toward Cody before Brentwood could give a response. "Mr. Gabriel, you are allowed to go. Ms. Cameron will have texted directions to your facility to agents Foy and Albright. I...." Jackson saw him look around and knew Ellery was wishing he had a private moment to thank Cody Gabriel. "Mr. Rivers and I will be in touch to see how you're doing. That's a promise."

"I appreciate it," Cody said humbly. He stood from the witness stand, and Jackson could see that underneath the charm and humor, his much-too-large suit was soaked with sweat.

Cody left, escorted by Albright and Foy, and the courtroom rustled. The members of the press ran to text their editors to see if there was anything bigger they needed to pay attention to, and the people who just liked to watch went running for the bathroom while the going was good.

Ellery sat down at the defense table and turned around partially so he could talk quietly with Jackson, Henry, Jade, Arturo, Annette Frazier, and her husband.

"You two are free to go," he said quietly. "And thank you."

"Do we have to?" Annette asked. "I... I would really like to see this through for Ezekiel."

Arturo leaned forward and touched Ezekiel lightly on the shoulder. "Did you hear that, Zee? We've got more people in our corner."

Ezekiel's speech was muddled, between the jaw wire and the disability, but Jackson could hear "Thank you" loud and clear.

Ellery nodded. "That's fair. I think after Jackson's testimony, they will probably break for deliberation." He gave a game smile. "I think they're swinging our way," he said hopefully.

"I don't see how they can't!" Annette Frazier protested. "The ADA even agrees we should drop the charges."

"What's right and obvious doesn't always get fair play in the justice system," Ellery said grimly. "We need our A game until the bitter end." He looked at Jackson then, and Jackson could read pleading in his eyes. "Speaking of which—"

Jackson's back ached, the skin and muscle exhausted from holding itself together while he was maintaining his rigid posture. His head ached, the joy of the muddy vitamin coffee having worn off in the sympathy sweat of watching Cody Gabriel testify. Still, he tried a perky smile and a waggle of the eyebrows.

"Should I strip off my sport coat before I go up to the stand?" he asked.

A double line formed on Ellery's forehead, and Jackson knew he was a heartbeat away from calling the whole thing off.

"C'mon, Ellery," Jackson baited. "You know you want to."

Ellery took a deep breath and said shortly, "Henry, check his shirt first. The effect will be lost if he's bleeding through."

Jackson turned slightly and let Henry lift his sport coat from his back. Henry sucked in a breath, and Jackson knew the answer.

"Leaving the sport coat on?" he asked.

"It's a good thing it's an old suit," Henry said.

"I like this suit," Jackson replied mildly, turning back and smoothing the coat down.

"I'll get you a new one just like it," Ellery growled under his breath. "Are you sure you're up to it?"

Jackson glanced over to where the four police officers were shifting in their seats, whispering unhappily to each other.

"Try to stop me," he said, and he met Ellery's eyes, letting Ellery see the rage he kept tamped down much of the time.

Ellery gave a grim nod. "I'll get you a real coffee tomorrow," he said. "A ginormous frappe—no vitamins this time, I swear."

Jackson smiled tightly and let the bubbles of anger in his blood settle back down to a simmer. "I'll hold you to that," he said. There was a rustle up at the front of the courtroom, and the bailiff said, "All rise!"

After Judge Brentwood was seated, they all sat back down. Ellery looked back at Jackson, who winked impudently, and then turned toward the bench.

Vitamins

"I CALL Jackson Rivers, investigator for the firm of Cramer and Henderson, Attorneys at Law, to the stand."

Jackson stood and moved up to the witness stand, hiding his wince as he raised his right hand to be sworn in. Ellery could see, in his mind's eye, the extent of the long, irregular wound on his back, the more than fifty stitches that tracked their way through a rough patchwork of former scars. Once the knife had gotten past Jackson's rib cage, the assailant had dug in, but had been too close to Jackson's side to catch an organ or anything else important. Still, the gouge could be seen. It had been bleeding for most of that morning. It was probably bleeding now.

Jackson made himself comfortable at the witness stand, although comfortable still involved keeping his back ramrod straight and his shoulders even, probably to reduce the pull on his stitches. He wasn't going to be fully comfortable unless he was lying down, probably on his stomach or his other side, hopefully asleep.

But Ellery worked very hard not to let any of those thoughts walk across his face. The legal community might know who Jackson Rivers was to Ellery Cramer, but it was imperative the jury not guess.

"Mr. Rivers," Ellery said, keeping his voice level and measured. "Cody Gabriel's testimony tells us he was rousted by the police department from a homeless encampment and put on a bus and driven over a hundred and fifty miles away to Redding last night. Were you with him?"

"I was." Jackson leaned back in his chair, putting his weight on his elbows and crossing his legs. It was theatrical; it made him look completely relaxed.

"Can you tell us why you were there?"

"Well, I wanted to prove Ezekiel Halliday hadn't committed assault," he said. "And if his disability and eye-witness testimony from Effie Kleinman wouldn't do it, I needed to find the person who *had* committed the assault. We interviewed the victim—and we were the first. Her story pointed to an undercover cop. We didn't know his name yet, but I have some sources in the department, and it took me about fifteen seconds to get a name and a location."

"Why is it important that it didn't take you long?" Ellery asked, blessing Jackson for the opening.

"Because it was an open secret. I passed on Ms. Frazier's description and said it was a cop who might have been under for too long and bam! Name and locale. One more call and I had a picture. So I went to talk to Mr. Gabriel."

"Why didn't you turn this information over to the police and ask for their help?"

For a moment Jackson stared at him like he was stupid, and Ellery actually saw the moment he remembered they were doing this for the all-important audience of twelve.

"Because the people implicating Ezekiel Halliday were also police, in spite of all evidence pointing to the fact that he couldn't possibly have committed the assault. Ms. Frazier's description of the man involved in pressuring Mr. Gabriel to commit assault led me to believe one of the witnesses for the prosecution had an active part in the crime committed against Ms. Frazier. This meant that Cody Gabriel was more in danger from his fellow cops than he was from anybody else, including himself. It's why we called in the Federal Marshals and asked them to help us keep Cody Gabriel safe, including through rehab. His testimony was *not* good for Engall Goslar's happy little gang of nut-busters, so we needed to not tell them until absolutely necessary."

He and Ellery both paused then, looking to see if Arizona was going to object, but she waved them on.

"So you approached Mr. Gabriel on the streets. Tell us what happened next."

Jackson recounted his night then, from the tentative contact with Cody through the horrific bus ride as the unwilling participants fell into a drugged sleep. He finished with getting off the bus and trying to hide their identities from the police officers waiting on the ground by the bus door.

"Tell us why you didn't want to be taken in by the policemen who had escorted you to this unexpected place," Ellery instructed, ignoring the roiling in his stomach.

"For one thing, they were brutal to the people on the bus, and nonconsensually medicating them was a criminal act. Obviously we were not comfortable with what they might do to us. And for another, I heard them talking about 'Do you see him?' 'Not yet—maybe he's not here.' 'Let me know if you find him,' as Cody was dozing off next to me. He was a hunted man, and nothing good was going to happen to him if we were found."

"Objection," Arizona snapped. "Calls for speculation."

"Mr. Rivers is here with proof that it's true," Ellery said. "It calls for demonstration."

Arizona raised her eyebrows at his rhyme, and he raised his back blandly. So he was frickin' Dr. Seuss. Sue him.

"We need to get to this proof soon, Mr. Cramer," Brentwood warned.

"Oh, we will. So what happened when you got to the ground and they recognized you, Mr. Rivers?"

Jackson inhaled. "Well, they grabbed for us, but we went running into the dark. They didn't identify themselves or warn us, and then they shot at us. Twice."

"Do you know which officer did this?"

"McMurphy. Goslar yelled at him not to because he was using his registered weapon, which means they were aware that if they *hit* us, it was an illegal shoot."

"What happened next?"

"We kept running, they followed, and I rolled my ankle and tumbled down a hill into a campground. They caught up with us, and Fred McMurphy got me in the back with a three-inch fixed-blade knife, which is an illegal weapon, by the way."

"When you say 'got you,' could you explain what you mean?"

Jackson stood. "How about I show you."

Ellery turned his eyes to Brentwood, who was staring at Jackson Rivers like he was the demon from which there was no escaping. "Your Honor, with your permission, Detective Rivers is going to demonstrate what sort of damage a three-inch fixed-blade knife can do."

And Brentwood nodded, seemingly incapable of resisting. "Go ahead," he said gruffly.

Jackson slid his jacket off, and Ellery kept his gasp of dismay to himself. The blood had soaked through the lining and into the wool of the jacket—Henry was right. The piece was toast. Then Jackson turned around and unbuttoned his shirt and cuffs with minimal movements.

When he was done, he reached to his neck and hauled his dress shirt and his T-shirt above his head, making sure the jury got a good look at the patched-together line of bloody gauze bandages that tracked from his shoulder blade down to his waist.

Ellery bit his lip, using the stunned silence to control his own beating heart. He hated this. He hated putting his lover's pain on display. But Jackson stood defiantly, glaring at Judge Brentwood with the full force of his recrimination, and Brentwood had to look away.

"One last question," Ellery said. "Because I know the prosecution is going to want to know this. Do you have anything that links the wound on your back to Fred McMurphy, who is sitting in the witness area?"

"We grabbed the knife," Jackson said. "It was raining, but the prints were pretty solid, and the knife has my blood on it. We also grabbed the knife that Goslar was holding to Cody Gabriel's throat after we incapacitated Goslar, before he could use it."

"Where are those weapons now?"

Jackson looked directly at Brentwood. "With the Federal Marshals, waiting to get processed by their crime lab so the DOJ can bring charges if the county does not."

Brentwood blinked, and Ellery saw the full implications hit him. If the Department of Justice became involved, Brentwood himself would be targeted in the investigation.

"I'm sure that won't be necessary," he said grimly.

"Well, that will be up to you, sir," Jackson replied.

Brentwood swallowed, and Ellery said, "J—Mr. Rivers, you can pull your shirt back on now."

"Sure," Jackson replied. "It was getting chilly in here anyway."

ARIZONA'S CROSS-EXAMINATION was minimal at best and seemed to focus on why Jackson hadn't alerted the authorities when he'd been abducted—the most significant thing about what she'd asked had been her use of the word "abduction," which both Ellery and Jackson had seized upon.

Ellery was pretty sure it was a gift.

When she was done, they broke for lunch, and Ellery did his damnedest to make Jackson leave.

"You look like shit," he said as they sat, wearily, in the nearly vacant courtroom while Annette and Larry Frazier fetched them some sandwiches from the cafeteria. Jade and Henry were going back to the office, and under strict instructions from Jackson, Ellery, and Jade, Henry was to go promptly back to his apartment and get some sleep while Jade drove Galen home. Arturo was escorting Ezekiel to the bathroom, and for the first time, Jackson let his mask slip. Some of the ferocity that had animated his features drained away. The lines by his eyes and mouth tightened, and some of the color faded, leaving him pale with red crescents at his cheeks.

Ellery didn't ask permission to hold his hand to Jackson's forehead. The "Are you sick?" "No I'm fine" bullshit could go on forever, and they had maybe ten minutes to be alone.

Jackson gave him a tired smile. "How'm I doin', Doc?"

"Not great." Ellery sighed and reached into his briefcase for the small touchless thermometer he'd placed in the pocket.

Jackson jerked back from it instinctively, but he was laughing as he did so. "You brought a *thermometer* here? To the courthouse?"

Ellery regarded him impassively. "Yes. I'll make a deal with you. You sit still and let me take your temperature, and if it's high, you don't get to give me crap about it."

"What if it's normal?" Jackson was still laughing, and some of the strain had eased from his face. Still in pain, Ellery surmised, but a chance to laugh, to smile, to enjoy sweetness when it came—that was one of Jackson's gifts.

Ellery held the thermometer up to his forehead in a brief gesture. It beeped, and Ellery grimaced as he glanced at the readout. "It's not, so we'll never know. I've got some ibuprofen—take it with your sandwich and I won't send you home before the verdict."

"You wouldn't!" he protested indignantly, and then coughed into his elbow. Ellery waited patiently for him to be done.

"I would," he said quietly. "Mike is coming over tonight, and maybe Lance and Henry, to keep you company while I'm gone. No hospitals this time. Not on my watch."

Jackson gave him a fond look. "You know, I really *can* take care of myself. Odds are good I'm just going to curl up and—"

"Not sleep," Ellery finished for him, voice cracking. "You're not going to sleep. Not after last night. I don't think either of us will sleep for a little while, but especially not you. So yeah. I'm calling in babysitters, I mean company, because...." He swallowed, thinking about all of it. Cody Gabriel, who was—God!—so much like Jackson it made his stomach clench. He'd started out thinking he was working for the good guys, and then the good guys had betrayed him and everything he'd believed in. Ezekiel Halliday, who was one of the people the good guys were supposed to protect, but who the police had gone out of their way not only to arrest and jail but to beat. The displaced homeless, who had at least known where they were, but who were now in a completely alien place without any support, any backup whatsoever.

The evidence of full-scale corruption at the DA's office that had led to this moment and that Ellery could only do so much about.

So much—so much to do—and he and Jackson could only do a small part of it.

The very least, the absolute minimum, Ellery could control right now was Jackson taking care of himself. Ellery was not going to fuck that up.

Jackson's hand on top of his as it rested on the barrier between the defense table and the audience, made Ellery realize he'd stopped speaking midsentence.

Well, maybe Jackson wasn't the only one who'd had a rough night.

"We need to find out who ordered the forced relocation," Jackson said softly. "And we need to alert the DOJ. And we need to push for charges to be filed against the police boy's frat club for brutality. These are urgent things, Counselor, but even I know they can't be done until later. We'll rest up this weekend." His eyebrows arched playfully. "I might even get you naked."

"Not until you're better," Ellery said primly.

"Wanna make a bet?" Jackson needled. "If I win, I get to have you naked."

Ellery gave him a droll look. "What if I win?"

"You'll get to have *me* naked, and I wouldn't mind that either."

Ellery covered Jackson's warm, dry hand with his own. "Unless you get some rest, I think we'll both lose, but it's a good goal to have."

Jackson nodded and sighed. "You're no fun." He sat back and winked, pulling his hand away as he struggled to make himself comfortable. "But you're very good to me. So you're going to stand up and knock this summation out of the park, and then we're going to go home and I'll get to see you and Jade dressed up for Halloween. I mean, the being sick's gonna suck—" He paused to cough into his elbow some more. "—but there are definitely some plusses to the weekend."

At that moment the bailiff approached, asking Ellery if he could join a conference between Brentwood and the ADA in chambers. Jackson and Ellery looked at each other uncertainly.

"Go," Jackson said with a crooked smile. "Big boys only. I'll stay here with the kid's table."

Ellery glared and pulled the ibuprofen out of his suitcase. "Take it as soon as they get back with your soda and sandwich. Annette likes you. She won't let you get away with dodging out."

Jackson managed a creditable "Who me?" expression as Ellery packed his briefcase and then left, following the stocky young woman who was their bailiff today.

Brentwood's chambers were tucked behind the courtroom, and they looked exactly like Ellery thought they should. Lots of heavy oak bookcases, with a massive oak desk right beneath the window and Brentwood's Harvard degree on the wall. There were also pictures— legitimately warm, it seemed to Ellery, and he'd seen the other kind—of Brentwood and his wife, an elfin, charming woman in her late sixties, like her husband, along with what looked to be two grown children, a boy and a girl. The boy was photographed frequently with another boy, this one seen sometimes in his dress whites, so a Marine at some point, but many of the pictures were casual. Some of the shots were camping, some at Disneyland, and some were obviously taken earlier when the children were in their teens. Some had other people the kids' age in the photos, and Ellery recognized the kind of family that attracted people to it. They probably had lots of people over for Thanksgiving, and judging by the photos, many of those people were not white, and there were at least two same-sex couples who were frequent visitors.

The pictures of Brentwood's son and his Marine boyfriend were the most surprising—but all of it, as a whole, didn't fit Ellery's picture of who Judge Clive Brentwood really was.

It was hard to hate a guy when he seemed to be living a good life, regardless of what his politics were, and Ellery took a deep breath and tried to remember to be reasonable.

Arizona was already seated in one of the chairs in front of Brentwood's desk, and Brentwood was behind it in his own massive ergonomic chair. He was over six foot five—sometimes that sort of height came with back problems, Ellery knew, and dammit, some of his hatred bled away.

"We have a problem," Brentwood said after dismissing the bailiff, and Ellery was pleased that he wasn't one of those people who minced words.

"We?" Ellery replied, keeping the archness from his voice. God, they'd brought in an alternative witness who'd *confessed*, for God's sakes, as well as provided proof for an alternative case theory.

Brentwood gave him a thin smile and closed his eyes, tilting his head back. "Fine," he said. "We as in Arizona and I have a problem. Are you going to help or to gloat?"

"Did you see the wounds sustained by my investigator?" Ellery asked harshly. "Or the way Cody Gabriel's hands shook? Did you hear Zeke trying to talk through a broken jaw? Not gloating here, Your Honor. This isn't a game to me, where I get a notch on my belt if I win. We are talking about very real people here whose lives have been impacted, and that doesn't even touch on the roughly two-hundred people who were forcibly relocated last night. You're absolutely right—this problem involves *everybody*, but it *shouldn't* involve Ezekiel Halliday."

Brentwood let out a breath. "No, it shouldn't. But it does. And I can't fix that. And if you're telling the truth, and the DOJ is already involved—"

"I am and it is," Ellery said. "Although your office and the DA's office have yet to be implicated."

"Well, aren't we lucky," Arizona said sourly. "Because Cartman's the one who refused to deal."

Ellery stared at her. "*Still?*"

"Here's the truth, Ellery," she said, sounding exhausted. "Raw and unvarnished. Clive here is a year away from retirement. He does *not* want the DOJ investigating his tenure. My hands are tied by my boss. He won't let me drop the charges. I've been begging him for weeks. And those fucking bozos who tried to kill your boyfriend aren't going away soon, even if the DOJ brings up charges. And they should. And that doesn't even cover how bad nobody in this room wants to see that poor kid in jail."

Ellery blew out a breath. "We could always, I don't know, trust the jury."

She gave him a sad look. "Do you really think that bunch out there is going to draw the line at jury tampering? I've already spotted two people who look like they're in the middle of an intestinal aneurism. Either someone's got their nuts in a vise about the verdict, or they haven't crapped in a week. I don't want to lay odds it's the second one."

Gah! She was right. He'd noticed them too, over the past week. He figured Jackson had been too busy trying to hunt down Cody Gabriel. With Jackson it was all black-and-white. He *found* the bad guy. Shouldn't it be over?

Ellery agreed with him, and not just in theory. He agreed it should be over. Even better, he agreed with Jackson that it never should have happened in the first place, but here they were, and his absolute— *absolute*—priority was to keep Ezekiel Halliday from going to jail.

"Wait," said Brentwood, staring at Ellery. "You and Rivers are dating?" He cracked a weary smile. "How did I not know that? I thought I knew all the LGBTQ couples in the law community." He looked embarrassed, like a tired dad and not a thundering authoritarian. "My family gets really excited that the community is expanding."

Arizona gave Ellery a baffled smile, and Ellery shrugged.

It was like two different people, but he'd seen it before. Judges had to be infallible, and they tended to take law enforcement's word for it. Even the liberal judges didn't let a lot of humanity escape as they were sitting in front of the courtroom.

"We live together," Ellery said, allowing a real smile to show. "Which means I'm on nursing duty for the next week. He's already running a fever."

Brentwood's own smile faded. "Christ," he muttered. "This needs to be addressed. But I can't do it from the bench. The DA needs to bring up charges—or the DOJ needs to do it for them. But we can't let what those officers were doing get in the way of justice for Ezekiel Halliday, and that's what we need to work on here. If I declare a mistrial, not only am I under investigation, but Mr. Halliday is going to go through all this again. And I do not want to be implicated in the unholy mess that you introduced today."

Okay. Ellery could work with that.

"How's this?" he said. "Arizona, you call Cartman and tell him that if he agrees to drop all charges, he *won't* be mentioned in the civil suit Galen Henderson is planning to file as soon as this trial is over. Right now it's our four boys in blue out there, but given the evidence we have now, we can name the DA's office with intent to cause additional harm."

Arizona nodded. "That might do it. What about the DOJ?"

"Well, right now we've got the county buses and the boys in blue. Try to convince him that the DOJ might not look any further than that if he agrees to drop the charges."

She gave him a level look. "*Might* not look any further?"

Ellery gave her a hard-eyed glance. "It's all I can give you right now, Arizona. McMurphy's knife and my boyfriend's back have already instigated an investigation. How far it goes depends on how much of a prick Cartman wants to be about this, and that's not coming from me. That's coming from my liaison at the Department of Justice, whom I had to awaken at two in the morning to get protection for Cody Gabriel, so he's probably in a really shitty mood!"

He was also a friend of Ellery's mother, but Ellery declined to say that.

Arizona nodded. "I'll give him the civil-suit thing and tell him he doesn't need the heat." Her mouth looked thin and strained, and for the first time, he could see she wasn't really young anymore. She'd always been such a fierce opponent, but fighting for the bad guys apparently took it out of her.

"Do that," said Ellery. "I'd love to go home early."

"I'M SO pissed," Jackson said an hour later, as Ellery piloted the Lexus home.

"I know." Ellery wasn't pleased either. He'd heard Arizona's side of the bargaining with Cartman, and he couldn't have done any better, but the terms had been heinous.

"Drop the civil suit? We had to *drop* the civil suit?"

"Zeke and Arturo agreed to it," Ellery said patiently, but it was as much to soothe his own temper as it was to soothe Jackson's. That had been their ace in the hole—everything brought up in the criminal suit was game to be brought up in the civil suit. And Galen Henderson had been prepared to skin the powers that be for their last nickel in Ezekiel's defense, but Cartman had been adamant. If the DA was going to drop all charges, the civil suit had to go.

"But Zeke needed that money!" Jackson protested. His little trip to jail had pretty much exhausted the social security and family stipends that paid his rent in the care home, not to mention the hospital bills.

"The city is paying his medical expenses," Ellery reminded him. It had been the biggest sticking point, and frankly, the reason for the suit. Ezekiel would need far more in the way of medical care than the average person to recover from his injuries. "And his care-home expenses for the next five years."

"It's not enough," Jackson said bitterly. "Zeke's in his twenties. Do they think he's going to drop dead at thirty and that'll be that?"

"It was nice of Annette to suggest the GoFundMe," Ellery said, but that was never the silver lining people thought it was.

"*The fucking police broke his body*!" Jackson roared before coughing wetly into the crook of his elbow, and Ellery couldn't even reprimand him.

"I know," he said on a sad sigh. "And we didn't want them to do it again." His voice wobbled. Oh Lord, his voice was wobbling. How could he be the grown-up when his voice was wobbling? But he'd had to. He'd *had* to present the offer to Arturo and Ezekiel. That was his *job*, and Arturo wasn't stupid. He'd watched the jury too, during deliberation, and he'd seen that the verdict was not guaranteed. It never was in cases like these that involved the police. People didn't *like* going against authority, no matter how much they complained about corruption. Arturo had looked at Ezekiel and promised him that he'd always have a home as long as Arturo was in charge of the Sunshine Prayers Care Home, and Ezekiel had started to cry.

And that had been it. Any hope of them getting some sort of recompense from the city for the copious amounts of pain and suffering inflicted upon them had been traded in for the certainty that Zeke wouldn't have to go through all that again.

"I'm sorry," Jackson said, when he'd recovered his coughing fit. "I don't want to yell at you." His voice had hit the raspy, thin stage right before laryngitis. "Particularly because I'm not going to be able to say anything shortly, and if I'm talking to you it should be good. I'm just... I'm mad. And I shouldn't be. Zeke's out of danger, and that is absolutely where our focus should be."

Ellery gave a choked laugh and reached across the console for Jackson's hand.

Jackson didn't disappoint him, and because they were at a stoplight, Ellery could raise their laced fingers to his lips.

"You're perfect," he said gruffly. "I've rarely felt shittier about anything in my professional life as I have about this deal. It's not fair. It's not even close to fair. Would you believe Brentwood looked appalled? *Brentwood*? And Arizona kept shaking her head, like she could shake off the stigma of being a part of an organization that would do this. This isn't what they signed on for. It's an abomination, and I don't know how to make it right."

"We keep Zeke out of jail," Jackson rasped. "We keep going." And then he said something else, but that was it. No voice. And the traffic light had turned, so Ellery had to let go of his hand and drive.

Interlude to a Storm

JACKSON KNEW Ellery would be 100 percent about getting them home so he could baby Jackson before dressing for the party and doing his own recon into the dangers of the night. Ellery would have claimed that attending the party was not nearly as hazardous as what Jackson had done the night before, but Jackson knew that playing the political game was no less risky, particularly not when he'd had his opponent on the ropes earlier that day.

And as disappointed as they all were in the bargain Ellery had struck, Jackson knew, deep in his bones, that there would have been no bargain at all if Ellery hadn't used every knife in his drawer to carve through the lies to the hidden motives of the DA's office to put Ezekiel Halliday in jail.

Ellery was treating the DA's annual costume party like a frivolous gesture—a social obligation that was important in appearance only, but Jackson knew the truth.

If they wanted to see how big the nest of snakes they'd kicked truly was—and how venomous—the surest way to count scales, tongues, and teeth was to attend that party, Jade in tow.

Before he'd gotten his back sliced to ribbons, Jackson had entertained fantasies of infiltrating the party from the kitchen, Henry working coms, to see what was being said when Ellery *wasn't* in the room, but even he could see that wasn't an option right now.

He'd taken his ibuprofen like a good boy, but that didn't mean he didn't feel like absolute two-day-old reheated crap.

Still, as he stripped off his bloodied shirts and tossed them in the hamper, he watched Ellery cluck over the sports coat that could probably never get clean and felt a flutter of want.

It wasn't that he was horny, hot, and bothered—not really. If he'd been alone after a day like this, he would have curled up in bed and shaken out the fever, existing on pain pills until everything stopped hurting or his stomach exploded. It was that with Ellery there, fussing over him, he knew he didn't have to do that, and he was grateful.

And he wanted to do the same for Ellery, because even though Ellery's skin was intact, Jackson could see he was still hurting.

They'd consoled themselves, all of them at the firm, with the idea that as soon as they got Zeke off the charges, they'd turn Galen on the city and the police force and the goddamned DA's office and make those fuckers pay for what they'd done. They'd call the press, make it front-page news, and push for reform like caped crime crusaders. They would by God get their pound of flesh, because it was no goddamned fair, and they *all*, all wanted to see Ezekiel taken care of for the rest of his life after this.

But that hadn't happened, and big boys knew they couldn't always get what they wanted. But dammit.

Jackson wanted to make it better for Ellery. He just did. Ellery's disappointment in himself, in the justice system he still believed in—it was all acute, and it left a wound.

He left Ellery to fussing over the sports coat and padded to the bathroom, coming back with clean but frayed towels. He stripped the covers down and shook the towels out on the bed so he didn't wreck Ellery's nice sheets. Then, glancing covertly at Ellery to see if he was paying attention, he stripped off his slacks, laid them nicely on the dresser, and then removed his boxer shorts, which he left puddled on the ground.

When Ellery turned around to get the slacks, he saw Jackson sitting, naked and predatory, on the bed.

Ellery's eyebrows shot up to his hairline.

"You think so?"

"Mm-hmm." Jackson hurt; he could admit it to himself. His throat hurt, his voice was completely gone, his back was on fire, and his joints ached from fever. But Ellery's adorable shock did release some dopamine, and that suited him just fine.

For a moment, there was naked hope on Ellery's face, and Jackson knew Ellery was craving that moment of being taken out of himself, of being answerable only to pleasure. It was a thing sex could give you, but only if you trusted the person you were with. In the past year, he was starting to see what a gift that sort of trust was—and how it kept on giving when you gave it back as much as you received it.

Then Ellery's face fell, and Jackson could see him pulling his big-boy panties up so he could say no.

"Jackson," he began, approaching the bed like he'd approached the bench in court. "You know you're not feeling well enough to—oh!"

He'd gotten close enough for Jackson to reach out and start undoing his belt.

"Jackson, you can't even talk!"

Maybe not, but his hands worked okay, and he had the belt undone and was tugging Ellery's pants down around his knees before Ellery could protest. He tugged a little on the pants with both hands, and Ellery stumbled forward, putting his crotch right at face level.

"Jack—"

Jackson stuck his tongue out and licked the head of Ellery's cock, and Ellery didn't finish that thought.

Encouraged, Jackson kept licking, shoving at the pants until Ellery took the hint and toed off his dress shoes and stepped out of his pants and boxer shorts even as Jackson tried to keep Ellery's cock in the game—or in his mouth. After a moment of scrambling, Jackson took him in. Not all the way to the back of his throat, but deep enough. Deep enough to pull a needy groan from Ellery. Deep enough to really get a grip on it and start stroking.

Ellery braced himself by putting his hands on Jackson's shoulders, and Jackson glanced up, mouth wrapped around Ellery's cockhead, and started to lick, while Ellery tried not to whimper.

Then, when his head was thrown back, his hands shaking on Jackson's heated skin, Jackson found the lube under his pillow, and while one hand and his mouth were busy on Ellery's cock, the other hand slid to his backside.

He ran his fingers along Ellery's crease, every suspicion about how badly Ellery needed this right now confirmed when Ellery moaned and spread his legs, giving Jackson better access.

Fabulous.

His fingers were dripping with slick because he wanted to slide in easily, one finger making its presence known, then two.

Ellery spread his knees enough for Jackson to scissor his fingers while taking his cock into his throat, but he knew it wasn't going to last like this for long.

"Losing… balance," Ellery grunted, and Jackson pulled his mouth away from Ellery's cock long enough to wiggle to the side.

Ellery fell face-first, sans dignity, splayed crosswise across the bed with Jackson's two fingers still lodged solidly in his ass, and the fact that he didn't try to adjust himself but merely pulled his knees up to his chest, told Jackson that surrender was everything his lover needed and the one thing he wouldn't have asked for.

Jackson stood, rotating his wrist so he could keep his fingers right where they needed to be, working in, first knuckle, second. He bottomed out, and Ellery wiggled his ass and begged some more.

Jackson added more lubricant and a third finger, gently stretching, and he felt Ellery's groan all the way to where his fingers were buried in Ellery's flesh.

He bent over Ellery's back, sliding his fingers in and out, the thrusting unmistakable—and not enough. "What do you want?" he taunted, the words barely audible.

"Your cock," Ellery said succinctly. "Inside me. Now."

"My pleasure." *He* couldn't even hear himself with that one.

He used the towel to wipe off his fingers and then added a little more lube before positioning himself at Ellery's clenching and unclenching asshole.

Ellery wanted him.

He thrust inside gently, bigger than three fingers, he knew without conceit, and pushed until he had bottomed out.

Ellery's breathy little sobs of need vibrated right to Jackson's balls. He stroked Ellery's smooth, pale back, loving the feel of his skin, and pulled out slowly, slowly, oh-so-slowly, before slamming in again.

Ellery screamed, *"Yes!"* as Jackson's hips smacked against his backside, and Jackson couldn't play the teasing game anymore.

He was wanted—he was *needed*—and he knew without a doubt that he was the only one who could fill the void in his lover's heart right now, just as he was filling his body.

He rocketed his hips forward and back, fast enough to drive Ellery to a frenzy, not so fast he lost his rhythm—or pulled too drastically at the stitches in his back. Still, he knew there was another race going on, a race against time as he struggled to make Ellery come before Jackson's own body gave out.

Sweat spattered from his forehead to Ellery's back as he thrust, welcoming Ellery's thrashing facedown on the bed as he fucked, but he could admit to a certain amount of relief when Ellery stopped thrashing and grabbed his own cock to stroke.

Normally Jackson liked dirty talk during sex, loved taunting Ellery, loved the give and go, even while they were fucking each other blind. But when Ellery clenched around him, spasming on the bed, his entire body convulsing, Jackson's moan of impending climax was merely a whisper, so he probably caught Ellery by surprise when his thrusts stuttered, orgasm washing over him like a boiling wave, cleansing him of his own anger, his own disappointment, his own poisonous fears. He buried himself to the hilt in Ellery's ass and came, collapsing over Ellery's back as Ellery's knees slid off the bed, leaving them facedown, sprawling, sliding down the mattress to the carpet in an inglorious puddle of come.

Finally they came to rest, Jackson on top of Ellery, his cock sliding out, their lush cream-colored carpet no longer pristine.

He had zero regrets.

"Jackson?" Ellery mumbled, and Jackson's mouth opened, but no sound came out. He realized that he'd poured every ounce of himself into what they'd done on the bed, and he barely had the energy to slide to the side to let Ellery up.

He did, and Ellery rolled to his own side and said, "Jackson?"

Jackson's mouth said, "Yes?" but his throat had peaced out. Silent as a goldfish.

Ellery squeezed his eyes shut and held his hand to Jackson's forehead and grimaced.

"Proud of yourself?"

Jackson nodded, tired but emphatic. "Worth it," he mouthed.

"Good, because you're going right to bed." Ellery was trying to sound prissy and like he was the one giving orders, but Jackson just grinned. They both knew who had been in charge two minutes ago, and it hadn't been Ellery.

Ellery gave him a sly peek from under his lashes. "Thank you," he said after a moment. "I… I needed that more than words can say."

Jackson leaned forward and pecked him on the cheek, not wanting to give him whatever virus or bacteria had taken advantage of his shitty night to move into his throat. "Love you, Counselor," he wheezed into Ellery's ear, and Ellery kissed his jaw, then his neck, finishing up by nibbling on his ear.

"Love you too, Detective," he said, nuzzling Jackson's neck again. With a sigh, he pulled away. "Now, let's get you into your briefs and into bed. I think we have a nice little area rug with an abstract print that would look great on this spot, don't you think?"

Jackson had no idea, but if they did, he was sure Ellery would find it before anybody had a chance to ask what happened to the carpet.

HE REALLY had put himself out of the game, though. Ellery managed to get him into his briefs and pajamas and basically poured him into bed before dashing off to make dinner and get ready for his evening. An hour after fucking Ellery through the mattress and into the carpet, Jackson was dozing on his side, Billy Bob parked solidly behind his thighs and Lucifer in a small circle of black fur up by his head, when there was a tentative knock at the bedroom door.

"You up?" asked Henry, and Jackson squeezed his eyes closed tighter.

"No," he mouthed.

"You are too, you big baby. Now sit up and let me stuff pillows behind you. I'm supposed to feed you soup."

Jackson snapped his teeth, because the day he let Junior here feed him was his last day on the planet.

"Oh yes. You're very fierce," Henry taunted, coming to set the tray of soup and juice on the dresser. "Much scary. So rowr."

"Fuck off," Jackson mouthed, but he'd managed to sit up and was plumping pillows so he could eat from bed. It wasn't until he put pressure on his back and felt nothing more than a dull ache that he realized Ellery had given him the really *good* pain pills and not only the ibuprofen. "Goddammit," he grumbled, but he grumbled while he was sinking against the pillows and gazing at the soup in front of him. He looked at Henry so Henry could read his lips. "What are you doing here?"

Henry gave a thin smile. "Babysitting," he said blandly. "Mike's in the front room, helping Jade get ready. He'll be staying too."

"Lance?" Jackson mouthed, and Henry's face fell.

"Another night shift. I miss him." He sighed. "I'm also fuckin' horny. I'm only telling you that because you can't talk and tell the world what an asshole I am."

Jackson smiled a little at that, but he got it. Busy schedules, busy lives. Sex was one of his favorite things too, but he and Ellery'd had precious little time these last three weeks. Ezekiel Halliday had taken all their extra energy.

Well, not *all*.

Henry must have seen something in his face because he raised a suspicious eyebrow. "You are looking exceedingly smug for a man who's supposed to be incapacitated. What can't you tell me because you're too sick to talk?"

Unwillingly, Jackson's eyes darted to the side of the bed, where a four-by-six area rug featuring geometric shapes in shades of brown on a blue background sat next to the bed now. Jackson had no idea where Ellery had gotten the rug: The garage? The guest room closet? A secret magic compartment that was passed down through Ellery's family for times of great need—or great potential embarrassment?

Wherever Ellery had gotten the thing, it sat now, complementing the décor of the room nicely and hiding the evidence.

Henry wasn't stupid. He tracked Jackson's gaze to the area rug and then back to Jackson's face and very quickly put two and two together.

"You're kidding, right?"

Jackson looked at him blandly, refusing to incriminate himself.

"You don't fool me with that innocent look one bit!" Henry said, sulking. "You're too sick to move and you managed to get lucky?"

Jackson widened his eyes and mouthed, "I'm a lucky boy."

Henry growled at him. "Okay, lucky boy. You eat your soup or your luck's gonna run out." He indicated the tray next to the bed with an irritable gesture, and Jackson grimaced back.

"Living room?" he inquired hopefully.

"No," Henry replied, folding his arms. "I am under strict orders to stay in here with you. Mike's bringing a chair in from the guest bedroom, and we're watching TV while you get some sleep."

"Video games?" Jackson mouthed, truly offended. "PS4?" Ellery had recently hooked a television up on the wall across from the bed. He *said* it was so he could watch the news at night before they fell asleep, but Jackson knew the real reason was so Jackson could watch television from bed if he woke up with nightmares. Too many nights Ellery had come to fetch him from the couch after he'd nodded off, trying to find some peace. Jackson had let him—and let him tell a story about why he'd done it—but he'd insisted that they at least have some headphones and a PS4 in the bedroom so Ellery could sleep while Jackson was fighting his demons. Both the demons in his heart and the ones on the screen in the games.

"Mm-maybe," Henry said, frowning. "Let me go ask him. You eat." He pointed emphatically at the food next to the bed. "And before you give me any crap, you need to know that your behavior tonight directly affects what's going to happen Monday morning. I've been told in no uncertain terms that Jackson can't come out and play Monday if he doesn't get some rest this weekend, so there. I'm just looking out for you, buddy."

Jackson scowled. "Ask," he mouthed, pleased when Henry held up his hands.

"Fine. I'll ask. Ellery!" he called, turning to stride through the bedroom to the hall. "Jackson wants to know if he can play video games!"

He had no sooner gone into the living room than Mike came in, carrying the tapestried Queen Anne chair from the guest room.

"No video games," he said, and Jackson glared at Jade's boyfriend in disgust.

A blue-eyed boy from West Virginia, Mike was in his forties with prematurely white hair and a socially backward mindset that he had been gamely pushing forward on a daily basis since he'd met Jackson. He'd been Jackson's tenant when Jackson still lived in the duplex he'd bought before hooking up with Ellery, and he'd become part of Jackson's family, attending holiday functions and summer barbecues with Jackson, Jade, and her twin brother, Kaden, and becoming comfortable enough—and learning enough about social justice—that one day when Jackson wasn't looking, Jade fell in love with him.

Mike had been counting his blessings since.

Mike and Henry got along like a house on fire. Both of them had been brought up in households in which anybody not straight, white, or male was not particularly valid as a human being, and while they were working hard to fight those ideas, they were both forgiving of the other when someone fucked up, used the wrong word, or voiced an opinion that wasn't particularly progressive. They were both living examples of "progress, not perfection," and Jackson treasured them as friends.

But maybe not as babysitters.

"Why not?" Jackson demanded, wondering if this was what most kids felt like at ten. His mother had been on the streets when he'd been ten; video games hadn't been a thing in their shitty apartment, but then, neither had food. Jade and Kaden's mother had taken him in and had mommed him until his own mother had gotten pregnant again when he was fifteen and kicked him out. Toni Cameron had put him up on her sofa until he and Kaden had moved out to their own apartment, shortly before Kaden got married and Jackson joined the academy. That small apartment had been the first real home he'd ever known.

But the experience had left him not great with rules.

Mike eyeballed him like any babysitter would eye a recalcitrant ten-year-old. "Because your boyfriend says so," he said grimly, not appearing to think this was odd in the least.

Jackson wanted to say that video games helped him relax and that he would be bored if he was stuck in bed without anything to do, but at that moment, Ellery hustled in and Jackson lost his mind.

"Charlie Brown!" he croaked happily. "Oh my God!" He clutched his heart dramatically, and Ellery paused to let a tiny smile of appreciation escape. Jade had outdone herself, buying the costume with the bald cap and the bright yellow shirt with the black zig-zag and shorts, which Ellery complemented with black knee socks and white tennis shoes.

With a little duck of his head, Ellery met Jackson's eyes and said, "Good grief!" sending Jackson into another puppy-wriggling paroxysm of sheer cuteness overload.

"Best. Thing. *Ever*!" he mouthed. Then he got down to business. "Video games?"

"No," Ellery answered, mouth twisting in appreciation of Jackson's single-mindedness. "Video games will keep you awake. We want you to *sleep*. Mike and Henry are authorized to stream any movie you want— Disney, Sony, and Dreamworks are your oyster. But no horror movies—"

"It's almost Halloween!" he rasped, and then wished he hadn't.

"Fuck Halloween," Ellery snapped. "You just lived Halloween." His face softened, those sharp brown eyes becoming limpid pools of pleasing that Jackson could never resist. "Wouldn't want you to have bad dreams," he said softly.

They'd been getting better. At the end of November the year before, he'd been having sit-up-and-scream dreams almost nightly. All the self-care Ellery had begged him to invest in had paid off, and now it was more like once a week, but they were still there. Still waiting for something like the night before—or the entire Ezekiel Halliday trial period—to send his emotions into a spin, to send his subconscious on a feeding frenzy and leave him naked and vulnerable and shaking in the dark of night.

So Jackson knew what Ellery was really saying here, and he hated it. He was saying he wanted Jackson to fall asleep, lulled by the television and by the thought that there were people in the room who cared for him. He was telling Jackson not to keep himself awake, make himself potentially sicker, by battling the digital demons instead of battling the demons in his own soul.

Jackson hated relying on them. Hated it. Since the day they'd moved in, he'd gone out into the living room if he could, to let Ellery sleep when he couldn't. It hadn't always happened that way. Some nights he woke up, heart pounding, breath screaming in his chest, and he could fake needing a drink of water and disappear.

But some nights he woke Ellery with this bullshit, and it pissed him off. He didn't want to trouble Ellery, but Ellery seemed intent on sticking with him through the whole freakshow that was his subconscious, and dammit, couldn't loving Jackson not be so fucking hard?

Ellery was telling him to have some faith in their friends and to sleep. Jackson knew it wasn't that simple.

"So maybe stay awake with video games," he managed to rasp in response to Ellery's bad-dreams comment, but Ellery shook his head.

"Please," he asked quietly. "For me?"

Jesus. Ellery only played that card when it was important. Jackson closed his eyes.

"I don't want them to—"

"The dreams?" Mike asked, popping their little bubble of spoken intimacy with a snort. "I know about the dreams. You had 'em when you lived next door, remember?"

Jackson gave him a sour look. He remembered. He'd had to give Mike a key to his own half of the duplex. Before Ellery, when Jackson knew the night was going to suck, he'd find a hookup. The warm body would keep the dreams at bay, but the lack of intimacy of the impersonal sex didn't obligate anybody to stay with him. On the nights he couldn't find a hookup, the dreams would be bad. So bad that Mike had busted down his door more than once to shake Jackson awake to make that noise stop before somebody called the police. Jackson had finally given him the keys so if somebody *did* call the cops, Mike wouldn't get caught breaking into his house.

"So you're still having them?" Mike asked, catching his hostility and softening his voice.

"Fine," Jackson mouthed. "No video games. Not talking about it."

Mike's face, smooth-skinned behind his white beard, softened. "I guess you've got more worse shit to dream about," he murmured. He looked at Ellery and said, "No video games. I get it now."

Ellery's mouth twisted; it might have been a smile. "Thank you," he said. Then he moved closer to Jackson and leaned forward. Jackson raised his face, anticipating a kiss and got the little touchless thermometer instead.

"High," Ellery commented with a sniff. "And you don't get any more meds for another two hours." He handed Mike the thermometer and showed him how to use it, saying, "Test him once an hour. If it goes above 102 I'm calling for antibiotics. I can't believe all they sent him home with was pain pills."

"*I* got the pain pills," Henry said grimly. "He was going to leave without them."

Jackson tried to glare at him, but his eyes were gritty. "You're fired," he mouthed.

"Oh, color me shocked," Ellery snapped, and then he took a deep breath, the expression looking very Charlie Brownish to match his costume. "C'mon, Jackson. Don't fight me on this."

"Don't worry about me," Jackson told him. "Be careful. Stay sharp. Cock out, tits up, cut them to ribbons."

Ellery gave Jackson one of his most scathing looks. "They won't know they're bleeding until I'm gone," he said with smug certainty.

Jackson smiled proudly. "That's my boy."

At that moment Jade came bustling in, her little blue dress and black wig looking very Lucyish. She'd even found saddle shoes from somewhere and had made a sign that said Psychiatric Help 5¢.

Mike grinned at her and held his hand out. She gave him hers, and he raised it to his lips. "All my best fantasies as a little boy. I am *so* confused."

She laughed wickedly. "Wait till we get home. I'm gonna make you wear Ellery's costume and things are gonna get *kinky*!"

Jackson, Henry, and Ellery all groaned.

"And thanks for making it weird," Henry said. "Someday I'll tell you what Lance and I dress up as and revenge will be mine."

"Someday?" Jade asked, eyeballing him skeptically. "Why not now?"

"Because we've only been together since June! Give us some time to think about freaky shit like costumes. For all I know, his fantasies involve being Freddy Krueger fucking Pennywise, and then sorry, I'm out of there."

"Jesus," Ellery muttered. "Jade and I will get out first because no. Just no." He took a step toward the door and then went and gave Jackson the kiss on the forehead Jackson had wanted since he walked in. "No video games," he reiterated before glancing at the dinner on the tray on the dresser. "And don't think I haven't noticed that you haven't eaten. Gentlemen, make him eat," he ordered, before heading out for real this time.

"Ta-ta!" Jade trilled. "Off to charm the cobras!" And then they were out the door.

Jackson sighed and picked up the bowl of soup, noting that it was tomato bisque, like he'd told Cody it might be. He took a couple of moody bites and saw that Mike was flipping through the streaming menu, looking for Marvel something or other, and Henry was regarding him quietly.

"What?" he demanded, just *over* the lack of voice.

"Dreams?"

Jackson breathed in and out. "They're not as prevalent," he said, wondering if Henry could even read his lips for that last word. "For a while, before my heart surgery, they were almost every night."

Henry nodded. "I… every now and then I wake up thinking I can smell Malachi, that he's there in my barracks and he's about to…." About to rape Henry, who had begged his ex-boyfriend not to do anything to jeopardize their military careers. His ex—also his sister's husband—had done anything he'd pleased, just to prove to Henry that he held all the power.

"That's terrible," Jackson whispered, heartsick.

Henry looked away. "That's once a month or so," he murmured. "It's more than enough." He turned back. "Eat your soup, Jackson. Get some sleep. We'll be here if the scary monsters come. There's no shame in having friends to watch your back when your eyes close."

Jackson nodded and turned back to his soup, not sure what to say. He was starting to really feel the fever Ellery was bitching about, and his body was listing all the terrible things he'd done to it in the last two days. The spoon was getting heavier and heavier as he dragged it to his mouth, and about the time he realized Mike had picked *Monsters, Inc.*, a cartoon about scary night monsters that were conquered by laughter, Henry was pulling the bowl from his hands.

Mike did a little shuffling with his pillows, and he rolled to the side, too tired to even complain. Sometime between the lying down and the falling asleep, he realized that he really did have two friends who had his back, and it was that thought that let him close his eyes.

Charming the Cobras

THE DA'S office had reserved the dance club at the top of the Hyatt Regency for their little shindig, which was a lovely venue with black couches, scintillating lighting, and a view of the city to kill for, and Ellery fought the temptation to judge. Wasn't the district attorney's office supposed to *serve* the people? But he had been born into money and privilege, and he enjoyed both. He wasn't going to feel bad because he had them, but he was going to devote his vocation to service, because that was only fair. If you had the means, you fought for others, right?

At least it had been in his house. Taking a look at Trey Cartman, he wasn't sure Mr. Cartman had been raised with the same ideas.

A skosh over forty, Trey Cartman was almost the anti-Jackson in appearance. He had Jackson's dark blond hair, but it was crisply and professionally cut instead of perpetually in his eyes. He had Jackson's height, but he worked out enough to lead with his chest; he looked taller than Jackson because of it. He had the knife-blade cheekbones and full mouth, but instead of Jackson's habitual expression of sardonicism and ready fierceness, there was something condescending about Cartman's mouth, much like the way his murky green eyes raked over the people in his scope, weighing their usefulness to him.

Ellery's first impression had been *soulless*, and as he spotted Cartman now, his costume—a brilliant cloak made of peacock feathers, along with a peacock-feathered harlequin's mask that he perched on the top of his head—didn't do much to change that.

As they made their way around the black leather couches circling the dance floor to the open bar, Jade, glancing in the same direction, made a little hissing sound in Ellery's ear, and he knew she felt the same. Stone-cold like a dancing snake: Trey Cartman all the way.

The two people Cartman was talking to didn't look comfortable either.

Taller and rawboned, Charlie Boehner had "cop" written all over his ruddy face. Ellery could spot a drinker's nose a mile away, and Boehner had a beauty, lit up like a Christmas tree from his first—or fifth—drink of the day. He was wearing a bear costume, with the big fluffy head tucked under his arm. It must have been sweltering inside, because his face and his drinker's nose were sheened in sweat.

Ellery had seen him with that nose at 10:00 a.m. when he was in court as a witness.

He wasn't sure how the man did it. His eyes didn't get red, his breath didn't smell—he must have known all the tricks, from Visine to Tic Tacs, but he couldn't hide the broken blood vessels on his skin or the sallow complexion that spoke of a beleaguered liver either.

Somehow, though, he managed to be competent and ruthless, particularly when it came to defending police officers from any appearance of wrongdoing. Ellery knew that for such people, a crash was coming—you couldn't push your body as far as Boehner was pushing his without a reckoning—but he wasn't sure of how much damage Boehner could do to the police force before it happened.

The other person Cartman was deep in conference with was Judge Clive Brentwood, and he did not look pleased. In fact as Ellery and Jade approached, he glanced up at them, and his face relaxed with relief that seemed a little acute for social discomfort. He was wearing a stunning tuxedo with a Phantom of the Opera mask, and given the good and the bad Ellery had spotted in the man, he couldn't have chosen a more appropriate costume himself.

"Wonder what they're talking about?" Jade murmured.

"I forgot to bring my pet fly," Ellery said back, thinking that the proverbial fly on the wall would be a very handy employee to have sometimes.

"Mr. Cramer," Brentwood said, a desperately congenial smile on his face as he came to shake Ellery's hand. "So good that you and your—" His eyes assessed Jade, and Ellery could tell he came up with zilch to quantify what she could be in his life. "—date," he finished awkwardly, and only Ellery heard Jade's gentle snort.

"Gentlemen," Ellery said, smiling with his teeth only, "this is Jade Cameron, the world's best paralegal and office manager, and my private investigator's sister."

"Charmed," Cartman said, taking Jade's hand and raising it to his lips. "Is this a private investigator I haven't met yet? Or are we still talking about the ubiquitous Mr. Rivers?"

"Oh no," Jade said. "It's Jackson. We were raised together."

"Ah." Cartman's razor-thin smile indicated he was unappreciative of being made to feel off-balance. "I didn't know Mr. Rivers had been in foster care."

"He wasn't," Jade said, looking amused. She turned toward Judge Brentwood. "Good to see you again, Your Honor."

Brentwood gave her a pleased smile. "I wasn't sure if you remembered."

"Oh no, of course I did!" At the other men's bemused looks—including Ellery's own—she said, "Gentleman, back when I first got my license, I was working for Pfeist, Langdon, Harrelson and Cooper. Lyle Langdon had given me this *humongous* file box to cart by my lonesome to the courthouse, where he was trying a case, and there I was in the elevator when some jackass behind me decided to practically shove me over and knock my file box out of my hands as he dashed for the door."

"He was an unconscionable prick," Brentwood confirmed. "Used to work for my firm when I was still in private practice. Anyway, the lovely Ms. Cameron here actually *called* him a prick to his retreating back, and he whirled around in complete surprise, and while she was on her hands and knees picking up files, she managed to give him an, er...."

"Double-barreled salute," Jade said with a smug little smile.

"It was something to behold." Brentwood laughed at the memory. "I helped her pick up the files, and together we put her box in order, and then we realized we were headed to the same courtroom. Her firm and I were on opposite sides of a civil suit, as it were."

Jade laughed. "Yes! We were! And Lyle Langdon was *so* surprised when you offered to take me out to lunch afterward. It was brilliant!" After a moment of sharing the memory, she sobered. "I never did tell you this, but my brother, Jackson, was in the hospital about then, fighting for his life. I was so stressed. That lunch really saved me. It was so damned decent of you."

"You were fearless, my dear," Brentwood said fondly. He smiled at Ellery then. "And so it's no surprise she and Mr. Rivers have ended up working with you, Mr. Cramer. You three are a force to be reckoned with."

"A big storm?" Cartman interrupted, apparently annoyed by the surprising bond between Jade and Judge Brentwood. "I'm not afraid of storms. They tend to be—what's the term? Full of sound and fury, signifying nothing."

"I thought that quote referred to the life of a corrupt man," Ellery said politely, knowing his *Macbeth very* well.

Cartman's eyes flashed, and Ellery thought with clinical detachment that he was used to being the smartest man in the room. "Well, one of the reasons that play hasn't become obsolete is because its meaning is flexible," he said.

"Flexible and universal are two different things, I should think. Corruption and abuse of power are timeless themes—there's no reason to distort the meaning of the words associated with them. The clearer the language, the more easily the reader can see directly to the truth."

Another flash of anger, this one bright enough to make the others in their group step back. Cartman opened his mouth as though to say something and then took a breath before smiling brightly. "Enough time debating the words of a dead man. Have you all met my wife? She's floating around here somewhere, dressed as a butterfly of all things. You should say hello. She'd be pleased."

It was a clumsy segue, and Ellery wondered if he'd gotten to the man. "I'll be sure to look for her," he said with a polite smile. He turned to Brentwood, remembering the photos in his office. "What about you, Your Honor. Did your lovely wife come tonight?"

Brentwood gave an almost sweet smile. "Indeed not. About ten years ago we came to an agreement. She wouldn't drag me to the craft store on my day off, and I wouldn't drag her to these things on hers."

Ellery laughed, thinking that sounded very much like the agreement he and Jackson had. "She sounds like a wise woman. What's her craft?" His sister had taken up crocheting as stress relief from her job as a doctor, and he'd heard from her in detail that all crafts had their special niches.

"Quilting," he said promptly and held out his luxurious velvet-lined cape. "With a side hustle for sewing her husband costumes for affairs like this one."

Ellery laughed again, finding himself surprised to like Judge Brentwood. He remembered the man's growing dismay that day and realized that a judge trying to be impartial must have a very hard job indeed.

"That's beautiful!" Jade exclaimed.

"You should give her my compliments," Ellery told him. "She did a lovely job."

"So, Cramer," Cartman interposed, and Ellery realized that he seemed to resent having the conversation pulled away from himself. "Where's your wife? Not that the lovely Ms. Cameron doesn't make a fine date," he added with a thin smile.

"He should be so lucky," Jade jibed, and when Brentwood and even Boehner, who had mostly been gaping at them like a fish, burst into laughter, Ellery was grateful for her. She was trying to deflect the question so he wasn't obligated to discuss his personal life.

He very much wanted to discuss his personal life.

"Well, my date was planning to attend," he fibbed, "but at present he's dealing with a course of antibiotics and ninety-three stitches in his back, so dancing in costume was off the table."

And the absolute truth of the last part smacked them all in the face.

Brentwood was the first to recover, possibly because Ellery had already told him about the relationship. "How's he doing, by the way?"

"He's currently home with friends and the cats," Ellery said, not wanting to be nasty to the judge anymore. "Sulking because I wouldn't let him patrol the streets of Gotham in a cape and cowl."

Brentwood's laugh had a bit of an evil edge to it. "He does seem to be a bit larger than life, doesn't he?"

"Yeah, but even heroics didn't buy you that deal you wanted, did it, Cramer?" Cartman asked meanly, and Ellery was aware of an icy hot rage boiling in his veins.

"He didn't put himself in danger for me," he said, hoping his voice stayed level. "He put himself in danger for our client. Don't forget, your office was trying to put an innocent *disabled* man in prison today. If that's the way you want to make a name for yourself, go to town, but those things tend to come back to bite a career in the ass."

"I don't know," Cartman said with a roll of his eyes. "That disability seemed awfully suspect. How could four police officers not spot it—"

"Of course they spotted it," Brentwood said, surprising Ellery *and* Jade. "The entire case spoke of sloppiness on the part of law enforcement, and if Cody Gabriel turns out to be a reliable witness, it speaks to corruption as well. Or at least some damned poor decision-making. I was in the room as Mr. Cramer here was making that deal, and you know what I didn't hear him promise, because he can't?"

"I'm sure I don't know."

Brentwood stopped and caught Ellery's gaze while Ellery tried not to let his heart quail. Ellery knew exactly what Brentwood was talking about. Ellery had made no promises about keeping the Department of Justice from investigating the DA's office, and certainly no promises about keeping Cody Gabriel from testifying.

But if Cartman didn't think about that he couldn't anticipate it, and suddenly Brentwood, who had seemed to be so very much above politics in the courtroom, was completely in the game here at the Sacramento Law Enforcement Annual Halloween Soiree.

The corners of his mouth turned up, an almost impish look crossing his distinguished features. "Well, then," he said, with all the aplomb of a fourth grader, "I'm not going to tell you. Now if you gentlemen will excuse me, Trey, I'm going to go give my regards to your lovely wife."

And with that, the judge whirled around, his cape billowing behind him as he went in what Ellery had to admit was a ferocious exit.

Cartman watched him go with murder in his eyes.

"Do you have any idea what he was talking about?" Boehner asked, and unlike Cartman and Brentwood, who could keep their apprehension to themselves, Boehner was eying Ellery with open hostility and fear.

Jade snorted. "You people really have no idea who you're dealing with, do you? Do you think my brother got his back sliced up for glory or for something to talk about at a cocktail party? He did that because he cares about Ezekiel Halliday and Cody Gabriel. That doesn't go away because Ellery here was forced to cut a shitty deal with a guy who only *thinks* he holds all the cards."

Cartman's rage flashed dangerously, and Ellery found he had taken a step slightly in front of Jade, because he was suddenly afraid for her.

"As long as those cards don't involve going after my guys, he can play any game he wants," Boehner said with disgust, and Ellery eyed him coldly.

"The Marshals have the weapon your guy used to slice and dice a civilian without identifying himself. It's an illegal three-inch fixed-blade knife, and it has your guy's prints. Don't worry, either of you," he said through his teeth. "Now that Ezekiel Halliday is safe, we can take the gloves off. This is all *far* from over."

He let that shot fall where it landed and glanced at Jade. "You know, I'm not excited about the scotch, but those desserts look first-rate. You in?"

"Sure. But I want some scotch too."

"Well then, we should stop there first," Ellery said indulgently. He turned toward Boehner and Cartman. "Now, if you'll excuse us...." And with that, he and Jade made for the open bar.

He waited until they were out of earshot and there were a couple of people behind them before he let out a sigh.

"That was not as smooth as I would have liked," he muttered.

"Speak for yourself," Jade muttered. "I wanted to put an oxford shoe down that asshole's throat."

Ellery gave a sharp bark of laughter, feeling marginally better. "He is not nearly as self-contained as he should be," he muttered, not liking this at all. Powerful men who didn't know how to control themselves were exceedingly dangerous. "Not for someone in that position."

"And Boehner couldn't have his lips more firmly positioned on his ass," she returned, as deadly serious as Ellery. "And we've already seen him abuse his power. The surprising one is Brentwood. Going by how much he let happen in the courtroom, I thought he was a lock for corruption, and I was really disappointed in him."

"I don't think that's it," Ellery said with a sigh. "I could be wrong— but I do know he's run on a conservative law-and-order platform his entire life. Maybe he's seeing what that can mean when the system's being abused?"

Jade let out a frustrated sound that Ellery couldn't blame her for one bit.

"It doesn't hurt that Ezekiel is white," he agreed softly.

"No it does not." She sighed. "But I don't think Boehner was ever personally that way. I think political parties are comforting—you have all your friends, they all vote for the same people. It's like rooting for a basketball team. It's not until individuals take a deeper look and realize that hey, the guys on the basketball team are blowing away the other team with howitzers that they can start to change things."

Ellery gave a humorless bark of laughter, and at that moment they got to the bar. He ordered a seltzer water for himself and a double Macallan for Jade.

"Isn't that a little highbrow for someone who grew up on Johnnie Walker Red?" she asked as the bartender went to get the premium liquor.

"You found us costumes and showed up ready to tango with snakes," Ellery said. "That deserves Macallan."

She let out a soft breath. "And you're not drinking."

He shrugged, thinking about Jackson at home fending off his demons. "I'm exhausted," he admitted quietly. "A glass of wine would put me right out. We'd have to get an Uber."

She laughed like she was supposed to, but then she went into mother hen mode. "You should be catching up on *your* sleep too!"

He grunted and tried not to let his shoulders twitch. "We only just got here," he said softly. "I have the feeling we have many more conversations to go."

At that moment, he spotted Arizona and saluted her from across the room. She was dressed as a tree sprite, in flowing white with a framework of wings like mist trailing behind her. Ellery found himself smiling fondly, particularly when she hauled Siren Herrera along.

Siren was a stunning woman, and her costume took advantage of her dark skin and striking bold features to wear the uniform of the royal guard of Wakanda as Okoye. She normally wore her tightly curly hair cropped close to her head, as well as large gold hoop earrings, so the rest of the costume was just dressing. Her warrior's spirit was never far from the surface.

And Jade was extremely jealous. "I could have worn that," she muttered.

"Of course you could have," Ellery said soothingly. "You were only trying not to humiliate me, which I appreciate. The only person I could have been from that movie was Martin Freeman's character, and that's sort of, you know, embarrassing."

"True," Jade allowed with a disdainful sniff that hid nothing. Siren Herrera was tall, shapely, and didn't look the slightest bit amiss in the sarong with the spear, and Jade would not have had quite the same effect.

"Besides," Ellery said, lowering his head so only she could hear the comment, "we all know you'd be Suri, because she's the genius behind the operation, right?"

She grinned at him. "God, I'm glad Jackson's keeping you."

"Me too." And with that thought, he felt fortified enough to wade into the political fray with only seltzer water to sustain him.

Arizona and Siren reached them as they walked from the wet bar to the dessert table.

"Do you want anything?" Jade asked, continuing their trajectory. "You can stay and chat."

"Coward," he said, barely loud enough for her to hear as she peeled off and aimed for the table.

"Ellery," Arizona cried, drawing near. "So good to see you." She eyed him up and down, then cast a look at Jade at the dessert table as she piled a plate high with cookies. "Nice costumes."

A year ago, he might have taken exception, but he couldn't now. Besides being a fair competitor as well as helping them in the past, she'd been as devastated as he'd been that day—and as infuriated at seeing the perversion of the law that allowed Ezekiel Halliday to suffer bodily injury and indignity with not a shred of recompense or even remorse. He'd seen the humanity in Arizona Brooks, and he knew now that the snark was between friends.

"Well, Jackson needed his rest, so we couldn't come as the Hardy Boys," he said with a smile.

"Which Hardy Boy are you?" Siren asked, drawing near Arizona. "Frank or Joe?"

Ellery laughed. "I think Frank was supposed to be the methodical, thoughtful one and Joe the impulsive, intuitive one. I'll let you guess."

They all laughed because that was a no-brainer.

"How is he?" Arizona asked soberly when the laughter had died down.

Ellery shrugged with a nonchalance he didn't feel. "Pissed-off, feverish, and in pain," he said honestly. "We know that getting Zeke free and clear was the endgame, but we sure did want to see justice done."

Arizona nodded and then lowered her voice. "Any chance the DOJ will investigate?"

Ellery's eyes sharpened as he remembered their one bright spot. "Count on it," he said. "And I've been looking for a contact in the press."

Arizona sucked air in through her teeth. "Do you really want to do that?"

Ellery swallowed. Drumming up outrage in the press was a double-edged sword. Ezekiel Halliday and Sunshine Prayers Care Homes did not need the backlash that an investigation against the police might incur. Police unions were known to get ugly when officers were implicated and charged. Having a credential inspector pressured to turn up at the care home and find a reason to shut the place down had been an implicit threat in everything Trey Cartman had said that afternoon.

"God no," he admitted, hoping he was right to confide in a friend. "But if we have to, we have our spin and we have our press release drafted. Arizona, this can't happen again—and just as important, what the hell is he doing with the homeless population? This entire thing started when the police tried to vilify the homeless so they could illegally relocate them. I don't think I have to mention Ezekiel Halliday to make that headline pop."

Arizona nodded soberly. "Do you trust me?" she asked.

Ellery pulled in a sharp breath. He'd been asking himself the same question. Without meaning to, his eyes flew to Siren's, and she looked soberly back.

"Do you trust *us*?" Siren asked softly.

"With what?" he replied, thinking he might already know the answer.

"If a source from the DA's office leaks the forced homeless relocation to the press," Arizona said. "No mention of Ezekiel Halliday, no mention of Cody Gabriel, just a suggestion to go up to Lake Whiskeytown and check out some of the homeless encampments that have disappeared from Sacramento. If it comes from us, they'll do it, and if you're not implicated, they can't look at the inciting incident." Arizona blew out a breath. "I sure would like to make something about this case right, Ellery, but I'd like to do it without losing my job."

"Right?" Siren chimed in. "You can't enact prison and sentencing reform without people on the inside *on* your side, but it sucks to be on the *wrong* side, if you know what I mean."

Ellery nodded, a grim smile twisting his mouth. "I do," he said, looking up and catching the eye of Lyle Langdon, one of his former employers at Pfeist, Langdon, Harrelson and Cooper. "I'll be honest—I don't have a job to lose for that exact reason."

Lyle Langdon, tall, silver-haired, with a narrow handsome face, gave him a respectful salute, and Ellery wondered if he had enough in him for one more intense conversation. At that moment, Jade showed up at his elbow with a plate piled high with cookies that she held out to Arizona and Siren first.

"You guys want some? I had to elbow a nun to get these!"

In spite of himself, Ellery glanced quickly to the refreshment table, and when he saw, indeed, one of the junior ADAs dressed as the Flying Nun, complete with a wire frame for the fluttering habit, he had to control his semihysterical laughter.

Siren and Arizona didn't bother to control theirs, but they did thank Jade for the cookies, and the rest of the conversation was about how Jackson could get injured in a pillow fight at a marshmallow farm. Before they parted to mingle with other guests at the "recreational" function, Arizona touched his elbow.

"Not a word about you, Halliday, Rivers, or Gabriel," she said softly. "I swear to you, Ellery, I wouldn't do you like that."

It had been a long, long day on little sleep, and Ellery felt his eyes burn. "I'll hold you to that," he said. "Thank you."

"Tell Jackson to stay out of marshmallow farms, okay?"

Ellery managed a tight grin. "Will do."

He and Jade had almost made it to the coat check when Lyle Langdon intercepted them.

"Ellery! So good to see you here. I wasn't sure if you were coming."

Ellery smiled at his old boss and mentor, unsure if the words were sincere or not. He and Jackson had met when they'd worked for Langdon's firm, and he'd considered Lyle Langdon a friend. However, his and Jackson's pursuit of the truth behind the Dirty/Pretty Killer had irritated some of Pfeist, Langdon, Harrelson and Cooper's more important clients. Ellery had been politely asked to resign, and Jade and Jackson had quit—colorfully—in protest.

"Lyle. Good to see you too."

Langdon's expression sobered. "I heard about Jackson. I do hope he's okay."

And because Ellery knew that Langdon really had been fond of Jackson—to the extent of telling Jackson that he and Jade could stay with the firm even though they'd asked Ellery to leave—he took this for the sincerity it was.

"I do too. It's one of the reasons we were out the door." The other being that he was dead on his feet and Jade was a little giggly after that double Macallan.

"Well, give him my best." Langdon bit his lip—an uncharacteristically tentative gesture from a man who had made his name in the courtroom as being cold as ice. "Ellery, if you can spare an hour next week, I have a consult for you. I'd pay you for your time, of course, but we would expect complete confidentiality."

Ellery was about to say yes. Yes of course he'd do this favor for his old friend and mentor. He'd be happy to. And being paid, after all the work on the pro bono Halliday case? That would be amazing!

He wasn't sure what made him cautious.

"I would of course have to see the name of the client before I accepted the consult," Ellery said.

Langdon nodded, looking, of all things, relieved. "Of course. You might recognize it, in fact." His eyes flickered furtively, as though he was afraid of being overheard, and he leaned into Ellery, close enough that nobody in the crowded venue could hear.

When he whispered the name, Ellery recoiled, and Langdon gave him a significant look. Ellery opened his mouth to say he couldn't possibly listen to anything this man said, and he wouldn't take a *dime* to help defend him, when Langdon paused for a moment, one eyebrow raised.

"You'll let me know next week," Langdon said coolly, and Ellery remembered that yes, he was still dancing with snakes.

"I'll have to check my schedule," he replied, voice even, expression mild. And he recognized this for the gift it was. "But thank you for thinking of me."

"Of course. You're the best man I know."

Not the best lawyer—or the smartest man or the best counselor. The best man.

"Next to Jackson," Ellery said, almost like a test.

Langdon nodded as if in relief, as though Ellery had passed. "Of course."

With that, Langdon strode off—hopefully to the bar, because he'd need it—and Jade took Ellery's arm while they strode to the elevators. There were people in the elevators: a group of men dressed like basketball players, but all of them were five feet ten and white, with buzz cuts. Cops, if Ellery had to judge, and he must have made their radar because they scowled at him and Jade all twenty stories down to the garage. Ellery watched as they made their way to their own cars while he waited for the valet to fetch his beloved Lexus, and every time Jade opened her mouth to ask, he gave a subtle shake of his head.

It wasn't until they were in the car and headed back home that Ellery took in what felt to be his first deep breath.

"Oh my God, you have *got* to spill," Jade said, probably feeling the tension in the car ease. "You're killing me. You actually turned white, Ellery. I mean white-*er*. You are damned pasty right now. What in the hell happened?"

"He asked me for a consult," Ellery said, mind racing. "For a case I think he knew I wouldn't take."

It happened sometimes. There were people and actions that were indefensible. Jackson and Ellery had founded the law firm on the idea that they were there to give people a fair shake; they were *not* there to help dangerous people escape the penalties of their actions. Their contracts were written with that thought in mind. Setting a monster free because they thought they were helping a guy with an assault charge was high up on the list of their mutual nightmares, and they'd done what they could to stop it from ever happening.

"Why wouldn't you take it?" she asked, all traces of expensive scotch fading from her voice. She'd been tricked into scheduling one of those monsters on their consult roster, and Jackson had suffered nightmares for a week that featured that guy in particular. She'd vowed to never make that mistake again.

"It was for the policeman's union," Ellery said grimly. "Specifically to defend Neil Freethy and Keith Brown."

Jade sucked in a breath. "Those two assholes?" She frowned. "Why not Goslar and McMurphy? They're far more liable for criminal proceedings."

Ellery nodded grimly. "I know. And that's what's got my knickers in a twist. Langdon was trying to tell me something—warn me somehow—without violating confidentiality. You remember that guy, Jade. He's canny, smart, and as principled as he can be. He wouldn't have asked me to consult for a case he *knew* I didn't want to have a fucking thing to do with if he didn't want me to know something was up."

"Oh, I agree," she muttered. "*Damn.* I thought we were going to play who's a bigger gaping asshole, Trey Cartman or Charlie Boehner. But this is a whole new game."

"Or is it the same game?" Ellery murmured.

"What do you mean?"

Pushing through the rattled clutter of his brain right now was painful, like cleaning out an old room that had been used for storage for years. But something Jackson had said....

"Jade, what was Jackson going to be doing tonight before he got sliced and diced?"

"Hunh."

God, that sound drove him crazy when Jackson made it and made him even crazier when she did.

"That's not a word," he muttered.

"Sure it is. Right now it's a word that means Jackson is a fucking genius. He was going to go to the police station and see who was working tonight, because the people on the DA's and the union's good side would be at the party."

Ellery nodded grimly and waited for her to get there.

"Oh," she said. "My God! None of those assholes were there!"

"No they were not," he said, remembering that he'd been looking for them when they'd first arrived. "And we know there were policemen there because that entire elevator was balls to the walls white boys with crewcuts and cheap shoes under their costumes."

"Those weren't costumes. Those were some Kings jerseys they bought on Groupon."

Ellery snorted because it was true—not particularly imaginative, and definitely not individual. "So our four choirboys weren't there tonight. Why?"

"Because," Jade said slowly. "Because they must have pissed somebody off."

Ellery nodded. "And Cartman and Boehner were working Judge Brentwood enough to make him really uncomfortable."

"He *did* look really happy to see us," she murmured. "God, Ellery, I feel like we should do something with all this information but...." Her voice wobbled.

"You're going home with your boyfriend to sleep," Ellery ordered gently. "So's Henry. So am I. It's the weekend. We're sleeping late. We're eating more cookies. We're resting. We saved Ezekiel Halliday from jail, and damn if it didn't cost us. Even Jackson has to rest this weekend if I have to drug his soup."

She gave a weak chuckle. "You're a good boss," she said with feeling. Then after a pause, "But we're still chewing this fat when we wake up tomorrow, right?"

"I don't bring home my laptop for nothing," he said grimly.

"Yeah. Good. Because those assholes can get up to all sorts of trouble if nobody's there to stop them."

"I'm aware," he said, and there didn't seem to be anything more to say about that.

OR MAYBE it was just that he was done with words. When he got back to the house, Henry was asleep in the bed next to Jackson, Mike was asleep in the chair, his head tilted back, and Jackson was curled up on his side, the cats parked—Billy Bob behind his shoulder blades, Lucifer behind his neck—and a Marvel movie was drawing to a close on the TV.

Ellery let out a sigh and said, "You guys want the guest room and Henry can take the couch?"

"We can't," Mike said, sitting up and scaring Ellery badly. "We have to let the dog in. Don't worry. I'm awake."

"Does that all the time," Jade admitted. "Scares the shit out of me, but he seems to really be okay."

And with that, they gathered their things to leave. Ellery leaned over Henry and touched him softly on the arm. He grunted, squinted up at Ellery's face, and then groaned.

"You can take the guest room," Ellery said, since Jade and Mike were leaving. "When's Lance off?"

"Ten a.m.," Henry murmured. "I'll do that and text him. He can pick me up in the morning on the way home."

"Fair enough. I've got some sweats if you want them."

Henry rolled off the bed and stretched, yawning. "You're a good man, Charlie Brown."

Ellery blinked at him and realized that, besides Jackson, nobody else had used that line on him all night. He chuckled, grateful that Henry had wandered into their orbit, then got him some sweats to sleep in and sent him to bed in the other room.

Jade and Mike let themselves out, setting the alarm and killing the lights, and Ellery changed into pajamas, brushed his teeth, and climbed into bed. After he displaced Billy Bob so he could at least tangle his legs with Jackson's, Jackson let out a sweet little sigh.

"'Lo, Counselor," he rasped, laryngitis not much better. "How were the cobras?"

Ellery leaned close enough to kiss his shoulder and then pulled away, not wanting to brush his back, even a tiny bit.

"Deadly," he said, meaning it. "But they can wait until the morning."

"Good. Love you. Glad you're home."

"Love you too. And God, I'm glad I'm home with you."

Something about the physical contact, Jackson's sleep-slurred words, the normalcy of the two of them in the same bed, allowed Ellery's buzzing brain to quiet down, and he fell fast asleep.

Wrong Guy

JACKSON'S PHONE went off right before he heard the pounding on the front door Monday morning, and he groaned. God. Didn't they have another two hours? The hell time was it, anyway? Five a.m.? The fuck?

He checked his phone and saw a text from Crystal, the tech genius who still worked at Pfeist, Langdon, Harrelson and Cooper.

Don't be mean to Christie. They're fishing.

He stared at the text and tried to put the pounding at the door together with it, and the resulting car crash in his brain woke him up enough to think—sort of.

With a grunt he rolled out of bed, careful not to wake Ellery. At Henry's request, Lance had shown up at their house with antibiotics for Jackson bright and early Saturday morning. By then, Jackson's back had been on fire, and his fever had been raging, and he'd been too weak to put up a fight. By Sunday morning everything had started working, including his immune system, and the two of them had spent most of Sunday sleeping and talking, texting their circle with ideas, and sleeping some more. Ellery had insisted that nobody go in to work, everybody take extra naps, and everyone but Jackson got to go in Monday morning to try to figure out what Freethy and Brown were doing by going for legal help without their union guy.

Also, everybody was *really* keen to know whose orders were responsible for the forced relocations and if their four choirboys in blue were acting on directive or instinct when they'd gone after Jackson and Cody Gabriel.

Somebody had to fix it. Somebody had to pay, and that couldn't happen until they got to the truth, and they couldn't get to the truth when they were falling asleep where they sat.

As Jackson padded through the front room, bare-chested, the stitches on his back finally not aching like he'd been skinned alive, he had to admit he wasn't up to much more than what he was doing right now. But Ellery planned to wake up and conquer planets, so if Jackson could answer the goddamned door at fuck-you in the morning, he was going to do it.

He was not prepared to see Detective Andre Christie and his interim partner, Leslie de Souza, standing at the door. Behind them stood four police officers that Jackson didn't recognize—but who didn't look particularly friendly.

Jackson blinked rapidly, trying to assimilate this new threat. "Detective Christie?" he asked tentatively. Andre Christie was a dapper, spit-polished Latino man, usually partnered with Sean Kryzynski, who was currently out on injury leave and whom Jackson and Ellery considered a friend. In fact, they considered Christie a friend as well. The weekend before, Jackson and Henry had spent a few hours at Kryzynski's place along with Christie and Billy Barnes, one of the Johnnies kids who'd offered to help Kryzynski out while he was healing.

In response to Jackson's sally, Christie shook his head, looking furious—but not at Jackson. "This. Is not. My idea."

Jackson's eyes widened, and he looked to Leslie for clarification. "Was it *your* idea?" he asked, and she shook her head grimly.

Leslie was a smart, tough woman, scary fit, with wildly curly brown hair pulled back at her nape and a sunburned pink nose. "No. No it's not. And given how shitty you look, I'd wager it's about to blow up in Trey Cartman's face."

Jackson suddenly saw where this was going. "What is it I was supposed to have done while I was laid up with fever and a fucking river of stitches down my back?"

She and Christie shared a look that was part anger and part triumph.

"I don't suppose you could prove tha—" Christie began, and Jackson turned around before he could finish. If he guessed right, his dressing needed changing. It must have, because Christie and de Souza both sucked air in through their teeth.

"I'm going to take a picture of that," de Souza said.

"Sure. You do that. Be sure to send it to Cartman, blown up with a diagram since half of Sacramento's already seen it. What else do you need?"

"Do you have any proof you were here last night?" de Souza asked.

"Besides my boyfriend to alibi me?" Jackson parried. "That depends. From when to when?"

"From ten p.m. to two a.m.," she responded, and Jackson thought for a moment, and then brightened.

"In fact, I do!" he said. Then, "But do me a favor and give me some of those evidence bags. I need to preserve the prints on the remote control."

He led them into the living room, after making sure only two of the officers were allowed in and they'd agreed to keep the front door shut. To make extra double sure the cats didn't get out, he tiptoed to the bedroom and shut the door, not surprised that Ellery had barely stirred.

"Here," he said, after bagging the remote control, showing everybody that he was being careful to preserve prints. "This is my own special remote. Ellery got it for me for Flag Day or something. Nobody touches it but me, and sometimes Ellery to get it out of the way. You should find those prints on it and nobody else's, and if you do find someone else's prints on it, let me know, 'cause there's gonna be a beatdown, you all feel me?"

Christie and de Souza nodded, but the other cops scowled, because apparently they had no sense of humor. "Okay—so what I'm doing here is calling up my play log on the game—see that?" He made the figure on the screen dance. "That's my guy. I've built him up plenty. See that?" He scrolled to the play log. "What's that say?"

Christie let out a low whistle. "Three hours last night? You played video games from ten to one in the morning?"

Jackson didn't tell him why. "Yeah. Felt like shit because fucking duh! Got up, played until my back stopped aching enough for me to sleep. Do you need to bag and tag the video game?"

"Uhm, we saw a video security system for the front porch—" Leslie began.

"Ellery will send you our footage, time stamped, as soon as he wakes up."

Christie frowned. "Uhm, Jackson, why aren't you waking him up now?"

Jackson scowled at him. "Guys, I've been running a fever all fucking weekend, and he's been nursing me through it. How much sleep do you think *he's* gotten in the last three days?"

Christie and de Souza met eyes. "Thank you for your time," de Souza said. "We're sorry for the early hour."

Jackson nodded. He got it. They were following orders. "What, exactly, was Trey Cartman trying to pin on me?"

They met eyes again. "It's probably already hit the feeds," Christie murmured, and de Souza nodded.

"Charlie Boehner was shot to death in his home last night," she said. "No forced entry. He was standing in his front room with a drink in his hand, and somebody blew him away."

Jackson stared at them. "Oh, you guys. Not only was this *so* not me, but this city is in big, big trouble."

Christie's jaw clenched, and he swallowed. "We are aware. We're sorry—so sorry—to have wasted your time."

Jackson raised one shoulder and winced. "I'd say it was nothing, but it's not, and now we all know it. You guys watch your six—something wrong—very, very wrong—is about to go down."

"You don't think that was the end of it?" de Souza asked warily, and Jackson met Christie's eyes.

"Do you trust me?" he asked.

Christie nodded decisively. "I know you had Sean's six when the department didn't."

"Then believe me. I know what shit smells like when it's about to go boom. You all can show yourselves out."

They did, and Jackson made sure the door was locked behind them. He stopped at the kitchen counter for his medication and his painkillers before making his painful way back into the bedroom to talk to Ellery.

Ellery was trying hard to move. "Time'zit?" he mumbled.

"Early. You have another two hours."

"Wuz-someun-attedoor?"

"Misunderstanding," Jackson said quietly, sliding into the bed and making sure to lie on the side he hadn't been sleeping on when he'd gotten out of bed. "Don't worry about it."

"'Kay."

Jackson scooted into Ellery's warmth a little, and Ellery returned the favor by rolling over so Jackson could spoon him.

"Sleep-now-kay?"

"Yeah." Jackson kissed the nape of his neck. "Get some sleep."

"I NEED to *what*?" Ellery demanded, staring at Jackson over the breakfast table while in the middle of stirring his coffee.

"You, uh, need to send our footage for the security system to Andre Christie at his work email so he can eliminate me as a potential suspect." Jackson took a bite of the english muffin Ellery had set in front of him and chewed experimentally. Not bad.

Ellery blinked rapidly, a sure sign he was having trouble assimilating information.

"Suspect for what?" he asked, still blinking.

"Killing Charlie Boehner," Jackson said, taking another bite. "He was shot to death last night in his home."

Ellery's mouth slowly fell open, and Jackson eyeballed the melon slice. His stomach grumbled under the antibiotics, and he figured what could it hurt?

Ellery had been quiet too long, and Jackson looked up in time to see him distracted by his phone. "Ellery Cramer, Esquire," he said automatically as he picked it up. Then his eyes focused on Jackson and narrowed dramatically. "Yes, Galen, I *did* see that Charlie Boehner was killed. Yes, apparently he was shot in his home." He glared. "And apparently Jackson needs to be cleared as a person of interest."

"I've been cleared as a suspect," Jackson corrected, ignoring his fork and picking up the melon with his thumb and forefinger. "Because the DA set the detectives after me, and they felt compelled to come see if I had an alibi."

Ellery stopped blinking completely. In fact his eyes grew wider. "Excuse me, Galen. I need to send Christie our security footage and kill my boyfriend."

Jackson swallowed a hurried bite of melon. "What?" he demanded. "What'd I do?"

To his surprise, Ellery's voice dropped with hurt. "You talked to the police without your lawyer?"

"Aw, Ellery." He reached across the table to cover Ellery's hand with his own. "You were beat, man. I heard them knocking and opened up thinking it was a neighbor complaining about the minivan or something." Henry had left it in the driveway when Lance picked him up, and it was definitely not up to neighborhood spec. "It was Christie and de Souza, and they really didn't want to be here. Cartman apparently sent them here directly, with four flatfoots to supervise, to see if I had an alibi. I don't know what made them think I'd be compelled to leave my sickbed to blow that asshole away between ten and two in the morning, but I convinced them I hadn't, and Christie asked for the security footage around our house to make sure."

He smiled prettily, but he wasn't out of the woods yet.

"How, exactly, did you convince them you were here?"

Jackson's smile froze. "My, uh, winning personality?"

Ellery stood up abruptly and stalked into the living room. He came back with the remote control, which the detectives had left after seeing Jackson's game stats. It was still covered in the evidence bag.

"How long?" he asked gently.

"Three hours," Jackson muttered, figuring giving in was easier on Ellery than fighting it. "I'm sorry. I was restless, and you were so tired." He met Ellery's eyes. "Please, Ellery? Don't make a big deal out of it this time? Everybody needs a rest. You can't take care of me when you're falling apart yourself. Let me spare you some of the scary shit sometimes. You know it's there. I don't think you're going to forget. But you needed to sleep. Everybody did. You're going to burn out on worrying about me if you don't take a break."

Ellery swallowed and gave a small smile. "I'll never burn out on worrying about you," he said softly. "But point taken. Just... just when you have to do that, tell me in the morning? Tell me if it was a bad one? Tell me what it was? I'll be more okay with you self-medicating if you don't try to hide it from me."

Jackson nodded. "Deal," he said, feeling unaccountably emotional. "I... you just looked really tired."

Ellery let out a weak laugh. "Yeah, baby. But this time it's really not your fault."

Jackson laughed slightly. "It's a little my fault," he admitted.

Ellery's laugh grew stronger. "A little," he conceded, squeezing his eyes shut hard. When he opened them, they were red-rimmed and shiny. "I... you brought backup this time," he said, sounding raw. "You contacted me as often as you could. You came home right into my arms. I have nothing to complain about."

Jackson heard what wasn't said, and he stood and crossed the space between them, then wrapped his arms around Ellery's shoulders.

"Except...?"

"Except I worry about you," Ellery mumbled, face buried against his neck. "I worry about how long you can keep doing this. I worry that someday your luck or your lives or whatever will run out. I… I want you for as long as I can get you, but God, Jackson, I want you for longer than a few years."

His voice broke, and Jackson pulled him tighter, thinking that they'd both been so tired three days ago they wouldn't have had the energy for this discussion then.

"Don't give up on me," he whispered into Ellery's ear. "I'll learn to duck, I swear. For you? I'll learn to walk on fences or fly or anything you need me to. I'm not as smart as you, though. It's only been a year."

Ellery's shoulders shook for a moment, and then he relaxed, giving Jackson some of his weight. "You'd better," he said. "I know you joke about me moving on if I lose you, but I don't think that's what would happen."

"No?" Jackson asked tenderly.

"It's hard to look for another man when your sky turns black and the world has crumbled up and turned to powder. I don't have a spare heart in my pocket in case you *don't* learn to duck and I lose you. You have to have faith in the world to love, Jackson. You *are* my faith. Don't take my faith away from me."

"No," he agreed, humbled. "Someday, you and me, we'll stand in a park, in public, and we'll tell the world that we love each other. I can't promise much, but I promise I'll make it to that day, okay?"

Ellery jerked sharply, as though slapped. "Did you just promise me we'll get married?"

Jackson opened his mouth and closed it, appalled. "Did I?"

"You *did*! You promised me we'll get married, and then you *tempted the fates* by saying you'll drop dead the day after!"

Now Jackson recoiled. "I did not!"

"Oh, you did too!"

"I didn't! I swear! Jesus, Ellery, if we go to all the trouble to get married, don't you think we should at least make it a couple of years after that?"

"I'm pulling for fifty!" Ellery snapped. "Now say it again, but don't spoil it with the bad part."

Jackson racked his brains desperately. "Uhm, I promise, you and me, we'll stand in a park, and we'll tell the world that we love each other—oh my *God*. I did. I *did* just promise we'll get married! Shit!"

"Are you going to take it back?" Ellery glowered.

"No." Jackson folded his arms across his chest and then grimaced when the movement pulled his gods-be-damned stitches. "No, I'm not going to take it back. But you know. Not a proposal or anything." For a moment Ellery looked like he was going to crumble again, and Jackson hurriedly jumped in to save the moment. "Yet."

Ellery's smile through his tears was like… like ice cream after a shit pizza. Like a perfect chord after a middle-school band. Like sunshine and rainbows and birds and butterflies after a hurricane. "But it's coming," he said, like Jackson had offered him a lifeline in a storm.

Jackson felt a little hurt. "Of course, Ellery. You know I couldn't love anybody like I love you, right? Of course it's coming. I'm just…." He shifted uncomfortably. "You know. Slow."

Ellery gave one of those big smiles again. "It's like the cavalry," he said, wiping his eyes with the back of his hand. "I just have to know it's coming. I can hold out forever if I know it's on its way."

Jackson moved in close again and used the hem of his soft T-shirt to wipe Ellery's eyes. He was throwing it in the hamper as soon as Ellery left anyway.

"Okay, Counselor," he said softly. They both heard his phone buzz from the table. "Is it enough to get you through your day?"

Ellery nodded, content and sweet in Jackson's arms as he very rarely was. His phone buzzed again, angrier this time, as though it knew that Ellery had put his work concerns aside for a few moments to be human and vulnerable and needy.

Jackson kissed his forehead. "Good, because I think your day is about to hit you like a sledgehammer, so you need to have your shit together."

Ellery took a step back and nodded grimly. "What are you planning to do?" he asked, and before Jackson could protest in all innocence that he was going to mooch around the house and heal as ordered, he gave Jackson a droll look. "I'm well aware that you're not about to sit this one out."

Jackson chuckled. "Well, let's say I've been thinking about the DA sending Christie and de Souza out here. Don't Christie and K-Ski have the best record in the department?"

Ellery nodded. It was common knowledge that when Sean Kryzynski and Andre Christie worked together, they were pure gold.

"So why would the DA send one of his best teams out here to chase down a bullshit lead with the added benefit of harassing the boyfriend of the guy who had just annoyed him?"

Ellery slow-blinked. "He knows something," he said softly. "Something he doesn't want anybody to know, including the police. They weren't sent here because he thought you did it. They were sent here because he might know who did."

"Yeah." Jackson nodded. "And the only way to figure out what he knows is to solve the case ourselves. And I bet ol' Sean is feeling mighty bored by now...."

Ellery's smile was completely self-satisfied. "And he can't go running off into the wild blue yonder either."

"No he cannot," Jackson said. "You have found yourself the perfect babysitter."

"Better yet," Ellery said brightly, "you found him for me!"

Jackson grinned, relieved that Ellery seemed to have located his center again. "Lucky you."

But Ellery sobered. "Yes. I'm *very* lucky. And I haven't forgotten that you're talking marriage, and that it's going to be in a park, under a blue sky, with all our friends around us."

Jackson felt his cheeks heat. "That's pretty romantic," he said, wondering what had possessed him.

"And practical." Ellery gave a decisive nod that fooled neither of them. "If you're anywhere near a candle, odds are, you'll burn the place down."

"Heh heh heh heh heh heh...."

Ellery stalked toward the table, obviously intent on his coffee and on getting to the office close to on time. "It's not funny," he huffed.

"It's hilarious."

"It's pathological."

"It's the best thing I've heard all day!" Jackson said on a laugh.

Ellery turned a smug smile toward him. "Not me," he said, and Jackson abruptly stopped laughing. As Ellery bustled around the kitchen and then into the bedroom again for a final lint roll, he sank down next to his breakfast plate and waited for the panic to assail him.

I said we were going to get married!

But by the time Ellery had hustled out, filled his travel mug with coffee and doctored it, and then kissed Jackson meltingly on the mouth before disappearing into the garage to leave, Jackson realized no panic was coming.

When he realized that the only thing in his chest at the thought of marrying Ellery Cramer was a deep and abiding sense of peace, he let out a breath and stood. He'd mull on the proposal later. But right now, they had so much work to do.

Breadcrumbs

THE THING about Galen Henderson's Sahara-dry Southern sense of humor was that Ellery could tell him anything and only be the recipient of a long slow blink of the eyes as feedback. Given that Ellery came from stolid and practical New Englanders who *also* tried very hard not to overreact, it meant that when Galen reacted to something that Ellery reacted to, it really had to be beyond the pale.

"So," Galen said, regarding Ellery over his desk, "there were detectives at your door at five o'clock in the morning. Jackson convinced them he hadn't moved—nor should he have moved, nor should he move for another week, although I know he will—and then patted them on the head and asked them to leave, giving you two more hours of uninterrupted shut-eye, and you are upset?"

Ellery made a frustrated noise. "Galen, what do we tell every client who walks through the door. Every. Damned. One."

"You shouldn't have fucked up, but now that you have, we're glad you're here?" Henry supplied, strolling through Galen's door without invitation.

"Ooh," Jade added, coming through right behind him and cutting in front of him so she could sit in the comfortable chair next to Ellery. "I'm going to put that on our letterhead! We should have business cards that say that. It's classy, doncha know."

Ellery snorted at their foolishness. "That's not what I was talking about. Galen, *you* know what I'm talking about, right?"

Galen was chuckling too, but he sobered and grew patient. "I do. You don't say jack to the police without your lawyers, even if the cop's name is Jack and he's your long-lost brother."

Ellery slow-blinked. "I don't really phrase it that way, but yes. And he just... I don't know—"

"Answered the door in his pajama bottoms and convinced two detectives and four flatfoots he was nowhere near a murder without even getting you out of bed." Galen rolled his eyes. "I understand. Your feelings are hurt because your boyfriend proved to you that he doesn't need you for your lawyering. Boo-hoo. I'm so sad for you. It must suck to have a man in your bed who loves you. I know I wake up every morning looking at my man and think, 'God, if only he loved me for my law degree.'"

Ellery managed to keep a straight face, but then Jade said, "My God, if only Mike was turned on by higher education, my life would be perfect," and he barely controlled himself.

Then Henry said, "Yeah, it's a good thing Lance is pretty or that cardiologist thing he's doing would be a real turnoff," and that was it. The four of them lapsed into a fit of the giggles that Ellery didn't even want to try to control.

Finally, they had the laughter out of their system, and Jade was the one who brought them to order. "As entertaining as this was, the fact is, Ellery was right—they sent those guys out to bother Jackson to keep them away from the crime scene. Now we know the DA did that for a reason. One option could be he didn't want anyone connected to us to see something there. Jackson and K-Ski are looking at crime-scene photos, and K-Ski is apparently calling up *his* contacts in the department, but Jackson asked us to have Crystal and AJ run financials and phone records. Which they did." She paused. "Crystal said Jackson made a very good impression on the police officers, given that she didn't have much time to warn him they were coming when she woke up this morning."

Ellery and Galen took a collective breath, because that "psychic accountant" thing was still a little rough on both of their practical psyches, but Jackson had shown Ellery the text that morning when he'd been retelling the incident.

"That's good to know," Ellery said dryly. "Does she have any ideas as to why they were sent to our door?"

"She did. She said it was to send you a message, and while I think you and Jackson are right about someone not wanting the good detectives to see anything, I think she's right about that too. What if Jackson *doesn't* have an alibi the next time something like this goes down. I mean, somebody could be offing guys right and left, and if they had a beef with Jackson, the cops could end up on his doorstep every time."

"But Jackson hadn't even *met* Charlie Boehner," Ellery protested. "What would his motive possibly be?"

Henry, who'd been slouching against the doorframe after Jade came in and made herself comfortable, moved to sit in the straight-backed chair to the side of Galen's desk.

"See, I've been thinking about that. That thing Jackson and I did Thursday night—that's going to have repercussions. Did you see the piece Arizona's contact did in the *Bee*, about the illegal relocation?"

Ellery shook his head, feeling off his game. "No. I'm sorry, I—"

"You were too busy tending to the crankiest patient in the world," Jade excused for him. "Which is too bad, because it got its own headline, and if you get the email newsfeed, that means it got its own email. It said, 'Reporter Investigates Forced Homeless Relocation; Finds Troubling Answers.' Would you like to know what those answers were?"

"Yeah," Ellery said, "considering Arizona promised to keep us—and Ezekiel—out of it."

"Well, first of all, she found out that California Department of Corrections buses had been used *five times* to bus people from Sacramento streets to Redding. The governor has sent a contingent of volunteers and social workers to Redding to investigate the camps and to try to get the people with connections in Sacramento back home. The reporter drove there and did interviews on Saturday—to a one, they reported being thrown on a bus and drugged. There were even witnesses who recalled police officers, and I quote, 'chasing some guys and shooting at them because they wouldn't do what the cops said.' Goslar and McMurphy were interviewed, and she got video of the two of them telling her to fuck off and to—and here's another quote—'talk to Charlie Boehner if you want to question our procedure.' So while she's dug up plenty to implicate Boehner and our four choirboys, she's also dug up a motive—but a thin one—for Jackson to have killed Boehner."

"But he didn't," Ellery said. "And we can prove it. So what are they going to try to pin on him next?"

There was a silence, which Henry broke with a wisecrack. "I don't know. Whatever crime they're gonna go out and commit next?"

Ellery and Jade gave a burst of laughter at that, but Galen sucked in his breath.

"No. No. That's not funny. Because that's *exactly* what sending those detectives is implying. It's saying that you and Jackson had better keep your noses clean of this investigation, or the next time somebody involved in this gets popped, they're going to come looking for you, and like you said, Ellery, the alibi might not be locked in. But it's also giving away his hand—the DA's, or whoever is pulling his strings—because it's saying that he's *planning something else*. So besides needing to keep you and Jackson well alibied, we're also in sort of a time crunch here, because Charlie Boehner might not be the only body to hit the floor."

"Alrighty then," Ellery said, putting this new angle together with what they had so far. "That means we *really* need to see what Charlie Boehner was involved in with Cartman. Also—show of hands. Who thinks Cartman is responsible for the forced homeless relocation to make himself look good for voters?"

Everybody in the room raised their hands.

"Okay, so we're on the same page. Now the question is, was Boehner aware his men were being asked to do something illegal, was he behind pulling those men for the job, or did Cartman do it behind his back? Because if he was working in league with Cartman and backed out, that's a good motive for Trey Cartman to murder him and then threaten me and Jackson. If Boehner wasn't in league with Cartman, that means someone else is involved, and things get muddy. So if we're looking through the financials and the phone numbers, we need to look for Cartman and Boehner, as well as Boehner with another number belonging to someone who's either dangerous or who has a lot of political clout. Does everyone follow me?"

"Yup." Jade held up two files that she'd walked in with. "Henry and I have phone numbers, you and Galen have financials. Do we want to work here or in the conference room?"

"Conference room," Ellery and Henry said in unison.

"Meet there in ten minutes," Jade said. "I'll go make sure we've got coffee, snacks, and highlighters. Are we good?"

They nodded, and Jade said, "Break!" before she and Henry filed out.

Ellery stood and stretched and looked at Galen. "You don't like the conference room?"

Galen smiled slightly. "I do," he said. "I'm always surprised to be asked. I don't know if I say this enough, but I do enjoy working here with you, Ellery. Thank you so much for making me love what I do again."

Ellery was going to answer, but then a ferocious yawn took over and he had to pause. "Thanks for being willing to work with us," he said when he was done. "It's not often you find someone who's willing to put his law degree to use for less money, longer hours, and no interest at all in politics."

He expected Galen to laugh, but instead, his colleague and friend looked at him soberly. "When John found me, I was living on the last of my settlement, and I spent my days trying hard to stretch out my supply of oxy so I didn't blow through it all in one go. I… I could have been homeless. If John had arrived a month or two later, I would have been. This case—it feels like amends from Narcotics Anonymous, but like I'm paying back the universe for sending me somebody who gave enough of a shit to get me out of that, to get me clean. Not many jobs give you a chance to redeem yourself or to pay back a karmic debt. You make sure this firm keeps doing that and I'll keep working here."

Ellery nodded. "It's why Jackson and Jade and I founded the place," he said. "It just seems like the deck is stacked against entirely the wrong people far too often."

"Indeed it does," Galen said, nodding. "I'll see you in five."

Ellery nodded and set off toward his own office for his notebook, files, and pens, and wondered at the complicated series of karmic weights and redemption pulleys that it took to keep the universe from falling into complete chaos. He'd gotten down the hall before he decided he could barely function as it was that morning. Perhaps he'd let Jackson figure it out for him.

Guys, Just Hanging Out

Sean Kryzynski seemed achingly young at twenty-eight, but maybe that was because, until he'd met Jackson and crushed on Ellery a little, he'd still believed in Santa Cop and the Easter Police. He'd only had a little time to be cynical and distrustful of his colleagues and his chosen profession, and sometimes his innocence showed.

"Jackson, I know it's frustrating, but just because your name came up in an investigation doesn't mean there's a conspiracy behind it."

Jackson pinched the bridge of his nose between his thumb and forefinger and prayed for Ellery's patience before speaking into the phone again. "Sean, they sent their best team on a wild-goose chase during an active crime-scene investigation. Andre *should* have been at the crime scene, but no, he was here, checking my video-game logs. Do you see the problem with that?"

He found hope in the beat of silence.

"Yes," Sean said, dismayed. "Yes, I do. Look, I'm going to call Christie and see what's doing." He ended the call without ceremony, and Jackson stood up tentatively and started clearing away the breakfast dishes. He'd wiped down all the counters and run the dishwasher—and given Lucifer and Billy Bob their morning helping of soft food—all while singing loudly to old Neil Young songs, when his earbud buzzed again.

"Jackson?" Sean sounded troubled… and urgent.

"Yeah?"

"Billy and I will be over in an hour with copies of the crime-scene photos and case files. Billy's getting them from Andre right now. He's putting his career on the line for this. There must be something really fucking hinky in there."

Jackson breathed out through his nose, a shiver of excitement coursing down his spine to celebrate the lucky guess. "I'm interested to see what it is." And then, because Ellery had been feeding him muddy "supplemented" coffee all weekend that he was starting to suspect was tea, he asked, "Hey, you guys wouldn't want to stop at a Starbucks and get me something ginormous, frozen, with sugar, would you?"

"Did Ellery say that you could?" Sean asked suspiciously.

"He didn't say I couldn't," Jackson hedged.

He heard Sean's careful breath, in and out. "Do you have cookies?" he asked quietly. "Because Billy keeps trying to make me healthy snacks with apple juice, and, you know, they keep me regular, but—"

Jackson turned carefully and checked the top shelf, then brought down an unopened box of fudge-covered Oreos. "I'll hook you up," he said with satisfaction.

"You're a good friend," Sean said in all sincerity. "We'll be there in an hour."

Word.

JACKSON GOT bored easily. By the time Sean and Billy, his totally hot live-in nurse/porn model, showed up at his door, he'd already found the purple-and-orange lights and synthetic pumpkin that Ellery had bought the year before, on Jackson's insistence, and decorated the alcove around the front door. He figured they had at least a week before trick-or-treating, so he ordered a shit-ton of other decorations, skeletons mostly: skeletons of dogs, skeletons of cats, skeletons of scorpions, rats, and possums. He figured that entryway was big enough that they could have an entire plastic skeleton zoo to welcome the bravest of the brave, and he added a set of faux-human bones that dropped down and screamed when someone tripped the sensor and then recoiled back up afterward, so they could hang it on the tree.

As soon as the payment went through, his phone rang again. This time it was Hurricane Joey, oh he of the nine-inch dick, a thing Jackson never called him to his face. However, given Joey's propensity for spreading chaos—and Joey's pride in his own endowment—Jackson never regretted calling him that behind his back either.

"So yeah, Jackson," Joey began, and Jackson sank into one of the straight-backed kitchen chairs that were easier on his stitches but tougher on his spine and sighed.

"What's up, Joey?"

"Well, yeah. About that car."

Jackson's breath froze in his chest. "The one I'm driving or the one you're supposed to be fixing?"

"Well, see, both. You know how we had to work on the CR-V because of the electrical system, right? Because it was haunted?"

"Yeah." This had been *after* Joey had done the bodywork and given the car back "good as new" when Jackson paid him cash.

"Yeah, well, I admit I haven't been hurrying much on that car because my sister's been driving it, see? It's better than her car—her car's this shitty Chrysler minivan, brown, you've seen it—"

"*I'm driving it*!" Henry had left the shitty brown minivan at Jackson's when he drove to the office with Galen that morning, because that lucky bastard had managed to figure out a way to live without a car of his own.

"Oh! Yeah. Sorry. I forgot—I was doing a lot of musical cars there, bro. I forgot which one you ended up with. But see? So she was driving around your CR-V to, uh, test drive it for a day before we gave it back to you, right?"

"Sure." Translation: My sister has been driving your CR-V around for the last three weeks while I shined light up your sphincter because it's a better car than the Town & Country and I love her more.

"So, uh, anyway, she was rear-ended. It's no big deal, but she called me up hysterical because she's in Arden Hills—you know, that swank country club place, right?—and the guy who hit her, he took one look at her, saw that she was brown, and told her to pay for the damage herself. And she's got his license plate, but she don't want to call the cops unless the car's hers, and the guy was an asshole and—"

Jackson took a deep breath and tried to sort out the conundrum. He got it. He did. The guy who hit her deserved to be hit with a lawsuit and a hit-and-run charge and a two-hundred-pound dead fish. "So what do you want me to do?" he asked.

There was a deafening silence on the other end of the line.

"Oh my God, seriously?"

"Sell your car to my sister for a dollar and postdate the receipt. I swear to God, Jackson, I'll fix that Town & Country until it gives up the ghost, and then I'll find you another car and fix it up sweet and fix that one for free too. Please? Jackson, my sister thinks I can do anything, but I can't go chasing down some white country-club asshole and tell him to pay insurance on a car that's not hers!"

At that moment there was a knock on the door, and Jackson stood stiffly to his feet. "Text me the address, Joey. I've got to go put on some fucking shoes."

He opened the door and ushered K-Ski in, saying, "Make yourself comfortable, Sean. You too, Billy. Turns out I've got to do a thing for a friend in Arden Hills. I'll be back in an hour."

Sean shoved a giant sugar-cookie Frappuccino into his hand, glowering, and Jackson let out a sigh. "Oh God. I'm such a bad person. I want this so bad."

Sean whispered, "Cookies, Jackson. You promised!"

"Top cupboard on the right, behind the rice flour," Jackson whispered back. "Can you reach that—"

"I'm right here," Billy interposed, and Jackson grimaced at him.

Sean Kryzynski was five eightish, young, blond, blue-eyed, and slender—pretty in an American-boy way. Billy was a few inches shorter with long, silky black hair, shoulders as wide as Jackson's refrigerator, and the smoldering dark-eyed beauty of a young Spanish don. Of all the kids Jackson had met who had roomed in the flophouse, Billy was the one who spoke the least and seemed to have the most painful secrets. He was also the most self-contained. Jackson had been frankly surprised when Billy volunteered for nursing duty, although he'd been less so when he realized that another one of his and Henry's rescues had been healing in the other half of Billy's room, and the guy he shared the room with was on twenty-four-seven nursing duty himself. Still, Billy needed a place to stay, Sean needed help doing everyday things until his punctured lung healed, and he thought they should get along fine.

He'd been unprepared for Billy's diligence and damned pit-bull-like determination to keep Sean Kryzynski healthy, or the baffled way Sean reacted to being managed by a surly porn model who seemed almost terrifyingly competent at his job.

The more Jackson had been around the two of them, seen their body language, the soft looks one would give the other when the other wasn't looking, the more he thought he may have set something in motion that had far-reaching consequences.

He was hoping that'd be for the best, actually. He sort of liked it when people found their others. It made him feel better, surer, even happier about having found his.

But he was also unsure of what to do about an upset Billy who didn't want Sean to eat sweets. He was pretty much on Sean's side for this one.

"Just to keep me company while I drink my coffee?" he said, giving what he hoped was a winning smile.

Billy regarded him with narrowed eyes. "That thing in your hand is an abomination, and I have the feeling your boyfriend would not approve."

Jackson turned his smile up a watt. "Well, Ellery doesn't have to know *all* the things I drink—one sugar cookie frap isn't going to kill me, right?"

Sean was suddenly glaring at him. "Don't you have a heart condition?"

"I'm allowed coffee!" Jackson protested. "Do you want to see my file? I just…." He groaned. "Wheatgrass, Sean. He's putting lawn clippings *in my coffee*."

"Yeah." He turned to Billy. "All things in moderation, right?"

Billy rolled his eyes. "Sure. How'd you know to drive to Arden Hills?"

"Well, *I* was going to drive there and let you guys chill here until I got back."

They glanced at each other. "But that would be sort of dumb," K-Ski said, giving a tight smile. "Because that's where our crime scene is, and I'm telling you, you're going to want to see for yourself."

Jackson's smile grew at the same time it relaxed. "*All* the cookies," he said, meaning it. "You get *all* the cookies."

Sean looked smugly at Billy, who rolled his eyes.

"Excuse me while I go put on some shoes," Jackson said, turning around toward the bedroom. It wasn't until he got there that he realized his dilemma: he'd only worn his battered oxfords on Friday. He'd been able to slide those on without bothering with the laces. The weekend had been slippers only—and sweats only, which was what he was wearing now.

Bending over to lace up his shoes made everything on his back cry out in sweet revenge.

"Fuck," he said, before he even thought of controlling his voice.

To his surprise, Billy barged in before Jackson could even think about anybody hearing.

"Sit down," he ordered gruffly, and Jackson opened his mouth to protest. Billy glared at him and gestured with his chin.

"Don't give me any shit. I get plenty from Sean, thank you. I blew out my back last year. The guys at the flophouse got really good at tying my shoes for me, so don't make it a thing. Sit down."

Bemused, Jackson sat on the chair by the bed since the bed buckled too much under his weight and compensating hurt.

With crisp movements, Billy slid a shoe on each foot and tied them before backing up and waiting patiently for Jackson to stand slowly in his own sweet time.

"Thank you," Jackson said uncomfortably.

Billy rolled his eyes. "You take care of us all the time," he said. "Cotton thinks you're an action hero."

"I got Cotton into that mess," Jackson reminded him, talking about another one of the flophouse boys who had recently been on his own adventure.

Billy snorted and was about to turn away when, to Jackson's surprise, he paused. "Why me?" he asked. "When you called and asked for a nurse to come help Sean. Why me?"

Jackson thought about it. "You're ready for a way out," he said after a moment, not sure how he'd sensed this. "You're still going to school to be an engineer, but you're…. God, you just seem so alone. Sean had a shitty breakup *while* he was in the hospital. I thought… I don't know. Two lonely guys might at least be friends."

Billy nodded. "Yeah," he said softly. "We could definitely be friends."

"More?" Jackson queried.

Billy swallowed. "I'm a whore, Jackson. How's he ever gonna trust me?"

"You're a human, and whoring's an honest business if an honest man is in it. Give him some credit, Billy. His world's getting bigger all the time."

"Yeah." The corner of his mouth lifted a little, like maybe he'd seen some hope. "Thanks. Maybe I needed to hear that now."

"You tied my shoes," Jackson said, because perhaps he'd forgotten. "Talking to you like a person is no big thing."

"For you, maybe," Billy said, and then took a step, only to catch his foot on Lucifer, who had chosen that moment to zip across the bedroom from under the bed to the closet, the better to hide from the people he didn't know.

Billy went sprawling on the carpeted floor, and Lucifer let out a yowl and disappeared into the closet.

And then, of all things, Billy Bob leapt from God knows where like an avenging angel to attempt to beat the shit out of Billy, the interloper who'd kicked his baby brother.

"Augh!" cried Billy.

"Billy?" called Sean.

"Werewolf fucking Jesus!" snapped Jackson, reaching carefully down to grab Billy Bob by the scruff of the neck. "He didn't do it on purpose, No-thumbs. Would you fucking leave him alone?"

He tucked the cat under his arm and tried to calm him down. "Look, you no-thumbs-having motherfucker, we do *not* jump on top of people in the house unless they *broke in* to get here!" He pulled heavily on Billy Bob's ruff, massaging his ears while he did so, feeling every muscle group in the cat's body relax.

"There," Jackson cooed as Sean helped Billy up and it looked like the world might not come to an end. "See? Not the devil. It was Lucifer's fault for tripping him, okay? Go make him feel better. Tell him you no-thumbs people need to avoid the feet, okay? No-thumbs-having motherfuckers got small feets. You don't understand about the big size twelves. He gots to learn."

And with that, Jackson took Billy Bob to Ellery's closet, wincing because it was open enough for the cats to get lots of fur on any low-hanging sets of slacks, and set Billy Bob down in the corner. Billy Bob found Lucifer—which was no easy feat, given he was just a set of green eyes and white teeth—and started licking his ear in solace, and Jackson figured that was about as calm as the sitch was getting. He closed the door enough to block out most of the light but still leave a gap so they'd be able to get out and turned toward where Sean was trying to patch another Billy's pride up.

"Oh Jesus, Jackson, did I kill your cat?" Billy asked unhappily. "I *like* cats. That's no good!"

"Naw," Jackson muttered, making sure the guy was unhurt. "And that cat's something special. He's the stompiest, loudest roommate I've ever had, and that includes Ellery. Vocal motherfucker. I'm surprised he hasn't tried to kill anyone sooner."

"Was that why you named him Lucifer?" Sean asked.

Jackson shook his head. "Oh no, that was after Ellery's mother. Speaking of which, we should go. Just mentioning her is like saying Beetlejuice three times. She's likely to pop up on our porch out of thin air. Hey, it's happened. I'm not shitting around here."

Sean and Billy gave him skeptical looks, but Jackson just gestured them toward the door, grabbing his denim jacket from its spot on his closet doorknob as he went, shaking it for the reassuring clink of his keys. Unlike his sport coat, the frayed garment washed just fine, and his wallet was in the pocket as well. A grab from the table for his phone and he was good to go.

When they got outside, Billy gestured to the Dodge Charger sitting next to the minivan, and Jackson groaned, thinking about getting in and out of the low-slung vehicle.

His two companions looked at him, and he gestured to the turd-brown minivan that he was about to go purchase for keeps.

"Uhm, it's comfy?" he suggested.

"Sure," Billy said, deadpan. "And when we're done with our errand, we can run snacks to your kid's soccer team."

"And there's bandages in the back!" Jackson added brightly. Without his prompting on the key fob, the lights started flashing and the side doors opened. "See? She's all excited about being taken for a spin."

He tossed the keys to Billy, who grimaced. "You know, I thought hanging with an action hero would make me cooler."

"Oh it does," Jackson retorted. "So much cooler. Icy cold. Now get in."

Jackson sent the address to Billy's phone, and he and Sean got in the back seat, where Jackson had room to look at the files while he trusted the driving to Billy.

"Okay," he said, settling carefully and drawing his seat belt closed. He was suddenly grateful for the room in the vehicle—he could stretch out his legs, and there was a cunning little pocket in the back of the passenger seat in front of him where he could stow files and organize. As far as mobile offices went, it beat the hell out of a motorcycle. "Let's see what we've got here."

He studied the photos for a moment and then read the report, frowning.

Then he studied the photos again.

"This… this isn't right," he murmured. "All Christie and de Souza told me was that there was unforced entry and he was shot in the chest. This…."

The photos showed Charlie Boehner splayed out on the ground, legs slightly apart and arms both bent at the elbows, hands near his shoulders, almost like somebody who'd been holding his hands up to show he had no weapon. But lots of people fell backward like that, and Jackson didn't think the rest of the evidence pointed to that being the case.

"That's a small wound in his shoulder for all that blood," he said.

"I agree," Sean replied. "I asked Christie about the slug, and he said forensics was looking for it as he and Leslie were being sent out to question you. When he left, they hadn't found it yet, and everything he heard from the lab since said it had gone through his shoulder, through three walls of the second-story apartment, and out over the street behind his apartment to spend itself in a nearby park, which is terrifying, by the way."

"Oh my God, yes," Jackson breathed. "And wait—second-story apartment?" He rifled through the pages in front of him. "Has Christie shown you any pictures of the exit wound?"

"Wait." Sean was texting madly as Jackson searched the file. "He's in with Toe-Tag right now."

Toby Tagliare worked in the forensic pathology department attached to Davis Med Center. Given the location of Arden Hills, Christie must have requested Tagliare personally, which made sense because he was one of the smartest death docs Jackson had ever met, and he was also a helluva nice guy. In Jackson's pre-Ellery days, going to Toe-Tag's house for dinner had been the high points of Jackson's year.

"Have him tell Toby hi for me," Jackson murmured. "What's the exit wound look like?"

Sean stared at his phone for a moment and then showed the picture to Jackson.

Jackson sucked in his breath. He knew that kind of exit wound; he had one of those himself. It was the kind that took all the king's horses and all the king's men to put back together again, except Charlie Boehner hadn't been shot on a city street in broad daylight. He'd been shot in a fairly nice second-story apartment.

"That wasn't a nine-millimeter," he said hoarsely. "That wasn't a Saturday night special."

Sean shook his head. "No, sir, it's not."

"That's a sniper shot," Jackson muttered. "Do we have any idea where the point of entry was?"

"Nope," Sean muttered grimly. "Why? Because Trey Cartman sent his two best detectives off to roust your scrawny ass at fuck-you a.m. That's why."

Jackson scrubbed at his face with his palm. "Okay. So we need to see that crime scene. How far away is my little errand from that apartment building?"

"About three blocks," Sean told him, looking at the address. "Let's do your little errand—what exactly *is* your little errand, by the way?"

Jackson grimaced. "Oh God. Seriously. You would not believe me if I fuckin' told you."

At that moment they were passing the corner of Fair Oaks and Walnut, and Jackson had Billy turn left. A few houses down on Walnut, parked in the driveway of a nice little house with rainbow banners on the front lawn and freshly painted windcatchers, was Jackson's CR-V.

"Wait," Sean muttered. "Isn't that your car—the one Ellery *just* bought you, because the Tank was totaled?"

Jackson let out a sigh. The Tank—a highly modified Infiniti QR-X—had been destroyed in their last little adventure. Sure, Ace and Sonny said they could fix it up, but it would take a while, and Jackson and Ellery told them not to make it a priority. They had a living to make. Although he didn't miss the thing's noise or its gas consumption, he was fully aware that he and Ellery might not have survived that car crash if they'd been in anything else. Ellery had bought Jackson a new vehicle—the CR-V in front of them—on what was probably the last of the insurance company's sufferance.

When the CR-V had been damaged—*through no fault of Jackson's at all*—Jackson had turned in desperation to Joey, who ran a housecleaning business and fixed cars on the side.

And that led him to the thing he was about to do, which he hated himself for.

He looked at the rear end of the CR-V and saw that all of Joey's admittedly decent body work had been squashed into powder once again, much of that powder littering the driveway in a patter of red, yellow, and clear glass.

He let out a sigh. Yeah. Nobody was going to get *anything* from the insurance company if Jackson didn't go in there and bend a rule or two.

"I'll be right back," he said, reaching for the handle of the sliding door on the side of the minivan.

"Mm, no," Sean said, lips quirking up. "I think I'll come with you."

"I'm not staying behind," Billy said, parking in front of the house. "I'm super curious."

"You guys...." But before Jackson could finish his whine, Jennifer the minivan opened both side doors and died.

Jackson grunted and patted the back of the passenger seat. "You sure you want to ride with us, sweetie?" he asked. "I'm, uhm, sort of rough on vehicles. It's, you know, almost a curse."

The glove compartment popped open, and Jackson took the hint.

"Uhm, Billy, if you could grab the pink slip there? I, uh, gotta go trade cars." With that he let himself painfully out of the back of the car, and Sean did the same from the other side, using Billy's hand to steady himself. As soon as they'd both cleared the vehicle, the doors slid shut and the lights flashed, for no reason whatsoever.

"Oh Jesus," Sean muttered. "Jackson, are you sure about this?"

"One hundred percent!" Jackson said cheerily, making sure his voice carried to the car. As they neared the house on the walkway, he lowered his voice. "You gotta say nice shit about the car. Jennifer has KO'd suspects, and whenever Henry's shitty about her, she slams his hand in her doors. I'm talking full bodily harm here—you guys understand?"

To his relief, they both nodded like they believed him, and then they made the sign of the cross, which made him realize that both the cop and the porn star had started out as good little Catholic boys, which made him laugh.

He pulled himself together enough to ring the doorbell and was surprised at how happy he was to see Joey's sister, Sandra Kingston, on the other side of the door.

"Jackson!" she said, smiling painfully. "Oh, honey, I'd hug you, but...." She pointed to her neck, which had a classic seat belt bruise across the clavicle, emerging in purple. She also had a bruise on her head. "God, it's been the shittiest day."

"Yeah, aren't you supposed to be in school?" he asked. Sandra's position teaching at a local high school was a source of family pride.

"It was an in-service day," she said unhappily, letting them in to a sweetly decorated little suburban ranch-style.

The living room featured a cluttered children's corner, where baby toys and toddler toys all fought a war against containment, and an art table where a barely school-aged child had left a masterpiece of blue-and-red blobs to dry. In deference to the coming holiday, paper cutouts of cartoon monsters were taped around the walls in the living room and the kitchen, and a centerpiece in the kitchen was a playful plastic skull filled with wrapped chocolates.

"Scotty had just gotten the kids off to day care and school because I didn't have to leave until later," Sandra explained, "and I was getting ready to back out of the driveway. I swear to you, Jackson, I hadn't passed the sidewalk when—*bam!*—that fucker took out the right rear quarter panel. He was up on the sidewalk! He left tire tracks in the lawn! I got out of the car and—well, I was pissed. I was like, 'The fuck you doin', *puto!*' Which if you ever talk to my students, I will deny saying to my grave. Anyway, he took one look at me...." She shook her head. "I watched his eyes go up and down, and he sort of raised his upper lip and said, 'Good luck proving it.' And then he got in his black fucking dented Mercedes and drove away."

Jackson frowned. God, that was ballsy. "Did you get a license plate?"

She gave a fierce smile. Sandra was a pretty woman with an oval face and Joey's curly black hair, but unlike Joey, she had the sense God gave a mountain goat. Still, they adored each other, and while Joey had never been more than a fling for Jackson, the two of them had been good friends for nearly ten years.

"Oh I did. Wasn't too hard, either. One of those fancy license plates. I don't understand what it means, but I got it!"

She held out a kitchen notepad with block letters written on it. *D8 WA DA.*

Jackson raised his eyebrows. "Oh wow." The guy couldn't be that brazen, could he? "Okay, so Sandra? I'm not going to sell you the car right now—I'm going to write a note that says you're my permittee. Then I'm going to give you Ellery's insurance company, in case your insurance company needs it, and you're going to call them and see what you can do to not have this end up on Ellery's deductible."

She nodded like people asked her to deal with bureaucracy all the time. Well, schoolteacher. Maybe they did.

"So after you get the insurance worked out, I'll come back and we can swap pink slips. I've got no problem trading cars with you, but as soon as we do, everybody's insurance goes bye-bye, and you'll have to pay full price to get the rear end fixed. Can we do that?"

She nodded. "God yes. Bless you, Jackson. I'm so sorry about the dent. My kids *really* love this car. The Town & Country...." She leaned forward like she was going to tell a secret. "They seem to think it's haunted."

"Go figure," Jackson said with a straight face. "I have no idea where they get that." He gestured with his chin. "Get me some paper and a pen, and then I'm gonna make a call to Ellery. I, uh, think we can get a line on your scumbag."

She served them all snacks first. Billy's face as he was torn between accepting or rejecting hospitality—particularly Mexican hospitality, complete with horchata and pan dulce, which she claimed to have been practice batches before Halloween—was almost comic. He'd obviously been raised to respect *mamis* of all ages, but he had that fierce dietary regimen, and oh, the delicious decadence! Jackson and Sean dug in with no compunction whatsoever, and after a tortured glower, Billy took a few tentative bites. Watching him melt—both with the sweetness of the pastry and, Jackson suspected, Sandra's sweetness as a mami—was a thing of beauty.

Jackson ate a couple of bites, washing them down with horchata, and then excused himself, wishing he could be there for the whole meal.

"You'll come back and finish this," Sandra said. "You're still scrawny, Jackson, and Joey was totally freaked out when you had your heart attack. Snacks will do you good, and so will something without caffeine!"

"Your brother's a rat," Jackson replied mildly. "I adore him, but he's a rat, and we both know it."

She shrugged. "What's to do?" she asked. "But that doesn't mean you don't need to eat."

Jackson wrinkled his nose at her, a trick from his single days. "Business first, darlin'. I think I can get your car repaired."

"That's very sweet," she said. "But if you can't, you know, Joey can do it for free."

Jackson's eyes narrowed. "I have no answer to that. I'll be outside."

His back hurt, and he hadn't realized until he'd been eating that he was overdue for his pain pill and his antibiotics. He thought he had some ibuprofen in the glove compartment, but he didn't want to alert Sean and Billy because, God, was he tired of people worrying about him.

And also... he wanted to scope out the area.

Three blocks away, Billy had said, and the blocks were small, residential places. He could probably see three blocks away while sitting in the passenger's seat when he was on the phone to Ellery.

He rifled through the glove compartment first and found the secondary stash of ibuprofen, thanking Jennifer for holding it for him, because he was that superstitious. Then he called Ellery.

Connections Made and Missed

"HEYA," ELLERY said, picking up on the first ring. He had a client interview in ten minutes and had spent the past hour searching through Trey Cartman and Charlie Boehner's phone records, trying to find a connection between the two. Contrary to what the TV shows made it look like, it wasn't easy, even for someone used to scanning information quickly, and Ellery always ended up printing out the records, using highlighters, and then looking up the similar numbers. As much as he wanted to be done with this task two hours ago, he was grateful Jackson had pulled him away.

"Hey, how's it going?"

"Client interview in ten. You did the dossier last week. Don't worry, I'm prepared." Jackson had lectured Ellery frequently about letting Jackson do the background work on the clients before the interview. The one time—one—that they'd walked into a situation blind, they'd encountered one of the average, everyday monsters who frequently made the evening news. He'd been angry because his girlfriend's infant daughter had overdosed on the drugs he'd kept in the house, and had wanted Ellery to get him off on all charges, including beating his girlfriend into the hospital as she'd grieved the loss of her baby.

Jackson's nightmares had gotten worse for a week after that, and Ellery had sworn that never again would they walk blindly into a situation like that.

"Glad to hear it," Jackson said, and while Ellery could hear the smile in his voice, he could also hear some thoughtfulness too.

"What's up?" He leaned back in his chair and closed his eyes, relaxing them from the strain of scanning all those numbers.

"So I got a call from Joey's sister's house. Seems some dirtbag hit her car this morning, and she was hoping for our help. She was in the car, getting ready to back out, when the guy went up on the sidewalk and bounced off her rear quarter panel. She left the car where it was hit. Ellery, this guy wasn't even close to the road. Now here's the thing. The guy gets out of the car, looks her over, sees the little Mexican soccer mom, and says, 'You'll never get me to pay that,' and then takes off. Problem is, she got his license plate number, and I need AJ and Crystal to run it, so let me give that to you before I keep going."

Ellery's eyes flew open. "Wait. Wait. You're *at* Joey's sister's house? What happened to Sean and Billy coming by and 'guys hanging out'?"

"They're here with me. Seems Sandra's house is only about three blocks from Charlie Boehner's apartment building, if you can believe that bullshit."

Ellery took a very careful breath. "What a coincidence," he said hoarsely.

"Yeah, I don't believe in coincidences like those. Not when the car that hit hers is a black Mercedes with the license plate D8 space WA space DA."

Ellery had begun writing the letters down as soon as Jackson started speaking, but he didn't need to finish.

"Jackson, that's Trey Cartman's Mercedes. You don't even need to run those plates. I've seen that car."

"Mm-hmm."

"You don't sound surprised." Ellery was. Ellery's blood was thundering in his ears from shock.

"I'm not. Now I don't think Cartman did it—because that would be much too easy—and also because Sandra was pulling out around eight thirty in the morning, and Cartman would have no reason to be here at eight thirty if he blew Charlie Boehner away in the sweaty balls of the a.m."

"But still," Ellery pondered. "We could check the car's location out if we can have him brought in."

"I'll have the cops collect him," Jackson said. "And quickly. It's ten a.m., and I doubt he's had time to get his car fixed. You do the legal voodoo that you do, and I'll call some cop friends who would probably love to be the ones picking him up."

"Fair," Ellery said, writing everything down on his legal pad so he could remember what to tell Galen and Henry. "Anything else?"

"Yeah. They made it sound like Boehner was shot dead in his living room by somebody who walked in the front door. Even Christie and de Souza thought so. But we got a good look at the crime-scene photos, and Sean got a pic from the autopsy, and that's not what happened at all."

Oh Lord. "Tell me."

"A goddamned sniper, Ellery. The entry point was through the top of a window in a second-story apartment, aimed down. His front looked like he got hit with a nine-millimeter, but his back looked like a grenade went off in there. It was a sniper. We need to look at our players—everyone, including Brentwood, although I know you're developing a soft spot for the guy—and figure out who's got training, military or otherwise, in long-distance target shooting. Sean, Billy, and I are going to scope out the buildings around Boehner's apartment to try to figure out where the shot come from, and then maybe we can take a look at the primary shooting site. Yeah, I know every yahoo who plays a game thinks they're a sharpshooter, but it is, in fact, a *very specific* skill. Someone who hunts might be able to do it, if they've practiced enough, and it will be a lot easier to narrow it down once we get a line on the ammunition, but this is going to help us pinpoint our bad guy by quite a lot."

Ellery nodded, making a list of things to have Crystal run. "It will. And thank God, because I was going to go blind tracking down phone records without something specific to go on."

At that moment there was a soft knock on his door, and Jade stuck her head in. "Your ten fifteen?" she asked.

He held up one finger and then gestured her into the room.

"Jackson, I'm going to hand Jade my cell so you can tell her what you just told me and I can talk to this client. But in the meantime, I want you to stay put, okay? Only go—"

"Sean and Billy with me the whole time. Backup, Counselor. I haz it."

Ellery gave a tight smile. "I'm sending Henry out to you," he said. "I want you to have more of it."

Jackson grunted. "Doesn't Henry have something better to do today?"

"Yeah. Keep you safe," he said. "Here's Jade. Love you."

"Love you back."

And then Ellery had to go.

HIS TEN fifteen was heartbreaking—a nineteen-year-old picked up for a handful of party drugs and charged with possession with intent to sell. It was the kid's third nonviolent criminal offense, and even a guilty plea would get him sent away for twenty-five to life. Ellery was going to have to tap-dance quickly—and maybe even take the kid to trial—in order to get a sentence that would fit the crime, but that wasn't what his mind was on after the appointment.

"Did you send Henry?" he asked Jade, and she nodded while handing him a sheaf of papers with phone numbers highlighted on them.

"But Galen is co-opting AJ for some surveillance he's desperate to have done. I okayed that, and he's grateful for the hours."

AJ was a sweet kid, back in college now, who had almost died the year before, caught in the Dirty/Pretty Killer's web. Jackson had befriended him, helped him get clean, and then had given him a job in Ellery's fledgling law firm. He was smart, resourceful, and as good at computers as Jackson's other friend Crystal. Since Crystal was in recovery as well, she and AJ had formed an almost instant bond and were even rooming together, last Ellery had heard. Crystal worked for Jackson and Ellery's old firm, and although she wanted to join Cramer and Henderson as soon as they could afford her, her present situation gave her information they might not ordinarily have access to.

She was also—Ellery could admit it now—psychic as hell.

Ellery wasn't sure if Crystal's warning to Jackson had been funneled to her through Pfeist, Langdon, Harrelson and Cooper, or if she'd had some sort of vision or something, but Ellery knew Crystal would use both data and anything else at her disposal to keep Jackson safe.

He was fine with that. And he was fine with not leaving Galen in the lurch.

But he was... uneasy with Jackson, Sean, and Henry out in the world together. Sean had been a steadying influence when he'd worn a badge, but he was a civilian now, and Ellery had cause to know that the once rule-toeing, box-loving young officer he'd met over a year ago had done some very out-of-the-box things since he'd been released from the hospital.

"Jade?" he said thoughtfully. "Do I have any other meetings today?"

"Three," she said promptly. "Eleven thirty and one. I figured we'd do lunch around two, and then you could leave after your three o'clock." It was early—usually he'd be working at the office for another three or four hours to put his notes in order, make phone calls, and begin the preliminary work on the cases he'd accepted that day. Most of the time, Jackson would be done when he was, but he wasn't sure if that was by design or causality. It could be that Jackson just stopped working when Ellery was ready to go home, or it could be that if the caseload was high, they both worked late, and if it was light, they could cut out early. Ellery had simply been grateful for the company—he'd never asked.

He only knew Jackson was damned good at his job so that Ellery could be good at his.

Which was why he'd sent Henry off to supervise Jackson and his new playmates. Jackson *was* a good investigator, and he was damned smart and damned intuitive, and once he started putting puzzle pieces together, it was hard to keep up with him, although trouble always tried.

Would it try today?

"Ellery!" Jade actually snapped her fingers in front of his face. "Ellery, where did you go?"

"Jade, they're on to something," he said, hating that it was driving him crazy.

"I know it," she replied. "I can't argue with you. But we've got a job to do, and we can't help them research if we're driving all over the damned city. We do our part, they'll do theirs. Now you've got ten minutes before your eleven o'clock. I'm going to get your coffee, you're going to take notes on your last case, and we're going to trust our boys to call us if they need us, okay?"

Jade's brows were lowered, and her chin was thrust out, and all in all, she meant business. Ellery nodded and looked around his office to clear his head. He'd done the place in shades of blue, green, and teal, including an abstract mural wall opposite his desk that held his degrees as well as Jackson's credentials. Jade's also.

But mostly it showcased that complicated storm of color, which also featured notes of an earthy brown that helped to center him when he was having trouble concentrating. His desk was situated with the back to the wall facing the street, which meant clients could get a glimpse of the shade tree that graced that corner of the building. Leafy in the summer, it kept the room cool, and it gave people something to look at when things were particularly hard in their lives. Ellery's window to his left showed the same tree, as well as the rooftops of the nearby buildings, also partially obscured by naked tree limbs as October neared an end.

Still, something about the overcast sky on the horizon gave him the hope he craved, and he took a deep breath and followed Jade's orders.

"Five more minutes," he told her, and she nodded.

"Good boy."

He finished taking notes on the last client and tried to keep his eyes from straying to his cell phone. Something was brewing. He knew it in his gut.

HENRY CAUGHT up with them in Galen's luxury sedan as they were about to pull away from Sandra Kingston's house.

When Jackson told Sandra he was a friend of Joey's too, she greeted him warmly, gave him a napkin full of pan dulce, and begged him to be safe.

And then she asked them all politely to leave so she could call up the insurance company and play two truths and a lie.

"Okay," Sean said as they all lingered by the cars for a moment. "What are we up to?"

Jackson nodded grimly at him. "You and Billy are going to take Jennifer to the actual crime scene. We'll follow you and scope out the outside while you're talking to the cops on the inside. If you can get me a trajectory for the bullet, Henry and I can try to track it down. If Christie calls you with a type, let us know. Henry, you know your sniper rounds?"

"Mostly a .308. That's a quick and dirty little bullet. Good range, good accuracy, and a hollow point will make a gooey mess on the way out."

Jackson grunted. "Tell me about it. We need to take a look at the crime scene and the slug and figure out where the shooter was stationed. The cops are looking at this like a basic murder, but this was a long-range hit, and that takes a specialized skill."

"Tell me about it," Henry retorted, and Jackson frowned, thinking about a question he'd never asked.

"What were you rated in the military?"

"Expert," Henry grunted. "It was my least favorite skill, so I mostly took the shiny medal and the promotion and did anything but apply to sniper training."

Jackson felt a tug of affection for his friend. "Yeah, if I'm gonna kill someone, I'd rather it be personal." And it had been. Every time.

"Right?" Henry nodded soberly. "But I can tell you where to look and what to look for. It'll be fun. Like a scavenger hunt!"

"Did you hear that, everyone?" Jackson asked. "We're going on a scavenger hunt. Let's go find us some bad guys!"

THE APARTMENT complex Jackson and Henry followed the brown minivan to was gated, with golden stucco buildings, rounded archways, and a pool and clubhouse in the middle. The suburb itself was old money, much like Ellery's suburb. The houses were fifty, sixty years old, with big yards and gorgeous customized landscaping. Many of them had their own pools in the back.

Property values here were decent, Jackson knew, and an apartment complex needed to be well kept and tasteful. This wasn't a crappy cop-flop, and Jackson wondered how much the rent here was in relation to Boehner's salary. It wasn't a house on the hill, but with Sacramento rents, it didn't have to be.

But that wasn't even the most important consideration. As Jackson and Henry circled the parking lot, the true problem of the location hit them both at the same time.

"Shit," Jackson muttered.

"Oh, this is bad."

They were surrounded by one- and two-story buildings. Depending on the angle of entry—and Sean could not get there quickly enough with the pictures—there was very little way for someone to get a sharpshooting round through the front-room window of an apartment in the complex without standing directly on somebody's house.

The closest building that would work trajectory-wise was almost half a mile away—an empty medical office that stood four stories and could have provided the height needed to make such a shot possible.

Henry blew out a breath. "That's impressive," he murmured. "Providing that's where the shot was from. Because the bullet would have needed to be a small-caliber sniper round if it wasn't going to just pulverize a human, and small-caliber rounds aren't always as accurate from a distance. Too much can affect their course. Did you say it hit center mass?"

Jackson shook his head, remembering the photo. "Shoulder. He bled out very quickly."

"Okay. So not expert. Good, but if you're trained, you avoid arms and shoulders. Center mass is a sure kill, and of course the head shot's golden."

Jackson suppressed a shudder. "Of course."

Henry shrugged. "Killing's an art, like anything else. I was never Picasso."

"You know, I'm sort of glad you're on my side."

Henry grinned. "Me too. Lucky, right? So what do we do?"

"Okay, let's check out the medical building and poke around. If our killer got up there, we can too. Sean and Billy should have information to us at any time, and I need to see if Fetzer and Hardison got that warrant. Let me do phone and people, and then we can do B and E."

"Sure, boss. I'm pretty sure the B and E is more to my liking than the P and P. I'm just saying."

"I'm not arguing," Jackson returned mildly. "But you gotta do a little of both in this business. You could still go to law school, you know. Galen would spring."

Henry snorted—really snorted. While Jackson was looking up Fetzer's number on his phone, Henry was digging tissues out of the console to clean up the resulting mess, and Jackson figured Henry Worrall, Esquire, was a thing that was not destined to ever be in this world.

At that moment his phone connected, and Adele Fetzer did not disappoint him.

"Fetzer. What do you want, Jackson? It's not mine and Jimmy's fault you were rousted this morning, by the way."

"I know it."

"That was all Cartman. Would you like to hear all the ways he's fucking up Charlie Boehner's investigation, by the way? 'Cause I'll be a rat to take that guy down. I spend volunteer hours with the homeless population, and that fucker's shipping my friends off to Redding in the winter? I've got a cousin owns a deep freezer. I say we dunk the guy in the river and throw him in there until his weenie comes off. You want in?"

"I'd rather just arrest him. You want some of that?"

She caught her breath. "Oh, you sweet, sweet summer child. You know that's for people who make more money than I do, don't you?"

Jackson chuckled, low and dirty. "What if I told you that a woman who lives about three blocks from Charlie Boehner got rear-ended *in her driveway* by a black Mercedes this morning. She's calling her insurance agent right now with the license plate. Would you like to know who that car belongs to?"

She made a long, drawn-out sound. "How about you tell me the license plate and let me look that up myself."

Jackson did, enjoying her snort of derision *very* much.

"And this woman is filing with her insurance company?"

"As we speak."

"Hit-and-run," she said with satisfaction. "Can I have her number? I'm going to make filing that police report she needs *really* easy."

Jackson rattled it off—with Sandra's approval, of course—and Adele said, "Wow, I didn't get you a damned thing. Is there anything I can do for you?"

And Jackson took a chance. "Adele, what have you heard about Boehner's murder?"

"Unforced entry, handgun to the chest. They're looking at fingerprint evidence, from what I understand."

"What if I told you K-Ski, Christie, and de Souza are looking for a sniper's entry point?"

"I'm saying that's not common information," she replied promptly. "What do you suspect?"

"I don't know, Adele. We're going to run background on everybody involved in the Ezekiel Halliday case—"

"Why would you do that?"

"Because Cartman had me rousted at fuck-you in the morning! What do you think that was? Just a chance to say hi?"

"A warning," she murmured. "A chance to get Christie and de Souza away from the crime scene. A twofer."

"Yup. And the only thing I've done lately that would get Cartman to stroke his meat on my irritation would be...."

"Getting sliced and diced by Boehner's lapdog," she said softly. "I'm starting to see how this might pull together for you. So Cartman's at the crime scene, he sees something that scares him, orders Christie and de Souza out of there so they *don't* see it, and is so freaked out he bounces off your friend's vehicle on his way back to work. And *we* have an excuse to call him in."

"Yup," Jackson said. "On a hit-and-run. You don't even have to tell your shit-for-brains lieu that's what you're doing." His assessment of Lieutenant Chambers had been "green and clueless" over the summer; he hadn't seen anything since to change his mind.

"Oh, *this* is how I wanted to retire, Rivers. You do bring me and Jimmy the prettiest messes."

Jackson grinned. "You're welcome. I ruined a suit in court the other day. I wouldn't mind a new shirt for Christmas."

Her laugh came from a lot of hard years on the streets as a woman of color working a white man's job, and it was, surprisingly, not bitter in the least.

"I'll make it bright Noel green," she promised. "I'll even let Jimmy check out the tie."

"I look forward to it. But will you let me look in on the interview? That's what would really turn my key."

"I'll call you when we hit the interview room. Let's hope he's too much of a bastard to lawyer up."

Oh, wouldn't that be sweet. "I'm getting all swoony just thinking about it. Go get 'em, Fetzer. Give my regards to Jimmy!"

"Oh, I will."

"So," Henry said as Jackson hung up, "do we go to the station and see if we can get in on the other side of the mirror? 'Cause I'm not gonna deny, I'm pretty excited about that."

Jackson's mouth twisted. "You and me both, brother. Even if all he gets is a traffic ticket. But before we do that, I want to know what scared him so bad. Let's find us the bad guy. Once we know his nightmare, we can give him a way to wake up."

Henry nodded and pulled up to a parking place on the cracked pavement right in front of a side entrance alcove to the building itself. Jackson couldn't have chosen a better spot. They both had lockpicks on them, and getting into the building shouldn't prove that difficult— it was old, obviously empty, and probably slated for demolition soon. Much of this area, nice to begin with, had been remodeled. Fair Oaks past Manzanita had experienced new life in the past three years: new restaurants, new businesses. This small medical center had probably once been an offshoot of one of the prosperous HMOs in the area, but new buildings had opened up for almost all of them, and now it was obsolete and out of place.

And easily the tallest building for a mile in any direction.

As they got out and headed toward the side door, Jackson's phone buzzed. He answered it and gestured impatiently for Henry to get on with the lockpicking.

"Me?" Henry gestured, looking pleased.

Jackson nodded, keeping his expression mild. He hadn't realized it would be a big deal. The truth was his back was on fire, and the idea of bending down right now to pick the damned lock made him a little bit queasy.

So he let Henry get to it and took Sean Kryzynski's call. "What you got for us?"

"Christie was here. Swears to God nobody saw the small hole right at the top of the window until I pointed it out to him. But then, as you know, he's been distracted, and not just by pursuing you. Cartman has had him and de Souza running around town trying to prove it's you or Ellery. Did you know they had to look through traffic-light footage around your house for an hour?"

"Oh for fuck's sake," Jackson muttered.

"Don't worry, they put an FNG on it while they snuck away to see what was left of the crime scene."

Jackson had to grin—Fucking New Guy had always been one of his favorite acronyms. "Okay, so are you there?"

"Yeah. Why?"

"Can you or Billy or Christie or whoever get up on a ladder and sight through the bullet hole at the right angle? I need to know what you see."

"Ugh. Yeah. Give us a few minutes. We'll call you back."

"Deal."

At that moment Henry gave an exultant, "Yes!" and stood up straight to pump his fist before turning the lever handle and letting them in.

"Good job, padawan," Jackson praised. "Now, did you bring a flashlight?"

"Yes, sensei," Henry said, reaching into his cargo shorts and pulling out a smallish but powerful Maglight. He proceeded to hold the thing up to his shoulder and shine it in either direction until they both saw the door marked Stairs.

"Sadly, the elevators were out of service," Henry narrated, and Jackson let out a pained gasp as they both headed in that direction. The door to the stairwell, which would have been locked during regular hours, was open now, the doorknob drilled out and removed. Jackson tapped Henry on the shoulder and had him shine the light on the ground, and they both let out a low whistle.

"That look like metal shavings to you?" Jackson asked.

"Yes, boss, it does," Henry agreed. "And fresh ones—all bright and shiny."

"Someone got here before us and bored out the door. What do you want to bet the door to the roof will be in the same shape?"

Henry chuffed. "No bet. It's like you can see the future."

Of course Jackson didn't count on trudging up four flights of stairs in order to see that future, and he was irritated to find himself sweating and breathless, his hands shaking on the stair rail as he pretended his back was just fine and everything was okay.

Henry went through the door first, and Jackson followed at a much more sedate pace, stepping over the predicted pile of shavings as he did so. He let Henry do the perimeter of the roof first, while he went directly to the northwest corner, which was the part of the building he was pretty sure faced Charlie Boehner's apartment complex.

He was standing next to the guard wall, wishing he had a sniper's scope or even an ordinary gun sight, when Henry finished his round and came to stand near his shoulder.

"Jackson? How you doin'?"

"Great," Jackson lied, still laboring to get his breathing under control.

"Really? Are you really doing great?"

Jackson became aware that Henry was eyeballing the back of his hooded sweatshirt and suppressed a groan.

"I'm bleeding through the fucking sweatshirt, aren't I."

"Yeah. Man, you could have just let me come up to the top of the building. You're so dumb, you're lucky your cat doesn't sleep on your face and end it all."

"He doesn't have any opposable thumbs. I'm sure if he could open his own bag of kibble, he'd think about it." It was a crisp day, and Jackson had soaked his sweatshirt with sweat—and apparently, with blood. Fabulous. It was even one of the newer ones Ellery had bought for him. He shuddered and very carefully didn't say anything about how badly he wanted to teleport down the stairs he'd just managed to haul his way up.

"Okay, sensei," Henry said on a sigh. "So we're up here, you've proved you're perfectly fine, now what are we looking for?"

"You tell me," Jackson said. "Boehner's apartment is about six hundred meters that way." He waved his hand in the direction they'd come from. "K-Ski is getting us some trajectory measurements. Where would an optimum place to shoot from be?"

Henry grunted. "About where we're standing."

Jackson took a few steps toward the cinder-block "wall" that traveled the perimeter of the building. "Burton told me once that a sniper's long-range rifle often has to be secured to a stable base—I don't see any marks like that here. What else could he have used?" He poked around on the gray cinder block, looking for tool marks that would show the rifle'd been anchored to the wall.

"Wait," Henry said, kneeling on the ground. "Not the wall. Look here."

Jackson backed up a foot and found the idea of getting to his knees and then back up again was just not working for him.

"Can you tell me?" he hedged, and Henry gave him a patient look.

"I'm taking pictures now," he said. "You can see the tripod markings. Whoever it was knew enough about ballistics to pick up his shell casings—"

"One," Jackson said. "One shell. Went through the edge of the window, through Boehner, through the far wall of the apartment, across the street, and into the park."

Henry let out a low whistle. "Okay. This is just a guess, mind you, but deer shot and elk shot are designed *not* to do that. You want a game animal to go down hard and fast and die as soon as possible. That doesn't work with shot that passes through their bodies. It needs to do bigger damage. Humans are a lot more fragile, but often there's technology or buildings in the way. Military ammo is often designed to go *through* things—walls, Humvees, body armor. So whoever we're looking for, I'd put money down on the bullet being military grade, and often but not always—you know this because there's always nutballs out there who want to burn the world—this means military trained."

Jackson nodded. "Jade's having Crystal and AJ look up our players: Brentwood, Cartman, the four choirboys from the trial. I don't think it's Cartman. He would have had no reason to be driving away so quickly at the time he nailed Sandra's car if he'd been the one to actually put Boehner in the ground. But I *do* think he knows *why* Boehner was killed, and that's important too."

"Okay," Henry said after getting some pictures with his camera. Per Jackson's training, he held up a small ruler to measure the width of the tool marks left from the tripod. "I'm going to forward these to Burton. He might recognize them and—"

Jackson's pocket buzzed. "And it's K-Ski." He pulled out his phone and answered the call. "What do we have?"

"Well, for starters, I can see you assholes on top of the old medical building using Christie's scope through the bullet hole. He carries it around so he's fun at parties, I guess."

"It's why we invite him," Jackson responded. "Do you have a—"

At that moment, Henry stood up, and a small red dot appeared immediately on his chest.

"Bwah!" Henry squawked as Jackson said, "Laser pointer? And yes, you do."

"Sorry, Henry!" Sean said over Jackson's phone. "It's just the laser sight—no gun attached. We wouldn't do that to you!"

"Glad to hear it," Henry said sourly. "Excuse me, I need to go piss."

Jackson wrinkled his nose at him. "You're made of stern stuff, padawan. I'll never wear these shorts again."

Henry rolled his eyes. "You're just saying that so I'll keep working for peanuts."

Jackson laughed and then spoke into the phone. "Okay, now that we've established where the shot came from, we need Christie to get hold of traffic cams in the area. You have a three-hour window, but I've driven around here in the fuck-you a.m.'s, and it's practically deserted. It shouldn't be too hard to find a guy in a vehicle that makes a half-hour stop to do some B and E so he can kill a guy."

"Christie and de Souza are going to do some interviews near you and see if they can't narrow down the time frame a little," Sean added. "So far they haven't been able to get any response to 'Did you hear a shot fired?' But if the building's nearly a half mile away, they wouldn't, would they? So they're going to requisition traffic cams and do some interviews, and what are we going to do?"

Henry took the phone from Jackson before he could object. "Well, *we're* running by the house so Jackson can take some pain meds and I can rebandage his back—"

"Goddammit!" Sean sounded legitimately pissed. "Our entire job was to keep you from overdoing it!" He dragged in a labored breath, and then Billy spoke on the phone.

"We'll meet you at the house," he said grimly. "Because you're both done. That's it. I'm calling a halt."

"K-Ski should go home," Jackson conceded, but Henry still had the phone, and he turned his back.

"Billy, we'll meet you at Jackson's place. If you love me, if I've done anything for you at all in the last few months, you'll stop for food. I'm in the mood for Thai or Chinese, but I'll leave it up to you."

"I can do that," Billy agreed, and Jackson was reminded that Henry had roomed at the flophouse for his first few months in Sacramento, and Billy was one of the kids who looked up to him the most.

"Excellent. Now remember, no matter what we do, we absolutely, positively can't let them overdo it."

"Roger that. See you there."

Then Billy hit End Call and Jackson was left sputtering.

"Dammit, Junior, I just need a rest. Like you said, pain meds, change of bandages—"

"Rest," Henry said implacably.

"But—"

Henry put his hands on his hips. "Jackson, answer me this. What can you do at this juncture?"

"I was going to be in the interview room when Fetzer and Hardison brought Cartman in—"

"Do you think that's going to happen right now? Be honest. I know we were all gung ho because you had a witness and a license plate, but he's the DA. When do you think that's going to happen at the earliest?"

"Tomorrow," Jackson replied grudgingly. "But Junior, do you think this guy's done?"

Henry shook his head. "No. And I get it. We need to find him, and we need to figure out his agenda and who he's after next. You and Ellery are probably on that list. Do you think I'm not worried? And we can do some of it from your house. Christie, I'm sure, will send you the footage to go over. Fetzer and Hardison will be calling to see how to bring in the DA. Crystal and AJ will have some reports to run. But all of that is *working*, and right now, your body is *not*. So c'mon, man—let me do my job, okay?" Henry's face, which had never been boyish in spite of the All-American blue eyes and blond hair, took on a hauntingly gentle cast. "I was sent out to be your backup, but also to help you call it when it got too hard. I'm calling it. You and Sean are done for the day. Now let's get you down the stairs."

Jackson involuntarily winced with the thought.

By the time he was down the first flight, he was holding on to Henry's hand for balance. By the time he got to the ground floor, he was sweaty and shaking and ready to throw up and his vision was doing that great sci-fi strobe thing from dark around the edges to gray in the middle. Still, he was pissed at himself for giving in until his phone pinged as Henry pulled away from the hospital and headed back to American River Drive.

It was Fetzer. Her lieutenant said they needed statements from Sandra and pictures before they got the warrant to bring Cartman in. She told him it would be tomorrow at the earliest, and he texted his thanks.

Then he got a text from Christie, telling him he'd have the tapes from the surrounding area to Jackson later that afternoon at the earliest, and that—*that* was what it took for Jackson to calm down.

Henry was right. They'd hurried up; now it was time to wait. Waiting may not have been his favorite thing to do, but he could admit to himself his body wasn't up for much else at the moment.

Noodles and Knowhow

WHEN ELLERY walked into the house, it smelled like Chinese food and sounded like a military op center.

He'd spotted K-Ski's Charger in front of the house, as well as the horrible minivan in the garage, and there was a little red Mazda in front of the neighbor's house that was so battered Ellery couldn't imagine it belonged to anybody who didn't know Jackson, so he was semiprepared for people, but he was unprepared for the low hum of purpose that echoed throughout the dining room and living room.

A young Adonis with dark curly hair and big brown eyes stood at the kitchen sink, washing dishes, and Ellery took a moment to smile at Cotton, who had helped to care for an injured military man after their last adventure. From what Jackson had said, the two had separated amid much angst and denial of pain, but Cotton's sad, clear-eyed smile in return told Ellery that the boy still had hope, and so he would too.

Jackson, Sean, and Henry's boyfriend, Lance Luna, were all sitting at the kitchen table, poring over their laptops, while Henry and Sean's nurse, Billy, wandered from person to person, peering over their shoulders and nodding.

Ellery took a moment to digest and realized this must be the traffic footage they'd been sent. He would imagine each laptop hosted the footage from a different traffic light, and they were probably looking to see if they could identify anybody who had been near the shooting site.

Jackson had texted him the plan; seeing it in action was pretty impressive.

What Jackson had *not* texted him, however, was that he and Sean had been overdoing it. That he could see for himself.

Henry looked up as he stood at the bar that divided the kitchen from the dining room and nodded, squeezing Lance's shoulder before he walked over.

"Find anything?" Ellery asked, knowing he should care more. He wasn't stupid—the implications of a sniper with an agenda that would terrify Trey Cartman were not lost on him. Yeah, sure, it could be something *not* connected to Ezekiel Halliday or the forced relocation, but Ellery would bet every startup loan he'd gotten for his business that there was a connection. Sometimes it didn't matter which side of the bench you were on; any connection could lead straight to him and Jackson at the wrong end of a sniper's scope.

But his house—designed in the sixties with absolutely no thoughts of open windows or flow-through—was uniquely protected in that regard. The siding was faux stone, which while bordering on unattractive at the moment, was surprisingly good at masking heat signatures, so that was helpful. The sliding glass door opened out onto a pool, and Ellery had checked the lines of sight that afternoon. There wasn't a building closer than a mile that had more than two stories. To complicate things for a would-be sniper, the trendy graphite vertical blinds that he used to keep out the sun were also damned near impossible to see through.

The next biggest window was in the guest room, and since there were no guests at present, that left their bedroom as their most vulnerable place— or it would be if Jackson hadn't installed steel plates under the drywall during his last week of leave after his heart surgery. Since they'd been threatened by stalkers before, Ellery had okayed the expense, and also the expense of the bullet-resistant glass and the special blinds on their windows.

And as Ellery had determined that morning, the only place for a clear shot through their bedroom was on top of their neighbor's roof. Good luck with that guy. He owned his own arsenal and was crazy enough to use it.

So the risk of getting hit by a sniper seemed minimal compared to the risk of watching Jackson keel over as he sat.

Henry grimaced as he saw the look on Ellery's face, and Ellery tried to crank it down a notch and failed.

"I got him home," he said. "And I fed him." They both looked to the half-full bowl of noodles by Jackson's elbow and winced. "And I changed his bandages and watched him take his meds. Ellery, he's a grown man, and he's worried. Not just about you and him—about everybody. He suggested Lance and I take a vacation. Thought maybe Sean and Billy could go stay with relatives. Suggested having you warn Judge Brentwood or post a police presence in front of Ezekiel Halliday's care home—or Effie Shaw's or Annette Frazier's. And I'll be honest, I can't argue with any of it. We're not the police. We don't have the authority to do any of it, and only a few of us are trained in any sense of the word. But you didn't see that shot. It was long, and it was scary. Somebody out there is really good with a rifle."

"Are the police working on this at all?" Ellery asked. He'd told Crystal and AJ about the shot from half a mile away, and understanding the situation, they'd both put their entire day on hold to run deep background on all of the players in their little drama. Ellery was expecting some files in his email as soon as he sat down, but he had to admit he felt like Jackson looked.

And Jackson was pale, with bags under his eyes. His hands shook as he ran his fingers through his hair, and Ellery had the feeling he was due for another pain pill.

Ellery let out a breath, suddenly exhausted and starving. "Is there any more Chinese food? That smells amazing."

"Billy and Sean brought enough to feed an army for a month. There's even cauliflower noodles with broiled chicken and teriyaki sauce."

Ellery's mouth started to water, and he gave Henry a naked look of supplication.

"All right, all right. You sit and talk to him. I'll get you a bowl."

"Thanks, Henry," he said, feeling the gratitude to his toes. "Maybe throw in some extra. I'll see if I can get him to eat."

Henry snorted. "Good luck with that."

Ellery nodded, but this time he couldn't really blame Jackson, either. Wearily he sank into the vacant chair next to Jackson's and peered over his shoulder. Footage from the traffic light on Fair Oaks at Arden sped by in triple time, and Jackson scowled at it. Ellery watched as he hit Pause and then wiped his eyes, giving Ellery a weary smile.

"Hello, Counselor," he said, stifling a yawn. "How's it going?"

"Crystal and AJ should have background on everybody involved in the cases before I'm done with dinner," he said lightly. "And then I, too, can become a data zombie like everybody else."

"Where's Jade and Galen?"

"In their respective homes," Ellery said. "Jade and Mike are thinking about taking off to spend a couple of days with your brother in the hills." Kaden and his wife, Rhonda, and their three children lived up near Truckee. They'd been stashed up there for protective custody during Ellery and Jackson's first case together and had loved living in the mountains so much they'd stayed. The place was out-of-the-way and unexpected. Jade and Mike were minor enough players for them to be pretty safe up in Todd Valley.

Jackson's eyes widened appreciatively. "Ooh, that's a good idea. I should have thought of it. I'll text her."

"In a minute," Ellery said gently, watching as he squeezed his eyes shut repeatedly in order to clear the sand of too much video analysis from his vision. "Henry said he had to change your bandages."

Jackson grimaced. "I know you heard me bitch about this all weekend, but, you know, it's your fuckin' *back*. You never think about the skin on your back unless you're trying to scratch an itch. Who knew it was connected to *everything*? Sitting down, standing up—"

"Walking four flights of stairs to check out a sniper's nest," Henry said, setting a bowl of chicken and cauliflower noodles at Ellery's elbow. "I felt like shit when I realized how much pain he was in, and we still had to walk down."

Jackson grunted. "I swear, I only thought we were leaving the house to…." His eyes darted to Ellery's, and he gave a game "I'm not hiding anything" smile.

"To what?" Ellery asked curiously.

"Yeah, Jackson. To what? I never did catch what you were doing out there by the crime scene."

Jackson shot Henry a look of pure venom. "I almost liked you today. Almost."

"Don't give up on me. You might almost like me sometime next week. I'll hold out hope." Henry gave an evil smile, and Jackson growled at him. Ellery chuckled, because while he and his sister had never engaged in sibling schtick, he imagined this was probably what most people meant when they talked about brothers.

"Joey's sister's car was rear-ended this morning," Jackson said. "I told you that. Talking to her was how we realized Cartman was fleeing the area. You both knew that."

Henry frowned. "That was Joey's sister's car? I swore that was the—" His eyes got big. "No," he said.

"I have no idea what you're talking about," Jackson lied. Ellery knew he was lying, Henry knew he was lying, but only Henry knew what he was lying *about*.

"Ellery," Henry squeaked, "he totally traded his CR-V for that brown piece of—"

"Sweet sugary goodness!" Jackson inserted. "Oh my God, Henry! Have you learned nothing in the last four days? If we want that car to not try to catapult you out of the front seat, what do we need to do?"

Henry gave him a bleak look. "She's a lovely car, Jackson. I just thought she was *somebody else's* car. But apparently she's not. I'm so happy. We get to drive her *forever*."

Ellery gaped at them both, trying to fit the pieces together in his tired brain, when an epic war broke out in the living room. It started with one of the cats growling, and then both of the cats yowling, and then the tiny, sad yelping of a little brown ball of fur as he hauled ass through the house, screaming at the top of his miniscule lungs.

"Aw, Poppy," Billy said, moving from his place soldered to Sean's side to bend down and pick up the little dog that Ellery hadn't noticed until now. "Baby, did those two terrible cats try to eat you?"

"I thought he was going with Cody Gabriel?" Ellery said, staring at the dog.

"Well, yeah," Henry said. "But right now Cody's in the part of rehab where he's being sedated and detoxed. He can't care for the dog at *all*. We're bringing him back at the end of the week, and I'm sure it will help."

At that moment Billy Bob leapt onto the middle of the kitchen table, wiggling his ass and knocking laptops right and left, meowing his displeasure. Jackson grunted and stood painfully, and Ellery watched as he picked the big furry goober off the table, straining his stitches as he did so.

"Come on, No-thumbs," he said, even his voice aching with weariness. "Let's get you into the bedroom where the big scary five-pound dog is not a threat." As he left, he picked up a shadow as Lucifer followed at his heels, meowing pitifully the entire time.

Ellery and Henry watched him go, concerned, but Ellery blew out a sigh of relief when the door closed.

"What?" Henry asked.

"He's not fond of crowds," Ellery reminded him. "And he's exhausted. If we're lucky he'll linger there to settle the cats and maybe fall asleep."

Henry nodded and gave Sean a meaningful glance over the computer screens. "Did you hear that?" he asked. "'Cause, you know— it could be catching."

Sean gave him a dead-eyed look. "Junior, do you have any idea how long I can live on irritation and coffee?"

"Oh dear Lord," Ellery muttered. "You sound like Jackson's ventriloquist dummy. Go into the living room and close your eyes."

Sean gave him a look of sheer horror. "Shut your mouth."

Billy leaned over his back and gave him the small brown dog. "Look, Jackson's calming down the kitties, so you go calm down the puppy and let the rest of us kids look at the screens, okay?"

Sean leveled him a look of pure bathos. "You are not endearing yourself to me, you realize that."

Billy's smile had a hint of smugness to it. "Of course I am. Now go sit."

For the first time, it occurred to Ellery that Sean and his "pretty nurse," as they'd all thought of Billy, might have a relationship a little deeper than first supposed. Well, given Sean's rather strict Catholic family, that could be awkward.

"Stop looking at them like that," Henry murmured as Billy helped Sean up by the elbow and walked him into the living room.

"Like what?"

"Like they're doomed."

Ellery smiled faintly. "I was surprised," he said. "I don't think they're doomed. I think Jackson is… I don't know. Magic."

"That's sweet," Henry said dryly. "Do you want to go check on your magic human to see if he's asleep?"

"Ten more minutes," Ellery told him, taking another forkful of noodles and sliding behind Jackson's laptop. "In the meantime, tell me what I'm looking for."

"This is the video footage from the intersections surrounding the shooting site. We didn't find any brass—which probably means whoever is military trained—but they had to get there from somewhere. Each computer has a different intersection, and basically we're forwarding between cars and then checking out the faces of the people driving through."

Ellery sighed. "If this was the movies, there'd be a pile of cigarette butts or shells and we could do DNA testing."

"Hey, if Jackson and I hadn't found toolmarks where the sniper put a tripod, we wouldn't have shit."

"Oh, we'd have shit," Sean said from the couch. "We'd have the shittiest union rep who ever wore a badge in a casket like a turd, that's what we'd have."

Ellery frowned. Of all the things they hadn't checked out yet, Charlie Boehner's enemies hadn't even come up. God*damn* Trey Cartman and his impulse to cover the truth up instead of discovering it; he'd cost an entire day's worth of investigation as Jackson and Henry had investigated the cover-up instead of the murder.

"He was hated?" Ellery asked, hitting Play on his video footage. "Why?"

"Well, for one thing, he had his head so far up Cartman's ass, he could taste what Cartman had for breakfast."

Ellery grimaced but kept his eyes on the screen. "Charming. What impact did that have on you guys?"

Sean grunted. "You know that LGBTQ chapter of the union we used to have?"

"Yeah?" Then Ellery's eyes widened as the implication of "used to" sank in. "Oh."

"But it's more than that. The guy could fight for us like a pit bull, but it was always the wrong stuff. He fought to get cops out of trouble for excessive force, fought to get them overtime for bullshit duties, fought to give them second chances when they failed sensitivity training. You know what he *didn't* fight for?"

"Family leave, mental health care, de-escalation training, confidential substance abuse counseling?" Ellery hazarded, because he was starting to see a pattern.

"See? You *did* know the guy," K-Ski finished sourly. "Every bad stereotype about the police—*that's* what he fought for. The stuff that would help make us better? Didn't even rate." He grunted. "And to make matters worse, I seriously think he cheated on the last election."

There was a chorus of groans from a group of people who had heard that *way* too often in the past year, and Sean laughed.

"Yeah, I know how it sounds. I'm just saying. Christie's cousin Jaime was running for the position, and she was running progressive, and she had mad support. I'm not sure what Boehner said or did to make Chambers declare him the winner, but he was the kind of guy who cheated, and I'm not taking that back."

Ellery was about to snort derisively and write it off as sour grapes, but something kept running through his head. Something about the Halloween party and Brentwood's desperately unhappy expression immediately after he'd flip-flopped so noticeably on his support for the trial. "I'm not sure what Boehner said or did...," Sean had said—and that usually meant coercion.

Brentwood's behavior indicated a pattern common to blackmail. Except Brentwood hadn't been able to go through with it, had he? He'd pushed to make a deal in the end, to exonerate Ezekiel because he couldn't watch a perversion of justice.

And Cartman's desire to hide the true killer—would that mean Cartman had been blackmailed too? Would finding the killer lead them to the dirt on Cartman that he seemed so desperate to keep hidden?

Things were starting to fall into place. Now if only they could get a bead on who the sniper—

"Shit," Ellery said, hitting pause on the film in front of him. "Guys? Are we sure our perpetrator was in a vehicle?"

There was silence all around, and for the first time Henry's boyfriend spoke up, his natural sarcasm ringing loud and clear. "Hey, Henry, do you think that might be important?"

Henry's response was pained. "Well, yes. We assumed they were in a vehicle because it's drizzling and it's cold and dark, and the old hospital is in the middle of a residential neighborhood. There's no place a pedestrian could really come and go from—"

"Then where'd this guy come from?" Ellery said quietly, pointing to a figure crossing the street with the traffic light, head covered in a hoodie, slender form gliding like their feet were on greased rails. Whoever it was had a massive duffel over their shoulder, something that swung like there was weight inside. But the person carrying it must have been strong, because their gait never wavered.

"Good question," Henry murmured, looking at the time-and-location stamp visible on the video footage. "Who's got the intersection east of this one? The place this guy would have been coming from headed west?"

"Me," Lance said promptly. "Ellery, what's your time stamp?"

"Eleven forty-two," Ellery told him, excitement rising in his belly like the tide.

"Damn, Jackson flew through that footage," Lance muttered. "Here, wait—I've got your guy. Passed in front of this camera at eleven thirty-seven. Billy, do you have them?"

There was a pause as Billy searched K-Ski's laptop. "No," he said, and then before they could all deflate, he added, "but I wouldn't. If he was on foot, there's a walk-through behind the grocery store that's right in line with Jackson's camera. I've been looking over your shoulders, remember? So whoever this was, they were walking from the east. They hit Lance's intersection, proceeded to Jackson's intersection, and then disappeared behind the grocery store, where a walk-through to the block behind the store could cut ten minutes off their path."

"Okay, then," Henry muttered. "So everybody scan from this point on. Given that whoever it is had to drill out the locks to the stairwell and set up the tripod on the roof, as well as wait for Charlie Boehner to appear in his own damned front room in the middle of the night." Henry paused. "How do you think he did that, anyway? Got Boehner to walk into his front room in full view of that big window?"

"Called him," Lance muttered. "Why not?"

Ellery swore again. "Dammit! I've got phone records of our key players in my briefcase. I was going to look through them for Boehner's number—"

"We can do that when we're done here," Henry said decisively. "Come on, guys, we're close. I feel it."

"Henry, I need your eyes," Lance said, hitting Pause and leaning back.

Henry moved playfully to sit on his lap.

"Hey!"

With a quick twist in the chair, Henry pecked Lance on his lips and grinned. "You let me sit down, I'll take your spot," he murmured.

Lance seemed to melt. "I'll get you some coffee, okay?"

"You love me," Henry said happily, standing up to let him out. He promptly sat down again, and Lance bent over his shoulders to kiss his temple.

"Highly probable," he said softly. "I'll let you know, if we can wrap this up in an hour and get home tonight."

"Oh boy," Henry cackled. "I'm gonna get laid tonight."

Lance ruffled his hair, and Henry went back to scanning his video footage while Ellery went back to looking at his own. It was funny how exhausted he'd been when he walked through the door—and how settling in to work some more had seemed onerous and taxing in the extreme.

But working with friends, *talking* to friends, had made it seem easier. He'd wondered at Jackson's sanity when he walked in, but now, as he attacked the video footage with renewed fervor, he understood.

This was Jackson's idea of fun.

And it was starting to be Ellery's as well.

HALF AN hour later he stood and stretched before checking his cell phone to make sure the best image they had of their perpetrator was on it.

Henry had been close—the shadowy figure in the cheap tracksuit hoodie had taken a good forty-five minutes to re-emerge onto their traffic cameras. Their figure had been careful not to expose his or her face, and Ellery couldn't help thinking military training.

Henry had echoed that opinion, and given his eleven years in the military, his word had some weight.

But it was late, and the people in his kitchen and living room had been working without break and without pay since early that afternoon. Ellery told them all to go home, promised Henry he'd text in the morning so Henry could be there for Cartman's interview, and made sure the Thai food was boxed up so Lance and Henry could eat it later.

On their way out, Billy paused to shake his hand, the little brown dog tucked under his arm like he'd forgotten it was there. "I fussed a lot about him overdoing it," he confided, "But I think this made him remember how much he likes his job."

Ellery smiled before looking pointedly at the dog. "You're taking that home with you?"

Billy grinned. "Sean loves it! He won't say anything, but the minute Cotton set it down, he just lit up like a sunrise. I think he really wants a dog at home, so yeah. We can keep it until that Gabriel guy is ready for his comfort dog."

It was almost too cute to stand.

But finally everyone was out the door and Ellery could go check on Jackson. Much like he'd supposed, he hadn't heard much at all from the bedroom since Jackson had retired.

Ellery found him on his stomach on the comforter, his knees curled up underneath him, almost like a toddler. His arms were tucked underneath his chest like he was cold, and his shoes were still on.

Ellery gave a sigh and started pulling off his shoes.

"Going out in a minute," Jackson mumbled.

"No," Ellery replied softly. "You're stripping down to your briefs and getting under the covers and going to bed. It's almost eight o'clock."

"Wow. You said that like eight o'clock is a sane time to go to bed." He let Ellery pull off his shoes before creakily swinging his legs over to the edge of the bed and standing up. Ellery helped him with his pants and hooded sweatshirt—one of his old, frayed ones—but left the T-shirt on. It was another shirt that was nearly transparent with age and washings, and since Jackson had gotten better about dressing like he cared if he lived or died, Ellery assumed it was because he didn't want to get his good T-shirts dirty.

"It is for good boys who did a lot of work today," Ellery said softly.

"I can't sleep," Jackson mumbled. "There are people here."

"I sent them home. Enough is enough."

Jackson groaned. "Man, you're right. It's so late. Just let me nap—"

"Jackson, we found the sniper. Sean sent the footage to Christie to see if video forensics can clean it up and identify the guy with the duffel bag over his shoulder. Or girl—it could go either way. Fetzer and Hardison are set to bring Cartman in tomorrow at nine. He's probably already lawyered up, but you and I will be there in the briefing room, so that may change things—"

"Both of us?" Jackson lay gingerly down on his side, and Ellery held his hand to Jackson's forehead. A faint fever relapse, but not too high.

"Yes," he said. "It was pretty easy for Cartman to write you off when he heard about you over the phone—much like it was easy for him to write Sandra off because he thought she couldn't hurt him. You in the same room with him? That's a two-pronged attack. He thinks of himself as a shark in negotiations, but let's see how he deals with real bloodshed." Ellery realized his distaste of the man was bleeding through his voice, and he tried to rein it in, but Jackson had caught it anyway.

"As long as you're not carrying a weapon into the briefing room, Counselor, I think he'll be okay."

Ellery snorted. "Stay right here. I'll be back with some water, and we can get you some pain meds."

"You just want me to pass out," Jackson slurred, and Ellery narrowly avoided saying, "You're damned right I do!" by the twitch of a jaw.

"Yeah, Jackson, everything's a conspiracy" was what he did say. "Now stay put."

By the time he got back with a glass of water, Jackson's medication, and some soft bread to pillow the meds, Billy Bob had lodged himself solidly behind Jackson's thighs and Lucifer was behind his neck.

"I don't think I can move," Jackson murmured.

"It's fine. I brought a straw. Now drink and eat."

He did so obediently, which was a relief. When he'd swallowed everything, including the bread, he handed Ellery the cup and napkin and snuggled back into the pillows.

"We got anything else we're doing tomorrow?" he asked.

"Going to visit Clive Brentwood," Ellery said. "We have an appointment with his secretary, but he wasn't in today, so he won't know we're coming."

Jackson grunted. "Brentwood. Interesting. What are you thinking?"

"Blackmail," Ellery said thoughtfully. "Brentwood flip-flopped, Cartman's terrified, and Boehner was known for playing dirty. What does that smell like to you?"

"Like Boehner blackmailed the wrong person and it burned him," Jackson said, and Ellery felt validated all over again. "Good thinking, Counselor." He took a deep breath, and Ellery thought he was going to say something else, but he didn't, so Ellery thought he was asleep.

Jackson stayed quiet while Ellery put on his pajamas and then got a glass of wine from the sparkling-clean kitchen, bless Cotton and his urge to take care of people. He was quiet as Ellery climbed into bed next to him, laptop open, and set the television to something quiet and mindless for background noise. About the time the first program was over, he spoke again, his words so unexpected Ellery startled and almost sent his laptop skittering to the floor.

"Are your parents coming here for Thanksgiving?" he mumbled.

"Yes," Ellery said, closing the computer carefully and setting it on the end table, because that spill had been a near miss. "Why do you ask?"

"I'd like Lucy Satan to see me when I'm not a mess," he said. "I figure my stitches will be out by then. I should be healthy. The firm's almost been running a year. Wouldn't it be nice to have everybody here and nobody hurt or sad?"

Ellery didn't correct him this time, remind Jackson that his mother's name was, in fact, Taylor and not Lucy Satan. He couldn't. He remembered the year before, when Jackson had barely been well enough to travel and they'd gone to Ellery's parents' home in Massachusetts. He'd been so traumatized by their run-in with the Dirty/Pretty killer and his subsequent stay in the hospital that Ellery's family had walked around him on tiptoes, doing anything they could to put him at ease. His mother—Ellery's *mother*—had elected to have Thanksgiving in the family room on TV trays so Jackson could curl up in a ball and sleep after a few bites. It was probably all Jackson had eaten all week. Suddenly Ellery very much wanted his parents to see them both happy and healthy, to see how much more solid Jackson had become since then.

Ellery's mother had always loved Jackson. She would feel so much better about the both of them if she knew Jackson Rivers was capable of taking care of himself—and of Ellery too.

"It would be," Ellery said, running his fingers along Jackson's arm. "But I'm surprised you think so too."

"Your mom is terrifying, Ellery. She's larger than life and super smart, and she loves you like a mama mountain lion loves her cub. But that doesn't mean she's not good people. I'd just like Lucy Satan to see that her baby boy is okay, you know? He's not saddled with a neurotic mess. His boyfriend is okay too."

"I was never saddled with you," Ellery said softly. He turned off the TV and the light before lying down behind Jackson, close enough to tangle calves, but not close to his back.

"I beg to differ," Jackson slurred. "But it's okay. I'll heal from this. This isn't so bad. You and me, we can host dinner. We can have Galen and John and Lance and Henry—"

"We can't take Lance and Henry from the flophouse boys," Ellery murmured. "We'll have to have them here."

Jackson made a tiny sound that probably meant he was thinking about all the people. "My brother was coming down from the mountains, and Jade was coming over, and—"

"Shh…," Ellery calmed him. "Maybe we can have an open-house thing. We'll have a caterer and all the food out, and people can visit whenever they can fit us in. It's sort of like an all-day party."

"Sounds complicated," he mumbled. "But you always know how to make things work."

"Never needed to until you came into my life," Ellery said quietly. "Never cared about so many people. Just so you know, I'm always grateful for you. You are my Thanksgiving."

Jackson let out an inelegant snort. "The way my body looks, I'm more like your Halloween."

Ellery resisted the urge to thwack him on the back of the head. "Your body isn't scary. It's seasoned," he said with a sniff. "And as long as it's keeping you alive, I have no problems with it."

"Augh!" Jackson gave a muffled groan into his pillow. "It's the perfect line. I should have you on your hands and knees and be pounding into you going, 'You got a problem with my body *now*, Ellery? Hah?'"

Ellery erupted into snickers and allowed his fingers to brush Jackson's neck, well above the stitches. His body reacted to the image, and he *was* pleasantly aroused, but more than that, he was pleased. Because Jackson hadn't tried it. A year ago, he'd be trying to sex Ellery up and prove he was okay, but he wasn't. He was letting himself be cared for. Letting himself heal.

"Another week or two, and yes," Ellery said softly. "I plan to be having lots of problems with your body." He leaned forward enough to kiss Jackson's neck. "But not now. Sleep, baby. I love you."

"Love you too," Jackson mumbled. "You'll never know how much."

But Ellery did. Sure, from pretty much the beginning of their relationship he knew Jackson cared enough to die for Ellery—he'd tried to a couple of times and had come damned close. Jackson had already proved that he would kill for Ellery as well, although Ellery knew it haunted him. But right now, allowing himself to be comforted, asking about family, about holidays, about how he wanted Ellery's mother to see him whole and healthy, Ellery knew the truth.

Jackson Leroy Rivers wanted to *live* for him. And not just subsist—to live fully, like an adult. To have a share of happiness. To allow himself to be loved.

Ellery couldn't ask for anything more. In his entire life, he couldn't recall ever wanting anything with the purity and the passion that he wanted time, so much more time, with Jackson.

We All Have a Past

THE MORNING before, it had been the police pounding down the door that had woken Jackson up.

This morning it was Ellery's mother's ringtone on his phone—"Lucy in the Sky with Diamonds." Or as Jackson sang it, "Lucy in the Satan Tree with Boostifer," which was something he'd thought of coming out of surgery the first time he'd met the woman and that Ellery really never would understand.

"Lucy?" he mumbled, unsure if his rather loopy, pain-med-and-antibiotics-relaxed state had summoned her in his mind or in reality. "Did you hear me talking?"

"No, darling," Ellery's mother said, her very upper-class Boston accent seeming to brace him for harsh winters and people of fortitude. "What were you talking about?"

"You guys are coming for Thanksgiving," he mumbled. "Making sure."

"Well, we plan to," she purred. "That is if there's anything left of you in a month. Did something happen last week that Ellery forgot to tell us about, dear?"

Oh God. "I, uh, got a little bit sick. Ellery was pretty busy this weekend taking care of me. It was no big—"

"No big deal? Is that what you were about to say?" she asked sweetly.

"Absolutely not," he said, swinging his legs over the edge of the bed and wincing. He squinted at the face of his phone—7:00 a.m. It was like a conspiracy of people trying to wake him up early. "It was... well, it was blown out of proportion in the legal community, but—"

"How's your wound, Jackson?" she asked, voice flinty.

Jackson actually closed his eyes to assess. "Not bad? Stiff. Could use some vitamin E oil?"

"Good," she said. "You're at least being honest. How's the fever?"

"How did you know I had a—"

"Because you told me yourself you'd been sick. It's what your body does—first there's trauma, then all your defenses get lowered, then you have a fever. It's like a priming switch for your immune system. You bleed out all your antibodies, and your body needs more."

"Said no doctor ever," Jackson began, laughing.

"I am not interested in the medical community's attempts to rein you in," Taylor Cramer replied, in a voice like expensive wine frozen over. "What I care about, Jackson, is that neither of you bothered to call me and tell me you were hurt! Did you think I wouldn't care?"

Jackson sighed. "I think Ellery was just too busy," he said truthfully, because Ellery usually made time to call his mother during the weekend, and it was out of character that he hadn't.

"And you?"

"I'll live," Jackson told her. "I didn't want to worry you if it wasn't important."

"Jackson? It's always important. Your new kitten is important. Having to expose a war wound in court is important. Being ill and feverish and being stuck on the sidelines and hating it is important. I... I know you don't know how this entire process works, son, but I guarantee it doesn't unless you tell me and Ellery's father what's happening in your everyday lives!"

"Most of the time it's sort of boring," he confessed, and she snorted. Ellery's mother. Snorted. Into the phone—on purpose.

"Try again."

He thought about it. "Well, yesterday I officially traded my mostly new and only a little bit battered CR-V with my friend's sister's ten-year-old Town & Country that Henry thinks is haunted," he said. "That was fun. She, the sister, uhm, apparently had just been rear-ended by the city's district attorney, who took one look at her and assumed nobody would believe her when she said he did it. Just drove off. Damnedest thing."

He heard her counting under her breath. When she spoke, she sounded perfectly composed. "Jackson, about what percentage of the story is that?"

He thought about it. "Five, maybe seven percent. I have no idea how much Ellery's told you."

"Assume nothing and start at the beginning," she instructed.

"Okay, but I've got to make it fast. Ellery and I are out of here in a couple of hours, and taping my back up before I shower takes forever."

He heard her grunt of frustration, but he didn't have an answer for it, so he started on the story without preamble.

She knew part of it, of course. Ellery's contact at the DOJ was her contact at the DOJ, and he'd kept her filled in. She knew, for instance, that Cody Gabriel had been installed at a super-secret rehab facility for people turning over state's evidence and that the DA's office was under investigation.

But as Jackson detailed the bus ride and the DA's attempts to implicate him and Ellery in the murder of Charlie Boehner, she grew frighteningly quiet on the other end of the line.

"Oh, this is not good," she said softly. "I feel like I shouldn't have to tell you how not good this is."

"There's no reason to think the sniper would be after Ellery," Jackson said. "I don't think Cartman would be so hot to implicate me if he thought the guy who took out Boehner would get rid of the two of us for him."

"It's possible that's true," she conceded. "But it's also possible that there's a sniper loose in your city, and he's going after people connected to this case. And that your DA is looking for a reason to sweep the homeless displacement under the rug."

"*That's* what has me worried," Jackson said, sighing. "The story came out this weekend, and people made a big fuss about it, but without lawmakers pushing for an investigation—"

"Give your governor a chance," she said. "He's worked hard on this problem. And there is no easy solution. Remember, it's easier to spot a disaster than to fix it, and our justice system is made to move slowly on purpose."

Jackson emitted a low growl, because he couldn't manage words for how frustrated he was, but Ellery's mother apparently spoke that language too.

"Because if it moved faster it would be fascism, Jackson, and we've come damned close to that and would rather not."

Maybe it was the crisp way she discussed politics as though she were teaching him how to tie his shoes, but he had to laugh. "Point taken," he admitted. "But I spent a night on that bus, in their shoes. I can't imagine spending more and still being—I don't know. Human, I guess—by the end of it."

"Which is why we keep fighting," she told him. Her voice lowered. "And you're wrong, you know. You were taken in by the Camerons, but before that I think you knew very well what it was like to not know where you would be sleeping one day to the next and to not know when you would be eating as well. You kept your heart, son. Don't think we don't know that."

Jackson shifted uncomfortably. "I was just a kid. It wasn't—"

"Stop," she ordered softly. "I believe you when you say Ellery was busy all weekend taking care of you. Did you help him?"

Jackson tried not to smile. "Didn't fight him."

"We'll call it a win. Now I'm going to hang up and see what I can find out about your DA that can help your investigation. And maybe light a fire under the DOJ's ass to speed up theirs. People think corruption in the police force is what they have to worry about, but once it goes higher than that, we are on very dangerous ground. Take care of yourself, son, and take care of Ellery too."

"That's my job," Jackson said, knowing damned well he'd failed at it. "I keep trying to do it better."

"I know you do. Remember Ellery's family loves you too, and Ellery's father is very excited to come meet the new kitten over Thanksgiving. He claims it's as good as a grandchild, but there will be no diapers."

Jackson chuckled. "Uhm, Lucy?"

"Yes, Jackson?"

"Thank you. For calling. I... you know. Ellery appreciates it when you call."

Her stony silence on the other end of the line let him know she was not impressed with his weak shit.

"And so do I," he added. "It's kind of you to worry."

She gave an elegant, ladylike snort. "My family does not do kindness, Jackson. We do practicality. My son is better off with you, so it's only practical that I make sure you are well. I shall call Ellery later this morning. Take care."

And she hung up before he could call bullshit—not that he would have. One did not call bullshit on one's boyfriend's mother.

Particularly not when she'd flown out to California on a dime before to make sure Ellery or Jackson or both of them were going to be all right.

"Who was that?" Ellery asked, emerging from the bathroom wearing a robe and toweling his hair.

"Your mother," Jackson told him grumpily. God, he was tired already.

"What did she want?"

"To mess with my mind," he said, and then moved on before Ellery could respond. "Can I really come play today?"

Ellery rolled his eyes. "I told you no yesterday, and you ended up with a porn-star op center in our front room. So fine. You and Sean want to come play—"

"And Henry—"

"Yes. You may all swing from the monkey bars and fall off the jungle gym. It's fine."

"But can we come watch the interview with the DA? The jungle gym's gonna kick my ass. I'd rather do that." Jackson gave him a hopeful smile that was all teeth, and Ellery laughed.

With quick strides, he reached Jackson as he sat on the bed and leaned over, taking his mouth in a minty-fresh, shower-soft-and-scented kiss, and Jackson drank him in.

"How are you feeling?" Ellery asked after he'd pulled back, looking adorably flushed.

"Better now," Jackson told him, giving a game smile. Teasingly he ran his palms up Ellery's thighs, exposed by the robe. "If I didn't need a shower myself, I'd do something about this…." He brushed Ellery's cock under the fabric, and Ellery's quick intake of breath told him the touch had meant something. "Never mind," he murmured, his voice going sultry. "Turns out you don't need to smell me."

And with that, he parted the robe and leaned forward, lowering his head just enough to lick the soft skin. Ellery gasped again, and Jackson chuckled, licking again, teasing Ellery's inner thighs gently and then pulling him into his mouth. Ooh, he sort of liked this—Ellery's skin soft, the blood flowing underneath his cock and making it swell. Engorging it until he it could no longer fit in Jackson's mouth without thrusting down his throat as Ellery's fists tightened in his hair.

Long strokes now, his mouth and hand working in concert. Ellery thrust gently, his breaths harsh, his precome starting fast. Jackson wondered if he'd been thinking about sex in the shower, telling himself he shouldn't because Jackson was still hurt, and he sucked Ellery in deeper, throat working hard, to make him forget any thoughts of being gentle.

Sex felt good, and it made Jackson feel powerful. Making love to Ellery—or fucking his brains out, or getting fucked by him—was something he refused to trade or cheat on. He wanted Ellery's come down his throat. He wanted to hear Ellery calling his name roughly, his voice broken a little. He wanted Ellery to be thinking of him and only of him, and not of his injuries or his vulnerabilities.

As Ellery let out a groan and pumped his hips furiously, trusting that Jackson would take the face-fucking and give back with tongue and fingers, Jackson's body flushed with endorphins, and when Ellery cried out, pouring spend down Jackson's gullet, Jackson flew.

Moaning a little, Ellery pulled out of his mouth and sank to his knees, burying his face against Jackson's stomach and breathing shakily into his T-shirt.

"Proud of yourself?" he asked weakly.

Jackson lowered his head to kiss Ellery's crown. "Yup."

"Want to know what I'm going to do to you when your back's all healed?"

Jackson's mouth, glazed with his own spit, curved into a smile. He licked a last rivulet of come from his lips and said, "Tell me."

Long and creatively, talking about sex acts they'd joked about but hadn't yet performed, Ellery exacted his revenge. When he got to the part about shoving a vibrator up Jackson's ass while riding Jackson like a show pony, Jackson's cock was hard enough to pound nails. With a vicious tug, Ellery leaned back and yanked on his briefs enough to expose it before taking Jackson into the back of his throat with a certain maniacal glee.

Jackson was left to finish the scenario in his mind as Ellery gulped him down, ignoring the smell of sweat and sleep and sucking Jackson until his orgasm exploded, sending white light through his body, cascading through his vision, spurting out his cock in a series of short, hard jets. When he was done, Jackson fought hard not to collapse against the mattress and knew he had this coming for trying to make love to Ellery without letting Ellery give back.

"Proud of yourself?" he rasped.

Ellery rocked back on his heels, his robe hanging off his shoulders, his beautiful lean body fully on display as he wiped his mouth with the back of his hand.

"Yes, I think I am." He gave a huffy little sigh. "But we're going to be late if you don't get a move on, so let me help you up."

Jackson let him stand and then took his offered hand up… and then stepped into his offered hug as the two of them touched, skin to skin, and let the warmth seep in.

"I want to play too," Ellery murmured, his head on Jackson's shoulder. "And I don't mind a little sweat."

Jackson rubbed his lips against Ellery's temple, feeling sexed and energized and weak and exposed at the same time. "I thought we didn't have time for both," he defended.

Ellery stepped back and gave him an evil look. "We didn't even have time for *one*. Now go into the bathroom and let me take care of your back so you *can* shower. You can tell me about your conversation with my mother while we're on the road."

"You're bossy," Jackson told him mildly, but he did as Ellery commanded.

He wasn't going to argue with sex. That way lay madness.

AFTER THE shower, the breakfast, and yes, the muddy coffee, he was a little more up to speed. Ellery drove them the familiar route down J Street, but this time going farther down to Freeport Blvd, where the police station sat.

Fetzer and Hardison had texted as they were on their way, saying they'd picked up the suspect in the hit-and-run and taken him to the police station for booking, but Henry wasn't going to make it in time. His text to Jackson was pissy and to the point: *Everybody's going to the shrink today, and I'm needed. Meet you at the office at ten.*

Jackson read the text to Ellery and sighed. "God, he is needed, but I got to tell you, I've gotten used to him having my six."

"What about me?" Ellery asked mildly. "Don't I have your six?"

"You do," Jackson conceded. "But Henry's a better shot." He'd managed to wheedle Ellery to the shooting range a few times since August, mostly to make himself feel better, but a few times at the shooting range was no match for an expert marksman.

"I'll have to train more," Ellery promised as he turned into the parking lot behind the station.

The building was relatively new—it had been built in the nineties—but as Jackson and Ellery walked through the parking lot, Jackson couldn't help but look over the sidewalks, which had held a tent city less than a week ago. A few panhandlers wandered there now, looking surreptitiously up at the four-story building like an evil overlord lived there, ready to sweep down and wreak havoc on their lives.

Jackson wanted to tell them that the evil overlord was eight blocks northeast, at the courthouse, but he didn't think they'd understand.

Besides, he'd apparently been transported in the back of a cop car to this very location. Lucky for everybody.

"Can you guys go any slower?"

Jackson and Ellery looked up to see an older, graying police officer holding a service door open for them and gesturing them inside. Jackson, who was still walking stiffly, bit the bullet and broke into a steady jog that made his stitches ache, but not with the same ferocity as the day before. Recovery time—it was a thing.

Jimmy Hardison, Adele Fetzer's partner, grimaced as they drew near. "Shit. I'm sorry. Whole world's talking about how McMurphy got a piece of you, and I fucking forgot. My bad."

"No worries," Jackson said through clenched teeth. "If we don't figure out what happened to Charlie Boehner and get Cartman to tell us the scam, McMurphy's got every likelihood of going back on the streets, so this is good."

"Your life is too complicated," Hardison grumbled. "I'd shiv the guy when he wasn't looking and go on my merry way. Your boyfriend could get you out of it, no problem."

Ellery's eyes widened in outrage, but Jackson had been with Jimmy and Adele through a firefight in August. Jimmy had taken one in the calf and had just been put back on active duty in the past week, and here he was hanging his ass out for Jackson and Ellery again.

Jimmy was good people.

"Well, that's why Ellery's got the big brain," Jackson said. "You and me, Jimmy, we're footsoldiers. The big brain here—he's got a plan."

Jimmy grunted and started leading the two of them through the back hallways and offices of the station. "I hope his brain is big enough to get us out of this. We had to pretend we didn't know who Tray Cartman was, which was hard given how many times he asked us, 'Do you know who I fuckin' am!'"

Jackson snickered. "Is it just me, or is that the easiest way to tell the world you're a tool without shouting, 'I'm a fuckin' tool!'"

"Yeah, no. He should have skywritten 'I'm a fuckin' tool.' Fewer people would have guessed." At that point, they came to an intersection that Jackson guessed would lead either to the elevators or the stairs.

"We can take the elevators, Jimmy," Jackson said softly. "Nobody has to know who we're here for. Remember, we get called in to post bail all the time."

"I hear ya," Jimmy muttered, turning right. "It was mostly my pride talking."

"Your leg bothering you?" Dumb question. Jackson had been shot before, and he'd been operated on before, and the leg hadn't *stopped* bothering the man.

"Yeah. It's okay, though. Promised Adele I wouldn't turn in my papers until she was ready. Dumb, isn't it? I mean, I love my wife, but I wouldn't want to do the job without Fetzer."

Jackson reckoned the only reason Jimmy could even voice such a thing was that Fetzer was a woman. But he got it.

"I hear you," he said. "Henry and I wanted to kill each other when we first met. Now he helps make the job fun."

"Weird." They came to the elevators, which were apparently relics from the Murder Room collection: cramped, stainless steel, and smelling of sweat, urine, and sanitized vomit. Jackson almost wished they'd taken the stairs.

They stepped in, nonetheless, and Jimmy saw their looks of distaste.

"Yeah. Most days, Adele and me take the stairs anyway. Better for my heart."

"We'll try the way down," Jackson told him, getting it in a big way.

"Sadly, we won't," Ellery said sharply. He gave Jackson's back a meaningful look, and Jackson grunted.

"It's never gonna stop fuckin' bleeding, is it?"

Jimmy chuckled. "I hear you looked real pretty stripping for the judge. Wish I coulda been there."

Jackson scowled at him. "You'd better check your sources. If it was McMurphy or Goslar saying that, they have questionable choices in everything."

Jimmy's expression softened. "They weren't the only cops in the room, Jackson. Some cops know what's what."

Oh. Well, that was nice to know. "Have them introduce themselves sometime," Jackson told him. "It would be good to know we're not all alone in the city."

The elevator doors opened at that moment, so Jimmy didn't have time to answer. Jackson and Ellery found themselves being walked down one more hallway—this one done in sort of a beige-rust—to the interview rooms.

Yes, they had the double-sided glass with the mirror on the suspect's side, just like in the movies. They also had an intercom in the observation room.

"Have you read him his rights?" Ellery asked, looking to where Trey Cartman—impeccable in his suit and tie—glared daggers at Adele, who stood sentry at the door looking very, very bored.

"Yes. And he's put in a call to his lawyer already. We figure you've got about twenty minutes with him before the lawyer gets here and we have to let him out on bail."

"Good. If we can't get the truth out of him in twenty minutes, we'll have to get it out of Clive Brentwood."

Jackson looked at him sharply. Ellery sounded like he knew something he hadn't before, but he didn't have time to ask him what he'd figured out.

"Jackson, I need you in the room," Ellery said. "Officer Hardison, you're taping this, right?"

"Oh yeah," Jimmy said grimly. "And you'd think he would have remembered that before unloading some pretty racist shit on Adele there. Fucker. Does he think she's stupid?"

Jackson gave Jimmy a level look. "Remember, that's why we're here. Because he *does* think she's stupid, just like he thought Sandra was stupid too."

Jimmy sucked air in through his teeth. "Easy to get fooled by the guys who don't have dirt under their nails, am I right?"

Jackson thought of Sandra's blatant puzzlement. He'd hit her car while it was in *her driveway* and had casually announced that nobody would believe her.

"Don't be," he said grimly. "You're worth ten of him." And then he followed Ellery through the door.

Adele let them in when they knocked and then told them she'd be "right outside." Which meant she would be in the observation room, probably hoping they'd find a crime to nail this guy on, but Jackson wasn't so sure. Still, it was good to know they were recording the whole thing. Footage helped.

"You're not my lawyer," Cartman said, scowling at Ellery. "What the hell are you doing here?"

"Trying to save your life," Ellery replied pleasantly. "Although the big question there is why we should bother."

"I don't have to talk to you." Cartman was leaning back in his expensive suit, his golden blond hair still perfectly coiffed, but his expression and demeanor were that of a sulky child.

"You don't," Jackson admitted cheerfully. "In fact, Ellery? You know—" He held his hand to his forehead and coughed weakly. "—I'm feeling faint. We should leave. I'm sick, Father, it's the black lung. I know he'll die, but I can't be fuckin' bothered to save his life."

"Poor baby," Ellery murmured, giving Jackson an amused look from the side of his eyes. "You're right. Who are we to intrude on the machinations of great men? We should leave him to the sniper roaming the city who probably wants his head on a platter just like Charlie Boehner's."

Jackson shook his head, looking as sorrowful as he could manage. "Poor asshole. Didn't even know it was coming. Wandered into his living room and pop!" Jackson mimed taking a sniper shot. "No possible way he deserved that, is there? No way he could have pushed someone too far."

Cartman's mouth had gone sulky. "It wasn't our fault," he said. "We didn't know—"

"Didn't know what?" Jackson asked. "That people had limits? Or that people are people? You wrecked your car leaving the crime scene, sir. Fetzer and Hardison have your car at the repair shop yesterday afternoon, and we've got an eye witness, a teacher, who says you smashed into the back of her CR-V, and she has evidence—*evidence*, mind you—that says it happened in her driveway and not on the road. You literally drove up onto the curb, wrecked the car, got out, looked at the damage, and said nobody would believe her because she was, what? Brown? Female? I'm still unclear on that. But you shit on her and drove away. And you thought that wouldn't come back to bite you in the ass. So we know brown people aren't people to you. Women aren't people to you. Disabled people aren't people to you. Homeless people aren't people to you. Who else did you think wasn't a person who picked up a gun and decided to make Boehner not one and might just be coming after you?"

"You have no proof he's coming after me—" But they had him, because desperation cracked his voice.

"We have *you*," Ellery said clinically. "You sent your best detectives to roust Jackson when there was no way he could have done it. Why? Because you wanted to take attention away from who *did* do it. Because something about who did do it links right back to you."

"You have no proof of that," Cartman said, drawing himself upright.

"Only your fear stink, soaking up the room," Jackson said dryly. "And seriously, given that I practically wear antiseptic and medical tape as an aftershave, I'm totally excused for saying that's foul as fuck. So let's look at the things that happened this weekend that could have led to Charlie Boehner's demise, shall we?"

"Well, the city's attempts to ship the homeless to other parts of the state was revealed," Ellery said, his voice dry. "That was obviously not your favorite part of the Sunday *Bee*."

"It was a hatchet job," Cartman said, but Jackson saw the sweat starting at his hairline, so he ignored that.

"That wasn't the only news in the *Bee*, was it?" Jackson asked musingly. "Wasn't Ezekiel Halliday in there?"

"Yes!" Ellery said happily, as though they were discussing this over the dinner table. "He was! Something about the four policemen who beat him up being investigated for... what was it again?"

"Brutality," Jackson said, nodding. "But that wasn't the only mention they got—lessee... lessee...."

"Oh!" Ellery exclaimed. "They were linked to Charlie Boehner, who defended their actions, and to you, Mr. Cartman, and your attempts to illegally clear out the homeless. So we've got four rogue police officers who aren't really rogue, collusion between the DA's office and the union representative to basically kidnap people and drug them to stay out of the way, and the DA's obvious willingness to turn a blind eye on the brutality of his officers as long as they subscribe to his agenda. And a DOJ investigation. Did I get that right? Did I get *all* of that right?"

Jackson turned to Cartman, whose little line of sweat had coalesced and was now beading and running down his temple.

"I don't know, Mr. Cartman. Who did we miss?"

"I don't have to talk to you guys," Cartman snarled. "You're a couple of ambulance chasers with an axe to grind—"

"You set the cops on us for no damned good reason," Jackson replied, keeping his cool. "And Ellery's a better lawyer in his sleep than you could dream of being. Do better."

"Nothing you say makes any difference," Cartman retorted. "You could accuse me of committing murder in here, but you're not the police and you're not the DA's office and—"

"But we do have the ear of the Department of Justice," Ellery said mildly. "And Jackson just talked to one of our contacts this morning. How'd she sound, Jackson?"

"Pissed-off," Jackson told him thoughtfully. "Wanted to know what sort of chicken outfit we were running out here in the Wild West anyway."

Cartman's color went a little wonky. "You threatened me with that on Friday, and nothing's happened," he said from lips that looked nearly blue.

"Oh, I'd say plenty's happened," Ellery said, laughing. "Lots of fantastic investigative journalism for one. And now your office is under investigation by the Department of Justice, and if you haven't been given notice, it's probably because you're in here, being arrested for a traffic ticket."

"Which, on the whole, is much less frightening than an obstruction of justice charge, which is coming," Jackson bluffed.

"Or a sniper's bullet, which probably has your name on it," Ellery added sweetly.

Oh, that was it. Cartman's hands had started to shake.

"The sniper is probably not interested in me," he said, and his voice was shaking along with his hands. Jackson and Ellery met gazes because they heard the unspoken word there.

"Anymore?" Jackson added delicately.

"How come you're picking on me?" Cartman yelled suddenly, as petulant as a child. "Why isn't Brentwood in here answering your stupid questions?"

Jackson and Ellery met eyes again. Interesting. Jackson nodded at Ellery to keep going.

"How do you know he hasn't been?" Ellery asked. "We're investigating everybody on the case—the better to facilitate the DOJ's efforts."

"Oh, you people always think the judge is the big grown-up in the room," Cartman sneered. "Some grown-up. Man can't even parent his own goddamned children."

"Hunh," Jackson said softly, and Ellery nodded. Interesting.

"What do Brentwood's children have to do with it?" Ellery asked, laughing slightly. "He's a devoted family man. What's the harm in that?"

"They make you weak," Cartman said sulkily. "Vulnerable. Guy thinks he's got all the principles in the world until you threaten to bring down the press on his kid."

"You blackmailed him?" Jackson asked, not surprised but disgusted nonetheless.

"I put pressure," Cartman said, adjusting his lapels. "If you live a clean life, you've got nothing to hide."

Jackson tilted his head. "That's a lie," he said. "It's usually a lie told by someone with the blackest soul and the most skeletons. You were blackmailing Brentwood by applying pressure to his kid, which was why he originally let your choirboys get away with, well, murder, am I reading that right?"

"They didn't kill anybody!" Cartman retorted.

"Jackson, show him your back," Ellery said, his voice so cold Jackson had to look at him twice to see if he meant it.

"Ellery...." He didn't want to whine. He didn't. God—one more time?

"This is the last time," Ellery said softly. "Go ahead."

Gah! Jackson turned around so he didn't have to see the mockery in Cartman's eyes and hauled his shirts over his head. In the reflection of the two-way glass he saw Ellery at Cartman's shoulder, forcing his eyes to track the layers of bandages.

"See that part up near the scapula?" Ellery growled. "That was where the knife hit bone. If McMurphy had hit soft tissue, or Jackson's spine, Jackson would be in the hospital or dead or paralyzed right now, but he didn't. Instead, McMurphy just slid that sharp, illegal knife down through his skin and muscle like butter, until he got to the soft tissue under the rib cage. See that? That's where the knife went through, and he was lucky. He's put on a few pounds since June, or McMurphy would have perforated intestines or organs, and Jackson wouldn't have made it out of there. He'd be dead, and so would Cody Gabriel. This was *your* guy, Cartman, under *your* orders. You're getting a little pale. Does it look painful? Does it look like it hurts? It does, right? You can see the blood seeping through. He was almost *dead*, you piece of shit, and *you* did it—you called the shots. That makes you responsible. So tell us the lie again, okay? Jackson's stood naked twice for something he didn't do. *Lie to us again!*"

Jackson hauled his shirts back over his head and turned to see Ellery, his face an inch away from Cartman's, his mouth open as he shouted.

And Cartman curled like a salted slug. "Boehner was good at finding the pressure points," he gasped. "The cops he pulled for duty were all on the take, and he knew. He had the proof—he'd defended them. Goslar, McMurphy, they were on the line for unnecessary force, but the case wouldn't go to trial for another month. It was his say-so whether they hang or walk. I asked for a puppy, he asked me what breed." And this right here explained why Freethy and Brown had gone running for another lawyer Friday night. Knowing that Cartman was displeased about how the trial had ended, they hadn't wanted to place their fates in Charlie Boehner's hands for another nanosecond. It was all starting to come together.

"And what breed was Clive Brentwood?" Ellery snarled, but at that moment, they heard Adele Fetzer demand to see someone's ID.

Jackson and Ellery locked eyes, and judging by Cartman's smug expression, they all knew his lawyer had arrived.

"You can't hold any of this against me," Cartman sneered, and Jackson rolled his eyes—but Ellery spoke.

"Do you think the DOJ isn't going to get this already? You may have just saved your miserable life, which could be the worst thing I've done all day."

And with that the two of them burst out of the room. Jackson paused to let the lawyer in, bowing and gesturing like a maître d', and Ellery met the lawyer's eyes and said, "We were discussing another matter. The interview was recorded, so you can see for yourself."

"If you dare," Jackson added, and the two of them moved to the observation room.

"What do you need?" Fetzer asked.

"Is your lieu going to press charges?" Ellery queried.

Fetzer and Hardison shrugged. "Probably not," Hardison replied. "She's weak sauce. I was hoping it was green and new back in August, but it's weak shit. I can say it now."

"Then leave someone here to deal with the paperwork," Jackson said. "We're going to go interview Brentwood and see if we can get a bead on the sniper who killed Charlie Boehner, and we will probably need backup."

Fetzer and Hardison both pulled in a breath. "This piece of shit knows who killed *Boehner*?" Fetzer asked. "And he wasn't going to tell you? Isn't that obstruction of justice?"

"A charge we just sacrificed," Ellery said wearily, "because we have the feeling this guy isn't done."

Jackson had known that, from the very beginning when they'd made plans to corner Cartman and question him. But unlike Cartman, their priority wasn't putting people in jail. It was saving their lives.

"Then it's decided," Fetzer said. "You go talk to whoever you need to talk to and tell us where you think the sniper's going next. We'll meet you there. We know your guy Henry on sight. Is there anyone else we should look out for?"

"We were going to tag Christie and de Souza," Jackson said, starting to move toward the door. "I'll blast everybody when we know."

And with that, he followed Ellery out into the corridor and back toward the elevators, knowing that Fetzer and Hardison had just signed on for hours of unnecessary paperwork and hassle on their say-so.

There had better not be any more dead bodies on their watch.

Things We Cannot Control

ELLERY KEPT an eye on Jackson as he piloted the Lexus back toward their American River neighborhood. They'd called Brentwood's paralegal, and she'd said the judge was working from home that day, and she'd postponed the trial he'd had scheduled to begin. It was a rare move—the wheels of justice may have turned slowly on a normal day, but when a judge didn't show up for work, they ground rapidly to a halt.

"I'm sorry," he said after a couple of uncomfortable moments that he'd used to negotiate the tricky turn onto J Street.

"For what—oh!" Jackson's sudden surprise told Ellery that he really *didn't* hold Ellery's command for him to strip against him. But he should have.

"I'm sure you're tired of being used as an object lesson," Ellery said, intent on getting his full repentance out now. "I mean, the first time, you walked into the courtroom knowing what was going to happen, but this time...." He shook his head. It would have been forgivable if Cartman hadn't been such a pile of excrement.

"It got to him," Jackson said softly. "I hadn't expected it would. Your description was... chilling, Counselor."

Ellery shuddered. "Well, I've had to look at it for the last four days and realize how close I came—again—to losing you."

"Not so close," Jackson reminded him. "There was backup and a plan and contact with you. All the good things."

Ellery knew this, but unreasonably, hearing it still helped to calm him down. "Except you getting hurt again."

Jackson let out a little chuckle. "It's weird. All the times I've been hurt, and hurt worse, and this wound gets all the attention. You know why?"

"Because you're still up and moving around?"

Jackson put his finger on his nose. "Yahtzee. I'm still up and moving around. I'm calling it a win, or at least I will if the damned sniper doesn't take out a scumbag. I mean, not that I'd mind if Goslar tripped on the cement and fell on a rake or something, but a sniper would make him look like an actual police officer, and that would be a fuckin' shame."

Ellery nodded. "Yeah. But still, I'd rather the sniper gunned him down than came after us."

"Just remember, if the cops find the sniper, there won't be much left of him or her to pin Cartman with. If we find the sniper, we get to defend them in court, and guess what happens then?"

Ellery felt his lips twist and was surprised he had a smile—a real one—in him this morning. "We get to make Cartman's scumbaggery public," he said, liking that idea very much.

"God, wouldn't that be nice. Maybe we can give Arizona's source at the press an exclusive. See? So worth it."

"Sure."

But only if they could walk away.

At that moment, Jackson jumped as if bitten and pulled his phone from his pocket. He grunted.

"What?"

"Goslar is our only player with military training," he said sourly. "He was a marksman, but not an expert. Just an everyday grunt, coming back home."

The puzzle was still scattered and out of focus, but Ellery had a feeling they were about to discover a big piece.

CLIVE BRENTWOOD lived about a mile away from Ellery's house, in a neighborhood about two clicks up income-wise. His two-story ranch-style house was bigger and nicer, and his yard was bigger and nicer, but they were still right next to Sacramento, so nothing mansion-worthy. Just... nice. Well-heeled. Hiring someone to decorate your house tastefully for Christmas, Halloween, and Easter nice. Consulting with a gardener and a landscape designer and a graphic artist in order to decide where to plant nasturtiums kind of nice. There was nothing gaudy or depressing about the house, but Ellery wasn't surprised to not see a cat in the window, either.

If there had been a cat, it very probably would have been a purebred something or other, professionally groomed so as not to leave dander everywhere. No three-legged split-eared street cats allowed.

Jackson stood visibly on the stoop as Ellery rang the bell, and when the door was opened by Jackson's friend Joey, he hardly batted an eyelash.

"Jackson?" Joey said blankly. "The fuck... erm, hell you doing here?"

"We're here to talk to Judge Brentwood," Jackson said, and Ellery could tell he was wondering if Joey was having affairs with older married guys now. "What the hell?"

"Oh, I just clean his house," Joey said cheerfully, obviously reading Jackson's mind. "He's a nice guy." His face fell. "He's... there's something weird going on today." He lowered his head and whispered, "The judge and his wife have been in the study crying all morning."

Jackson and Ellery met eyes. "You need to show us in, Joey," Jackson said. "I think... I think we may know why."

Joey grimaced. "Jackson, I-I'm supposed to make everyone go away."

"Trust me, Joey, he's not going to hold it against you."

Joey had a wickedly handsome face with the kind of smile that bracketed his mouth in dimples. He pulled one of those out now and said, "I don't know, man. Last time my client ended up dead, and I'm pretty sure he's cursing us both out in hell!"

Jackson chuckled. "Extenuating circumstances. Notice *I'm* still alive, and I'm apparently keeping your sister in CR-Vs."

"Fine, but only because you took her haunted... erm, electrically challenged minivan. Man, nobody wanted that thing."

Ellery wasn't aware he was going to smack Jackson in the shoulder until his hand flew out.

Jackson winced and turned to give Ellery an apologetic smile.

Ellery shook his head. Haunted. Fucking haunted minivan. Dammit.

Then they were following Joey through the Brentwoods' home, and he forgot everything but the case.

It was a big place, but it wasn't "spacious." It had been built with lots of bookcases and window boxes which took away from the space. And pictures. Pictures in every corner, just like the judge's office. As they walked down the hallway, Ellery saw the two kids again, with friends and partners. He saw the young man holding hands with the young man in a Marine uniform, heard Jackson's sharp intake of breath, and knew Jackson saw it too. The young man—who had brown eyes and a hawklike nose, obviously Brentwood's son—grew thin and wan in some of the pictures. Sick? Drugs? Ellery couldn't be sure. Then he saw the plaque: In Loving Memory of Nathan George Brentwood, with a birth and death date and a picture of the young man when he'd been healthy, smiling, and full of promise.

He'd been twenty-five.

Jackson grunted, and then they both looked back along the wall to the picture of the young man and his Marine.

And Ellery heard Brentwood's voice in his head. *My kids get excited when I tell them about LGBTQ in the law community.*

Not his *son*, but his *kids*. And apparently his son-in-*law*.

Ellery's heart was pounding in his ears when Joey knocked on the door to what was apparently the study. "Judge? I'm sorry, Judge, but they're friends, and they said they needed to talk to you, and maybe they could help."

The door opened and Brentwood appeared, looking decades older than he had when Ellery had seen him not more than four nights ago, his eyes red-rimmed and a beard starting at his cheeks.

"Joey—"

"Judge Brentwood?" Ellery said softly. "I think we can help."

Brentwood rubbed his mouth with the back of his hand. "Nothing can help," he whispered. But then he stepped back and gestured them in.

Ellery remembered when Brentwood had told them about his wife and how she'd sewn his costume—how proud he'd been. The study showed touches of that talent when the rest of the house was obviously professionally decorated. Curtains in a print Ellery would put money had never been in a catalogue, for one. A homemade fleece throw and a beautiful, intricate quilt in a wedding-ring pattern on the small couch for another. Both blankets were draped over a sleeping woman, whose shoulders rose and fell every so often in a trembling motion, as though she'd only now fallen asleep, sobbing.

A part of him wondered what had happened there, but a part of him thought he might already know.

That damning plaque of the young man whose promise had not been fulfilled would haunt him.

"Would you like to speak somewhere else?" Jackson asked softly. "So she can sleep?"

He shook his head. "I… she took a sedative. Sometimes it makes her sleepwalk. I don't want to leave her alone."

Joey spoke up, and Ellery startled because he'd forgotten the man had followed them in.

"I'll sit with her, Judge. It's no worries. I've got my assistant lined up to take my next house." He gave a game smile, one that probably put the judge at ease as someone who didn't know anything but was simply being kind, when the truth was none of Jackson's friends were stupid, ever. "Rivers here shows up, and I know shit's bound to get complicated, you know?"

Brentwood gave a weak smile, and they left Joey to sprawl on the guest chair, playing a game on his phone.

Brentwood walked them back down the hall to a small sitting room off the foyer. It looked like it had started as a place to take off boots and jackets and had grown to a meeting place, with a coffee table and a couple of chairs, and he gestured for them to sit down.

"Can I get you anything?" he asked on automatic, and they both shook their heads no. Ellery wondered what he would have done if Jackson had asked for water or a soda. Would he have gone to fetch it, his eyes as vacant as he moved about the kitchen as they were now?

"What can I do for you?" he asked, sounding exhausted, as though the two of them showing up on his doorstep was the least surprising thing in his life.

"You know who the sniper is," Jackson said softly, "and we need a name."

Brentwood's face crumpled, his carefully even expression shattered by Jackson's brutal honesty.

"You can't kill him," he begged. "You… you can't kill him. I know… I-I… it's basest hypocrisy. Do you think I don't know that? But he's all I have left of my son…."

Jackson was sitting closest. He was the one who put his hand on Brentwood's shoulder.

"Why don't you start at the beginning," he said softly. "We know part of it. We know that Cartman put pressure on Boehner to clean up the streets, so Boehner came up with the scheme to bus the homeless population to the middle of nowhere. No amenities, no legal help, no communication. You didn't know about this when you were trying the case. We know that was a surprise to you Friday. How am I doing so far?"

"Frighteningly well," Judge Brentwood said shakily.

"Do you want me to keep going?" Jackson met Ellery's eyes, and Ellery nodded. Jackson had broken through the judge's reserves; it was time for Ellery to pick up the thread.

"We're pretty sure," he said slowly, "you were being pressured on another front. You were supposed to put Ezekiel Halliday back in prison, regardless of the prosecution's case, am I right?"

Brentwood nodded, looking ill. "My whole life," he whispered, "I prided myself on being fair. Hard-line? Sure. But fair. I listened to both sides. Wasn't that my job? But you're correct. Cartman was putting pressure on me the whole time. He… he never said anything outright, mind you. Just told me he could make things very difficult for my family." He shuddered. "My… my wife, she's been through so much. You… she couldn't go through any more. She's…. I took all the guns to a storage locker. I hid all the medications, including Tylenol. I-I make sure there's always a housekeeper or Joey or our daughter here with her. I don't want to leave her alone. And Cartman knew that. But… but Friday I just couldn't. Part of it was you," he said, looking frankly at Jackson. "You were in pain, but you were there. You showed up to do the right thing." He met Ellery's eyes. "And part of it was you. What you were willing to risk to do the right thing. Part of it was Halliday himself and all of the people who showed up to speak for him, including Cody Gabriel, who risked everything to come out of the cold." He let out a little sob. "But what mattered most was that I just, I couldn't do it. I just, I couldn't. I called Cartman and told him to deal with you or I'd go to the press, and you know what happened that day."

"What happened that night?" Ellery prodded.

"Well, that night is when he called Boehner in to make sure that next time I'd heel."

Brentwood's shudder was so deep, so visceral, it knotted Ellery's stomach.

"What did Boehner have on you?" he asked, steeling himself for the answer.

But Brentwood's eyes were anything but clinical. "My son," he said hoarsely. "He… he was such a good kid. So sweet. And we were so excited when he started dating Lance Corporal Adler. Myron was… he was steady and kind, and you worry so much about your children. The world can be so cruel to queer folks. You worry a little more. You want kindness in their lives, and Myron…. God. He was so kind."

"What happened?" Jackson urged.

Ellery's stomach was so tight he couldn't breathe. Jackson had to feel it: the urgency, the need to haul ass out of the house and find a killer. But Ellery forced his chest in and out and made himself wait. Brentwood *was* a decent man, and his story was so painful.

"Nathan got into a car accident," Brentwood rasped. "About three years ago. He suffered nerve damage, and God—he was in so much pain. And the hospital kept prescribing morphine, and by the time we realized he was an addict, it was… he was already buying fixes on the street." Brentwood's voice broke. "By the time Myron's deployment was over, Nathan had OD'd in his bedroom in our home. Elaine was the one to find him, and… and we were the only family Myron had. His own parents had kicked him out, and we were his birthdays and his Christmases, and we kept trying to be there for him. He and our daughter, Lindsey, were the only people holding Elaine to the planet, you understand?"

"Yes," Jackson said. He took the man's hand, and Ellery *did* hold his breath until Brentwood relaxed and squeezed it.

"And Boehner called my house Saturday morning and told me he would put Nathan's death in the papers. He'd smear our boy all over the press if we didn't fall in line with Cartman's agenda. He wanted me to reopen the Halliday case, to void it and try it again, and… and I couldn't! I couldn't! And Elaine heard me arguing and called Myron, and Myron heard the whole story and…." He broke then, sobbing into his hands. "He's all we have left of our son, and he's so lost. He's just trying to protect us, and I just want to retire so I can care for my wife…."

Jackson changed position and wrapped his arm around Brentwood's shoulders, comforting the man in a way Ellery was pretty sure he'd needed for a long time.

Everybody had their pressure point, Cartman had said smugly, and Ellery wanted to go back into the interrogation room and have Jackson push a nerve in his wrist until he passed out.

"Who's he going after next?" Jackson whispered. "We need to know, sir. We can't save him if the cops get him first."

"Cartman," Brentwood hazarded. "He heard the conversation and knew Cartman was the one applying pressure—"

"Cartman's in the police station," Jackson told him. "I think he's got another hour or two there. For the moment he's safe. Who's next on his list?"

Brentwood grimaced. "I'll be honest," he murmured, sounding detached. "I was really hoping it would be Cartman. God, all the bad things people say about lawyers...." He shuddered, and Ellery found himself oddly sympathetic.

"Judge," he said, his voice kind.

Brentwood nodded, understanding. "Goslar," he said after thinking about it. "He'll go after Goslar. It was Goslar's idea to pressure Cody Gabriel, and once Myron heard that... I could see it falling into place. I could see it clicking behind his eyes. He's needed to make someone pay for Nathan's death. He's said it a thousand times. If it wasn't going to be Cartman, it would be Goslar. These people were threatening Elaine and me and Lindsey and all the happy memories he had in his adulthood and—"

"And he couldn't take it," Jackson said softly. He pulled out his phone and unlocked it before handing it to Ellery, mouthing, "Text Fetzer."

Ellery did, making it brief. *Keep Cartman at the station under police protection. Where's Goslar right now?*

"Sir," Jackson said softly, "I'm going to be honest. I can't guarantee we'll take him down alive. Do you understand?"

Clive Brentwood covered his eyes with his hand and nodded, once.

"Do you have someone you can call? A doctor you trust? A pastor or priest?"

He shook his head despondently, and Ellery had the feeling he'd been very, very much alone these past weeks. Well, of course. He couldn't talk to his colleagues, and he'd been worried—so worried—about his partner, the one person he would have talked this over with. His daughter, his son-in-law? He wouldn't want to worry them. All it took was one moment of weakness to isolate and alienate a human who lived for the love of others.

"I want you to call an ambulance for your wife and take her in for a suicide watch. Make sure she's in the hospital when all this goes down. I have a friend I'm going to call for you. I know you're not Jewish, but he's a good guy, and he'll walk you through the mental health system and be someone to stand with you two. Don't worry. He won't even try to get you to go to temple. I haven't gone, and I've been talking to this guy since January, okay?"

Brentwood nodded, still obviously distraught.

"And I'm going to get Joey to sit with you and Elaine until the ambulance gets here and Rabbi Watson gets here, okay?"

"Okay," he whispered.

"You're going to have people to take care of you, but we've got to go."

"Okay." He wiped his eyes with his palm and looked at Jackson and then Ellery. "Thank you both," he rasped. "Do what you can." He swallowed. "Hurry. I haven't heard from Myron since he stormed out of here Saturday, determined to stop Boehner and Goslar and the other three cops. I don't know if that's going to satisfy him. If someone doesn't… doesn't call him back… he may…."

They nodded. Ellery already feared it was the truth. Lance Corporal Myron Adler may have signed his death warrant already with the first shot.

Sometimes violence was the only recourse, even for good men.

JACKSON NEEDED to make some calls—he had all the contacts—and Ellery escorted Judge Brentwood back to his study.

On their way back, a touch of the shrewd judiciary Ellery had come to respect returned.

"You know Joey, the young man in charge of our housecleaning service?"

Ellery let out a snort. "Yes. He's… well, helped us out is the wrong choice of words, but there is no right one."

For a moment, Brentwood allowed himself to be distracted. "I'm sorry?"

"Jackson and cars," Ellery said bluntly. "He destroys them. He doesn't even have to be touching them. It's…. If I believed in curses, I'd say he's cursed. His last vehicle was parked in a grocery store parking lot, and he and Henry came outside after doing business in the store and found the car damaged, and my insurance company is about to quit on us, and Jackson has had it with me buying him things. So Jackson gave the car to Joey because…." He resisted the urge to flail his hands, and Brentwood's mouth quirked up, the tiniest bit.

"Joey knows a guy," Brentwood supplied.

"I suspect Joey *is* the guy," Ellery responded darkly.

"Also likely." Brentwood nodded as they drew near the study, and he paused to let Ellery finish.

"Anyway, long story short, Joey's sister now has a recently repaired brand-new CR-V, and Jackson now owns the ugliest minivan I've ever seen in my life. Our assistant swears it's haunted."

For a moment Ellery heard strangled breathing.

"Judge Brentwood, are you all right?" Oh Lord, please don't let the man be having a heart attack. Of all things—now?

Brentwood held up a hand and took steady breaths. When he could speak, he said, "Oh, I must tell my wife that." He sobered. "When she awakes. All of the tragedy surrounding us. I think we've both forgotten how to laugh."

With that he went into the study a little straighter to sit by her side, and Ellery called Joey to him.

"Don't leave them," he said softly. "Jackson's calling Rabbi Watson over right now since they don't have a counselor of their own, and we'll stay as long as we can before he arrives. If you can get the judge to call his daughter, you may want to do that too."

Joey nodded and blew out a breath. "I knew Nate. Myron grew up in my neighborhood. They... the judge was my first big contract. This is all kinds of fucked-up, you know?"

Ellery grimaced. "I know." He felt a sudden heartsickness, a weariness, for all the things that haunted these people. Brentwood had taken it all seriously—his home, his family, his job. He'd cared about people and had done his best in all the ways that should have counted. He wasn't sure if anything would be left of Brentwood's career after this, and he didn't think the man cared right now. But he would. When everything had fallen out, he'd remember spending twenty years on the bench and hoping he was doing good in the world and having that destroyed by someone looking for a free pass. Brentwood would be treated much more harshly in the press—of that, Ellery was certain. Cartman would be forgiven; he'd spin it like he was trying to find a solution to the homeless problem, when the truth was he'd been trying to fix the way the homeless looked on his record.

None of it was fair, and when that was a child's cry or an argument in a coffee shop, it meant one thing, but right here, when a good man was holding on to the people he loved for dear life, it was so much more painful, so much more dire, and Ellery could only hope he and Jackson hadn't made it worse.

Into the Breach

RABBI WATSON was—lucky them—less than ten minutes away, and Jackson spent that time on the phone.

"Adele?"

"Waiting on your call," she said. "Cartman's lawyer filed the paperwork, and he's trying to get out of here. He thinks the police-protection thing is bullshit, and he's probably filling out mine and Jimmy's termination papers as we speak."

"I don't think he's going to be employed that long," Jackson told her grimly. "Put him on."

"What?" She sounded genuinely shocked.

"I said put him on," Jackson told her. "And start finding out where Goslar is right now. Is he on shift?"

She grunted. "They have roll call at eleven. A lot of cops do their PT the hour before they come in."

"Find out where he's at. We know who our sniper is, and we know he's after Cartman, and if he can't get to Cartman, he'll take out Goslar next. He's had three days to learn everybody's habits, Adele, and he's a Marine."

She sucked in a breath. "Well, that's higher than my paygrade. Got a name? Any pictures?"

"I do, but...." Jackson let out a curse. "I don't want a big deal manhunt here. Do you understand? For one thing, if you send the entire police force against him and he's got the high ground—"

"We're going to end up with a lot of dead cops," she said, sounding desperately unhappy.

"Yahtzee. And for another, he's got one murder under his belt, but he's not a serial killer. He's not a sociopath. He's *heartbroken*. Cartman, Boehner, and Goslar were blackmailing Brentwood about spreading his dead son's drug habit all over the press. Our sniper was his boyfriend, and he thinks he's protecting what's left of his family. Do you understand?"

"Oh Lord," she muttered. "Jackson...."

"I know I can't save everyone!" He was shouting, and he pulled his voice back under his control. "I know that. But I can save the cops who would go after him blind. And maybe if I can save them, and if I can save the scumbags he wants to kill, I can save him."

She let out a breath. "What's your plan?"

"First I need to know where Goslar is," he said. "Then we'll see."

"A sniper in the city—"

Jackson sucked in a breath. "Do you think I don't know?" he asked, and his bones ached with memory. "I lost a year of my life, Adele. A year. I can't go inside a hospital anymore. I just… a *year*. I know what a sniper can do. I know the damage his bullet can do. And I know a sniper in a crowded area is like a stealth freight train with the dead man's name on the bullet. But who's going to negotiate with him? Your lieu, who's stupid, corrupt, and green? Cartman, who's the reason he snapped? Brentwood's a mess, and his wife is suicidal. We've got an ambulance on the way to take her to the hospital because whether this ends well or not, the two of them are exhausted. If we go in quiet, maybe everybody doesn't have to die."

He heard her let out a breath and realized what he was asking.

"I mean, Henry and I can do it. Maybe Christie and de Souza. You and Jimmy have done plenty, Adele. I'm sorry, I was just—"

"Just expecting people to be their best selves," she said, her voice dry. "I hear you. You talk to Cartman. I'll have Jimmy try to get hold of Christie."

The next voice he heard on the line was Cartman's. "Give me one good reason I shouldn't—"

"Because I'll find the dirt, Cartman," Jackson told him, his voice low and venomous. "You stay there. You wait until we get this situation under control. You let us step in and save your worthless, gutless, brainless ass, and I'll let the DOJ have you and you can consider yourself off easy."

"Don't you threaten me—"

"One word to the press," Jackson continued as though he hadn't spoken. "One attempt to try to spin this on Brentwood, on Boehner, even on Goslar, God rot his soul, or on Ellery, or anyone I know, and I will find the dirt. I'll find *all* the dirt. Did you grope a secretary's ass ten years ago? I'll have it on the front page. What porn do you like, Cartman? What do you whack off to at night? Which waiters do you stiff? Who do you vote for? Who shows up at your family barbecues that you wish wouldn't? What's your favorite TV show? Who in your political party has deemed it inappropriate? Have you looked at any children lately? How long? Why? What was the last dog you kicked? You think you know how to put pressure on people? You think you know how to make them look bad? That's what I *do*, you sonuvabitch. There is no skeleton in your closet that I won't find, and there's *nowhere* you can hide the bodies that I won't dig them up. It took me one night—one night—to blow a hole in your prosecution's case. Give me a week, and if I can't find enough to throw you in a supermax, you can *bet* I'll find enough to crucify you in the press, on social media, hell—you'll have an entire TikTok channel devoted to what a puppy-eating bastard you are. You'll be the most hated man in the state, I guarantee it."

"What do I have to do?" Cartman asked, seething, if Jackson knew his douchebags.

"Sit down, sweetheart, and shut the fuck up. Like I said, the DOJ will find plenty, but unless you want me to help them, you will sit down, shut up, and let us work today. You don't know how to do this fuckin' job—"

"And you do? I have a law degree, for Christ's sake—"

"So does Ellery. And he's got me. So you sit down, shut up, and let us get the sniper out of the city. If I get wind of one cop tipped off, one order given on your behalf, one bad decision that you personally had a hand in, I will smear your cockcheese all over the internet and the whole world will know how bad it smells."

Cartman made a sound—a helpless sound—and Jackson had to hope that was enough.

"Give the phone back to Adele," he snarled.

"Sac City," she said. "Engall Goslar runs the track there. Likes to think he's an athlete. He should be there for another half an hour."

Fuck. A school on a weekday. "Call the administration. Have them clear the community college away from the track. And I take it back, send in units to help clear the school quietly and without panic. Call it a drill. Have them leave on the side away from the track. I know that campus. You can evacuate ninety-eight percent of it out of the north and east entrances, leaving the track and stadium alone."

She grunted. "Fair enough. I'll have units there in ten—no lights, no sirens unless there's shots fired."

"We'll be there in fifteen," he said. "You tag Christie?"

"Done. He'll meet us there."

"Good. Update him on the sitch and the strategy for me. Ellery and I are on our way as soon as we know the judge is okay to be left alone. And don't forget to keep an eye out for Henry. Don't want him shot."

"I'm sure he hears that a *lot*. Be safe," she added.

"You too. Out."

And with that he hung up. He dialed Crystal, and while he was waiting for her to pick up, he texted Henry. It usually took her a minute to pick up, and Henry had responded before he heard her voice.

I'll be there. Should we lock down the school?

In progress. Christie, de Souza, Fetzer, and Hardison are the only ones who should be in the stadium.

Word. Do you want me to get in position?

Jackson slow-blinked and then did it again. Henry meant should *he* get in position to take the sniper out. It hit him what a terrible responsibility he'd laid on the shoulders of all his friends in telling Cartman to sit in the back seat.

Get equipment and permission from Christie and de Souza, he texted. *We should be on site before you go.*

Roger that. There was a pause, and Jackson was about to round up Ellery when his phone buzzed again. *Don't be afraid to use me, Jackson. I was good at this. Not Burton good, but good.*

Nobody's Burton good, he texted, referring to their friend in covert ops who had helped them out on many occasions. *Be safe, padawan.*

Always, sensei. Out.

And just then, his phone rang.

"Jackson? You have your guy already, don't you?"

"Yes, we do, sweetheart. But I appreciate your help. It was the friend of a friend sort of thing—there was no way for you to know who to research."

"I understand, but what did you want?"

He let his eyes narrow and his voice go grim. "I want the dirty on someone, sweetheart. Trey Cartman, recently elected district attorney. He's hurt a *lot* of people, and I need to make sure he's not in a position to hurt any of them ever again."

She sucked in a breath and then let it out slowly. "Oh, so many dirty pockets involved," she said softly, and he had no doubt she'd just gotten a hit or saw a vision or felt a shiver. Something, somewhere, was telling her where to look. "Where do you want me to send the information?"

"Arizona Brooks. She's got a contact at the press who can do what we can't with it. Either way, I don't want him to get away with a damned thing."

"I got it." She paused, and he was about to sign off when she said, "Be safe, Jackson. I can feel the danger—in your voice, in your breaths. Keep yourself safe. Keep Ellery safe. You can only do so much."

"I know," he said, but he hated it. "Thanks, honey. I'll call you later."

And there was a knock at the door.

Jackson got there first and welcomed Rabbi Watson in. An ordinary man with a full brown beard who only wore his yarmulke on the sabbath, Rabbi Watson had become Jackson's friend—and counselor—by complete accident. Jackson hated hospitals, didn't really trust shrinks, and resisted anything resembling "treatment" if he could at all avoid it. But the rabbi was low-key, and he liked to laugh, and he arrived late to his own services because he still wasn't comfortable talking in crowds.

And all he ever wanted was to make the people he was talking to feel better. Jackson understood now that rabbis had specialties—some specialized in scripture and some in politics. He'd always gotten the feeling that the reason Ephraim Watson had become a rabbi was because he liked people and wanted to help them. The end. No ambition, no flaming political sword. Just a community leader who found his community in his faith. It wasn't Jackson's faith, but he respected the hell out of the man's commitment and regarded him as a friend.

"There's an ambulance on the way to take the judge's wife to treatment," Jackson said quietly, leading the rabbi into the hallway without preamble. "Ellery and I have to go. Its urgent, and the judge may get more bad news. The family needs someone—an advocate, a counselor, and—"

"And you have other things to do."

Jackson opened the door, gesturing him in and nodding Ellery out.

At the same time, the judge and the rabbi looked up at them and said, "Be safe."

Ellery closed the door softly with a wave, and Jackson thought that somewhere in there was a joke: They had a judge, a rabbi, a lawyer, and a street rat. All they needed was a punchline.

"Everybody in place?" Ellery asked, pulling Jackson back from a semihysterical thought train.

"Except us," he muttered. "C'mon, Sac City college, the stadium."

"Oh dear Lord," Ellery muttered, and together they rushed out into the rainy October day. "It's going to be a madhouse."

"No," Jackson told him. "Go around the back way, like you're going to a football game. I've got all the police presence clearing out the school at the other entrances. By the time we get there, Christie, de Souza, Hardison, and Fetzer should be there to let us in."

Ellery stopped in his tracks as Jackson swung around the Lexus to open the door. "How in the hell did you manage that?"

"Manage what?" Jackson asked blandly.

"Manage to keep the whole thing from being a 'three-ring cops in a tank, SWAT team firing at innocent civilian' circus?"

Jackson thought about it and shrugged. "A few favors, a little blackmail, some threats—whatever, Ellery, come *on*! Henry's offering to put on a vest and go sniper on our sniper, and I've got to say, that scares the shit out me, so can we get going?"

"Yeah, sure," Ellery murmured, but he sounded a little lost. That was okay, though. When he got behind the wheel, he drove like a bat out of hell.

Jackson stayed wisely silent for most of the trip, keeping up by texts. He gave Ellery terse directions from Christie on the way to get in without running into a police blockade and answered a couple of "The actual fuck is Henry doing here?" texts by telling Christie and Fetzer to look up his service record if they didn't believe Jackson and to ignore the dishonorable discharge. Henry was honorable to a fault.

And in the middle of that, he got a text from K-Ski, asking Jackson what in the cold blue hell was happening at Sac City.

He had to pick up the phone for that one. "Stay the hell away from there," he said tersely.

"Billy's there. He's got class today!" Sean responded. "Dammit, Jackson—"

"Well, keep him away from the football stadium!" Jackson snapped. "Text him, whatever. Tell him to let the cops guide him out and—"

"And I'll be in the football stadium parking lot where Christie just texted me from," Sean snapped. "You couldn't have told me?"

"*You're on leave!*" Jackson shouted. "Isn't there some sort of clause about you not being involved?"

"Yeah, asshole. It's on the same paperwork that says *you're* a civilian, and last time I checked, *you're on leave too*!"

And like that, the adrenaline faded enough for Jackson's back to seize in a blaze of fire. "Excuse me," he rasped with dignity. "I need to take an ibuprofen."

"I'll see you in the stadium," Kryzynski said with the same dignity. "I'll have Billy meet us there."

"Fine. Whatever. Invite the whole damned world there. See if I care. It's only half a dozen people right now, hinging their lives on whatever the hell I'm saying. What's two goddamned more?"

He wasn't even aware that was going to come out of his mouth until he said it, but then he heard Sean's soft, bitter laughter and realized it had slipped out.

"Better you than Cartman or Goslar himself, Rivers. You made a good call. An all-out assault would be a disaster. A couple of people and a well-placed gun? That's the right approach. Don't get all soft and squishy on me now."

"Ew."

He heard Sean's cringe from the other end of the line.

"Yeah, I'm sorry about that."

"Fuck off. We're almost there."

"Me too."

And sure enough, as Ellery rounded the corner for the decently sized stadium, he saw the blue Dodge Charger fall in line behind them.

As he fumbled for an ibuprofen, he could only pray Sean was right and he hadn't sent them all into a meat grinder.

When Ellery pulled up to Fetzer and Hardison's unit and Christie and de Souza's unmarked, they both noted that Jennifer the minivan was there, but Henry wasn't.

"Your boy's already suited up and heading up the back way," Fetzer told them. "We had a coach give us the keys before we evacced his ass out of there. I guess Henry knows the campus—there's a little-used corridor and stairwell up to the top level of the stadium and the announcer's box."

Jackson gasped. "And he's alone?"

"And he will be," Adele said patiently, "if you keep talking our ear off." She and Hardison both had on tactical gear, and so did Christie and de Souza. They both had their weapons at the ready, and Jackson caught a clue.

"I know this campus too," he said as Sean limped up, breathing heavily. "I'm going to go down to the track through the athletes' entrance and try to find Goslar. Has anybody alerted him?"

The cops all wrinkled their noses at each other.

"Alerting Goslar is alerting the whole rest of the police force we're trying to avoid," Christie said. "You made the right call here, Jackson, but telling Goslar would fuck it all up."

Jackson swallowed. "I'll talk to him in person," he said. "You guys go back up Henry so he doesn't end up dead. Ellery, stay here and keep Sean out of trouble. I'll be right back with Goslar."

K-Ski was struggling to get out of the car as he spoke, and while Ellery's attention was diverted that way, Jackson took off at a jog, ignoring the pain in his back that threatened to turn his vision white and hoping he could make it to the track before Ellery caught on to what he'd actually volunteered to do.

A Different Proposal

ELLERY DIDN'T like to think of himself as a stupid man, but he'd gotten to Sean Kryzynski's side before it hit him.

He spun around on his heels to see Jackson disappear around the corner of the stadium and said, "He wants me to do what?"

Kryzynski took a deep breath and said, "I think he wants you to stay out of danger while he goes and gets between a sniper and his target."

Ellery turned wide eyes to Kryzynski and gaped. "He... he... what are you doing here anyway?"

"Billy's taking classes today," Kryzynski said, face pinched. "I texted him to follow the other students out and told him I'd be waiting for him here. I-I don't know how to worry about him, you know?"

Ellery nodded. "I know," he said, watching as Fetzer, Hardison, Christie, and de Souza disappeared into an exit at the opposite end of the stadium from the end Jackson had just gone toward. He studied the mental schematic of everybody's location, and he found he couldn't catch his breath either.

"He... he...." A kaleidoscope of images hit him: Jackson, the first time they'd made love, fierce, angry, determined to only have sex and stunned when Ellery wouldn't allow that to happen. Jackson, a year ago, feverish and despondent, sleeping off a night of a thousand horrors in their bed while planning to leave Ellery to simply curl up in a ball and die. Jackson, making tentative strides with Ellery's family, every interaction bonding him closer to Ellery's mother and father, making him their own. Jackson at Christmas, giving him shooting lessons so he could protect himself. Jackson, doing everything from baring his soul to help other people to saving Ellery from trained assassins to... oh God. Cuddling his mannerless street cat and promising him ear rubs while calling him vile names.

Jackson, running off to offer himself as bait because he didn't want anybody to die.

"Ellery?" Kryzynski said gently.

"Yes?"

"Go after him."

Ellery was charging down the blacktop—his hard-soled leather shoes sliding on sand or gravel over the pavement, his trench coat flapping behind him—before he could even question the logic.

A sniper had almost taken Jackson away from him before they'd even met. He'd gone on a basic fact-finding mission not five days earlier and had almost been gutted by a dirty cop with an illegal knife. Ellery wasn't going to give fate yet another chance to take him away, unseen and unsung, while the rest of the world watched but couldn't help.

He made it to where he'd seen Jackson disappear and took a few more steps before he found the thruway. It was a back entrance, he thought, for employees or athletes—hard to spot, easy to guard, easy to give private pass holders a way in. In off-hours, when the facility was open to the school and public use, it would make a handy little shortcut, and Ellery ventured through the darkness now, heading for the light on the other side.

JACKSON CAME out of the tunnel and stood in the entrance, scanning the track for a moment to see if Goslar was even there. He spotted the man sitting on one of the benches in front of the bleachers, where the football players would sit during the game. Goslar wore a SAPD sweatshirt with the arms and neck torn off, and a pair of running shorts, both items soaked with sweat as he shoved his cleats into a bag and put on regular tennis shoes.

Jackson ran up to him, putting his body between Goslar and the announcer's box on the other side of the track.

Goslar scowled at him with unfriendly eyes, and Jackson contemplated throwing himself on the ground and giving Myron Adler a clean shot, but he couldn't.

He just couldn't.

"The fuck do you want?" Goslar snarled, and Jackson grimly kept his temper.

"I'm here to save you from the same sniper who took out Boehner," Jackson said, keeping his voice low and pleasant. He was unprepared for Goslar to stand up, all six feet five inches of him, and shove rudely past Jackson on his way toward the opposite end of the field.

"Bullshit," he snapped. "You people and your tricks. It's all about getting me to confess, isn't it! Well, you'll have to work a lot harder than that!"

"I don't have to work hard at all!" Jackson retorted, his temper slipping. "We've got Cartman in custody. How long before he snaps! How long before we find dirt on him, put pressure on him, and the whole story hits the shit-covered fan?"

Goslar whirled on him, taking ground-eating strides until they were chest to chest. "I was following orders, you little puke—"

"Were you following orders when you were about to decapitate Cody Gabriel?" Jackson shouted back. "Were you following orders when you kicked an old man who just wanted his fucking dog? You're a sadistic bastard, and you've earned everything coming to you, and I'm still here trying to save your fucking ass because *somebody's* got to do the right thing, and it's certainly not you!"

"Oh, who gives a shit about the right thing!" Goslar kept advancing on him, and Jackson kept retreating, hopefully back toward the tunnel. If he could *lure* Goslar there with his anger, they could get one variable out of the way while Henry took out Myron Adler. "You don't care about that. All you ever cared about was winning the case! We put our *lives* on the line every fucking day, and what thanks do we get? Cody Gabriel was a trainwreck—"

"Cody Gabriel was your *brother*!" Jackson shouted, his voice breaking. "You talk about cops putting their lives on the line. He was your *brother*! And you blackmailed him and you pushed him and you pushed him too far—"

"He was weak!"

"He was *human*! And you exploited that, and you almost broke him. Does that make you proud, Goslar? You almost broke him? Because breaking people comes back to bite you—and it's about to now—*oolf*!"

Jackson's body hit the hardpan of the track, pressed down by a lean, tightly muscled weight, just as the crack of the shot hit his ears.

ELLERY'S BREATH labored in his chest, and Jackson let out a yelp underneath him as they crashed to the ground. Next to them, in front of the bleachers, the LED screen that lined the bottom front of the seats exploded into a fractured sizzle as the bullet hit home.

He'd known what Jackson was doing, of course, trying to lure Goslar back to the tunnel, but it was taking too long, and as Ellery watched, he realized that every step he took back was followed by a tiny red dot, flickering from Goslar's side to Jackson's, from Goslar's to Jackson's....

And Ellery couldn't take that fucking chance.

With a clumsy leap and a tackle that would have been the laughingstock of every Pop Warner football team in the country, he shoved Jackson to the ground, flailing on top of him as he lost his balance.

And apparently Adler had taken his shot at the same time.

"Ellery, get off me!" Jackson begged, his voice strained.

Oh shit. "Your back?" Ellery asked solicitously, but he wasn't moving.

"You! You are in the line of fire. Jesus, baby, get up and get to safety!"

"No," Ellery said, eyes closed. "He was going to hit you just to get you out of the way. I could see the way the target moved. Couldn't you see the target?"

Jackson's little huff of breath told Ellery he hadn't.

"Baby, we've got to get up so we can get to safety," he rasped, as Goslar, who had been studying the destroyed LED panel, turned around and peered at the opposite end of the stadium.

"Is somebody *shooting* at us?"

They both saw the red dot appear on his chest, and Ellery felt Jackson's entire body labor for enough air to be heard.

"*Adler!*" he called. "Adler, don't!"

The red dot stayed trained on Goslar's chest, but Adler didn't fire.

"Who the fuck is Adler?" Goslar asked, obviously not catching humility *or* a clue.

"A Marine sniper you pissed off," Ellery hissed. "Now shut up and let him work!"

"Adler!" Jackson called again, and Ellery put some of his weight on his knees and elbows on the track so Jackson could breathe, but he didn't roll off. No. He'd seen the tiny dot of the laser sight, and his heart had stopped. All those images of Jackson had whirled faster and faster to this point in time, in which Ellery absolutely would not sacrifice him under any circumstances. But Jackson still needed to work.

"C'mon, man!" Jackson continued, obviously aware of the absurdity of conducting negotiations from the flat of his back, but Ellery couldn't help that. "Just don't! No more shooting! No more death! We've got people on you now. You gave away your position. You can still make it out of here alive!"

"For what?" came the fractured voice, and Ellery turned his head along with Jackson, both of them searching the area round the announcer's box where the first shot had obviously come from. "What do I have to live for?" Adler's voice broke again. "He's gone. He's gone, and that's just the way it is, man. But I can do this for him."

"But this isn't what he wants!" Jackson cried. "His mother needs you, Myron. She needs you alive. She needs you to keep Nathan alive for her. His father needs you to keep *her* alive. They love you, man. You're their hope!"

There was a heavy silence, and Jackson looked up into Ellery's face.

"Baby, get up," he begged, all his air gone and his voice a bare whisper, and Ellery saw his eyes had grown red-rimmed. "I'm not sure if this is going to work. I need you to get to safety."

"No," Ellery returned. He bit his lip. "Just no. Not again. Just no."

"You make it sound easy!" Adler cried.

"Does this look easy?" Jackson retorted, some of his frustration coming out in his voice. "Can you *see* this? He won't get up! He won't go to safety! He doesn't want me hurt anymore, and all I want is for him to be okay! Do you think I don't know how you feel?" He labored for another breath, but Ellery wasn't crushing him anymore. Ellery realized his stomach was clenched tight against his own sobs. "Do you think I don't worry every day that this person who makes my life worth living won't be taken away? His mother called me this morning. His *mother*. And all she wanted was to make sure I was okay. And if anything"— his voice dropped for Ellery's ears only—"oh God, baby, get up. I'm begging you"—-then rose again—"if anything happened to him, do you think I'd want to live?"

Adler's voice drifted across the field to them, grief-stricken, dreamy. Only the damning red dot, unmovable on Goslar's chest, gave any indication he was still ready to follow through.

"I don't want to live."

"You have to!" Jackson cried. "You have to! Because Nathan's parents love you. And you're all that's left of their son. Don't give up on them. Nathan's dad was trying to protect you. Don't repay him like this!"

"They were going to spread it in the papers," Adler said, openly sobbing. "My beautiful, beautiful boy, and they were going to make him look like trash. *They're* trash. *They're* the ones who should be treated like trash—"

"And we're going to do that!" Jackson called. "Don't you want to live to see it? Do you think this asshole is strong enough for prison? Don't you want to hear how he breaks? Don't you want to watch Cartman get everything taken away? You'll have to do jail time, but you can do it with honor. Do you think these assholes have honor? Do you think they'll have Nathan's parents writing them? Keeping them human? Please, Myron. Please. I'm begging you. Put the gun down." He cupped Ellery's cheeks then, his palms sliding in Ellery's tears. "Please, baby," he whispered. "Please."

There was a heartbeat of silence. Then another.

The telltale dot on Goslar's chest disappeared.

Henry's voice sailed across the stadium. "We've got him, Jackson. It's all clear."

Ellery collapsed against Jackson again, all the strength gone from his limbs, just as Goslar took off for the tunnel.

As Ellery turned his head and scrambled awkwardly to his knees and then to his feet, he saw Billy, standing right in front of Sean Kryzynski, pop Goslar hard in the jaw before Goslar had a chance to react.

Goslar stumbled back, his knees watery, and then he fell on his ass.

Sean got behind him and pulled him to his feet, only a little out of breath as he cuffed the man, reciting his rights. The charge was obstruction of justice, and while Ellery thought even a shitty defense attorney would get that dropped, it was as good a reason as any to put Goslar under lock and key until Cartman folded.

He'd be a lot easier to track down if they had him in jail already.

Ellery realized he'd been on his feet for quite some time, and Jackson was still flat on his back, eyes squeezed shut in apparent pain.

"Jackson? Are you okay?"

Jackson's voice, when it came back, was thin with agony. "Ellery, I think I popped all my stitches."

Ellery sucked in a horrified breath and offered his hand to help Jackson up. Billy was at Jackson's other side in a second, taking as much of his upper body weight as possible as Jackson pushed heavily to his feet.

The back of his hooded sweatshirt was a mess, and Ellery let out a groan.

"Oh my God, I'm so sorry. Jackson, I'm so sorry. I… I saw the laser sight, and I just couldn't let you get shot. Not again. I just couldn't—"

Jackson took Ellery's cheeks in his hands and pulled him in for a hard, almost desperate, hot kiss.

Ellery stood stiffly for a moment before melting into the touch, responding to the kiss, tasting the brine on Jackson's lips and on his own. Oh God. For a moment he'd seen it all so clearly—Jackson, dead on the field, his body torn apart by a sniper's bullet, death coming to reclaim him in one vicious punch, recompense for all the times Jackson had cheated the specter at the last gasp.

Ellery would rather die.

Jackson's mouth over his told him they were both alive. They'd both survived. They had days together. They had holidays and vacations together, and gentle moments in the sun.

They had so much work to do.

So much lay before them. And all of it, all of it, was possible because Jackson's mouth was hot on his, demanding every response he could give.

When Ellery was limp and ready, Jackson pulled back from the kiss and met his eyes, his own bright with tears.

"Don't ever do that again," he rasped.

"No promises," Ellery told him. "Don't ever leave me behind again."

Jackson grimaced. "No promises."

Ellery felt a watery smile twist his lips. "Well, we're at an impass—"

"Marry me."

Ellery's eyes grew wide, and for a moment he had no words. "Now?" he finally managed.

Jackson's mouth thinned in exasperation. "Marry me later. *Promise* me now, since it's apparently the only promise we can make."

"Yes," Ellery said, wiping his eyes with his palms. "Yes. Yes, of course I'll marry you. Now or later. Or whenever. I promise. I promise we'll—"

"Later," Billy said, his mostly impassive face actually sporting a droll expression. "Mr. Cramer, he's bleeding like a stuck pig. You guys go ahead and set the date, but do it at the hospital, okay?"

Ellery leaned his forehead against Jackson's. "Of course," he whispered. "You ready?"

"Not even a little," Jackson replied, mouth curved into a rueful smile. "Let's get it done."

THE HOSPITAL sentenced him to two days incarceration under the guise of being "under observation." Ignoring his protests, they sedated him heavily to help control his blood pressure and anxiety, and because the doctor who'd attended him Thursday night proclaimed he was no longer to be trusted with important things, such as his own health.

"But I could just go back home," Jackson protested, even as Nurse Dave was prepping his morphine shot. "I don't want to lose two days of my life!"

Dave scowled at him, clearly out of patience. "Look, man, you're here because you obviously can't rest at home, so here we are. We're keeping you sedated until this shit has time to heal, and then we're changing that number on that sign from ninety-seven to zero, and we're all mad about that."

Jackson blinked and actually looked at the sign, which was written in Sharpie on printer paper and tacked to the examining room wall. It said, "Days since Rivers was last admitted for care: 97." The number was on a Post-it, which had obviously been replaced every day since Jackson's heart surgery.

"Wow," Jackson said, a little stunned. "You, uh, keep tabs on that?"

"Yes, we do," Dave replied coldly. "And we were super excited too. We almost had you up to a hundred. That would have been a banner fucking day for us here. I mean, sure, you've come in for cuts and scrapes and shit—but no overnights." He glared. "Until now."

Jackson smiled apologetically, grateful for the layers of anesthetic they'd smoothed on his back before they'd restitched the entire thing. "I swear to God, Ellery tackled me. I was just standing, having a conversation with a guy, and Ellery jumped on top of me. Wasn't even my fault."

The loud snort from where Ellery sat at the end of the treatment cot told Jackson his understatement wasn't appreciated.

"There was a gunman *aiming for him*," Ellery said, his voice assuming that persnickety tone that Jackson had always found irritating—and adorable. "It was either tackle him or let him get *shot*!"

Dave paused and stared at Ellery. "Well done. I don't want to have to piece together *that* mess again." He turned back to Jackson. "No, I blame this entirely on you. You have got to get your shit together, man. We can't keep doing his!"

Jackson sighed. "I'm doing my best," he said honestly. "Living clean, calling in my backup…. I mean, I wasn't alone out there today, right?"

Dave harrumphed and disinfected the inside of Jackson's elbow to administer the sedative. Jackson knew that ordinarily they would have checked him in, had him cleaned up, gotten him on the hospital bed, and inserted an IV for this, but he was already shaking with anxiety. Dammit.

"But if you put me under and make me stay here," he said a little desperately as Dave picked up the needle from the tray, "I'll miss the two days of Ellery telling everybody I proposed! And we're getting married. Don't you think I want to be conscious for…?" Dave injected him without mercy, and the delicious wave of ennui that accompanied the morphine began to seep in through his bloodstream. "Goddammit. That."

"Married!" Dave said, as though Jackson hadn't just taken the stars-and-moon express. "Are you inviting Alex and me to the wedding?" He helped Jackson into a johnny, now that all of the tending to his back was over and the sedation had begun. Jackson assumed his pants would be removed when they got to the room.

"'Course," Jackson murmured. "You guys are my people. Ya hear that, Ellery? I've got people!"

Ellery snorted, but Jackson felt his hand, gentle on his calf through his jeans, as Ellery said, "You've always had people. You deserve people. Don't worry. Everyone's going to be there."

"It'll be in the sunlight," Jackson mumbled. "In the spring."

"In Capitol Park," Ellery told him. "You can have the rabbi officiate."

"That'd be nice," Jackson agreed. "Flowers. I like flowers. Dave, do you know Ellery buys flowers sometimes? Just to have on the table. Isn't that amazing?"

"It's really special, Jackson," Dave said, finishing cleanup and disposal. "Do you ever buy him some?"

Jackson grunted as Dave helped him off the table and into the wheelchair. "Not enough," he said, as Ellery said, "All the time."

Dave laughed. "Perfect balance, I can tell."

"Flowers at our wedding," Jackson mumbled dreamily, wondering exactly how much morphine Dave had been authorized to give him. "Ellery, promise me...."

"That's a promise I can keep," Ellery said softly, kissing his temple.

The next two days were uncomfortable and fraught with dreams, but Jackson clung to that kiss on the temple, the dream of flowers in the springtime, and Ellery smiling at him shyly while dressed nattily in his best suit, to get him through.

It was daylight at the end of the tunnel. A long, lifetime of a tunnel, into the best, most glorious day.

TWO DAYS after Jackson had been admitted, Ellery was pacing the floor of the kitchen, looking at his watch. Jackson was supposed to have been released from the hospital that afternoon, and Henry had been dispatched to go get him. That had been hours ago, and they were *late*, goddammit. So late.

Ellery had been in court that day and had given deposition after deposition about the events leading up to Myron Adler's arrest. The DOJ had finally stuck their nose into things when Arizona Brooks had sent them file upon file that suggested Trey Cartman had coerced and blackmailed law enforcement, judiciary officials, and gas-station clerks in his meteoric rise to the top. He was under investigation for everything from extortion to hit-and-run, and Ellery would be testifying in front of the investigative committee for another two days at least. Jackson would be at the courthouse for most of next week, Ellery assumed, which would serve him right for being late tonight!

Myron Adler had pled guilty to one count of murder with extenuating circumstances and had been given ten years in Leavenworth, since he was still enlisted. He'd broken down, apparently, as Henry and the others had processed him, and the story had been so pathetic—and Trey Cartman so monstrous—that Ellery would have intervened to have the case tried if Arizona had offered anything harsher. Cartman and Boehner had not only threatened to smear the circumstances of Nathan Brentwood's death across all media fronts but also Elaine Brentwood's subsequent emotional breakdown and the heartrending lengths Clive

Brentwood had gone to in order to shelter his daughter and wife from any of the brutalities of public exposure. They'd had pictures Cartman had illegally requisitioned from the coroner's files that they'd threatened to release, of Nathan Brentwood dead with a needle in his arm, and privileged files on Elaine's shaky mental health that they'd been ready to send to gossip rags. None of it legitimate, all of it ghoulish and in the worst possible taste.

A taped recording of Clive Brentwood in tears, pleading with one of the most vitriolic conservative news hosts in the country to keep his wife's name out of his mouth when he went live in a segment to be aired the following week had been Adler's trigger. He'd overheard the conversation firsthand, and hearing Cartman's threat to air the tape on social media had been too much to bear.

The fact that Cartman and Boehner had both been in positions of power that they'd abused to do this had helped keep Adler from doing life without parole.

Goslar and McMurphy had been arrested. Apparently Boehner had kept records on "his boys," and the ones on Goslar and McMurphy implicated them heavily, particularly for the assault on Jackson and Cody Gabriel. As a father confessor, Boehner had been ready to turn around and tell the next "God" up the line who was liable for doing bad things. The fact that Goslar and McMurphy had been brought down by the words of the man who had been supposed to be protecting them but who had enabled their sadism instead had seemed particularly delicious, in an irony-as-breakfast sort of way.

Ellery had been afraid that the displaced indigent population would get lost in all of this political intrigue—he'd mentioned his concerns multiple times during his deposition. He'd been reassured that morning when the governor had asked the legislature for emergency funds to house the people who'd been shipped upstate, as well as for an investigation to discover if there were any other "dumping grounds" for people who had been forcibly moved.

God, it was nice when there was another grown-up in the room. Ellery hadn't even wanted to vote for the guy, but he'd been the closest thing to progressive on the ballot. Now Ellery wanted to tearfully bow at his feet.

And Jackson had gotten a text from Cody Gabriel that morning. That day marked a week from the time Jackson had sat at Gabriel's side, pulling him from despair to hope, saving his life. He'd confessed to Jackson that rehab was a bitch, but remembering that he was warm, he was fed, he had people watching out for him—that helped. So had Poppy; one of the guys from the flophouse had brought the little dog by now that Gabriel was no longer being sedated.

And Jackson's stitches were healing nicely—the two days' sedation and immobilization had helped. This stay in the hospital had felt different to Ellery. Jackson hadn't fought it quite so much. It was like the feral part of him, the part that had been so afraid to trust in other people, had learned how to curl up and sleep when it needed to.

He'd learned how to heal, to fight another day.

And Ellery wanted him home. Halloween was in two days, and the decorations had arrived in the mail the day before. Ellery had gotten home from visiting Jackson in the hospital and found them on the doorstep and then put them up, feeling some of Jackson's joy seep into his bones as he did so. Halloween. Who knew it could be so much fun to decorate? He'd stopped by the store on his way home and bought ten pounds of candy, hoping the flickering pumpkin faces and multicolored lights would attract trick-or-treaters on Saturday night and not thrown eggs.

Chicken-and-rice soup simmered in the cooker, and the cats were on the back of the couch, tails and whiskers twitching on alert. They were—all of them—waiting for the one person to return who made the house a home.

As if on cue, Billy Bob leapt fluidly off the couch and hissed, and Lucifer rose to his three feet and fell off the long way, leaving claw marks on the leather back of the couch as he scrabbled for purchase. He landed with a squawk on his back and went tear-assing for the bedroom, where both cats preferred to be when there was company.

Lucifer hit the doorjamb on his way through, spit at it, and finally found his way into the room—probably to jump on the bed and complain about the unfairness of things to his big brother.

Well, cats weren't always graceful.

Two minutes later, the front door opened, and Henry, arms laden with stuff, gestured Jackson into the house.

Jackson smiled tiredly, looking decidedly *not* like a man who had come straight home from the hospital and napped.

"Sorry we're late," he said softly, moving in to kiss Ellery on the cheek. His eyes were doing a wicked little sparkle dance, indicating he knew Ellery was waiting for Henry to leave before he chewed him out. "We stopped for a few things."

"One minute," Henry said, running around the kitchen and dining room. There was a rustle of paper and packages, and Ellery tried to look over Jackson's shoulder to see what he was doing.

"Ignore me," Henry called. "Pretend I'm invisible. No Henry here."

"Did you hear that?" Jackson said wryly. "Henry isn't here."

Ellery lost his resolve to be irritated and chuckled, seeing where the crinkle of cellophane came from. "Invisible Henry is putting flowers on the table. They're lovely."

Jackson grinned. "Right? See? I may have been high, but I remember my responsibilities."

Ellery stepped into his warmth and let Jackson wrap his arms around him. With the idea that Henry wasn't there, he closed his eyes and buried his face in Jackson's neck. "You've never forgotten. So should I look at what else isn't there, or should I just close my eyes and be glad you're home?"

"The second one," Jackson murmured, breathing in at his neck like he was filling his lungs with fresh air. "A lot of this was his idea—it's sort of a gift."

"Mm." Ellery nodded, his anxiety about a late Jackson completely overridden by the joy of a *here* Jackson. Here was always better. "That's sweet. Can I open my eyes now?"

"One more minute!" Henry said anxiously. "Ooh, soup. Can I have some of that?"

It was on the tip of Ellery's tongue to say, "It's dinner!" but then the smell of Jade's lasagna hit him and he understood. Not just Henry, then. Everybody.

"Sure," he said softly. "Feel free to fill up a container."

"Thanks, Ellery! After I'm done with the thing."

Ellery kept his eyes closed, safe in Jackson's arms, knowing that if Jackson had any say about it, their bodies would be safe and alive for as long as possible. Their hearts would be safe and bound forever.

"How long is the thing?" Ellery asked, for Jackson's ears only.

"A heartbeat," Jackson said. "Two. There seems to have been some protest, you see."

"Protest?"

"Yeah. While I was in the hospital, my phone kept blowing up. Apparently my proposal was amateur hour at the romance café. My, uhm, friends have insisted on something a little more professionally done."

Ellery snorted, shoulders shaking. "Would you believe Galen said something similar?"

Galen's exact words had, in fact, been, "Oh. So you're engaged. I see no proof. I see no rings. No pictures. No romantic gestures. All I see is that neither of you got shot and Jackson's once again full of Bactine and cat gut. I maintain skepticism."

"The ration of shit I got from Jade and Henry has been...." Jackson breathed deeply. "Formidable."

"All to be remedied," Henry called. Ellery heard a click, and from under closed lids saw a burst of light. Henry took a deep breath, and Ellery heard a step, and another, and then another deep breath.

"Perfect," Henry murmured. There was another little bit of motion, and Henry said, "Remember, Jackson, you promised."

Jackson started to pull away. "I could just knee—"

"You could just sit down. The photo op will look great. Ellery, keep your eyes closed."

Ellery dutifully did his part, and Jackson kept hold of his hand while he situated himself, Ellery assumed, on a chair.

"We ready?" Jackson asked.

"Yes, boss," Henry said. "Let me get my camera out and... go."

"Ellery, you can open your eyes."

Ellery did and smiled.

Flowers—yes. Red roses, because classics were classics for a reason. The vase was new, a stunning green cut crystal, and Ellery saw the hint of an engraving on the base. Wow.

Henry had set the table with a pristine white tablecloth, red place mats on top. He'd set out a bottle of champagne in a bucket Ellery had never seen, although Ellery was pretty sure Jackson was not ready to drink so soon after being sedated.

There was a cake—simple, with white icing and red piping, and "Ellery, will you marry me?" piped in a graceful script.

"The cake's awesome," Ellery said, because his throat was closing and he didn't have words for the big things.

"Crystal's contribution," Jackson said, blinking hard. "The champagne is from Dave and Alex, and Toby is responsible for the tablecloth and napkins—they're apparently a gift, not a loan."

Toby, a medical examiner, had been one of Jackson's earliest friends and touchstones, and his family was still a big part of Jackson's life, and Ellery held his hand to his chest, moved.

"Christie and Kryzynski did the flower vase," Jackson said, surprising him.

"Galen and John sent the champagne bucket and candlesticks," Henry reminded him. "And AJ and the Johnnies kids ran around for two days ordering things and making sure they were the right stuff."

Jackson laughed a little. "And Mike made dinner on Jade's instructions."

"You should have been there to listen to Jade give him orders." Henry snickered. "That was classic."

Ellery's eyes were burning. "So everybody," he said softly. "Everybody who loves you had a hand in this."

"Well, Kaden and Rhonda and the kids mostly sent offers of support—for you," Jackson said, mouth twisting in a smile as he talked about Jade's twin and his wonderful family. "Apparently they're ready to kick me to the curb if I screw this up."

"Which is why there must be pictures," Henry told him, taking one more of the table setting, which deserved its own shot.

"I did do one thing," Jackson said, and Henry reached into his pocket and handed Jackson a small box, and even though Ellery knew what was coming, he still let a happy little sob sneak through. He didn't even have to open the box to know what they'd look like.

"Yeah?" he asked. "You did this thing?"

"Amazing what you can order from a hospital bed when you're high as an eagle," Jackson told him, smiling. His smile faded. "I was going to go down on one knee—"

Ellery dropped to one knee without a moment's thought. "My turn," he said gruffly. "You proposed last time. And you made it perfect this time. My turn."

Jackson gaped, and Ellery shook his head.

"Your fault, you know. You opened the door. I'm going to take advantage."

"That's your job, Counselor," Jackson said, smiling slightly.

"I do my best, Detective." Ellery loved—*loved*—that Jackson had turned his vocation into an endearment. It somehow made the thing they loved doing—and loved doing together—important. It acknowledged a part of each other's soul.

"Jackson," he said, his voice shaking. "I... I boss you around a lot. And tell you how to do things. Wear this shirt, give this gift to my mother, don't get shot."

Jackson suppressed a laugh, and Ellery continued.

"But that's only because I've been taking human lessons from you for over a year. Things like loving people for who they are and judging less and helping more. Things like not dismissing people because of their mistakes, and treating every soul as a human being, whether or not they reciprocate. I... I may have believed in these things before, in the abstract, but you've made them very, very real. You've made me a better person, living these ideas as a part of our lives. A true soulmate is somebody who makes you better by simply being who they are. You talk all the time about improving who you are for me—I don't think you understand how much better I've become just because I love you. Hopelessly. Without reservation. You were going to ask me to marry you. I'm *begging* you to marry me, because I'm selfish. I want to keep being this person, this person who could have the friends you've brought into my life. Who's imbued a job I already loved with meaning I didn't know it could have. Together we're... we're perfect. I mean, we're not—"

This time when Jackson laughed, he sputtered tears, and so did Ellery, but Ellery had to finish.

"Neither of us. But together, we make the world a better place. Please marry me. Please build a life with me. I'm so spoiled by loving you. I couldn't love another person like this. It would break my heart."

Jackson nodded fiercely and opened the ring box. Two simple platinum rings sat in it, one with an onyx stone. Elegant and plain and perfect. "Yes," he said.

Ellery pulled one of the rings out. It had Jackson's name engraved inside in a bold print, and a he assumed it was his. He held the one with *Ellery* engraved in the center for Jackson to slip his finger into, and then Jackson took the other one and did the same.

"Yes," Ellery said.

He lifted up slightly, and they kissed, another briny disaster, but this kiss didn't have pain in it or stress or desperation.

It was absolute, 100 percent unfettered joy.

In the hazy background, Ellery felt his phone buzz in his pocket and heard Henry say, "Perfect. Congratulations, you guys. Henry out."

He wouldn't look into his pocket until later, as they lingered over the cake—and the sparkling cider Dave and Alex had provided along with the champagne. But when he did, he found the picture of them kissing, surrounded by the trappings of tradition and the thoughtfulness of family and captioned with a simple, "Yes."

Henry had sent it to everybody, including Ellery's family, and the congratulations had filled up both his and Jackson's phones.

"Would you look at that," Jackson said softly. "I guess people have been rooting for us."

"I know I have," Ellery told him, and they both put their forks down by mutual decision and kissed again.

This kiss ended up in the bedroom, where they made slow, careful love. This time, Ellery took care of Jackson, because he was the only lover Jackson had ever allowed the honor. This time he worked carefully around the hurts and took him, softly, sweetly, without pain. Jackson's crest was a breathless break of a slow wave, and Ellery came inside him as effortlessly as breathing, as spectacularly as a shooting star. He spent an eternity after that running his fingers through Jackson's hair, rubbing his hip, kissing his shoulder, soothing his lover until Jackson's even breathing told Ellery he was asleep.

Ellery let out a deep breath then and lay there, still inside him, both of them on their sides, as he waited for Jackson to sink a little deeper into sleep.

He would need to move to do some cleanup in a moment; his practicality wouldn't allow the exquisite cake to sit out or the bucket holding the unopened champagne to soak through to the table with condensation. He needed to blow out the candles and feed the cats and do the dishes— and very often Jackson helped with these chores, but not tonight.

Tonight, Jackson's only job was to sleep.

He'd done all the hard emotional work. He'd faced so many demons, and he had the scars to prove it, but he'd won.

For once, Ellery prayed Jackson would get a full night's sleep and wake up refreshed and happy to see that the world had changed around them, but they were still the same.

Together, heart and soul, burning with purpose, as long as they could march hand in hand into the battle.

They had so much work to do.

Author's Note: A word about *Crullers*

Crullers started out as a series of "thread the needle" ficlets on my Patreon—and boy did these shorts thread *every* needle, covering pretty much every couple mentioned in the Fishiverse toward the end of *School of Fish*. Altogether, they came to about 30,000 words—but there was no cohesion to the batch of stories if you *hadn't* read pretty much *every* word in the series. However, certain groups of the fishlets did manage to go together, and the whole work functioned better split into three pieces. The first chunk is in the back of *Constantly Cotton*, and the second chunk is here. The third will go best with *Under the Stars*, a novella about Jai and George, who are from the area of the Fishiverse occupied by Ace, Sonny, Burton, and Ernie. So enjoy this oddly shaped story. Something happens at the end that people have been asking for since Lucy Satan insisted that Billy Bob should get a friend.

Crullers

Part 1

GEORGE'S SPANISH was getting better, but it felt like not fast enough. The little girl sitting on the bench waiting for her mother was looking so dejected. George wasn't sure Duolingo was up to this one.

Amal grabbed him by the elbow just as George was moving in to try.

"What?" George asked, keeping his voice down. Amal had the same look in his eyes he'd had when he and George had helped a busload of children get back to their parents under the eyes of a watchful military commander who had *not* wanted the children returned because he'd been, in his words, trying to catch the "big fish."

George and Amal had told him that nobody ate fish in the desert, and he'd not been amused.

But Jason Constance and his busload of children had been on their way back to Sacramento, where, George had it on good authority, all the children had been returned to their parents.

George had apologized profusely to Amal for that. He'd put his friend in so many dangers: danger of getting arrested, danger of getting targeted by immigration authorities, even though Amal was a third-generation citizen, danger of losing his nursing license. George had no right, none at all, to ask a friend to do all that, in the name of—

"A busload of kids who only wanted to see their parents?" Amal had asked bitterly, his pretty, thin features crumpling to reveal the marks left by casual and not so casual racism, the pain he shrugged off as the price of living in a free land. He'd stopped George short, mid apology. "Don't you fucking dare apologize. I mean, don't make this some sort of underground railroad, home for all the people who will throw our ass in a sling, but don't apologize. So much of what we see here is awful and painful and we can't fix. *That* was something we could fix."

And the next day, when nobody had stormed into the ER of their busy urban hospital about two blocks from LA's Skid Row, they'd given each other a quiet high five and carried on about their jobs as though nothing had happened.

Two weeks later, George had taken a week off so he could go visit his boyfriend in the desert and quietly probe into a job closer to Jai. Because George missed him just that damned badly, and he was tired of Jai being afraid that he'd drag George down into his life of iniquity and crime.

The truth was, 98 percent of the time Jai was a garage mechanic with a select set of skills that he'd probably picked up working reluctantly for the mob. The remaining 2 percent of the time, he and his friends took it upon themselves to fix things that needed fixing. After having been called in on a few of those assignments—giving medical care to those afraid of deportation, helping a busload of kids get returned to their parents—and seeing that sort of reprehensible criminal behavior, George wanted to be a criminal too.

Or at least he wanted to live the 98 percent of his life he *wasn't* being asked to risk his nursing license next to the guy he'd gladly risk it for.

The week before, he'd been told that he had maybe a month before two of the ten nurses, four physicians assistants, and five doctors working at a tiny hospital in the middle of nowhere retired. He'd gone in to tell Amal that he'd put his hat in the ring for a job there immediately afterward.

He'd expected a couple of reactions. One was for Amal to say, "Fuck off, loser, I thought we were friends." Another was "I can't do this bullshit without you." And a third was "Fine, go be with your boyfriend and be happy ever after. Don't feel guilty or anything as I try to find a nurse who can read my mind and doesn't mind my shitty sense of humor."

What he'd gotten was the same steady-eyed look Amal had given him when he'd explained they were sneaking a busload of kids back to their parents right under Uncle Sam's nose. It was a look that said Amal trusted George, and trusted what he was doing, and was all in.

"So this place got any more openings?" he'd asked, and George hadn't been sure if he'd been kidding or not.

"Uhm, Amal, I can't promise there will be much more to do there besides give people Gatorade and zinc oxide."

Amal had just looked at him. "So those surplus supplies you keep co-opting—unused antibiotics, expired ointments, gauze that's got new packaging—that's going in a landfill unopened?"

George had flushed. He'd asked about taking those things every time. He hadn't wanted Amal to need to lie for him. He'd expressly told his friend not to. Because the truth was that whenever he visited Jai for more than two days, he held a small, unsanctioned clinic in the home of the girl who Jai's boss had sent to college. A home in which English was not spoken, at least not well, but people still needed checkups and medical care, and even if they were completely legitimate citizens born in the country, they couldn't be guaranteed that their hospital stay wouldn't turn into a nightmare in an ICE detention center, and so they avoided the hospital when they could.

"Well, my new work wouldn't know about that," he admitted. He shrugged and looked away. "I was probably going to pay for all that stuff out of pocket anyway."

Amal regarded him with that steady adult expression, the new one that had come after the former administration had destroyed everybody's innocence and COVID had taken their hope. "Just tell me where to apply," he said.

"Amal," George had protested. "You're... you're on a career track here. You're going to be head nurse in the ER by the end of the year. You'll be able to transfer anywhere you want! Pediatrics, OB/GYN—"

Amal just shook his head. "I want to do what you're doing, George. Whether you're doing it legally or illegally. It gives me hope to know you're doing what you do."

George had pinched the bridge of his nose. "I'll give you the name of the woman I talked to in HR, who is also their scheduling nurse because that's how small this place is. But don't mention the other shit. That has nothing to do with—"

Amal nodded. "I get it, George. You are off the beaten path with this one. It's okay. Have you told Analiese yet?"

"This weekend," George said with a sigh. Analiese worked in an entirely different hospital, and he was going to miss her coming over for wine and whine, as she called it now, on the weekends he wasn't visiting Jai.

"Tell me what she says."

But George hadn't had time to tell Analiese this last week, and Amal was looking at the terrified little girl sitting on one of the plastic chairs outside her mother's room with that level, grown-up look in his wide brown eyes, and George wondered what was up.

He was leaning against the counter to the nurse's station, smiling at the little girl and trying to get a smile in return. The girl was wearing jeans and a zip-up cardigan, both too warm for Los Angeles in September, and her face had that peaked look that he recognized from seeing too much of it.

Reaching under the station where Amal kept fresh fruit stocked, he grabbed an apple and sauntered over to the little girl.

"*Manzana?*" he offered, and she took it shyly.

"*Gracias.*" Without hesitation, she took a big bite, but then she looked around furtively, as though afraid somebody would punish her for eating it.

Great! Of course, the next part was a little more complicated. He tried once, but it came out as "eestass spando etso mwami," and her expression of abject confusion made him remember the musical voices in Alba's mother's house and how patient they'd been teaching him their language.

He tried again.

"*Estás esperando a tu mamá?*"

She nodded. "Sí."

He tried one more time and thought he might have done a decent job asking her what had happened, but she started to cry instead. The one word he got from her was "*Hielo,*" and just saying it made her cry harder. He pulled a melted Jolly Rancher from his pocket and offered it to her, and one of the obstetrics nurses hurried by out of nowhere and gave him an emergency teddy bear. That calmed her down for a moment, but when he looked up, Amal was staring at them both with troubled eyes.

"What'd she say?" Amal asked.

George touched the teddy bear gently and smiled as she held it tight, silent tears coursing down her cheeks.

"Hielo," George said, typing it into his phone.

Amal stiffened. "Shit. Shit. God*dammit!*"

"What?"

Amal's face was suffused with fury. "Her mother's being treated for trauma—sexual trauma, George."

"But what does hielo mean? Oh." It had popped up in his phone dictionary.

"Hielo. Ice."

"Shit." George took a deep breath. "But—but she's here. She's documented. I saw you take her insurance card myself."

"Yeah," Amal told him, shaking. "But it's been happening. Some officers abuse their authority. They threaten to deport anyway and then…."

George's heart was suddenly racing, whether it was with rage or with fear he couldn't say. He was facing the double doors that led through the metal detectors and the glass door separating the ER from the hospital entrance.

"They're here," he said, swallowing.

He and Amal met eyes.

"We've stitched her up and given her antibiotics," Amal said tonelessly, and then he took a deep breath and his spine straightened. "I can stall them for five minutes. Can you get them out of here?"

George looked at the tiny girl clutching the teddy bear and swallowed. He and Jai had talked about prison, and how Jai might someday have to go. George had thought he was awfully brave for facing the consequences of his actions, however well-intentioned, with such stoicism. George himself, he'd thought, could never be that brave.

"Down the freight elevator and out through the custodian shed on the employees-only floor."

Amal nodded and reached for a set of keys in his pocket. "My Jeep."

George pulled out the set of keys for the piece-of-shit Toyota truck that Jai kept tuned up by sheer force of will. "My POS. See you in two days."

Amal nodded, and they shook hands while exchanging the keys.

"Be safe," Amal said, and George turned toward the little girl, summoning up the words for *Follow me! Let's go see Mommy!* On his phone.

The girl's mother was distrustful at first, but she spoke enough English for him to get the message across. That one word, hielo, was enough to make her eyes widen, and with her daughter, Lola, in his arms, he found himself sprinting through the hospital at top speed, not caring who saw them, just caring that he got this woman away from the people who had claimed the right to harm her.

He was in Amal's Jeep, which was a damned sight more elegantly appointed than his own POS, that being what you got when you got scholarships to nursing school instead of student loans, and heading for Victoriana when his phone buzzed in his pocket. He fumbled for it and answered, expecting Amal's voice on the other end telling him that it was all sorted out.

What he got was their coworker, Sherri, telling him that Amal had been arrested and taken into custody for hindering government authority, and that there was a warrant out for George's arrest.

George thanked her, signed off, and then did the only thing he could think of.

He called Jai.

Jai told him, "Do not worry. We have people." Then he proceeded to give George directions to a gas station in Barstow with no video cameras in the immediate vicinity. "We are closer," Jai said. "Is there anything you need?"

George looked at the woman and her child, huddled in the back of the Jeep. "Are you hungry?" he asked, thinking that Mom might have enough English to understand.

"Sí," she whispered.

"Food and clothes," he said to Jai. Looking wistfully at Lola, he added, "Woman's medium—stretchy—and something in a child's size seven. Summery. With flowers."

"Da," Jai said. "Get there safely."

And that was when George remembered that Amal had told *him* to be safe, and George, thinking that Amal would be fine, hadn't said the same thing. He wiped his cheeks with the back of his hand and tried not to fall apart.

"WE'RE GOING where?" Ellery asked as Jackson started throwing clothes into a duffel. There they'd been, enjoying a Saturday morning swim after some rockin' sex—a celebration of Ellery's new 3-D printed mobile cast, of course—when Jackson's phone started going off with the *Avengers* theme music. Jackson had popped out of the pool so quickly it had been like levitation, and then he'd shouted, "Ellery, we've got to *move*!" as he'd run into the house.

When Ellery had gotten there, Jackson had been dressed already, dark blond hair slicked back against his head, wearing new cargo shorts and a *polo* shirt, which meant he was serious, and packing.

"Victoriana," Jackson said tersely. "One of Ace's people. He's in trouble, and it's bad, and we need to help."

Ellery scrubbed his face irritably and tried not to shiver as the air conditioner took advantage of the fact that *he* was dripping all over his carpet.

"Well shit," he muttered. They owed Ace's people. They owed them *everything*. "Drive or fly?"

Jackson paused in the act of throwing shit into his duffel. "What's quicker?" he asked. Then his phone buzzed again on the dresser— *Avengers* again. He lifted it up and said, "Drive or fly?" He blinked once and nodded to Ellery. "Drive, but only if I'm behind the wheel."

Ellery nodded. Fair enough. Jackson drove like a bat out of hell, and there was no arguing with that. Besides, Ellery's hips ached when he drove with the cast. That accident in August was not so far away as all that.

Jackson listened for a moment, his jaw tightening, and when he spoke next, he sounded almost angry. "Man, do not fucking insult me by asking me that. We will fucking be there—and so will his mother. Why would his mother come? Well, for one thing she's got contacts at the DOJ, and for another, you guys helped save her baby boy. So yeah. And fuck 'last favor.' Goddammit, Ace, there is no 'last favor' here. There's no 'favor.' We got your fuckin' back, 'cause I know you guys got ours."

Ellery swallowed hard on the lump in his throat brought by pride and started to dress in his own outfit, much like Jackson's. As he did so, he made lightning-quick decisions between his navy pinstripe suit and his summer-weight gray and made a mental note to pack the guns and Kevlar.

When Ace Atchison called, it was lawyers, guns, and money—and Ellery could provide all three.

And his mother too.

Part 2

JAI WAS waiting as George pulled up to the gas station, and so was Ace. Jai was driving a shitty minivan with big paint chips missing. Ace was driving the terrifying yellow car that Jai had taken up to the campsite once when he and George were still pretending that they were just fuck buddies who met in a tent.

Ernie poked his head of dark wavy hair out from Ace's passenger window, and George had to wrap his brain around what the plan could possibly be.

Then a young woman—dark-haired, dark-eyed, brown-skinned— popped out of the minivan from next to Jai, and George gave up. He had no idea. He was lost.

But as George pulled the black Jeep up to the motley collection of people waiting for him, he was mostly looking at Jai anyway. Tall, broad-shouldered, slouching against the minivan, he looked solid, safe, and kind.

George didn't even want to look at himself in the rearview mirror. He'd cried for ten minutes after he found out Amal was in jail. It was a good thing one of them looked calm.

He turned toward the woman and her child, but the young woman by Jai's side had already approached and rapped sharply on the back door so George would unlock it. As he did so, the young woman broke into a patter of Spanish so quick that George wasn't even sure he'd been trying to speak the same language. At the same time, Jai approached his door and opened it, and George found himself spilling out of the Jeep and sobbing on his giant boyfriend's shoulder in the middle of the cracked and weed-laden pavement of a Barstow parking lot, deserted because the Walmart, Laundromat, and gas station had all apparently gone out of business in the last couple of years.

Jai stepped back and cupped his cheeks. "We must hurry, little George. This place has no cameras, but if police come by, it will seem very strange."

George nodded. "Uhm, who's going with whom?"

"Alba is going to take your friends to her family's house in the minivan." He scowled. "And she's going to drive very carefully, because we don't have so many cars that we can give her another one."

The young woman, who was currently handing food over to the mother and her daughter, grinned impudently at Jai. "I drive as carefully as Ace does," she said pertly, and George actually saw Jai pale.

"I hope not!" Jai burst out, but Alba just laughed and turned back to the mother and daughter in the back of the Jeep.

"What are Ace and Ernie doing here?" George asked apprehensively.

"Well, you and I are going to take the SHO back to the gas station," Jai said frankly. "It's where the yellow car lives, and nobody will be looking for a black Jeep when they see the yellow car. Ernie and Ace are going to go to Los Angeles and pick a nice lady up from the airport in your friend's nice Jeep." Jai gave a very wide smile. "And you, me, and Sonny will be there to greet our lawyer friends when they get here from Sacramento."

George blinked. "Who's the nice lady?" he asked, confused.

"She is a lawyer too, but she has contacts at the Department of Justice. She is going to fight for your friend."

George's brain exploded. "Department of…?"

Jai looked wistful. "Sonny, Ace, and Ernie say she is a very good woman, but I was moving cars when she was here last, so I did not get to meet her. Anyway, Ernie says Ace will need him, because Ernie can keep the Jeep away from the police." Jai gave a grimace. "Also, we need the Jeep. It's really the best vehicle we have for transporting gracious women."

"Hey!" Alba protested, and the look Jai turned toward her was, at best, besotted. At its worst, it was the look a doting big brother gave his baby sister when she was playing too.

"You are an elegant young woman," Jai conceded. "When you have lived enough life, you too will get a car without worn upholstery and missing paint."

Alba's laugh was both delighted *and* delightful. "You know I love my old Beatrice," she said, gazing fondly at the minivan. "You know what I love best about her, though?"

Jai gave that smile again, the one that was all teeth. "She runs," he said, and she laughed again.

The laugh washed over George and told him that things might not totally suck after all.

JACKSON GOT another *Avengers'* phone call right before they were about to go over the Grapevine. He'd pulled over reluctantly because

Ellery, who had been making plans, covering their asses, and making arrangements for Henry to feed the cat, had demanded some sort of food-like stuff, since they'd barely remembered a granola bar for breakfast, and it was now nearly three o'clock in the afternoon.

Ellery had been understanding—to a point. Only once had he lamented the crepes he'd planned to try his hand at on their quiet Saturday off, but as the shadows had stretched long, as they tend to do in September regardless of the heat, he'd finally put his foot down.

Jackson, he'd said, could drive until his body turned to dust, but Ellery needed food.

Jackson had conceded, and as they'd stood in line at Chipotle, he'd told Ellery with a sigh, "I was really looking forward to those crepes."

The truth was, he didn't really know if he cared for crepes or not—the vote was still out there—but making the effort to say it was worth the glow he saw in Ellery's brown eyes.

They'd finished eating and were on their way back onto the freeway when the phone rang, and Ellery answered, putting it on speaker. The Tank was still undergoing the massive repairs it would need after their little episode in August, and Ellery was still wearing a brace on his knee and a lightweight breathable cast in concession to the injuries he'd sustained. They were driving the new CR-V, and while Ellery was a little trepidatious—Jackson had wrecked the last two—Jackson kept up his sunny optimism. Surely the third time was the charm, right?

It may or may not have been, but the inside was still a damned sight quieter than the Tank.

"So," Ace drawled. "We'll be at the airport in an hour and a half. Do I have the gate right?" He repeated what Ellery had apparently been texting, and Ellery replied.

"Yes. Her itinerary says she'll land in about two hours. I have no idea how she got a cross-country flight so quickly. It's like her superpower."

Jackson gave a sour grunt. "Not her only one," he muttered, but he wasn't sure either of them heard him.

Ellery went on. "We're going to need her. I contacted my friends at the DA's office in LA County, and they have no record of Amal Dara being taken into custody. This is purely ICE, and they're known for holding people without cause for days and weeks. They're going to need somebody with a voice banging on their door to get him out."

"We looked up the offices and detention centers closest to the hospital," Ace said. "I texted Jackson the number. We can meet you there but"—he sounded uncomfortable—"it's not the greatest area. Your mom's a classy woman. She's gonna need us."

Jackson felt a reluctant smile twitching at his lips. Apparently Lucy Satan had ensnared some more admirers. "Good thinking," he said with a grin. Then, more seriously, "Where are the victims?"

"Safe," Ace said, and Jackson wasn't sure if he kept his words terse because he was trying not to give too much info or because he was just Ace. "We figure they'll stay that way until we know they can go home again. We've got college students who are going to go check on their apartment and let us know if they've got people guarding the place or not."

Jackson grunted, not sure he liked the idea of that, but he couldn't control everybody in his orbit. "Understood. What about George?"

"Our place," Ace told him. "Although Burton may come and take him out to their place. I got Ernie with me so I don't run into anybody with an eye out for the Jeep."

"Does it really work like that?" Ellery asked, doubtful.

Just as Jackson started shaking his head to not ask those questions, Ernie chirped, "I know when someone has malevolent intent," he said. "Feels like bugs crawling up my arms and legs. No bugs, no high-speed chases. I get a little tickle, we go the other way."

Ellery palmed his eyes. "Just... just don't tell my mother that you're driving a car that might or might not be considered stolen and part of the ICE investigation," he said. "We can just... you know...."

"Leave that part out," Ernie said. "Understood. We'll meet you at the ICE office as soon as we pick up the package."

As Jackson pushed the little car up the terrible gradient of the Grapevine, Ellery wanted to groan. "We may or may not get there by six."

"You can only try," Ace told him. "I mean, at eleven this morning, you guys thought your day was gonna go a whole other way, didn't you?"

"We did indeed," Jackson said, keeping the irony out of his voice.

Ace signed off, and Ellery thumped back against the seat again. "God. You know, I hope we can get their friend out."

"You don't think we can?" Jackson was surprised. He was pretty sure Ellery and his mother could accomplish anything. Particularly when working together. If they had Ellery's father there, they could probably solve world peace.

"I have some ideas," Ellery admitted. "But...." He blew out a breath. "Jackson," he said, none of the arrogance or prissiness Jackson had once thought consumed him evident in his voice now. "Jackson, they have so much faith in us. I mean, here they have people who are completely innocent. Not even accused of a crime—they're *victims*. If we can't help them, what are we doing?"

Jackson's heart hurt. "Our best," he said simply. "And your best, Counselor, is terrifying."

Ellery grunted. "So's your faith."

"Ditto," Jackson told him, but Ellery, mind likely busy with how he was going to approach a government agency with such a prohibitive amount of power, didn't respond.

Part 3

ACE GLANCED in the rearview mirror at the formidable woman in the back of Amal Dara's Jeep and smiled nervously.

"So," she said, seemingly unperturbed at having been yanked cross-country at a moment's notice and thrown into the back of a Jeep Cherokee with two men she'd barely met, once, in pretty much the worst of circumstances. "Can you give me the situation, please?"

Ace took a deep breath and pulled into Los Angeles traffic, hating it with every fiber of his being. And then it hit him. "You don't know why you're here?" he asked.

"Well, Ellery didn't know much either," she said. "Details were sketchy, Mr. Atchison. But you and your friends helped my son when he needed it most, and you seem fairly independent. I'm reasonably certain he wouldn't have summoned me from three thousand miles away if this was a parking ticket."

"Ma'am," Ernie said, a sort of reverence in his voice Ace had never heard. "Would you adopt us?"

"Consider it done," she said, the faintest edge of humor in her voice telling Ace that she appreciated the sentiment. "Now, about your friend's situation."

"The situation, ma'am, is tricky." Ace frowned, hoping he could make this as concise as possible. "See, our friend Jai is seeing a friend who works as a nurse. He, uhm, has at times worked to help people who, uhm, ordinarily would not be seeking medical attention."

"Criminals?" she inquired, using the same tone one might say, "Golfers?"

"Immigrants," he said bluntly. Better she know them for who they were. "Not all of them legal."

"Oh," she murmured. "Understood. Not exactly legal, but definitely moral and ethical." She let out a short, almost bitter laugh. "Laws made by evil men are not necessarily laws we should obey."

Ace actually felt his eyes burn. "We agree, ma'am. But George, he's been growing closer to the community. So he sees a little girl in the ER waiting room, and he starts talking to her. Offering her an apple and such. And he asks her what happened to her mother. And she starts crying, and says, 'hielo.'"

"Oh dear," Mrs. Cramer, Esquire said, and Ace heard her comprehension and disapproval in those two syllables. "How long has the woman been in the country?"

Ace swallowed because he could hear her rage already. "That's the thing. She was born here. So was her daughter—and her ex-husband for that matter. She speaks English when she's not terrified. Apparently this agent threatened to deport her if she said anything. George and Amal didn't know that. They just knew that ICE was coming in through the front door."

"Amal Dara. This is the person who was taken into custody?"

"Yes, ma'am. He's George's boss, and he gave George the keys to this here vehicle and said, 'I'll try to stall.' George shot through the hospital with the woman and her daughter, thinking that the authorities were going to be after him, and ten minutes later he gets a call that Amal has been taken into custody."

"And do we know what the charges are?" she asked, and she must have been glancing at her phone because she gasped. "No. We don't. Because he wasn't reported as being taken into custody. That is illegal." She glanced up. "He was born in this country?"

"Yes, ma'am. I asked George, in case that'll be a hang-up. George says he's third-generation."

"Indeed."

Ace was finding it hard to breathe. The heat screaming off her body as he followed Ernie's quietly voiced directions coming partly from his phone and partly from his brain almost crushed his lungs.

"So, where are we headed now?" she asked.

"Well, the ICE office in the middle of the city," Ace told her.

"Will it still be open?" she asked, sounding surprised—and she should be. It was a good ten minutes past six now, on a Saturday.

"Well, according to your son, who got there fifteen minutes ago, he's going to make sure it stays open until hell freezes over, so I'm going to say yes." Ellery had texted just as her plane landed, and Ace had to give it to Jackson Rivers. The man had a bit of tornado blood in his veins, and Ace would like to see him in a souped-up muscle car someday—as long as Ace wasn't racing against him, because Ace only did that shit for money now. Or in the middle of the desert, when he and Sonny were in a mood.

The next noise that came from the back seat was the feral, dark sort of sound that might have come from a mother wolf after she watched her pup bring down prey.

"That's my boy."

JACKSON GLANCED around the utilitarian office building and watched Ellery slice through layers of receptionists and COs to find the AIC. He was not familiar with the hierarchy of this particular organization, but he did know it always came down to the Asshole in Charge, and since Ellery was a similar fish, well, he knew where to swim.

"I said," Ellery repeated, looking down his nose at the tall bulky man in the brown boxy suit, "that I am not leaving until I speak to my client, Amal Dara."

"And I'm telling you—"

"You should look at your duty log," Ellery said. "You had two agents, Cly and Tetley, who entered the hospital at eleven ten this morning and demanded to see Lara Martinez, who was being treated for a vicious sexual assault. Ms. Martinez had checked herself out AMA and had vacated her room. When the charge nurse on duty—Mr. Dara—couldn't produce the patient on cue, your agents took him into custody and have, apparently, been holding him here."

"We are allowed to hold immigrants—"

"Without charges for forty-eight hours, a law I'm sure will be overturned with the current administration," Ellery said, not even giving the man a chance for his voice to find purchase and give pressure. "It's a terrible law, but it doesn't apply here. Mr. Dara was born in this country, as were his parents, and a rudimentary search should have revealed that. He's a United States citizen, and the only reason he's being held is blatant prejudice because he has brown skin and you think you can."

Mr. AIC drew himself up to his full height—which was about two inches shorter than Ellery, a fact Jackson was sure he wished he hadn't noticed. "I resent the implication—"

"And I resent that you haven't called Cly and Tetley out here," Ellery said. "Or attempted to get hold of them if they are out in the field. Or to look for Mr. Dara in your holding facilities or interview rooms. I've just told you that you're breaking the law. It seems to me that you should be more interested in either proving you're not or fixing the situation than in telling me my rights. I know my rights, sir, and I know Mr. Dara's, and I'm telling you right now, I'm not the one who needs a refresher course."

The AIC sputtered for a moment and turned to the female officer in reception. "Call Cly and Tetley out here," he muttered, "so we can resolve this."

Jackson was afraid the next five to ten minutes were going to be *very* uncomfortable, but then he felt a faint whisper at his elbow and smelled the barest breath of Chanel No. 5. He hated to admit it to himself, but the scent lifted him somehow. It wasn't that he thought everything was going to be all right, but, well, there was just something about knowing Ellery's mother was there that made him think that even if it wasn't all right, the fight could still go on.

The AIC—he had a name badge, Friars, but Jackson wasn't calling him that. He would forever be the Asshole in Charge.

"How's he doing?" Lucy Satan murmured for Jackson's ear only.

"Really good," Jackson said. "Maybe wait a minute before you start throwing weight."

He glanced at her, and she gave him a complacent smile—sort of like one of those creepy animated creatures that was hiding lots and lots of shark teeth.

"Make no mistake," she purred, "whether he succeeds or not, there *will* be weight."

He gave her a not-quite wink and then watched in surprise as two guys—bulky, muscular men, dressed in the trademark black combat and tactical wear with ICE emblazoned on the front of their shirts—stepped off the elevator. The bigger one, older, shaved bald with a salt-and-pepper goatee, was clearly the leader, and his partner, a little shorter, a little less hulked out, with a head full of auburn hair and green eyes, appeared perpetually hurt and trying to be hard.

Jackson had to swallow… several times. He recognized that look on the younger partner's face. A thousand years ago, he'd seen it every time he looked in the mirror.

"Officer Cly," AIC Friars blustered, "This is Ellery Cramer. He claims to represent Amal Dara, but I've been telling him there's nobody here by that name."

Jackson was pretty sure everybody's eyes were on Cly, the big bastard with the scar over one eyebrow and the weather-roughened skin over his leather-burnt pinkness.

Not Jackson. He was watching Tetley, who swallowed convulsively and glanced behind him in a furtive manner, as though checking to make sure Amal Dara was right where he'd left him.

"Look, ya little ACLU puke," Cly blustered, upper lip curled into a sneer, "that illegal fucker's got no rights when he interferes with an investigation—"

"He's third-generation American, sir," Ellery said coldly, "and I'm not from the ACLU, although I'll be sure to send them your regards."

Cly slow-blinked, and then re-upped on the sneer, but Tetley didn't. His eyes grew much larger, and Jackson figured Cly had been trying to tell him that this Dara guy really *was* illegal and that's why he deserved to get roughed up or detained or whatever.

"What investigation is that anyway?" Ellery asked, eyebrows raised. "Because as far as I know, your division doesn't investigate forcible rape. Mr. Dara was the charge nurse of a patient who had been forcibly raped and who apparently heard her daughter yell 'hielo' and ran out of the hospital. Think about that. She'd been recently stitched up in two very uncomfortable places, and she *ran* out of the hospital to avoid you. Why do you think that is?"

"Fuck if I know," Cly blustered.

"Oh, I think you know," Jackson said, his eyes on Tetley. "Doesn't he, Tetley? Did he tell you he just had to talk to this illegal alone? Did he take about twenty minutes and come back saying, 'Bitch'd do anything to stay in this country'?"

Tetley blanched, looking a little sick, and Jackson was right there with him.

"Did he tell you he ripped her until she was bleeding? Did he tell you he did it in front of her *daughter*?"

Tetley hauled in air like a swimmer who'd been underwater for… well, months probably. Probably for as long as they'd worked together, and Tetley had wondered how hellish his life would be if he tried to extricate himself from this dirtbag. How would he feed himself? How would he get another job in law enforcement? He'd been to school for two to four years, right? What was he going to do with all that time? He had student loans up the yang—probably owned a beater car and paid rent on a shitty apartment. How was he supposed to live if he turned in his partner? How was he supposed to work? What if he said something to someone and they were just as dirty as he was?

Jackson lowered his voice and lowered the boom. "Did he tell you she wasn't illegal at all? That she'd been born in this country and so had her little girl?"

The sound that came out of Tetley's throat wasn't human, and Jackson stepped back to let Tetley charge Cly from behind.

Their struggle was short and brutal. Cly had seventy-five pounds on Tetley easy, and he fought dirty. Tetley caught an elbow in the eye socket that would probably impair his vision, and his head bounced off the tiles before his eyes rolled back and he was blessedly out. But Cly wasn't done with him—guy was probably roided to the gills. He stayed on Tetley's chest and hit him once…

And then Jackson swung his foot back and caught the guy in the side of the jaw, and he slumped to the floor, dazed, sliding off the man he'd been about to beat to death.

Jackson didn't trust him to stay there, though. He leaped on the guy and started raiding his pockets, unholstering his gun, his taser, and chucking them on the floor near Ellery, who neatly kicked them to his mother like an unholy game of soccer. Then he reached into Cly's belt for cuffs, and while he was unhooking them, he looked up at Ellery's mother.

"Lucy, before you call the DOJ on these motherfuckers, could you *please* call the cops on this one?"

To her credit, Taylor Cramer cleared her throat and straightened her spine and gave AIC Friars a disdainful look.

And then pulled out her phone and did just that.

Then Ellery turned toward Friars and said in his iciest voice, "And now, could you please get Mr. Dara so the police can take his statement?"

Friars looked around the crappy tile-and-beige walls of the reception area and then looked at the desk sergeant.

"Do we even know where they came from?"

"Conference room twelve, third floor," she said before standing up. "I'll go get him." She eyed her boss with her own brand of ICE. "I don't trust you to do it."

Friars was still gaping and sputtering when Taylor Cramer hung up and gave him the bad news about how the attorney general's office would be *very* interested in speaking to him, and he should, perhaps, start packing up his office now.

He waited until LAPD arrived before he fled, and as Ellery and Taylor were talking to the officers on duty, Jackson turned just in time to see the desk sergeant arrive with a slender middle-height man with tawny skin and sloe-brown eyes. He was still wearing nurse's scrubs, and he had a bit of a shiner and some bruises on his wrists.

Jackson made his way to the poor guy, who was looking exhausted and scared and probably angry as well, underneath that.

"Hey," he said, extending his hand. "I'm a friend of George's. Or rather, I'm a friend of George's boyfriend. You want to go find a vending machine? I could really use a soda. How about you?"

"Root beer and Oreos," Dara said with a faint smile. "Do you really know George's boyfriend? I was starting to think he was a myth, manufactured by George to get the hell out of the city."

Jackson grinned at him, and after checking to make sure Amal wasn't shying away, slung a companionable arm around his shoulders— sort of a stranger's way of saying, "You're safe with me," and a hug wrapped into one.

"Which, honestly, is what we all thought about George, if you want to know the truth. How would you like to meet him?"

"George's boyfriend?" They were making their way down the corridor behind the desk, and Jackson spotted the vending machines right off.

"Yeah." He reached into his pocket and pulled out his wallet, handing the card to Amal while he checked his phone. "Get me two diet cokes and a regular. And I hope that answer is yes," he added, before responding to the answer on his phone.

"Why?" Amal asked, tapping numbers into the machine while it read Jackson's card.

"Because once we get you free and clear of this shithole, it would sort of be a good idea for you to take a few days off work so we can make sure nobody's left here to wage a vendetta against you, for one."

Amal groaned. "Fuck me!" He paused and gave Jackson a once-over. "In fact, I'm single. You, uh—"

"Are taken," Jackson said, appreciating the offer, though. Amal was *very* cute. "But that's sweet."

"Bummer." Amal turned and handed Jackson the card and then started pulling out sodas. "What's the other reason I'm blowing town for a few?"

"Because the two guys who drove your car here to drop off my boyfriend's mother just turned back around, and we need to go fetch it."

Amal frowned. "Why'd they leave? I mean, I'm *right* here!"

Jackson cocked his head, raising his eyebrows compassionately. "Oh, Amal, surely you can see why someone might have an allergy to the po-po, after today especially."

Amal looked at the small package of Oreos in his hand, and the soda, and then his knees buckled, and Jackson was barely able to get him into one of the vinyl-and-chrome chairs that lined the wall.

Jackson slid down next to him, and when Ellery and Taylor came to find them an hour later so he could talk to the police, he was still sobbing into Jackson's shoulder with the heartbreak of innocence lost.

FOUR HOURS and forty centuries later, they'd all given multiple statements and were allowed to leave. Jackson had Amal direct him to a nearby taqueria, and for a moment they ate in exhausted silence.

Then Jackson said, "Amal, do you have a cat?"

"Yeah, but I have a roommate. She'll take care of it until I come back."

Jackson nodded. "I'm sure someone where we're going has some clothes you can borrow. And I've been getting texts telling me they have managed to scare us up some places to sleep. Guest rooms, couches, etc."

"No hotels?" Taylor asked, sounding horrified.

Jackson and Ellery exchanged glances. "Mother," Ellery said hesitantly, "this isn't.... I mean, there might be a Motel 6 out there, but I don't... there's not really...."

Her eyes widened, and then she laughed, self-deprecation evident. "Look at me, making a fuss over such things. I need to remember what's important."

Amal looked at her, and then at Ellery and Jackson. "Complete strangers came cross-country to save my bacon?" he hazarded.

"An innocent man is out of custody," she said firmly. "And between the DOJ, the FBI, and the LAPD, I think we may have begun to right the even deeper wrong that had you imprisoned there in the first place."

Her face fell. "I'm just so angry right now," she confessed, raw and vulnerable as Jackson had only ever seen her when Ellery had been hurt. "I've labored my entire life for a better world than this. It's such a step backward."

"Well, yeah," Jackson told her. He smiled briefly when she looked up. "But Ellery's here to pick up the fight."

Ellery's hand on the small of his back told him he'd said the right thing.

And her faint smile and the stiffening of her spine told him the same. "Both of you," she said softly.

He shrugged.

It was perfectly obvious to him that he hadn't been necessary at all.

THEY MADE it to Victoriana and followed Ace's directions out to one of maybe three *really nice* finished ranch-style houses in a deserted housing tract that had been meant for at least a dozen. This one had cream-colored stucco, white trim, and desert-chic landscaping of hardy succulents spreading over white gravel.

"The hell?" Jackson said and yawned, pulling up the driveway behind a large battered truck and a now-familiar black motorcycle. "How does someone even know this is out here?"

"If it's Burton," Ellery said practically, "he probably doesn't need anybody to know."

They sat there after Jackson killed the engine in the much-driven CR-V, and just when Jackson thought they were going to have to get out and do something, Ernie and Burton appeared in the doorway. Ernie hurried over to the back seat where Taylor sat and opened the door for her, while Jackson, Ellery, and Amal all stood creakily and stretched.

"Took you long enough," Burton chided before pulling Jackson into a bro-hug. Jackson returned it and grinned.

"Nice place you got here," he said. "I never saw it."

"Good," Burton replied. "Because Ernie asks that you stay tomorrow night too. He wants to have a dinner or something. Don't ask. He's excited. Is that okay?"

Jackson looked over at Taylor, who was smiling at Ernie in that way that indicated she was charmed but bemused. "Well, Lucy Satan is the boss. You'll have to ask her. But…." He yawned again. "Later. Ask her later. Man, what time is it?"

"Two in the morning."

"Is that fucking all? This has been the weirdest day!"

Burton laughed and ushered them all into a spacious home with a large living room and glass bricks separating the hallway from the three bedrooms and two baths. Jackson and Ellery had one case between them, and even Taylor had packed light. While Burton showed Jackson and Ellery their guest room, Ernie showed Amal where he could shower and fetched him clothes before bringing Taylor to their den, which had a twin bed against the back wall.

"Where will Amal sleep?" Jackson heard her ask.

"The couch is *super* comfortable," Ernie said.

Jackson blinked. There'd been something wrong with the couch, he vaguely remembered. Something that might make it difficult for Amal to sleep there. Something that—

Taylor's voice came drifting through the hallway.

"But where are you going to put all the cats?"

Part 4

ERNIE HAD the feeling that Amal Dara had never thought of himself as an activist or a rule breaker or a firebrand but that those things might change after the events of the past day or two.

Not now, though. Now, as Ernie and Burton's house filled with friends, Ernie felt relief from the young nurse, and amusement. The ember of anger had been lit, but Amal was going to see how hot it made him before he decided what to do with that fire.

Right now he was going to enjoy Ernie and Burton's home, which even Ernie had to admit was pretty damned awesome, and he was going to relish meeting the "secret" friends George had been hiding for more than a year.

And apparently he was going to enjoy petting as many cats as he could, which Ernie appreciated about him, because Ernie felt the same way. The landscaping around their ranch house consisted of the pool in the back and a great lawn in the front. But that was only because Burton and Ernie were there to do upkeep. Everything around them was a desert cat box, although Ernie had sprinkled catnip in one of the vacant lots about a block away that hadn't had ground broken yet, just to keep everybody doing their business in the same place. He figured that if someone came in to finish this development, well, they'd have equipment. Otherwise, the feral cats would be going out in the desert anyway, right?

And the indoor cats were good about using the cat door to the garage.

Which meant that everyone—even Sonny—got the tranquility of petting a people-friendly feline without the politely wrinkled nose that usually went with having quite so many.

Ernie wasn't really thinking about that right now, though.

Someone was... lonely.

He'd wanted this gathering as sort of an experiment. His psychic abilities had been overwhelming in the city, but he hadn't been equipped to deal with being completely alone either. This past year, as he and Burton had become closer, as he'd expanded his base of friends to first Ace and Sonny, then Jai and Alba, then Jackson, Ellery, and Taylor Cramer, and now George and Amal, he'd become… safer. More confident. More secure in the ties that bound him and Burton's people together. He missed Jason Constant—a lot, in fact. He had a stomach-rumbling suspicion that something big was going on in Jason's life, and Ernie knew it was only a matter of time before he and Lee and maybe everybody else got called in on that matter. But in the meantime, he'd wanted to see if he could *function* in a situation with more than three people at a time. He wanted to see if he could have a houseful of people who liked him—some of whom *loved* him—and be okay.

And he could! All these people had eaten the dinner he and Lee had cooked—well, Lee had barbecued by the pool—and then, after dark, they'd moved inside into the air-conditioning and eaten the desserts Ernie had prepared. They'd drunk sodas and waters and a couple of beers, and everybody had asked Alba how Lara Martinez and her tiny daughter were doing.

Alba told them… well, the truth. That Lara was traumatized and frightened. She'd had a good job in the city as a receptionist for a pediatrician; being bilingual had been a plus, but she was also competent and kind. But now whenever any of Alba's relatives asked her if she wanted to go home, she simply cried.

But Alba's mommy said that was fine. They could go in the city and get her things and find a place for her to live here, where she was surrounded by people who would take care of her until she felt strong again.

Ernie's heart ached for her in so many ways, but he knew this was not his wound to heal unless she befriended him. And even then he might not have been the voice she needed to hear.

But in spite of what had brought them all together, looking around the room, seeing Ellery's mother be worshipped as the queen she was, seeing George and Jai standing close together and smiling shy and secret smiles, seeing Sonny engaged in dynamic conversation with Amal about the differences between a twelve-pound cat and an eight-pound dog, it all seemed… perfect.

But someone was lonely.

Lee's heat slid along his back, and Lee circled his waist with those strong arms. "Whatcha thinkin', Club Boy?" he murmured, and Ernie smiled at the nickname. He used to use the clubs to turn all those painful thoughts into white noise, to deaden his pain. He didn't need to do that anymore.

"Somebody's lonely," Ernie said, looking through the crowd. Ellery was sitting in the corner of the L-shaped conversation pit, a large calico cat on his lap, stroking her thoughtfully. He was watching his mother talk animatedly to Ace about God knew what, but he was smiling in bemusement. He didn't seem lonely, even though he was....

Oh.

"Where's Jackson?" he asked, scanning the living room again. And it hit him. "He doesn't like parties, does he?"

"No," Burton admitted softly. "He was looking pretty drained, so I asked him if he wanted to sit in the garage and see the kittens."

Ernie turned his head to beam at this amazing man—assassin, badass, loyal friend, beautiful, beautiful lover. "Well done, Crullers," he praised, and Burton looked a little sheepish.

"I learned from a prodigy, Club Boy."

Ernie turned his head just a little farther and kissed his cheek, purring when he got a warm response back. Not an urgent one, but not the kiss of a man afraid of people knowing he was in love either. Sadly, it was Ernie who had to pull back.

"I should go see him," he said softly.

"No, no. Wait." Burton gestured with his chin, and Ellery paused in mid-cat-stroke and glanced around the room in concern. They both watched as he gave a pointed sigh and then moved the calico cat gently from his lap (she was displeased—he had to disconnect her claws from the hem of his cargo shorts) and stood, heading toward Ernie with a puzzled frown on his face.

"Have you seen—"

Burton and Ernie both pointed behind the kitchen door to the garage. "There's kittens," Ernie said quietly, and Ellery gave a sad little smile.

"He's not great at parties," Ellery apologized, but Ernie shook his head.

"I'm sorry. I shouldn't have made you come."

"Oh no!" Ellery looked genuinely distressed. "No, not at all." He gave a fond smile over his shoulder to his mother. "She doesn't celebrate her wins," he confided. "Jackson told me that last night before we fell asleep. We should stay so she could be queen for a day. Don't tell her he said that. He likes to pretend she's Satan."

Ernie laughed a little, delighted. "Not a word," he promised. "I just forget, not everybody likes parties."

Ellery shrugged and gave a shrewd glance to where Amal was talking to Jai, his face alight with awe. "Lots of people are walking around with arrows in their hearts," he said. "They just choose their places to bleed. For Jackson, it's parties."

But Ernie had met Jackson on one of the worst days of his life, had grabbed his hand and gazed into his soul and seen the torn edges trying to stitch themselves together. He wasn't bleeding quite that badly anymore; Ellery had seen to that. But even if he managed to staunch all the bleeding everywhere, there would always be scar tissue, ragged seams, sharp edges, where his soul had been patched.

"For Jackson it's a lot of things," Ernie said gently. "But I'm glad he found a place here where he could hide from all the people."

"I'll go check on him," Ellery said, obviously uncomfortable with Ernie knowing so much.

But Ernie couldn't help it. "Tell him we have a cardboard crate for the one you two pick out. They're eight weeks old now. One of them's ready to go home."

Ellery's eyes widened as he disappeared into the garage.

Ernie stood still, eyes closed, with Cruller's arms securely around his waist, until that arrow of loneliness passed, leaving only a vague ache in its wake.

In response Ernie fell back against Lee's hard body just a little more. "We should do this again," he said dreamily. "After Jason brings his boyfriend back to the desert."

"I beg your pardon?" Lee asked, his entire body stiffening.

Ernie sighed. "You know, I didn't even know I was going to say it until it came out. Can we just pretend it didn't?"

Lee sighed. "Sure. Sure. That's fine. That's great. I should call him. Do you think I should call him?"

Wonderful. Lee had gone an entire three hours without worrying about Constance that day.

"When everyone's asleep," Ernie told him, patting his hand. "It's brewing, but it's not ready to boil over yet."

Burton relaxed infinitesimally, and Ernie leaned into him again. "It's always something, isn't it?"

"As long as it's something with you."

ELLERY FOUND Jackson sitting on a carpeted box in the garage. There seemed to be a couple of them, for both feline and human use, and Ellery glanced around, noting that no cars had ever been in this garage.

There were, however, several cat trees, carpeted shelves in varying heights off the ground, and a wall of food and water bowls, as well as a bank of cat boxes, that, while not pristine, had certainly been changed that day.

And nearly twenty cats moving about—thin, feral, sleek ones and fat, fluffy, spoiled ones. The entire garage—and much of the house—was given over to cats.

"They make Ernie happy," Jackson said as Ellery sat down next to him.

"I can see why," Ellery told him, leaning comfortably against his side.

Jackson gave him a brief smile and then moved to squat next to the six-by-six-foot portable enclosure at his feet. "This one," he said, reaching down to pull up a black kitten with enormous green eyes.

"You want him?" Ellery asked.

"No," Jackson said, laughing. He flipped the creature onto his back and began playing with his tiny paws. "But I think he wants us."

As the kitten played, he began to meow. Not pitifully, just… vocally. Half meows, full meows, half purrs. A volley of cat sounds erupted from him as Jackson played, and Ellery laughed, sticking out a finger to rub the black fur. He was still a little spiky from kittendom, but in a few weeks he'd be a sleek mini-panther.

The kitten snagged Ellery's finger and began gnawing on it, keeping up the monologue the entire time.

"My God, he's chatty," Ellery said in wonder. "Does he ever shut up?"

"Probably only when he's sleeping," Jackson told Ellery, laughing. "See?"

The gnawing eased up, but the kitten kept talking, only licking Ellery's finger now.

"I thought I was going to choose!" Ellery protested—but not hard. He had to admit this guy was pretty attractive.

"Well, you can," Jackson said, indicating all of the other kittens in the enclosure. "There's five more in there, and while the tiger stripe there appears to have the personality of oatmeal, the two orange toms over there are promising."

The black kitten kept licking his finger, finally wrapping all his little kitten limbs around Ellery's hand in contentment.

And once he wasn't partially tucked against Jackson's chest, that's when Ellery noticed.

"One of his back legs," he said.

"Yeah, I saw." He heard the forced nonchalance in Jackson's voice, and his heart hurt.

One of the kitten's back legs was stunted—probably circulation had been cut off in the womb. A vestigial, withered back paw hung there, and a competent vet would probably remove it just to get it out of the way.

"He's perfect," Ellery said with awe. "He... he's us."

"He's you," Jackson said, so much affection in his voice Ellery couldn't take offense. "Like you were yesterday. Just kept talking, making sense, fighting the good fight, until those assholes kneeled before you." Jackson looked at him happily, green eyes soft and admiring. "You were fucking awesome."

Ellery gave half a laugh. "Jackson, you drove Tetley to confess. In fact, you made him jump on top of Cly, and then *Cly* pretty much admitted guilt by beating on him. I mean, I may have cut through the bureaucracy, but *you* cut through the crap."

Jackson shrugged and looked away. "Think Tetley will be charged?" he asked, and Ellery's chest ached.

Yeah, Ellery had seen the similarities between Jackson and the young ICE agent too.

"No," Ellery said softly. "He had his suspicions, but Cly never trusted him enough to confess to what he'd been doing. Tetley turned over their visitation logs and highlighted the women he thought Cly might have been abusing, but he was...." Ellery shook his head. "Destroyed. Realizing what his partner had been doing, being forced to be a party to it? Once you connected the dots, he was... he'll probably never work law enforcement again."

Jackson grunted. "He should have seen," he said at last.

"He thought he was working for the good guys," Ellery reminded him. Just like Jackson, Tetley had been used and disillusioned.

Unlike Jackson, Tetley might end up a salesclerk in a gas station or doing something else that required little responsibility and less power. Tetley had been appalled, but he hadn't been strong.

"He wouldn't have done what you did," Ellery continued, taking the kitten from Jackson and smiling as the little goober curled up in the crook of his elbow and started to purr. "You were strong enough to see, Jackson. You were strong enough to fight back."

"Well, you didn't come along to save me until much later," Jackson said mildly.

"You didn't need saving," Ellery told him. He was still tired from the day before, and as they situated themselves back on the carpeted wooden box, he leaned his head a little on Jackson's shoulder. "Just some training up."

Jackson laughed a little. "So," he said. "That one?"

"Do you think Billy Bob will like him?"

Jackson kissed Ellery's temple. "I think this one will talk him to death if he doesn't."

Ellery chuckled and let that vibrating little heat source pulse relaxation through his body.

"What should we name him?"

"Sammy-Joe."

"No."

Jackson laughed and tried again. "Cletus."

"God no."

"Azazeel?"

"As in Satan? No."

"Charlie Satan?"

"Jackson!"

"Johnny Satan?"

"I will name him Carl if you don't think of this seriously."

Jackson sighed. "There's really only one name. You know that, right?"

God, Ellery loved this man. So much. Enough to let the inevitable wash over them both and christen the little furry thing in his arms.

"Lucifer, then," he said sighing. "My mother will be thrilled."

And she probably would be. She adored Billy Bob already, and knowing Jackson had named a cat after her? Well, his mother did have a sense of humor.

And she loved Jackson almost as much as Ellery did.

But not quite. Ellery set the bar pretty high.

Clinging to the Curtain

A Fish Out of Water Ficlet

"JACKSON?" ELLERY grumbled, reaching for the empty spot on the bed. "Jackson, where are you?"

Jackson didn't answer, and Ellery listened for a moment for bathroom noises, but there were none—and no light on either. He almost fell back asleep then, but a sound from the living room got his attention.

"Billy Bob, you no-thumbs-having-motherfucker, did you do this?"

To his surprise, there was an indignant "Merowl!" in response.

"Don't lie," Jackson muttered. "This has you written all over it."

Another "Merowl!"—this one a definitive, "Fuck you, bub. This isn't my fault."

"I don't believe you," Jackson muttered flatly. Then, in a completely different voice, he said, "Okay, Baby Satan, it's fine. I'm here. I need you to let go, okay?"

The teeny-tiny "mew" that came next was not exactly a surprise, except Ellery had no idea Lucifer had started talking back. In the two weeks since they'd brought home the kitten, the tiny three-legged sleekly-furred tornado had been responsible for more broken plates, glasses, and vases than any other creature, human or animal, that had ever been in Ellery's home.

Ellery was terrible at discipline, but Jackson wasn't much better.

The day before, they arrived home from work to find a vase of flowers that had been on the table cracked into pieces on the floor. Ellery had been—finally—working up a real head of steam about how they had sixty-zillion different toys and an entire cat tree in the guest room, and how could the little shit know unerringly where to run to do the most damage, when Jackson had pulled out an old movie quote and stopped him with his mouth wide open to deliver the scathing comedown.

"That was a very expensive vase, you bitch!" he said with pitch-perfect inflection, and that quickly, Ellery couldn't stop giggling.

The kitten would live another day. Maybe.

Because right now, there was a wealth of worry in Jackson's voice that made Ellery deeply uneasy. He stood, throwing on a short robe because he was wearing briefs and nothing else, and followed the ambient light from the stove into the open-floor front room/kitchen/dining room.

Jackson was at the far end, by the back door, talking to the top of the curtains.

"Oh, Baby Satan," he crooned. "Little Beelzebub… whatcha doin' up there?"

"Mew! Mew! Mew!"

"Yeah, I know you're stuck. I can see that. Wanna help me get you down?"

"Mew! Mew! Mew!"

"Mrowl!"

"You stop it," Jackson admonished, looking down at Billy Bob. "You say you're not responsible for this mess, but I for one am not buying it."

"Mew! Mew! Mew!"

"Aw, Baby Satan, he didn't mean it. You just need to stop pouncing on his tail, that's all. It's the only part he's got that's still intact."

"Mrowl!"

"Don't tell him that," Jackson hissed. "He doesn't need to know about that part. It's next week, and we want him to stay!"

"Mrowl!"

"We do too, you big baby. Think about it. Me and Ellery are gone all day, and you're here all by yourself. If you can't treat this little guy right, we're gonna have to give him to Jade."

Ellery wondered if it was his imagination, or if the next, "Mrowl!" hadn't gained some extra force and volume.

"Yeah, that's right. Jade. And you know what? I bet this guy is so sweet to that big woof dog of hers and Mike's that he doesn't even miss you."

"Mrrroooooooowwwwwllll!!!!"

Yeah, that definitely pissed the big Siamese mix off.

"Uh-huh! So you be nice to Baby Satan here and Albert stays your buddy forever, and you'll be the only cat he'll ever love."

"Mew! Mew! Mew!"

Jackson turned his attention back to the curtains that were stretched across the back door. Deep in the shadow of the corner of the room, Ellery could see a tiny fuzz of darkness, legs spread, just out of Jackson's reach.

"I didn't forget about you!" Jackson chided. "I'm just giving big no-thumbs-having-motherfucker a talking-to. I know you didn't get into this sitch by yourself."

"Mew! Mew! Mew!"

Ellery watched appreciatively as Jackson stood on his tiptoes and stretched his arms over his head while he fiddled with his fingers. "Ah-ah-ah… there we go."

He relaxed his calves and stood flat-footed, clutching the kitten to his chest. The next sound that came was loud enough to fill up the room.

"Yeah, I know. You think I'm special. But I'm going to hand you to Ellery and spend some time with No-thumbs over there so he stops being a big jealous turd. Do you mind?"

"Purrrrrrrrrrrr…."

"You knew I was there?" Ellery murmured, walking forward to take the kitten from him.

"You were making weird sounds," Jackson said frankly. "It was like you were humming. Anyway, take him to the bedroom, and I'll give Billy Bob some kitty treats—"

"Do we even *have* kitty treats?" Ellery asked, not sure those were on the grocery list.

"No, but we have crab delight for the salads."

"Jackson, we can't give the cat—"

"Ellery, do you want me to rescue Baby Satan there from every curtain in the house before he nests in your hair?"

The kitten started kneading biscuits on Ellery's bare chest, having managed to find his way between the lapels of the robe.

"No." He winced.

"Then we're going to make that other furry asshole feel like the king of fuckin' American River Drive, you think?"

"Sure," Ellery gasped, trying to detach the ecstatic kitten. "Sounds like a plan."

He fell asleep with the kitten literally nesting in his hair on top of the pillow, waking up when Jackson slid in next to him.

"How's Billy Bob?" he mumbled and was rewarded by a big *whump*! on the bed and Jackson's "*Oolf*!" as the cat marched across Jackson's stomach.

"Fuckin' peachy," Jackson replied, and as Ellery peered through the darkness with slitted eyes, he saw the cat curl up behind Jackson's neck and, of course, start making biscuits in Jackson's hair.

"So," he said as the room filled with purring, "this is pet ownership."

"Yup."

Ellery smiled softly at him, remembering his street-smart, shoe-leather-tough lover mediating a dispute between the alley cat and the kitten and trying to help them both reach an accord.

"It suits us," he said, kissing Jackson on the mouth.

"Mm…." Jackson responded to the kiss and then jerked back. "It does," he said, hissing as Billy Bob kneaded some more. "It will suit us even better when these two morons let us have sex again."

"Tomorrow," Ellery told him, already making plans to buy something the kitten could climb up, like a rope or a cloth they could secure from the ceiling. "Right now, let's savor the peace."

"Fine," Jackson muttered, closing his eyes. They fell asleep like that, facing each other, while the rumbling of happy felines filled the room.

Like so many things, I blame this completely, unequivocally, on Jason Russell. You're welcome.

Jackson's Christine

A Fishlet

JACKSON AND Henry stood by the once-new Honda CR-V, stunned and in shock.

"This isn't my fault," Jackson said, taking in the completely concave driver's side and rear quarter panel.

"We parked it in a parking place," Henry said, looking around the grocery store parking lot with eyes haunted by ghosts of traffic misdeeds past. "For once."

"I... I... this isn't my fault!" Jackson almost moaned. "Dammit! Henry, this isn't my fault!" He had lost track—*lost track*—of how many new vehicles he'd gotten in the past year. Was this the fourth one? The fifth? It didn't matter. After the first one had been shot up, the rest had been on Ellery's dime, and on his insurance. But it didn't seem to matter. Shot up, shot up *and* rolled down a hill, smashed in by a drunk driver, *blown up*, then refurbished and *then* used in a demolition derby race that had yet to be classified, every vehicle had somehow met its unholy and untimely demise. Jackson, while not always the driver, was somehow the catalyst that had doomed them all.

"I'll swear on a stack of Bibles," Henry told him, nodding seriously.

"I... I don't know how to fix this," Jackson mumbled, watching as the rear bumper fell off. Almost frantically he tried to think of a thing to do that wouldn't bother Ellery, wouldn't inconvenience him, wouldn't get him *kicked off his insurance plan*. Jesus, how could he be so reliant on Ellery Cramer after only a year? What would he have done *before* they—and Ellery's seemingly inexhaustible trust fund—had hooked up?

Jackson smiled.

"What?" Henry asked suspiciously.

Jackson clicked the key fob and gestured to Henry, who had access to one of the doors that worked. "Start pulling shit out," he said. "There's grocery bags in the back. I've got an idea."

Henry's eyes narrowed. He'd been put in an uncomfortable spot before when Jackson had tried a workaround with Ellery. Jackson had never told him how that had fallen out. Henry probably had his suspicions that it had been bad, but whatever they were, he hadn't even scratched the surface. So bad. Relationship-breaking bad.

"This is unholy and unwise, and I want no part of it," Henry said, holding his hands up and taking a step back.

"Oh, put your testicles on and start cleaning house," Jackson told him. "I swear to God, this won't get you in trouble!"

"You say that," Henry protested, but Jackson noted he was actively engaged in getting the grocery bags and pulling out the stuff in the back seat. Maps, bottles of water, first-aid kit, Nikon camera with long-range lens, both their gym bags, extra bandages—all of it went into the grocery bags while Jackson grabbed his phone.

"I'll be in the coffee shop," he said, nodding to the place by the grocery store, "using my phone like a boss."

"Boss is right," Henry muttered, but he didn't have Jackson's brainstorm, so he could pout all he wanted.

Ten minutes later, Henry had purchased two iced coffees—decaf for Jackson and his tetchy heart—and Jackson was trying not to show his distaste as he continued to do things on his phone. Finally he finished, sat back, and took a swig, sticking his tongue out like a cat when he realized what he was drinking.

"Tea, Junior," he said in despair. "Iced tea, no sugar, is fine! Oh my God, that's vile. That's—"

"Stop bitching," Henry snapped, taking his own swig of Jackson's coffee. "It's—" He shuddered and swallowed, his entire body recoiling. "Fine," he rasped after it was down. "Tastes great. Go ahead and wimp out for tea if you need to. What's our plan?"

"Well, first of all text Andres and tell him that his perp just walked in while you were getting coffee. I think we had his workplace right but the time he started wrong. Be ready to watch the guy squirt out of here when his buddies warn him that we came in looking, 'kay?"

"Yeah," Henry said, all business. "Got him. Heading down the produce aisle. Look, he's got an apron. It seems weird that a guy with an apron should be wanted for grand larceny."

"As opposed to murder, when the apron keeps his clothes clean?" God, Henry could be dense sometimes.

Henry stared at him. "You are so weird."

"Whatever. Oops, there he is, talking to the manager. Looking around. You take the employees' exit. I'll be right outside."

"But our stuff!" Henry opined.

Jackson held up a twenty and waved it toward the barista. "Watch this?"

The woman—middle-aged, looked like she had kids and a mortgage—nodded happily. Jackson handed her the twenty and vamoosed out the front door, leaving Henry to make sure their guy, a stolid, plain white guy with a tiny mouth compressed in a scowl and a five-head, didn't go out the back.

He had just situated himself when Henry buzzed him. Jackson hit his earbud, and Henry barked, "Shit! He's out the back! Out the back!"

"He can't hop that fence," Jackson told him, because there was a tall, steep rise behind the grocery store, topped with a ten-foot chain-link fence.

"We're coming around from the east!"

Well, shit. Jackson jogged to the east end of the grocery store, hearing the pounding of feet and the whispers of muffled swearing as he did so. Jackson pressed his back against the rough granite of the outside wall and waited... waited... waited....

"Hang on, kid!" Henry panted from farther back, and Jackson took that as his cue. He grabbed one of the grocery carts just hanging around and shoved it, blocking the only exit their perp had just as the kid came barreling out from the narrow alleyway.

He went over hard, so quickly he didn't have time to scream or curse, and Henry skidded to a stop as he landed.

"Ouch," Henry muttered. "That's gonna leave a mark."

"Road rash of the face is never pretty," Jackson said.

At that moment, an unmarked car screeched to a halt in front of the grocery store entrance and Sean Kryzynski's partner emerged. Muttering to himself, Andre Christie strode over to where their perp was rolling on the ground, holding both his torn-up shins and moaning.

"So," he said in bemusement, "this is the guy who's been setting up truck hijacking operations throughout the valley?"

"He's been sleeping with the scheduling lady," Jackson said. "He told the hijackers where the trucks with the expensive shit would be, and they paid him a cut." Jackson crouched down by their poor moaning asshole. "Isn't that right, Julius?"

"Fuck you," Julius Warner sobbed. "I don't have to talk to you."

"No you do not. But you should probably talk to a lawyer." Jackson stood. "So, are you dropping charges against our guy?"

Christie, a dapper, handsome Latinx man, smiled grimly. "Since you were nice enough to run down the actual criminal, I'll talk to the DA about it." He scowled at their bad guy's injuries. "After I take him to the hospital." He eyed Jackson critically. "You need anything? Scrub and wash? Stitch and soap? Any bones set? New ticker?"

"No, and fuck you," Jackson told him pleasantly. "Junior and I have some car bullshit to take care of."

"Fine. Kryzynski's house, Sunday? The Kings are playing."

"We'll be there," Henry said before Jackson could give pushback about watching sports. Henry was right. Of course they'd be there, because Sean Kryzynski was their friend and being off duty while he recovered from a punctured lung was driving him batshit. Jackson just didn't like being easy.

"Yeah, yeah," Jackson muttered. "Don't let Junior here cater. He thinks iced coffee should be decaf."

Christie let out a horrified gasp. "Heathen! Jesus, no. I'll bring beer, chips, popcorn, and something with protein. You assholes bring whatever you want." He pulled out the radio at his side. "Now, if you don't mind, I've got this to take care of."

Jackson looked up to where the tow truck had just arrived and breathed a sigh of relief. "And we have our own date with destiny," he said. "Junior, go get our bags o' crap. We're catching a ride with the tow-truck guy."

Henry groaned. "Can't I just take a Lyft?"

"No. Because we've got two more cases to look into after this one, and I'm not stopping because somebody creamed our car."

"But Jackson," Henry said quietly as they walked away from Andre Christie. "What about insurance, getting the car fixed—all that?"

Jackson shook his head violently. "I've got money," he said, knowing he sounded stubborn and not caring. "I've got money, and I've got connections, and—"

"Wait a minute," Henry said, and the suspicion in his voice was fair. "This isn't... you know...?"

"Hurricane Joey and his Nine-Inch Dick?" Jackson said, nodding. "Yes. Yes it is. Because he's got some guys that do bodywork in their spare time."

"But what are we going to drive in the meantime?"

Jackson didn't want to think about it. "I got nothin'," he said. "But Joey reassures me he's got a vehicle I can borrow."

Henry scrubbed his face and groaned. "Oh, I am not going to like this," he muttered.

"You don't have to," Jackson reassured him. "This is all on me."

Famous last words. God, Jackson shuddered to think.

ELLERY GOT home about an hour after Jackson did, but part of that was because Jackson and Henry had been busy, and Ellery had been doing the paperwork that came with their productivity. Jackson had texted him, assuring him that everything was fine, just fine, and he was home broiling chicken and preparing vegetables, and all was right with the world.

Ellery didn't trust a world in which there were no wrongs. He trusted it even less when he pulled his beloved vehicle into the garage and saw the... the monstrosity parked in Jackson's usual space.

He was at a loss. At least ten years old, with primer spots where paint had been flaked off in the weather, it had once been a deep-brown-colored Chrysler Town & Country. Since then it had apparently been with a family that washed it with rocks and then passed it on to a company that believed in stripping big gouts of paint from the sides. Ellery could barely make out the printing where the plastic ad-wrap had gone.

Cleaning and Repair...

Oh dear.

Ellery shook his head. Not angry, really, just curious. Where *was* Jackson's car, and what was this abomination doing parked in its—

The car's lights went on.

Ellery stared at it.

The lights came on, blinked once, twice, three times, and then went off. Then the car horn beeped.

"What in the he—"

The back hatch slowly began to rise.

Ellery paused, thinking he could actually look inside the demonic machine, or he could go into the house and ask Jackson what in the world of fuck this thing was doing here.

"Jackson!" he hollered, heading for the garage step. "Jackson! The actual hell!"

Jackson greeted him at the door to the kitchen and gave him a brief kiss on the cheek.

"Is it doing it again?"

"Doing what?" Ellery asked, trying to keep his voice level.

"Is it acting possessed?"

Ellery hadn't wanted to say it.

"Yes," he admitted. "Yes. It is acting possessed. What is this possessed car doing in my garage?"

Jackson grimaced. From the garage came another small beep, then a powering down sound, like an airplane whose engines were spinning to a stop.

"Well, I borrowed the car from Joey."

"I figured that." Ellery didn't bother to get jealous anymore. If he got a bug up his ass every time he met someone who'd slept with Jackson—or wanted to sleep with him—he'd forget how to walk normal. "Where's the CR-V?"

"Joey's. Uhm…." Jackson finally met his eyes. "Ellery?"

"Yes?"

"Once—just this once—if I tell you I've got it and it wasn't my fault, can we not ask too many questions?"

Oh Lord. He looked *so* sincere.

"Were you in any danger?" Ellery asked, because this was the real sticking point between them.

"No. I would have told you if I had been."

Okay. "Am I going to have to report this to my insurance company?" His insurance agent was ready to come over and do an exorcism anyway. After the last vehicle had bit the dust, the man had seriously asked Ellery if his boyfriend was possessed by Satan. What was he going to say now? "No, Jackson's fine, but if we could smudge the car…?"

"I'm really trying to avoid that," Jackson said. "Please? I feel bad enough already."

Ellery let out a breath. They'd been together for a year and a month, and he wouldn't change a minute of it. Jackson had functioned just fine as an adult before Ellery had arrived. Maybe it was time to trust him.

"Sure," he said. "But, uhm, about that car. Did you know the back hatch was opening by itself?"

"Yeah," Jackson said. "Don't stick your hand in there—it's a trap. Henry needed ice."

Ellery closed his eyes and let out his tension. "Did you say chicken?" he asked desperately.

"Sadly, no. Lucifer stole the chicken just before you walked in. I think he's hiding in the bathroom, sharing with Billy Bob. I was about to pull out the lunchmeat." Jackson gave a game smile. "Sorry?"

And Ellery laughed helplessly. "Can I get a kiss, at least?" he asked.

Jackson's grin appeared, the full monty, the one that popped his dimples. "God yes. C'mere, Counselor. Let's neck."

Sometimes that kiss waiting for him when he got home really was the alpha and omega, wasn't it?

HENRY AND Jackson approached the recently repaired CR-V warily. They'd gotten it back the week before, and at first, they'd been just so damned grateful not to be driving the Town & Country that all the world seemed shiny and bright and all the things seemed good.

But then....

Then the wipers had gone on when they were in the middle of traffic. Then the horn would beep when neither one of them had been anywhere near it.

Then the back hatch would fly open as they approached the vehicle, and slam shut as either one of them tried to close it.

"Was it too much to ask?" Henry complained bitterly as the lights came on and the back hatch started to open.

"No," Jackson told him.

"I mean, it's like the Town & Country passed on the evil spirit."

"I know," Jackson said grimly.

"I mean, this thing hates me!" Henry had barely escaped getting his hand slammed in the back more than once.

"Hates us both," Jackson confirmed.

They were about fifteen feet away from the vehicle now, their attention so focused on what it could possibly do to them that they weren't paying attention to their surroundings. Neither of them saw the guy with the knife come whipping around the back end of the vehicle, aiming it at them both, shouting something about letting Julius Warner out of jail so his brother didn't have to go too until he was almost in Henry's face.

Henry took a step back, and then the car stepped in, the back hatch popping all the way open and tagging the kid in the head. Their would-be assailant pitched forward, barely avoiding getting impaled on his own knife, and then he lay there, out cold, while the hatch to the CR-V slammed shut and latched itself closed.

"Maybe not hates," Henry said tentatively, staring at their attacker.

"Maybe it's warming up to us?" Jackson suggested, pulling out his phone to get Andre Christie out there and help scoop up another one.

"Still not getting in it without backup," Henry said, as though making a decision.

"Smart boy," Jackson said. As he pulled up Christie's number, he wondered if they could get Rabbi Watson *and* the insurance agent out to their house. If they couldn't exorcise the vehicle, maybe they could bless it, put it in a good mood. A possessed car could be helpful, as long as it didn't maim Jackson or Henry as it did good work.

I've Got You

A Fishlet

"So, NO?" Ellery asked as they left the county jail.

"Fuck no," Jackson said savagely, still shaking. Ellery's hand on the small of his back told him he was dangerously close to losing his shit in a very public venue. He took a deep breath and an extra step away. He knew Ellery didn't like public displays of affection. He didn't want to obligate Ellery to break his own rules because he couldn't hold himself together.

"I'm sorry about that," Ellery said softly as they got into the Lexus. Jackson wished he could drive. It would give him an excuse not to talk about it.

"Somebody lied heinously to Jade when they called," he said, sliding on his belt.

"I know they did."

Jade had gotten a call from the jailhouse clerk saying Ellery's presence had been requested to represent a client accused of murder and possession.

Nobody had mentioned that the murder was of a four-year-old girl, and the possession had been the drugs she'd ingested from her mother's boyfriend's meth stash.

The boyfriend had been completely unrepentant, blaming "the stupid little bitch" for "stealing my good shit."

Not the cases they took. Ever.

Jackson had heard the one sentence and had stood up and told Ellery they were leaving. Ellery had made the polite noises about declining the case—it hadn't been a pro bono case or court assigned, after all—and they'd exited.

But Jackson was still shaking.

"Lunch?" Ellery asked politely.

"No," Jackson said. Normally he'd at least pretend to eat. He'd been doing so good, staying consistent, being healthy, not straining his heart or Ellery's patience. But anything he ate that day wouldn't stay down—not even a little.

"Home?" Ellery asked tentatively.

Jackson shook his head. "Work," he said. "Henry and I have some shit to check out today, and I think Jade has some leads for us. I'm fine, Ellery." He tried to keep the edge of impatience out of his voice, because it wasn't fair for him to take the shakiness, the sickness in the pit of his stomach, out on Ellery. This wasn't his fault. The world was fucked-up and always had been, and Jackson had to learn to live with it or lose out on the good parts he'd just discovered.

"If you're sure—"

"Ellery, I'm fine. Truly. Just… you know. We need to find out how that guy got our number."

"Sure. Sure, that's the problem. How that guy got our number."

Jackson breathed in through his nose and out through his mouth, and apparently the sound alone was enough to warn Ellery off the subject.

"Which I will ask Jade about immediately," Ellery finished pleasantly. "Message received."

"Good."

But it wasn't the end of it. He knew it couldn't be. Nothing was ever that easy.

"So," Henry said, his voice ringing with that same insincere, pleasant quality that had laced Ellery's voice on the drive to the office. "What ugly sphincter-eating cockroach crawled up your orifice and died?"

"Fuck off," Jackson growled, taking a sip of his coffee. He'd tried a smoothie back at the office, but it wasn't going to work. Apparently the only way to combat the thing growing in his stomach was more acid.

"No, really." Henry's eyes moved restlessly across the ugly little suburb in Citrus Heights. Sandwiched between the slightly more urban Carmichael and the picturesque, moneyfied Fair Oaks, Citrus Heights had adorable little rainbow neighborhoods with nice lawns and inclusive signs and happy flags, and it had war zones where the kids in the rec centers had to dive for cover at least once a week because of nearby assholes with guns.

This was one of the latter; they'd seen the white-supremacist graffiti on their way into the mostly Black and Brown neighborhood and had gotten the idea that they were on the right track for who killed the young Mexican graduate student who had been helping at the rec center.

Unfortunately, a transient with a shopping cart and a dog happened to be more visible than the Proud Boy who actually did the crime, and enter Ellery Cramer and pro bono work he would agree to do.

They were on the lookout for a bald twentysomething with a beard down his chest, a tiny Swastika tattoo behind one ear and a cigarette behind the other. Just to talk to him, right?

Just talk.

Jackson thought about the client that morning and wondered how much talking he could do before Henry pulled him off the guy.

Oh, he was in an ugly mood.

"I don't see this guy," Henry muttered. "And we've been staking out this place for the past hour. School has ended, parents have picked their kids up from the center—I think he's hiding out."

"Smartest thing he's ever done," Jackson muttered. Then, oh God! There he was. Six feet tall, ginger beard, oversized black jeans pulled low down his ass from the semiauto stuffed in the back. Jackson was out of the rental minivan and down the street before uttering a word. He heard Henry at his heels, but only in a peripheral way.

"Tab Miller!" he called out. "Tab Miller? I've got some questions for you!"

The guy turned, a sneer on his face, his bare chest showing off black-line tattoos in the October chill. "Who the fuck are you?"

"I'm a friend of Craig Munoz. Does that name ring a bell?"

Tab's jaw hardened, and his hand went to the gun in the back of his pants, and then Jackson charged and leaped.

He came to himself when Henry hauled him up by the armpits with the help of two uniformed police officers, one of whom moved in to cuff Miller.

"He killed Munoz," Jackson panted, wondering how long he'd just sat on the guy's chest and beaten him into the pavement. His jaw was swollen, and he tasted blood, so Miller must have gotten in some blows too. That made him feel better somehow. He didn't pick on the helpless. He didn't beat up the innocent.

"I know," said one of the uniforms, a fair-faced, blue-eyed boy. "He confessed while you were beating the shit out of him. Not sure if it will stand up in court, but it's enough to confiscate the gun and compare ballistics."

"Get Randy Caufield out of jail," Jackson mumbled. "Into a program. He... he needs to be off the streets."

"That depends, Mother Theresa," said the cop at his shoulder—older, female, Latina. "Are you going to stop beating random people on the streets and let us do our job?"

Jackson opened his mouth to retort that if they'd done their jobs in the first place, Ellery's services wouldn't have been needed, but Henry hauled him away, still sputtering, while he was trying to brain words.

He found himself shoved into the passenger seat of his own car—well, his own rental—before he could protest... well, everything.

"Why are you driving?" he asked as Henry pulled away from the scene, leaving four squad cars and an ambulance in the dust.

"To get us out of there before you got arrested," Henry retorted. "I ask you again, what crawled up your ass?"

"You don't want to know," Jackson told him. They were probably the most honest words he'd spoken all day.

"Of course I do!" Henry snarled. "Look at you! You're bleeding all over this great haunted minivan. You were *dying* for a fight. You didn't say five words to me in an hour, and then you were hauling ass out onto the street to fight with our suspect. And you may have a few bruises, but I use the term 'fight' loosely. You were going to *kill* that guy. And as shitty a human being as I think he is, I don't think he's who you want to kill right now!"

Jackson grunted. "I wouldn't have *minded* killing him," he hedged.

"I wouldn't have minded seeing him die," Henry said, no bullshit, and since Henry had fought in the infantry and had seen men die, Jackson took him at his word. "But before we go commit murder for the cause, I'd like to know who should be standing in his place."

Jackson's anger drained out of him abruptly, and he looked at his bleeding knuckles and grimaced and then pulled down the visor to check out his face. Swollen jaw, split lip, and a graze on his cheek. The guy had led exclusively with his right. Jackson had a vague memory of snapping his wrist. Well, he wouldn't do that again.

"We did an interview this morning," he mumbled. "Let his girlfriend's four-year-old overdose on his meth. It... touched a nerve."

"Oh," Henry said softly. "Oh. Damn. That's... that's awful."

"Yes."

Henry took a breath, and Jackson could hear all the things he was trying not to ask—like, what was it like to grow up with a junkie for a mother, and had something like that ever happened to Jackson.

"I got the shit kicked out of me if I touched the coke mirrors," he said after a moment. "Celia wasn't a great mother, but she didn't want me to die either. Small mercies." He touched his aching jaw and felt an echo from something that had happened a long time ago. Very, very small mercies.

"And you thought it was a good day to go out on the streets?" Henry asked, the sharpness in his tone soothing.

"I'm not broken," Jackson snarled, his anger up again. Oh God. When was he going to get a handle on this? He'd been working on it; weekly visits with Rabbi Watson when he wasn't even Jewish—or religious. All of that soul-baring honesty with Ellery. If he wasn't good at his job, what was any of that other bullshit worth?

"Oh, Jackson," Henry said softly. "We're all broken. You taught me that. Sometimes you just have to accept those edges will never really heal."

"Fuck off," Jackson said, giving up on trying to fix his knuckles, his face, his life. Wasn't going to happen right now. He leaned back and sighed. "You know, you can say what you like about this haunted piece of shit, but it is damned comfortable."

"As long as it's not trying to eat me," Henry muttered darkly.

"Or the alarm doesn't go off at fuck-you in the morning," Jackson added. It happened about once a week.

"When do you get your car back?" Jackson had given the thing to a friend of a friend to fix—it had needed bodywork. But apparently the bodywork had gone a little far, and then it needed a new radiator. And then the radiator had broken when they'd been giving it a test drive, and now it needed a new engine.

"Next week," Jackson said glumly. "Maybe. We may end up with the crap-mobile forever after."

"Maybe if we do," Henry said, sounding unreasonably optimistic, "we could paint it something besides brown. Then it won't be the crap-mobile anymore."

"Don't kid yourself, Junior," Jackson warned. "This thing will never be anything *but* the crap-mobile. You could paint it sky-fucking-happy-assed blue, and it would be the sky-fucking-happy-assed-blue crap-mobile."

Henry sighed. "But at least it runs."

Jackson patted the dashboard. "Good crap-mobile," he crooned. He could swear, sometimes it heard the tiniest bit of praise and that was all that kept it running. "What time is it?" he asked, head tilted back against the headrest, eyes closed against the autumn sun coming in the windshield.

"Six thirty."

"Drop me off at home and keep the crap-mobile for yourself," Jackson told him. Henry still didn't have a car, but given that part of their days were often spent at the office and the other part out and about, they ended up sharing custody of the vehicle. Henry said it was comfier than his boyfriend's car, so it seemed to work. "It'll save everybody half an hour of driving."

"And give you a chance to clean up the blood before Ellery sees you," Henry said, because he wasn't stupid.

"And give me a chance to clean up the blood before Ellery sees me," Jackson agreed.

"But you'll still tell him, right?"

Well, Jackson wasn't stupid either. "Yes. But you can't make it bigger than it was when you tell Jade about it at the office."

Henry grunted. "Ha!"

Well, it wasn't like Jackson didn't deserve it.

ELLERY SAT on the couch, knees drawn up to his chest, and watched Jackson doze off, one cat on either side of his neck, both of them purring. Maybe… maybe this time it would take.

It was getting so Ellery knew when the nightmares would come just as sure as Jackson would, and he certainly didn't have to be a shrink to know there'd be a doozy this night. Ellery figured if he was sleeping right now, he'd be having his own.

But Jackson—who had apologized briefly for getting into a fight with a suspect and assured him, in five words or less, that he really would be fine—hadn't given Ellery time to have a nightmare. First he'd swum laps until it was almost too cold to get out of the pool without the space heater Ellery had provided, and then he'd pushed his dinner around his plate until it gave up and disintegrated, making his plate look slightly less full.

Then he'd given Ellery a perfunctory good-night kiss and lay down on his little sliver of the bed like a prisoner going off to execution.

Ellery had dozed off before the first nightmare hit, but the screams had pretty much put an end to that. Jackson had pretended to drift off in Ellery's arms after that, but Ellery had felt him get out of bed and come out to the couch. Ellery had thought he'd be playing video games, but instead he'd been lying down, eyes closed, earbuds on, listening to old Green Day albums at top volume.

Ellery had sat with him, waiting for the album to end. Ellery could hear it, even from across the couch, and when he'd checked, Jackson had been mostly asleep, the cats in place, sentinels to dreamland who may or may not succeed.

"Why won't you let me help you?" he whispered, knowing that it was probably unfair of him to ask. So much progress in the last year. So much change. Jackson was entitled to some space in which to work out the more painful moments in his mind. He'd been up-front about his injuries, had kept to his exercise regimen, and had even cooked dinner, although Ellery couldn't blame him for not eating. He was trying.

Ellery just wanted to try with him.

In response to Ellery's quiet words, Jackson murmured Ellery's name, and Ellery had a sudden, desperate idea.

He moved to the side of the couch, on his knees, and gently disengaged Lucifer, now six months old and the fully sassy nightmare Jackson had anticipated when they'd chosen the sleek black three-legged creature from his cluster of quadrupeded slightly-less-sassy siblings.

"Go steal Billy Bob's food," Ellery told him, and Billy Bob, alert to any such shenanigans, uncoiled himself from Jackson's other ear and leapt over the arm of the couch smoothly to keep an eye on the youngster.

Jackson shivered a little now that he didn't have his furry ear warmers, and Ellery moved closer, close enough to rub his lips along Jackson's jaw.

"That hurt?" he murmured.

"No," Jackson replied. "You should go to sleep."

"Shut up and kiss me," Ellery teased, wondering if he was crazy or desperate or just needy. He wanted Jackson's warm body, wanted his sweetness, his surrender.

If he surrendered, allowed himself to be loved, maybe the nightmares would leave him alone tonight.

Jackson's mouth seeking his out was nearly as gratifying as what Ellery had planned. Oh, the kiss went on and on, and Jackson's hands gripping Ellery's biceps were needy and urgent.

"I've got you," Ellery whispered, pulling away. "I've got you."

He started undressing Jackson there in the living room, pulling off his ragged T-shirt, shucking his sweats. Jackson lay on the couch, staring at him from sleep-muddled eyes.

"I'm naked?" he mumbled. "Is that right?"

Ellery darted in and sucked on his nipple, giving it a little nip before pulling back and hauling his own shirt over his head. "Do you want it to be?"

Jackson had used sex for years to cover up his nightmares, Ellery knew. He'd tried not to do the same thing with Ellery, tried hard to be emotionally whole when they made love, not to come to Ellery's bed needing raw sex to staunch the bleeding in his soul.

But that's not what this was.

Ellery wanted to comfort him, but more than that, Ellery *wanted* him. Whole, broken, bleeding, healed—Ellery was shameless. If Jackson needed to use Ellery for sex, well, Ellery was there for use.

Or to use Jackson for the same thing.

Because sex between two people who loved each other and wanted the other to feel better was a healing act, and Ellery would take that for what it was.

"Yes," Jackson moaned, trying to shove up on his elbow. "Yes, I want to be naked, and you to be naked, and—"

Ellery kissed him again until he stopped talking and then kissed down his chest, kissed his nipples, sucked on them, enjoying Jackson's drunken wriggling as he tried to pull away from sleep, from the dream that had been coming, from the misery he was trying so hard not to share.

Ellery got to Jackson's cock and took it in, shucking his pajamas at the same time because he *rocked* at multitasking. There they were, naked in the living room, and Ellery was about to try the world's most awkward rim job, and he didn't care. He shoved himself between Jackson's thighs, spreading them with his hands and parting Jackson's cheeks with his thumbs.

"Ellery?" Jackson mumbled, sounding confused. "What are you doin—whoa!"

Ellery lapped at him, stretching, fingering, stretching more. Jackson's little moans and cries were almost unbearably arousing, but Ellery was having a little game of mental arithmetic while he serviced his lover's body. Did he need lube? Was it slick enough? Did he want to go get lube? Would that break the mood? He really didn't want to break the mood. Why didn't he think of lube before he started this—*oh*!

Jackson had rooted around in the side of the couch, found a small bottle from the last time they'd done this here, and was currently shoving it into Ellery's fingers.

Ellery took it and slicked him up, thrusting his fingers inside Jackson's asshole while licking his cock from base to tip, sucking at the end for the saltiness, letting every whimper of need stir his own cock to stiffness.

"Ellery," Jackson moaned. "Please. I need you!"

"Of course you do," Ellery panted, almost bitterly. He added more slick to his own cock and pushed up, positioning himself so he could thrust in. Jackson tilted is head back and moaned, shaking around Ellery's erection as Ellery closed his eyes and embraced being surrounded by home.

And then home began to thrash underneath him, and Ellery had a job to do.

He began to rock back and forth, his strokes long and hard. Jackson didn't like to admit to needing anything, anybody, and now that he had, Ellery had to deliver. He began to power-fuck, devouring Jackson's grunts of pleasure like sustenance, allowing them to fuel him, goad him into more.

Jackson's breaths quickened, and his legs encircled Ellery's hips.

"You like that?" Ellery taunted. "You want more?"

"Yes," Jackson pleaded. "Yes. Please. Please, Ellery. Please."

"*Yes*!" Ellery cried, because what he wanted to say, things like "Then ask me, you stupid asshole!" or "Why won't you trust me to talk about it, dumbass!" weren't going to come out now when Ellery's body shook with desire, with heat, with the need to come.

Jackson came first, hands locked around Ellery's biceps, legs locked around Ellery's hips, his body language, his sounds, all surrounding Ellery with the need he hadn't wanted to voice.

The shaking of Jackson's body spurred Ellery on to finish, and he cried out, a raw, loud scream of frustration and sex and power and need.

He poured his come into Jackson's ass in sex like he poured his soul into Jackson's in their lives together, and as his body shook in aftermath, he felt the gratification of pleasuring them both seep through the frustration in his bones.

He sank into Jackson's arms, hearing Jackson whisper, "It's okay, I've got you. Don't worry, I've got you. It's okay."

A part of him wanted to cry, because hadn't that been the purpose of this exercise? To catch Jackson when he was flailing, falling through the looking glass of his own tortured psyche?

But then, didn't he do what he did because Jackson was trying to catch the world?

"I got you," Jackson whispered into his ear. "It's okay. I got you."

And sometimes the world included Ellery.

"I know," Ellery mumbled. "I've got you too."

"I know," Jackson told him, wrapping all his limbs tightly around Ellery, drawing him in, protecting him, even as he protected Jackson's heart. "I know you do. Thank you. Thank you for catching me. Thank you."

Ellery pressed a kiss against Jackson's neck. "You could have asked me for help," he said miserably.

"I didn't want to hurt you."

Ellery let out a sigh. "Only when you hurt yourself." He shivered, and Jackson pulled the afghan over his back, letting it cover both of them. Ellery looked Jackson in those bottle-green eyes and stroked his tender jaw. "Are you ever going to tell me what happened here?"

Jackson grunted. "Only because Henry will make it sound super dramatic."

Ellery had the feeling Henry's version would be closer to the truth. "Then by all means, tell me," he said, collapsed on top of Jackson's damp chest. "Better from you than Henry."

"Sure." Jackson kissed him and held his cheeks, making sure they were eye to eye. "But first, I love you, Counselor."

"I love you too, Detective." Ellery sighed. "Even when you're pissing me off."

Jackson gave a slight smile. "So every day, then?"

"Yeah. I love you more every day."

Jackson looked away, shy, and Ellery wanted to crow.

"So, the story behind the jaw—" Jackson began.

"And the knuckles." Ellery hadn't missed the tape across them. "And the bruises on your knees." He'd seen them as he'd undressed Jackson. "And your day."

"Fine." Jackson smiled crookedly. "Wasn't sleeping anyway."

And then he launched into what seemed to be a highly edited version of the story.

Sometime in the middle, as he was talking, they both managed to get off the couch, gather their clothes, and move to the bedroom, where it was a little warmer. Ellery would hit the couch with fabric cleaner the next day, but in the meantime, when Jackson was done with the story, they were lying in their own bed, safe and warm in the cocoon of each other's arms.

Ellery had to agree with Jackson after days like they'd had. The world was fucked-up; there was no denying it.

But together, for brief moments, they could forge a world of safety that would sustain them to fight another day.

AWARD WINNING author Amy Lane lives in a crumbling crapmansion with a couple of teenagers, a passel of furbabies, and a bemused spouse. She has too damned much yarn, a penchant for action-adventure movies, and a need to know that somewhere in all the pain is a story of Wuv, Twu Wuv, which she continues to believe in to this day! She writes contemporary romance, paranormal romance, urban fantasy, and romantic suspense, teaches the occasional writing class, and likes to pretend her very simple life is as exciting as the lives of the people who live in her head. She'll also tell you that sacrifices, large and small, are worth the urge to write.

Website: www.greenshill.com

Blog: www.writerslane.blogspot.com

Email: amylane@greenshill.com

Facebook: www.facebook.com/amy.lane.167

Twitter: @amymaclane

Follow me on BookBub

Guess who's swimming in the same pond...

FISH
OUT OF
WATER
Amy Lane

Fish Out of Water: Book One

PI Jackson Rivers grew up on the mean streets of Del Paso Heights—and he doesn't trust cops, even though he was one. When the man he thinks of as his brother is accused of killing a police officer in an obviously doctored crime, Jackson will move heaven and earth to keep Kaden and his family safe.

Defense attorney Ellery Cramer grew up with the proverbial silver spoon in his mouth, but that hasn't stopped him from crushing on street-smart, swaggering Jackson Rivers for the past six years. But when Jackson asks for his help defending Kaden Cameron, Ellery is out of his depth—and not just with guarded, prickly Jackson. Kaden wasn't just framed, he was framed by crooked cops, and the conspiracy goes higher than Ellery dares reach—and deep into Jackson's troubled past.

Both men are soon enmeshed in the mystery of who killed the cop in the minimart, and engaged in a race against time to clear Kaden's name. But when the mystery is solved and the bullets stop flying, they'll have to deal with their personal complications… and an attraction that's spiraled out of control.

There's blood in the water and
death in the air...

RED FISH,
DEAD
FISH

Amy Lane

"Deliciously tense . . .
a satisfying mix of sweet
angst and steamy suspense."
KAREN ROSE,
NYT Bestselling Author

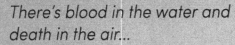

2

Fish Out of Water: Book Two

They must work together to stop a psychopath—and save each other.

Two months ago Jackson Rivers got shot while trying to save Ellery Cramer's life. Not only is Jackson still suffering from his wounds, the triggerman remains at large—and the body count is mounting.

Jackson and Ellery have been trying to track down Tim Owens since Jackson got out of the hospital, but Owens's time as a member of the department makes the DA reluctant to turn over any stones. When Owens starts going after people Jackson knows, Ellery's instincts hit red alert. Hurt in a scuffle with drug-dealing squatters and trying damned hard not to grieve for a childhood spent in hell, Jackson is weak and vulnerable when Owens strikes.

Jackson gets away, but the fallout from the encounter might kill him. It's not doing Ellery any favors either. When a police detective is abducted—and Jackson and Ellery hold the key to finding her—Ellery finds out exactly what he's made of. He's not the corporate shark who believes in winning at all costs; he's the frightened lover trying to keep the man he cares for from self-destructing in his own valor.

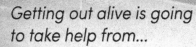

Getting out alive is going to take help from...

A FEW GOOD FISH

Amy Lane

3

Fish Out of Water: Book Three

A tomcat, a psychopath, and a psychic walk into the desert to rescue the men they love…. Can everybody make it out with their skin intact?

PI Jackson Rivers and Defense Attorney Ellery Cramer have barely recovered from last November, when stopping a serial killer nearly destroyed Jackson in both body and spirit.

But their previous investigation poked a new danger with a stick, forcing Jackson and Ellery to leave town so they can meet the snake in its den.

Jackson Rivers grew up with the mean streets as a classroom and he learned a long time ago not to give a damn about his own life. But he gets a whole new education when the enemy takes Ellery. The man who pulled his shattered pieces from darkness and stitched them back together again is in trouble, and Jackson's only chance to save him rests in the hands of fragile allies he barely knows.

It's going to take a little bit of luck to get these Few Good Fish out alive!

Hiding the
Moon

AMY LANE

Fish Out Of Water: Book Four
A Fish Out of Water/Racing for the Sun Crossover

Can a hitman and a psychic negotiate a relationship while all hell breaks loose?

The world might not know who Lee Burton is, but it needs his black ops division and the work they do to keep it safe. Lee's spent his life following orders—until he sees a kill jacket on Ernie Caulfield. Ernie isn't a typical target, and something is very wrong with Burton's chain of command.

Ernie's life may seem adrift, but his every action helps to shelter his mind from the psychic storm raging within. When Lee Burton shows up to save him from assassins and club bunnies, Ernie seizes his hand and doesn't look back. Burton is Ernie's best bet in a tumultuous world, and after one day together, he's pretty sure Lee knows Ernie is his destiny as well.

But when Burton refused Ernie's contract, he kicked an entire piranha tank of bad guys, and Burton can't rest until he takes down the rogue military unit that would try to kill a spacey psychic. Ernie's in love with Burton and Burton's confused as hell by Ernie—but Ernie's not changing his mind and Burton can't stay away. Psychics, assassins, and bad guys—throw them into the desert with a forbidden love affair and what could possibly go wrong?

5

FISH ON A BICYCLE

Amy Lane

If you give a
fish a bicycle,
how's he going
to swim?

Fish Out of Water: Book Five

Jackson Rivers has always bucked the rules—and bucking the rules of recovery is no exception. Now that he and Ellery are starting their own law firm, there's no reason he can't rush into trouble and take the same risks as always, right?

Maybe not. Their first case is a doozy, involving porn stars, drug empires, and daddy issues, and their client, Henry Worrall, wants to be an active participant in his own defense. As Henry and Jackson fight the bad guys and each other to find out who dumped the porn star in the trash can, Jackson must reexamine his assumptions that four months of rest and a few good conversations have made him all better inside.

Jackson keeps crashing his bicycle of self-care and a successful relationship, and Ellery wonders what's going to give out first—Jackson's health or Ellery's patience. Jackson's body hasn't forgiven him for past crimes. Can Ellery forgive him for his current sins? And can they keep Henry from going to jail for sleeping with the wrong guy at the wrong time?

Being a fish out of water is tough—but if you give a fish a bicycle, how's he going to swim?